WAITING FOR THE ELECTRICITY

WAITING
FOR THE

ELECTRICITY

A Novel

CHRISTINA NICHOL

The Overlook Press
New York, NY

This edition first published in hardcover in the United States in 2014 by
The Overlook Press, Peter Mayer Publishers, Inc.

141 Wooster Street
New York, NY 10012
www.overlookpress.com

For bulk and special sales, please contact sales@overlookny.com,
or write us at the address above.

Library of Congress Cataloging-in-Publication Data

Nichol, Christina.
Waiting for the electricity : a novel / Christina Nichol. — First edition.
pages cm
1. Georgia (Republic)—Fiction. 2. Georgians (South Caucasians)—
California—San Francisco. 3. Culture conflict—Fiction. 4. Satire. I. Title.
PS3614.I3326W35 2014   813'.6—dc23   2014007051

Book *design and type formatting by Bernard Schleifer*
Manufactured in the United States of America
ISBN: 978-1-4683-0686-6

FIRST EDITION
1 3 5 7 9 10 8 6 4 2

To Zviadi, Giorgi, Vanichka,
and both big and little Mananas

"It's like Pandora's Box. When Zeus opened it everything flew out. What was left? Just hope."

—Georgian worker, on the completion
of the Baku–Tbilisi–Ceyhan pipeline

WAITING FOR THE ELECTRICITY

1.

A TIDAL WAVE OF WOMEN, HUGE AND BUSTY, DRAPED IN LONG BLACK dresses, lumbered heavily, trundling toward the sea.

Watch out! Get out of their way.

This horde of buxom women was hiking down the hillsides like an invasion. On the minibuses they cracked sunflower seeds between their teeth, staring straight ahead, invested only in sunlight, in the promise of the sea. On the beach all these women would sunbathe. Some stood, holding a *pirozhok* in one hand and a beer in the other, thigh-deep in the water, yelling to little Shako not to swim too far. Those from the villages still bathed in their dresses, which clung to the folds on their bodies.

The air was hot. The air was drunk. The air had fermented into summer, a serious and committed summer. It was August 19, the last day of the season, also known as The Day of Turning, and everyone was trying to blacken their bodies before the weather changed. Armenians, Azeris, Georgians, and even Russians hefted toward summer, deep and late. Like an overladen table, the weight of summer groaned.

In the beginning, when God was distributing the land to all the nations, we Georgians missed the meeting. The next morning we looked around and realized we were homeless. "Hey!" we shouted to God. "What about *our* land?"

"Where were you last night?" He asked. "You missed the meeting. I already gave away all the land."

"We were drinking!" we cried out. "We were toasting Your name!"

God was so pleased with us that He gave us all the land He was saving for Himself. That's why we are supposed to relax and enjoy the beauty of God's earth.

The Armenians say, "We missed the meeting too, and all He gave us were the *rocks* He was saving for Himself." That's why their land is so strewn with stones, and also why they are now hogging up our beach.

We lived on God's land for thousands of years, enjoying its beauty and its bounty, always carrying a hoe in one hand to sow and reap the wonders of His holy dirt. But, because of our neighbors, in the other hand we had to carry a gun.

One day God came to see how everyone was doing. He visited each country in the neighborhood. First, He went to Armenia and asked, "How are you doing? Are you enjoying everything? Sleeping well? No complaints?"

The Armenians said, "Everything's well. We're living very nicely on these rocks You gave us."

God said, "I'm so pleased that you are living so well. This puts Me in such a good mood, in fact, that I'll grant you any wish you make."

"Well," the Armenians said. "As we said, we're content. But . . ."— and here they paused and started thinking very demonstratively, tapping their temples with their fingers—"if we *were* to think of something, our only wish would be that You destroy Azerbaijan. Those guys are always trying to steal our lake."

So God went next door to Azerbaijan to see how well they were holding up. "Hello!" He called. The Azeris were busy boating and fishing on the Caspian Sea and eating up all the caviar. "How are you doing down there?"

"Normal. Praise God."

"Well, what do you people wish for?"

"We'd really appreciate it if You decimated Armenia. They are bothersome neighbors, always trying to usurp one of our wheat fields."

Then God came over to Georgia.

"Victory to You! *Galmarjos*!" we cried out when we saw Him, thrusting high our sheephorns filled with wine. "We kiss You." We were already so pleased with His bountifulness that when He asked what we wished for we said we needed nothing more. We told Him, "We don't ask for anything. Just grant Armenia and Azerbaijan *their* wishes."

That's how the story goes.

It is said that in order to keep stories alive in our hearts, we have to tell them back to each other because when you only listen to stories and don't tell them back you become like the man who picks grapes but does not prune the vines, like the one who reaps the harvest but does not sow the seeds. You can become catatonic and easily led astray. In the olden days, when it was time for a boy to tell his own story but he didn't know how to begin, if his mouth wouldn't work properly, as if it were filled with rocks, the elders around the fire would say, "Start like this: 'Once there was. Once there was. Once there was not.'" This is the beginning of every tale. It means that what was true once, and even a second time true, is not always true a third time.

It was once true in Georgia that we only have one life and so we shouldn't waste it on material pursuits. It was also true that we lived in Paradise. But it took perseverance to remember every day that we lived in Paradise. Here we have dancing, love, wine, sun, ancient culture, and beauty. But no money. Therefore, we have become a little unfashionable because, these days, money is the hero of the world.

That's why I decided to try to tell the story of my country back, in order to keep some hope alive in our hearts in the midst of a living condition that had become extremely difficult.

For this reason, mainly, I was composing the following letter in English:

August 19th, 2002

Dear Hillary Clinton:

My name is Slims Achmed Makashvili and i am from the little town called Batumi, on the Black Sea. it is the very small town. So to say, it is beautiful and sunny. It is the town for me.

But then I worried: What if Hillary had never heard of Batumi? I didn't want her to feel ignorant, even though she *should* have heard of us because Inga Charkhalashvili and Maia Lomineishvili—both famous Georgian women—had great success when they played at the International Chess Championship in Batumi.

I continued:

Batumi is the little town that not many people know about. i know because i looked up Batumi on the Internet and there was only one picture of the palm tree. The tourist wrote, "this town looks like chipped paint." That is because we are under reconstruction. The local dictator is tearing down the old buildings and making many of the lawns in our town because no one can hide behind a lawn with a gun. In addition, the religious leaders are building 12th century spirituality huts. We are progressing civicly and religiously. We even have a bank. It is shiny and modern bank but has no money left in it. New certification requirement in 1998 decreased the number of banks from 200 to 43.

i really think we need little help over here in the farmer land, especially me! Especially because Georgia is the Christian country and it's difficult to have the Muslim name in a Christian country! If i had more Georgian name such as Davito, Dato, Temuri, or Toto, i could get a higher governmental position.

But now I will explain to You the more important information about how Batumi is the natural port. Port lies at the end of the railroad from Baku and is used mainly for petroleum product. Our town boasts of eight berths which have total capacity of 100,000 tonnes of general cargo, 800,000 tonnes of bulk cargo and six million tonnes of oil and gas product. Facilities include portal cranes and loaders for moving containers onto railcars. As You can see, Batumi offers You and Your country great business opportunity!

But then I reconsidered what I had written. After all, petroleum products were killing off all the fish.

I leaned back in the cafe chair and looked out at the sea. The Philippine and Turkish freighters on the horizon, on their way to the port, exhaled in slow motion a chalk-like substance. Everyone else still headed to the beach.

The Day of Turning is when everything changes. It is the day that the sea begins to slowly cool. Even the weathermen were predicting plummets in temperature. On TV that morning, *News Nostalgia* had reminded us what happened a decade ago on the nineteenth of August, with old footage of Boris Yeltsin in Moscow yelling at a tank to back up from Moscow's White House. That nineteenth of August was the day of the failed *coup d'état* in Russia, the day that our elders say in a voice thick with nostalgia and remonstrance, "Our country went from red to black."

Literally black. We hadn't had any regular electricity for eleven years. And we hadn't had any at all for the past eight days. Sporadic all summer, it only sparked intermittently in the stairwell. The government said the hydroelectric dam didn't have enough water to run the turbines, but when we saw the reservoirs at their highest capacity we remembered that—as with everything—what we witnessed was exactly opposite to what the government said.

I picked up the pen again and looked around the cafe to see if I recognized anybody I knew. I had to write surreptitiously because usually no one writes in cafes, they only recite poetry aloud, or sip ice cream coffees and complain about their mothers-in-law.

Jungles of grape vines were twining around the trellises, and around the abandoned buildings on the boulevard—traffic jams of shrubbery, green waves smattering like surf on the sidewalk. Pedestrians were trying to wend their way through them on the way to the beach. Off a railing, I plucked the thick stem of a large leaf and used it to keep off the sun.

Once I wrote a letter to Pink Floyd but they never wrote back. My best friend Malkhazi said my letter probably ended up in a wastebasket in Warwick. I was hoping that my letter to Hillary would have better results. In Georgia women have all the power in the home. I assumed it was the same in America.

A few weeks ago at the Maritime Ministry of Law, my place of employment, I had received a fax. Actually, it wasn't addressed to me, but to the chief deputy of maritime law. It was an application to enter a contest entitled "Small Business Proposals for Former Soviet Republics to Ensure Democracy and Security Throughout the Post 9/11 World," sponsored by Hillary Clinton. The winner got to visit America and attend a business conference that would address "The Challenges and Opportunities for Project Management in the Developing World." Usually only the local dictator, his family, and his closest friends ever received access to such opportunities. This one, though, had ended up in our fax machine.

This fax was like a falling star that I picked up and put in my pocket. And then it lit my pants on fire. To be precise, it was actually my pack of joke cigarettes that lit my pants on fire. But the little hole they burned created a sense of urgency reminding me of the fax, that the contest had a deadline, though January 7 still seemed a bit far off.

I had spent the last week in my village, located in the mountainous region northeast of the city, harvesting hazelnuts. To tell you the truth, I hate this kind of work. At least when we are working in the cornfields we can sing the old song:

Come all you and see my scythe
Look at it and see how beautiful it is
It is made of good metal
Come all of you workers out of the hills
Bless those who planted the cornfields

But do we sing songs about nuts? No, because we hate nuts. Actually, this is what we sang, "Fuck! Fuck!" as we shook the nuts off the trees.

Some say that the people in our village are lazy, that we grow Odessa grapes because even though Odessa grapes do not make such great wine, they are easy to grow and we don't need to spray them with some special fertilizer. Also, some people say that we like to grow big vegetables, like pumpkins, so we can pick one and eat it for a long time. They are only joking, of course, but it's true that we are not like Turkish people who work all the time. Turks look at us and say, "You have such a big house but you do not work much. How is that possible?" We tell them it's called The Great Georgian Mystery. Even Turkish people want to know the secret. But I can't explain what it is. Maybe it's God's gift.

But in Dgvari, the village on the other side of our mountain, they are very workaholic people. They can plant a violet on a stone. Recently, they worked so hard that they cut down all the trees on the hillsides, but then the soil lost its foundation, the mountain started to crumble, and their houses slid down the hill. The people had to move to the lower lands, into the abandoned tea packaging plant. "You see what happens if you work too hard?" my grandfather warned. "The mountains slide down and you lose your place in them. The Soviet Union was better," and he pointed to his gods, Lenin and Stalin, tattooed on his chest.

My grandfather was always saying everything was better during Soviet times. Green was greener and red was redder. He says the mineral water at the oldest cafe in Tbilisi was sweeter and the women who worked there could serve twelve people at once and dance the *Kartuli* at the same time. We had theaters and libraries then, and every village had its own parliament. We provided cotton pajamas to the whole Soviet army and we had our own toothbrush factory. The seaside resorts always had high quality magnetic sand. Now all the sand has lost its magnetic properties.

For my grandfather, Soviet times were *obviously* better. We were the richest republic then, a country of aristocrats, and people had such important employment positions they required uniforms. Georgia provided the entire Soviet Empire with mandarins! Tea! Wine! Roses! of such high quality they required explanation points after them. My grandfather could fill up two suitcases with roses that he grew in our village, take a subsidized flight to Moscow for the weekend, and sell his roses for a ruble apiece to all the romantic couples at the ice skating rink.

But now Russia had stopped buying our roses, which is why we were sitting in the middle of a mound of nuts, like workers in a Turkish factory, my hands raw from peeling the skins off. We had gathered five hundred kilos of hazelnuts from the trees. These nuts had paid my tuition for three years at the university, and for our flat in Batumi. I was hoping that this year, these nuts would pay for me to get out of this country.

In our village the air is so clear you don't need telephones. The voice easily slips through so that everyone knows all of your business and you must speak quietly if you don't want to be overheard. When I called in a low voice to Marika, a girl on the other side of the village, to make me and herself a cocktail, her mother heard. When Marika complained to me from her balcony, "Slims Achmed! My mother said I took a whole liter of vodka to make our cocktail, but I only took one little glass," her mother shouted back from the orchard, "I said no such thing. She just wants an excuse to run away to the beach and not help me bottle the plum sauce!"

In this way, through the crystal air, we also heard the rumor from the ice cream man, through his megaphone, that this year hazelnuts had lost their value. One lari per kilo. Or, one kilo of nuts for an ice cream cone. The hazelnut harvest was kaput.

Due to this news, on the bus back to Batumi, everyone had been in a terrible mood. Even the bus drivers argued about whose minibus got to go next. "You're after *me*," one said.

"Your mother!" replied another. Their tempers swooned like the heat and they started to threaten each other with the umbrellas they were holding to keep out the sun. Another man joined in, "Fuck all of you. Aren't you tired of shouting?"

A stupid man asked if he could sit in the seat next to mine. "Yes," I said. "I believe *all* the seats on the bus are going back to Batumi."

A woman carrying a beach ball got on, but when she saw the driver she said, "Oof! I hate the way you drive," and got off again.

"Stop at the big tree!" a passenger called.

"What big tree? They're all big trees," the driver complained.

"What kind of a donkey are you? You don't see the big tree?"

By the time we were descending the final mountain into Batumi I was starting to feel very irritated. I had to figure out another way to make four thousand dollars for a visa. That was the question, was always the question, was the main philosophical question for the drunk people on the sidewalk. And then they would ask, "What is the meaning of life, and who is to blame?"

Of course the question of how to acquire four thousand dollars for a visa was not quite of the same philosophical caliber as those of our ancient philosophers. No one knew why, exactly, four thousand dollars was required for a visa, only that anyone who had made it out of Georgia always had at least that much. I only knew one person who made it out of Georgia—my friend Vano went to America and overstayed his tourist visa. Now he works for a company in Detroit pouring concrete.

Fathers, wary of the philosophical question arising in their sons of how to acquire four thousand dollars had recently started telling them, "It's a sin to drink alone and become philosophical. Instead, you'd better learn how to drink in order to celebrate your unity with others. Otherwise, you will become too sophisticated. We are not like those Westerners, caught in metaphysical abstractions." But after the Soviet collapse, my father wasn't there to warn me of the dangers of too much sophistication, of too many philosophical questions. Georgian independence had coincided with the more immediate tragedy of his death. He was killed while driving a minibus near the border with Abkhazia. Some starving Abkhazian soldiers shot him through the windshield when they saw coins that he had collected from his passengers stuck to the magnet on his dashboard—a total of twenty-eight lari, about fourteen dollars. The soldiers claimed that they had forgotten what money looked like, and that they had gone crazy when they saw it.

After the funeral, my friend Malkhazi began to drink on the street. My little brother, Zuka, found solace in the company of Christian angels. My sister, Juliet, searched for an identity in English language novels, and I began to study the law of the sea, to figure out how to get across it and leave this dark country.

Returning to Batumi down the mountain, our little bus clunked heroically over the ruts, past the springs that gushed water onto the road. The driver had turned up the volume of his radio, and grandmothers, carrying their towels and picnic foods in their laps, listened primly to the tinny words of the Gloria Gaynor song "I Will Survive."

But up ahead was a roadblock. A small group of black-clad men waved us over to the side of the road, in the same slow and lazy way a lion in a nature show attacks an antelope. The driver should have driven straight through, but instead he slowed down and then stopped. The woman sitting beside me sighed and adjusted her bag on her lap. The roadside workers forced open the doors and hiked up the steps of the bus. "Not again!" I said. They yelled at the driver to turn down the radio, reached into their pockets, and pulled out grenades.

"Those are so little," the driver said.

They ordered him to drive into the forest.

"Which forest?" the driver asked, throwing up his hands. "Everywhere is a forest."

They pointed to a little meadow behind a cluster of trees and told him to park there. In the clearing we had to get off the bus, take off all our clothes, even our socks. As I squatted in the field, I gripped my last twelve lari in my palm. I hadn't been paid my salary recently and I knew that when they came to me they would say, "What? A grown man only has twelve lari?" I knew this because this was the third time I had been robbed this year on a public transport and it always went the same way. Since my physique isn't shaped the same way as my best friend Malkhazi's, who once worked as a security guard for the mayor and can bend a bicycle around a person's neck, I whispered to the man crouched beside me that I only had twelve lari. He passed me one of his twenty-lari notes.

I tried not to open my mouth when they came to me, just kept staring at the ground, at the little mountain herbs poking out of the trampled grass by my feet, so they wouldn't be tempted to pull out my gold tooth.

After the criminals took everyone's money, they thanked us. The oldest one shrugged apologetically and said, "My mother is sick at home. I need this to pay for her electricity." Another reached in his pocket and gave a few lari back to the women. "Take this," he said, patting their hands. Then they got into the bus and drove away.

I put my black trousers back on, my socks, my shirt, and my wool vest.

"It's that new Robin Hood phenomena," someone said. "Steal from the men and give to the women."

"It was the police," speculated another.

I rubbed the mud off my shoes with some grass and took out a Parliament cigarette. Just when I was starting to feel less nervous, *sheni deyda*! Your mother! I lit a cigarette from the wrong pack, my joke pack, and it cracked in my face, bringing me back into the explosive present, the fire crack-gunshot craving Georgian man's world.

I do not mean to suggest that gunshots were always going off in Georgia. It's true that we used to be known as the bullet-footed generation ever since we had to block bullets with our boots during the civil war with Abkhazia in the nineties. But we never resembled those gangland dandies, or those American leather-jacketed motorcycle-riding heroes. We didn't ride motorcycles. We didn't even ride bicycles. We were not a nomadic citizenry. We preferred to think of ourselves, as my sister Juliet would say, "a *proper* country of classical bandits."

I was getting tired of this bandit mentality. It was time to appeal for some help. We needed some foreign, good-natured, law-abiding policeman, someone who could intervene, one of those wholesome, American cops who rode around on a horse, someone who inspired dignity in the citizenry.

That is why when I hiked off the mountain I didn't go to the beach but to the umbrella cafe on Seaside Boulevard to ask for some help.

> *Hillary, i'll try to write to You more about myself, but i'm not as interesting person as You are, obviously, but still i'll write something. I love animals, especially fish. Once i had the fish which i called billclinton, but unfortunately it had eaten some poisoned thing and that was the end of his life. And what about You? Do You like animals or have You a pet? We've a small garden at home, but mostly i love cactus.*
>
> *i am the maritime lawyer but personally it is the very dull life. The bosses are old communists and the unfortunate circumstance is that the laws of our country can't change until they all die off.*
>
> *Now for important ancestral information. Have you heard of Buffalo Bill's Wild West? My great, great grandfather from my village in Guria followed Prince Ivane Makharadze to Iowa and introduced tradition of trick riding to cowboys. People thought they were Cossacks but really they were Gurians from my village. They could ride three horses at one time standing on their head. They were so skilled that even if they wanted to commit suicide it was impossible on a horse. Only on the ground.*
>
> *During Soviet times government always forbid American cowboy movies on TV. But sometimes, on religious holidays they showed them. Since we are such maniac religious people this was crafty method by Soviet government*

to trick us to stay home to watch taboo movies instead of going to the church. My grandfather watched these movies, The Magnificent Seven, Stagecoach, always trying to catch a peek at his relatives.

My grandfather, after watching cowboy films said, "The only hope is the cowboy!" He began to imitate the cowboy. He wore a straw hat and sat on the balcony plucking an instrument made of strings across a coconut.

He insisted that my father call me Slims, from Slim Sherman, after the legend of Ben-Hur. So, you see, Hillary, even though I come from ancient poetical culture, i am cowboy, and i come from cowboy family. True American, like Giorgi Bush.

Even though Slims Achmed resembles Islamic cowboy name combination, it is really a nineteenth century name, expressing same fervent Georgian dream for independence from Russia, like 19th century poets Nikoloz Baratashvili and Akaki Tsereteli. But Hillary, don't worry. If you do not know Georgian poets, that is normal.

The Muslim part, the Achmed part, is said in this way: Axkmed, from the back of your throat. It tastes like truth, like the sound of a Gurulian frog. Actually, it tastes like love. Hillary, i know that in English the phrase i love you is the very beautiful sound. And in French. Je t'aime. Again. Very beautiful. Perhaps you will think that our Georgian expression for love is not so beautiful: Meh shen meexhvar xhar. Yes, not so very beautiful.

But my dear Hillary, my grandfather wasn't thinking of love when he named me. He was thinking of his friend Achmed, from the Muslim village across the river. Achmed always stole our pigs to prevent us from eating their pork. My grandfather hoped that if he named me Achmed the Muslim village would stop filching our personal pigs. Also, he wanted to make the peace with the Turks. If we made the peace with the Turks, we could free ourselves from the

Russians. He said, "If the English colonize us, Juliet (that's my sister), with her English name will survive. If we regain our Independence, Zuka (my brother), with his Georgian name will thrive. And if the Americans or the Turks invade, then Slims Achmed will survive."

Now i wish to ask to You very important question: Have You seen the movie Jesus Christ Superstar? Do You know about the theme song in the movie, "Don't you mind about the future. Think about today instead." ?!!(!) We have been living that way for very long time now, for 15 centuries maybe, and i don't think it's very good advice. We have freed ourselves from Russia, are holding out our hand, and waiting for help up.

Respecting Your way,
Slims Achmed Makashvili

2.

As I was sitting on the boulevard, writing my letter, a cloud began to spread across the sky like a giant oil spill. Kerosene, diesel fumes, and the sharp smell of an impending rainstorm cut through the air. The shadows of the city's buildings were turning winter, the colors muted—the colors of a gun. Georgia still has its own poetry, I thought, could even be beautiful in a designer way, like the sandy white dune buildings in *Casablanca*.

I put my letter to Hillary away and set out to find Malkhazi. I had to tell him about how the prices for hazelnuts had plummeted.

If you looked at it now you wouldn't believe it, but it is said that when Queen Tamar entered Batumi with her soldiers in the twelfth century, the town was so clean she ordered them to take off their shoes. Even during Soviet times all was in order; the trees were like soldiers—all in one line. The Soviet national anthem of our town used to go like this:

If you go to the Adjarian mountains
sweet aroma will go through your heart
And if you look deeply into Batumi's eyes
you feel cured from every illness

Batumi, sparkling clean
Batumi, so breathtaking

You are the emerald, you are the paradise
If the town falls in love with you
It gives you all its soul
And, if necessary, it will die for you.

But I think the town has lost some of its powers. For example, I do not know anyone whom the town died for recently.

A bread truck stopped in front of the Paradise Cafe, its engine covering up the shouting of the men guzzling brown bottles of Kazbegi beer. The driver rushed out and carried loaves and buns in his dirty hands into the restaurant.

In the distance, to celebrate the last day of summer, Batumi's biblical artist was embroidering Georgian Orthodox crosses into the beach with stones the colors of young green wine and every shade of sunburn.

Across the square, I saw Malkhazi. He was standing with Gocha Abashidze under the stone monument to Gocha's great uncle, our city's godfather. Godfather, clad in the traditional Georgian outfit—the *cherkeska* with the special breast pockets designed for artillery cartridges, scabbard on his belt, *nababi* on his head—was supposed to remind everyone what a true Georgian man looks like, how he is a noble man and must constantly maintain his dignity. But Gocha hadn't inherited this expression at all. Instead, dressed in his new black silk shirt from Thailand—his "image"—he would chase anyone who stepped on his little piece of lawn, Batumi's new peewee golf course.

Gocha is from one of the *aristocratic* families, the ones who recently bought up all the real estate near the sea. He lives in one of the centrally located apartment buildings, the ones recently renovated to look like a Greek temple, with balconies carved by Batumi's most celebrated bronze workers. Gocha says he is related to a famous king from the fourth century BC, the one who owned a tile factory that all the archaeologists are digging up these days. But Gocha is not a noble soul. He thinks one thing, speaks another, and does some third one.

Malkhazi, standing beside him, looked like a character from one of my sister's Victorian novels, doomed and romantic, except for his gigantic nose. When Malkhazi swims in the sea on his back, the beachgoers point at his nose and shout, "Watch out! A shark!" He resembles the Armenian Little Red Riding Hood who says to the wolf, "Oh, what a big nose you have," and the wolf replies, "Well, look at yours."

Malkhazi was wearing the new pair of jeans he had bought the previous week at the Turkish market, and also his GEORGIA TECH T-shirt. Looking down at his boots, rocking back and forth, he seemed to be propelled by the weight of something he was considering. Malkhazi could stand like that all afternoon; it was his main form of amusement. He looked like the South American peacock bass I'd seen in Batumi's former dolphinarium, with brown and rust markings, never meant to be domesticated, languidly swimming back and forth. And then up go his fins and in one split second he eats the little goldfish; and then back to his languid ways as he spit out the scales. Malkhazi has the same jaw.

I whistled and when Malkhazi saw me he said goodbye to Gocha.

"Gocha offered me a job working for Herbalife," Malkhazi confided as we walked down Seaside Boulevard toward the sea. "But I refuse to work for a Russian company. Those guys drive around Georgia in their Volkswagens, preaching about herbal remedies but herbal remedies their mother! Georgians were writing poetry when they were still living in the trees. We should be driving around Yekaterinburg promoting wine and hazelnuts!"

"Good idea," I said. "Because right now one kilo of hazelnuts is now the same price as an ice cream cone."

"*Sheni deyda*!" he said. Malkhazi reached in his shirt pocket for some matches. If Malkhazi's lips were an art museum, the cigarette was the permanent installation.

We climbed through the boulders to the frayed hem of the surf. Malkhazi ripped the top off a new packet of Viceroys, set the aluminum paper into the wind, and shook out a cigarette for me. The surf was wilder than usual because of an impending storm, and a great tangle of jellyfish bobbed along the water's edge.

We sat smoking, gazed out at the cargo ships from Bulgaria, Odessa, Turkey. They sat there, shackled to the sea, as if waiting, like the rest of us, for something. Malkhazi scrutinized the water, as if he were its protector. The waves crackled over beach rocks and groveled to his boots. The Black Sea didn't look very romantic right now, so I looked across it, trying to see the other side, where I wanted to be. But the swimmers were in the way—innocent children playing on multicolored floating devices, churning the last of the sun's warmth into the water, the warmth, in turn, churning up the dormant radioactive material beneath.

A breeze blew, some water arced up, and a thin layer of crude oil spattered onto Malkhazi's jeans. He tried to wipe it off with his handkerchief but only smeared the stain. I thought about the Black Sea spiny dogfish population and how it was going extinct because of this crude oil, which congregates on top of the sea like a municipal meeting of politicians. I dug my hand into the beach stones and extracted one, rolled it around, gritted up my palm. "What about the Italian ship captain?" I asked Malkhazi. "Have you heard back from him?"

At the end of June, an Italian ship captain had told Malkhazi to send him a letter detailing all of his job experience. Malkhazi had written, "barn builder, farmer, toastmaster at village weddings, bodyguard, casino employee." He also included his height, age, and zodiac sign (192 cm. / 27 years old / Libra); his personality type (choleric); his favorite qualities in a person (woman: intelligence, honor, spiritual force; man: bravery, sociability, good physical protector); his most harmful habit (caught between two fires); his favorite country(Georgia); his education (no formal education); his language abilities (Georgian, Russian, a little English).

But no, Malkhazi hadn't heard back and now when he told me he acted annoyed as if he wanted me to shut up about it. I realized that Malkhazi, the mountain dreamer, was turning into one of those typical Georgian men who huddle together on the street near the bus drivers, forming their own private junta, making too many deals with Gocha on the boulevard.

"The Italian probably tried to call but the telephone didn't work," I told him. "Did you give it to the postman yourself, or put it in the postbox? They haven't been emptying the postboxes."

"I e-mailed it," he said.

"Oh," I said and threw the stone I was holding, aiming for the middle of a jellyfish. "Do you know the Koreans eat those?"

"Blexh," he said and threw his stone, avoiding the jellyfish.

"What if you had the chance," I asked, "to leave Georgia, to work on a ship, but you could never come back?"

Malkhazi didn't answer. He only became more village-heavy, gloomily glaring at the sea. Under his breath, Malkhazi quoted our poet Alexander Gomiashvili:

Among these mountains I was born,
Their songs and legends made me strong.

After that we just sat silently and stared at the sea.

"I don't think I could leave Georgia forever," Malkhazi said finally. "It's better to see what will happen here."

"But what is this place? It's practically destroyed," I said.

"Only Georgia can destroy Georgia," he said. "Two Georgians together can make a country. Three Georgians united make a world."

"The only problem is," I said, "these days, it's almost impossible to unite three Georgians."

"Unless it's you, me, and Shalva," Malkhazi said.

"Shalva. Which Shalva? The optician or the policeman?"

"The policeman," he said. "Listen Slims, today I met a foreigner, an Englishman who is working at the port. He's a geologist, a pipeline specialist. I think he's a very valuable man."

"And what do you want to do with him? Kidnap him?"

"I am not afraid of the electric chair. We have no electricity." It was an old joke.

"Don't be a donkey," I told him. "You can't get any money from the English government. Someone already tried that last year when they kidnapped the soccer player."

"Not money from the government. From Shalva. He said he'd give me his car."

"There's a chicken living in his car."

"We can eat the chicken and fix the car. You know how our police don't have any respect? People just use them to borrow a light? Shalva said he'd give me his car if I kidnap this English man so he can rescue him with television cameras, so that people view the police more heroically."

"Why would Shalva rescue him? It's always the police who kidnap the people."

"Pipeline workers can't be targeted. That's their rule."

"It doesn't sound practical."

Malkhazi raised the curved sword of his eyebrow. "Show me a man with his feet planted firmly on the ground, and I will show you a man who can't put on his trousers."

"Where did you hear that?" I asked.

"I read it in Juliet's book of famous English quotes. But seriously," he said, arms crossed over his mighty chest, inflamed cheeks incongruent to his little ears, "ask anyone what the name 'Makashvili' means. Everyone knows the Makashvilis are famous dreamers."

Even though Malkhazi and I have the same last name, he is not actually my blood cousin. Malkhazi lost his mother when he was born. I don't know all the details except that she was young; the local hospital hadn't opened yet; the midwives were at the cattle festival. No one could believe Malkhazi's misfortune when, three years later, his father was shot by Turkish snipers after he had tried to cross the border to Turkey to avoid being sent to Afghanistan. After the funeral, Malkhazi's uncle took it upon himself to teach Malkhazi all the Georgian traditions: how to hunt game; how to make wine, or at least how to know through smell alone which variety of grape it came from; and how to make the proper Georgian toast. Malkhazi's uncle, so intent on making Malkhazi self-sufficient, once tore down his barn so that Malkhazi could learn to build it back up. Perhaps he overcompensated.

"Our name is not written about in the history books," I said. "Probably no one outside of the beer factory district knows we're famous."

But Malkhazi was right. The Makashvilis are dreamers. During Soviet Union times, whenever we met on Seaside Boulevard, before we even kissed each other's cheeks in greeting, we began to dream. We dreamed of fishing for gold-speckled trout in the northern territories of Abkhazia. We dreamed of sharpening our swords to battle Turkish people. We would compose letters in awkward English to the cute European girls we had met at Batumi's International Chess Championship: *Hi sweet heart, Any time You want, You can come back and enjoy real life. If man doesn't worry about money, and if he has a car, Georgia! is exactly perfect place to feel all the true nature.*

When Malkhazi and I were still living in the village, we used to roam around in the pastures, mixing the milk of a sheep with the acids of a crushed-up fig leaf. The acids, mingling with the milk, made curd that we cooled under a stream and ate for lunch. I told him once, "That is a true romantic tourist image. You should be a tour guide. You could surprise the Russian tourists by pretending to be an uneducated sheepherder, and then confound them by answering their questions in French." It was only a joke because he didn't speak French. Nor did he like sheep. Nevertheless, after I moved to the town I pressured him to come too. "Georgia is beginning to privatize," I told him, "making many employment opportunities in Batumi. My friend is a photographer of Georgian doorways. Another is a window maker. I am studying the law of the sea." And so, Malkhazi, in his early twenties then, had come to live with us. Too young to marry, too old to enter the university, and he didn't even smoke.

He didn't approve of smoking either, especially for women. If he saw a young woman standing behind a corner with a cigarette, he would ask her for it, stick the filter part up his nose, and then give it back to her. But when he got his first job working in a wedding restaurant in Batumi, he shaved his mustache and took up the habit. He would smoke and sit under a nearby tung tree listening to his *Super Hits of the 90's* tape: Alla Pugacheva, Kino, Nautilus, or even "Aisha," the Algerian hit song. In the village he was known as Malkhazi the Disco King—ever since he had salvaged a tape recorder from an anthropologist and set up a disco venue in an abandoned boxcar.

But when people had stopped getting married, and Malkhazi lost his job, we dreamed of feeling the true nature of other places, hiding on an oil train headed to Kazakhstan and joining the Central Asian hash industry. Malkhazi's uncle in the village had taught us how to roll marijuana across our palms until they turned black: had described the whole procedure, how the women run naked through the oily fields of the steppe, the finest resin sticking to their bodies (the second quality resin is that which sticks to the horses). But instead we had squandered most of the past summer sprawled on the cobbled beach, listening to the new punk bands from Tbilisi on Malkhazi's radio. The lyrics asked God to save Georgia's soul, complained that there is no peace without bloody war, and that the world is tired of stupid needlework. Now we dreamed of getting a job at the port, working for an air-conditioning company, or a Swedish appliance manufacturer, a postal service, anything reliable.

"What about getting your job back at the casino?" I asked him.

"Nugzar, the owner, said I milked too many buffalo. He said that's why the cards always slipped out of my hands."

"What about the job you were offered in the forest?" I asked him.

"I don't want to be a woodchopper!" he said. "I am tired of selling our trees to Turkey so they can build up their towns."

"But I will never get a visa to leave this country if they find out I aided in a kidnapping."

"I told you, it's better not to leave. Anyway, the Englishman doesn't speak Georgian so I need your English."

"But I'm tired of criminal activity," I said. "I was robbed again today."

"Again?" Malkhazi said. He had a strange habit of blaming me every time I was robbed. "Anyway, the Englishman's name is Anthony. He is having problems with the pipeline. I explained to him how the pipeline is set to run through our village, how we could help him out. He already agreed to come to dinner tomorrow, for the Feast of the Assumption."

3.

THE WIND OVER THE SEA WAS NOW BUILDING IN STRENGTH—THE WAVES growing more impatient—carrying away the sound of the hefty mothers calling to their children to come in from swimming, reminding their children of the date, that it was the nineteenth of August, and time to leave the water.

I tuned Malkhazi's radio to the jazz station, tucked it under my arm just as the rain began to plummet. We ran home along the water's edge, cutting through the schoolyard before the floods moated our neighborhood.

We live in Piv Zavod, the beer factory district, in a block of concrete flats built in the 1970s. Although, because the beer factory closed down after the Soviet Union collapsed, it should really be called the oil train district because all the oil trains screech and bang together in our backyard in the middle of the night. We are located in Row 8 Building 7, but we don't really have an address. If anyone wants to find us he can just call out, "Makashvili!" And again, "Makashvili!" Everyone knows where we live.

Actually, if anyone wants to find us he can look for the building with the most disarrayed laundry hanging from it. The Sadzaglishvilis, who live above us, always drape their laundry right in front of our windows, without any order. The Makashvili name comes from the word meaning, "to dream," but the Sadzaglishvili name comes from the word meaning "sons of a disorganized family."

As we ran inside, the rain poured down sounding like the Great Toastmaster's giant applause. The only one doggedly unaffected by the weather was Batumi's new bishop, Father Mikhail. He had recently conscripted a whole clan of "groupies," as we called them, to help him build his twelfth-century hut, directly across from our flat. They had collected stones from the riverbed, transported them across town in a donkey cart, and were laying one boulder on top of another, smudging the cracks with plaster.

"Keep building!" we heard Father Mikhail intoning.

Malkhazi cupped his hand and shouted out the window, "Build!"

"Such twelfth-century fervor!" my mother exclaimed to Guliko, the kindergarten director, over on the next balcony.

"What does he think he is trying to do? Build something?" Guliko yelled back, expressing the current disbelief system that anyone would try to do anything as audacious as build something.

"Even Juliet is helping out!" Malkhazi scowled.

I looked out the window. My sister mingled on the periphery of the blessing seekers, making a little question mark in the mud with her boot. Ever since she had watched that new movie playing at Batumi's cinematography club, *Jeanne D'Arc*, she had developed a Joan of Arc complex. She wore her black turtleneck sweater, ate *lobiani*—bean bread—and frequented the new soybean restaurant near the university on Wednesdays and Fridays, the fasting days.

Malkhazi took off his shirt, draped it over a kitchen chair, removed his pants, and stood in his shorts by the balcony door ripping his oil-stained, Turkish jeans to shreds, which, in turn, were staining his fingers blue. "Look how cheap these jeans are," he said. In Georgia sometimes you feel like poking holes in things. It's supposed to mean you're in love. The nineteenth-century poet Chavchavadze says, "Georgian love is an injury."

While Malkhazi dropped strips of his jeans over the railing, one by one, I noticed more and more people across the courtyard gathering around the bishop. Perhaps some wanted to examine up close his stone building methods. Others seemed to be seeking his benedictions. "He's like a rock star," said Malkhazi, whose bare legs were splotched with oil, like a pied cow, the German variety that produces excellent beef, not the Georgian species better suited for butter.

"Father Mikhail says miracles are happening these days," my mother said from the stove. "He says the icons in the churches have started to weep for Georgia. Malkhazi, have you heard that the icons have started to weep?"

"It's not a good sign," Malkhazi said. "In history, they've always wept before an invasion."

"This new Christianity makes me carsick," I said and filled a pot with water to boil some macaroni. "I think I'll change my religion."

"Hmm," Malkhazi said and scratched his head. "How can a Georgian man change his religion?"

"I was only joking!"

"In every joke is a little bit of truth," he said.

My mother turned to me. "Slims," she said. "When you were in the village did you repair the corn lofts?"

"Yes, Deyda," I said.

"When your father was alive," my mother said huffily, "the corn lofts never needed fixing. Oh! If only your father were alive he would have harvested the corn long ago. This one just doesn't like to work." She pointed at me, sitting on the couch, looking up words in the English/Georgian dictionary.

I wanted to continue my letter to Hillary but it was difficult to find a quiet place to concentrate because at home everyone was always interrupting and forcing each other to eat soup or some other food. And everyone was so loud. I think the biggest problem in Georgia is noise pollution.

When my sister Juliet came home she changed out of the black Victorian dress she was required to wear for the English faculty at the university and into a housedress that made her resemble a buccaneer from Iran. Then she put on the bandit hat that our great-grandmother had worn during the Soviet Revolution. Juliet began wearing that hat after someone stole her umbrella, but continued to wear it because it made her feel like some sort of a classical bandit. She and my mother stood over the stove together concocting a skin lotion made from the cream of a goat and a bundle of rosemary.

I looked around the kitchen to try to describe to Hillary more details on how we live. We had too much furniture: the same huge China cabinet from Soviet times with glossy orange wood, staunchly situated against the wall, feebly proclaiming, "Stability!" Someone had stuck a cardboard candy box lid with a picture of blue carnations on the inside of the window of the oven door. The oven didn't work; we only used the stovetop. The tablecloth was not on the table. I don't know where my mother keeps the tablecloth. On the wall were paintings of palm trees and the sea. Juliet's guitar hung on the wall, next to a hollowed-out gourd for pouring wine and a metal casting of our great medieval epic poet, Rustaveli, dressed up in his twelfth-century knight outfit. A calendar of images from the new pipeline construction in Borjomi, published by the local oil company, hung next to that.

But then I realized that Hillary might not be so interested in our kitchen.

Contrary to my mother's beliefs, I wasn't lazy—the main problem was our business climate.

Dear Hillary,

Let me explain to You more about our business climate. The local dictator here has a monopoly on all the businesses: he raises ostriches for the eggs, and goats for their sweet milk. Everyone buys his sweet milk because he plays Viennese waltzes to them during the milking. He also has over one hundred Caucasian dogs for . . . i don't know, the good feeling in his heart. About ancient origin of Caucasian sheep-dog: it is pride of all peoples of Transcaucasia and Caucasus, but at the same time it is the trouble of these peoples. After the Soviet Union broke, each of the sover-

eign republics tried to appropriate to herself the right of the founder of this breed. What new names are not thought up? Arsak's dog? Longhaired Georgian wolfhound? Azerbaijan Gurdbasar? Alanian dog? In each area and each village the name is dispersed and it will become a tragedy for the breed. Have You an opinion on the name it should adhere to? Once when our dictator was on vacation to Switzerland, his favorite dog refused to eat so his guards sent the dog to him. As You can see, this illustrates the love between a man and his dog.

Since Juliet taught English at the university, I asked her if I could read her what I had written to Hillary so far. I was hoping she could help me out with the grammar.

She said she would be happy to but when I finished reading the whole thing to her she said only, "Do you think Hillary is so interested in dogs?"

"It's not only about dogs but about businesses," I said.

"If you are trying to write a business letter to Hillary Clinton, I think you must write straight and directly to the point."

"Well, how do I know what to write to Americans about if I've never met one or been to their country?"

"Well, Hillary's never met you either," Juliet said. "She's probably never even heard of Georgia. You should give her a more panoramic perspective."

"If she wants a more panoramic perspective she can look it up on the Internet," I said. "But what about the English? The grammar."

She looked it over. "*i* should to be capitalized," she said. "And *You* should be lowercase."

"But that is very impolite," I said.

"Why write anything if you cannot write the truth?" Malkhazi interjected. "Words are nothing because you can lie or hide something behind them, like your boss does, and it's going to be difficult to get any guarantee that what someone is saying is the truth. Especially in the city. It's better to rely on instincts, emotions, feelings, and good experiences with friendly people because they don't have the words to cheat. Slims, if you want to write a love letter to Hillary, you should go back to the village. Only in the village is where you can find any true love left in this world."

"I'm trying to ask America for some help. Otherwise we're all going to end up like you," I said, "supporting ourselves on criminal activity."

"I told you it's a good plan," Malkhazi said. "It's not a criminal activity."

"America! Dollars! That's all these young people think about," complained my mother, who was pounding the rosemary with a pestle in the mortar. "First it was rubles, and now dollars. What about our own dear little lari? *Opa!*"

"What is it?" Juliet asked.

"The pestle broke!" my mother said. Then she lost herself in her usual tirade about how all intelligent Georgians were leaving, how our population was diminishing. "Just like the anchovy population," she said. "Because of that dangerous American lady." She was referring to the *Mnemiopsis leidyi*, the alien jellyfish that had invaded our sea a decade ago, after so many oil ships sank and disrupted the pH balance.

"*I* don't want to go to America," Malkhazi said and brought his soup bowl to the sink. "And I'm sick of this complaining. It's not interesting."

"Where are you going?" I asked.

"I'm going to kidnap a wife," he said, strapping on his boots.

"Don't go somewhere!" my mother yelled after Malkhazi. "I need your help to bottle the plums." But Malkhazi was already out the door, running away.

"O! Nightmare, nightmare, they don't like to work," my mother said. And then she stuck her spoon in the plum jam and drowned a bee.

4.

THE NEXT MORNING THE TORRENT OF RAIN HAD STOPPED, AND I SAT outside the Paradise Cafe struggling over the words in another letter to Hillary. I watched a raindrop fall from the iron chain of a shopkeeper's sign. The sky was streaked with a combination of gray and white—the favorite color of medieval horses.

What I really wanted to describe to Hillary was how we didn't used to steal copper out of the electrical wires or smash up the state's electric meters with hammers. When we were younger the only thing we ever beat were the mulberry branches in order to feed their leaves to the silkworms. My father had hoped that our village would one day become a great communist hero village increasing the state productivity of silkworm products. He was the one who had organized our silkworm collective when the village Soviet was passing around those books with Lenin's picture that we now use as toilet paper in the outhouse. But since all the silkworms had died, and everyone was moving from the villages to the town, everything was changing. Even Malkhazi had started pacing around with a sort of strut, always making sure his boots were polished, and quoting lines from Al Pacino.

But we Makashvilis are not actors, I reminded myself. Especially we are not actors from the remake of that religious movie about Joan of Arc.

We don't need the Bible, I concluded. We don't need it in the sense of using it for any kind of advice anymore. We already know who we are, viscerally, without any thought. Our self-knowledge stemmed from the experience of having lost everything after the Soviet Union collapsed, and yet, we are still here. We remain.

I looked across the water, toward the United States—actually Bulgaria was on the other side of the sea, but I looked farther west than that, and pleaded to Hillary, "What else can I do in this tiny town where the only thing to do is to stand around looking at the dirt, argue about who it belongs to, play backgammon with the taxi drivers, or kick around pieces of metal pretending to be a shy and concentrated man who can't talk about love without wine?" I could feel myself caving. I decided that I would help Malkhazi kidnap the pipeline worker after all.

Actually, it was overnight that my mind had changed. I had fallen asleep on the coach, and I suspect that when Malkhazi came home he used his *Chidaoba*—Georgian martial arts—crystal gazer hypnotizing power on me, which he had once learned at a Soviet pioneer camp, because when I woke up all I could think about was how useful it would be if we had a car. We could buy a kilo of chewing gum, drive to Siberia with a trunkful of grapes, and use the profits to repossess my uncle's wine factory, which we'd lost during independence. We could follow in the tracks of my father and become drivers, and to be a driver was really a noble profession. We could give rides to widows for free. We could bring watermelons to the villages, and grain. I could help weave Georgia back together again into a network. "All right," I had told Malkhazi that morning. "I'll help you kidnap the Englishman."

I studied the pamphlet for tourists I had obtained from Batumi's Center for Democracy. It said:

> *Although kidnapping occasionally occurs in Georgia, it is only a significant risk in a few of the trouble-spots (notably Abkhazia and the Chechen border, and to a lesser extent in Svanetia and South Ossetia). Just as the intense nature*

of Georgian hospitality can sometimes feel like kidnapping, most reported cases of kidnapping in Georgia turn out to be less sinister than in other societies. Perhaps more dangerous are the driving habits. Georgia does not have an emergency road service.

I began a new letter:

Hillary, have you ever given much thought for our need of tow trucks?

(Or, had she given much thought to the fact that our roads were so filled with potholes that even very *good* kidnappers of pipeline workers couldn't make a fast action getaway plan while driving in a broken-down Lada being chased by the Georgian International Oil Association in *their* decrepit old Lada. No, not very exciting, not like that James Bond film about the oil pipeline.)

More importantly Hillary, have you heard the story of our kurdi, *our Georgian mafiosi? It's a story we tell in the kitchen about how after 1917 Russian Revolution, Georgians went to Italy and started Italian mafia. It is long story with many son-of-this and son-of-that. We have no real* kurdi *left now, only kids playing* kurdi *to get drugs, not to start a furniture business or something useful to support themselves. I worry that my little brother Zuka is spending time on the street with the imitation* kurdi, *the drug dealers. My mother is all the time complaining about this. But now is new trend. Real* kurdi *can't have diploma; they must acquire all their knowledge on their own. They hate communism so much they won't even eat the red Jell-O on top of a torte. They can't kill anyone for selfish reasons and they can't get married because they would be away from the house too much since they spend most of their lifetime in jail. They are the lawmakers of jail, the wise men. My friend Malkhazi is trying to revive old* kurdi *traditions but he is already a nobleman. He doesn't need this new profession. This is why I ask you to understand us. Please don't believe what you see on TV. If you soon see his face or mine on the news for criminal activity, it is probably only state sponsored communist propaganda. Or else it is only a joke.*

As always, respecting your way,
Slims Achmed Makashvili

In the courtyard in front of our block, the usual assortment of men clad in their felt mountain caps were huddled under the eaves because the empty fuel canisters in the yard were too wet to sit on. One man bellowed up to his sister to throw down some change. A low voice rose out of the huddle at me, "Slims Achmed! *Modi ak!*" But I waved aside the invitation to drink with them. "We are having a guest," I announced. They nodded and then turned their attention back to our neighbor Soso, who had just returned from his village and was expounding on how to steal electricity without getting electrocuted.

My little brother Zuka was asleep on the sofa. "Get up," I said. "You make the *chaadi* and I'll try to fix the electricity."

Since Zuka sculpts icons in his spare time, and icons and bread are the same—flesh-of-Christ, etc.—Zuka is our designated *chaadi* maker. Zuka is also the family doctor, ever since he found a blood pressure pump washed up by the sea. Personally, I think it is Zuka's method of attracting older women because the ladies love to know their pressure.

"God is sending us a foreigner," I told him so he would wake up a little faster. "We need to give our guest some unforgettable moments." Zuka got up and brushed some sawdust off himself—after Zuka works on his icons, a film of wood dust always sticks to him like hash resin in a Central Asian field.

Zuka ripped open the sack of *chaadi* flour, threw some handfuls into a bowl, added water from the water bucket, and squeezed it through his hands. "It doesn't have to be *exactly* eighty times," Malkhazi always tells him, impatient with housewife superstitions. While Zuka rolled the balls of batter back and forth in his palms, I spliced wires together in the electrical box and sang the new song I'd heard on the radio, "I'm tired of getting stuck in the elevator. I want electricity." Zuka dropped the rounds of cornbread batter into the red sunflower oil, and I salted the eggplant, and then squeezed out its bitter brown juice. When Zuka coughed, I asked him if he had started smoking. He denied it.

Irakli Khorishvili, the neighbor from downstairs, stopped by to watch what we were doing. Finally, insightfully, he remarked, "Ha! Two men cooking. Where's your sister?" Since Juliet had been reading so much English literature for the last ten years, she had been trying to become an independent woman. But I didn't know how to explain this—the neighbor was from an older generation and didn't understand such things. The consequence of my sister's philosophy was that now Zuka and I had to do all the cooking. It was Malkhazi's job to fix the iron, but the iron never broke.

I sharpened the knife on the bottom of a saucer and quartered the potatoes, and then fried them with the garlic and a fistful of coriander. My mother returned from the garden holding a cluster of beets, her hands black and her feet black, and she asked why we never had any napkins and why she always had to wipe off her hands on the pages of English grammar books. Then she scolded Zuka because he had trailed icon mulch all over the kitchen floor.

When Juliet came home and heard that we were going to have an English guest, she stood in front of the mirror by the door, tucking stray strands of her dark hair into a lump under a new hat—some sort of black, velvet, English-teacher outfit that looked like a piece of Victorian furniture.

Shoving on his rain jacket, Malkhazi said, "I'll go find some wine."

My mother turned to me. "Slims, if we are going to have a guest, we need to pound the garlic, and how can we do that with a broken pestle? Go find another pestle on the beach."

I walked the few blocks to the sea, which looked like unpolished silver and made me cold to look at. The waves uncrumpled to my shoes, and crinkled back over the chunks of beach rock that I slogged through, searching for a pestle. I found an oblong stone and tucked it under my arm.

Even though the weather was gray, my mood was cheerful. To have a guest—our lives became a holiday. Usually, all we ever did was gather together with the other men in the neighborhood, hold up ruby glasses of Khvanchkara—the young red wine of our village—and bunch up all our words of Georgian wisdom while trying to make one final announcement: *"In the end the earth unites and makes as one the king and slave."*

Tonight, I vowed, I would stay focused. I would not drink from my *kantsi*, my grandfather's drinking horn, made from the hollowed-out horn of a famous bison. Otherwise, I might become distracted, start endlessly toasting to Georgia, and forget about my plan, which was that after Malkhazi kidnapped him, I would ask the Englishman for a visa invitation.

As I walked home, I tried to imagine our guest. Would he look like the foreign sailors Malkhazi and I used to chase down in the boulevard? "Need English! Need English! Very badly," we would holler, jogging after them. If they didn't respond, we would shout, "Or German!" At that time, we had wanted to start an importing business. Through some South American sailors, we imported a few chickens from Brazil. We made an advertisement of a seductively dressed chicken and taped it to a palm tree on the boulevard: "Brazilian chickens. So sexy!" But unfortunately the chickens caught the bird flu. Then we started an ice cream business, importing specialty ice cream bars from Russia. But with the electricity continually going out, imagine our nerves! We kept the ice cream in the big freezer at the port because there they always had electricity. But then the local dictator moved the freezer to his private residence. "Too many people are sharing the freezer. We are not a communist country anymore," he said.

Maybe this Englishman would be a wrestler. I sang to myself a wrestling song from Eastern Georgia.

You are my brother
You look like an eagle
You are so strong
but your cap is on crooked
and you look like some sort of a boaster
I know that your town is far from where I'm from
but I came to meet you anyway
because I have no other business

What was his business anyway? And perhaps, since I had none, he could share his business with me.

When Malkhazi came home, he plunked down two glass jars of Kakhetian wine on the dining room table. "Were you able to steal some electricity?" he asked me.

"Even the third line is out," I told him.

"Come on, come on," he said to the electrical wires protruding from the wall, untangling them with the teeth of a plastic comb, "I'm tired of shaving with only cold water."

Unable to steal any electricity from the mayor's line, we decided to use the rest of our gasoline on the generator. When Malkhazi got the generator going, he yelled to me above the noise, "This Englishman works for an oil company. Maybe he can get us some more gasoline."

My mother looked at all the food we were cooking and shouted at Malkhazi. "Where are all the guests?" Malkhazi shrugged and said no one was home.

Zuka yelled, "He didn't invite anyone else! He wants to hog the guest all to himself!"

"Go call Tamriko," my mother said.

"Tamriko just left for the resort," I said. "With Gocha."

"Call Zaza. Call Guliko. Call the bishop," said my mother.

"Something is wrong with the phone," Malkhazi said.

"Then shout out the window," my mother said.

Irakli, the neighbor, still watching us cook, called all the neighbors to come join us.

* * *

We heard a little rap on the door. We knew it must be the foreigner because no one knocks on the door anymore. They only shout.

Anthony, the foreigner, stood in the doorway, wielding a flashlight and an umbrella. "You've got some wires that are sparking down there in the stairwell," he said.

"That's normal," I said in English.

He looked like one of the illustrations of the hoopoe bird from our reader in third form. He wore an olive-colored tie and had brushed his blond hair in a lopsided swath behind his ears. He was thin and would have looked jaunty in the English manner, except for his brow, which was furrowed and grim. His brow resembled that of the American president Bush when he was trying to think of something to say, but his boot was stuck in the mud and a combine harvester was heading his way.

My mother stared at him and turned to Juliet. "Ask him how old they must be in England before they marry? Seventeen? Tell him as soon as you marry, I can go back to the village. Tell him the water is purer there."

"Deyda," Juliet said, her face crumpling, "I told you. I have a good job. You don't have to wait for me to marry if you want to go back to the village."

"Oh, how I miss the village," my mother started complaining.

I quoted a Georgian proverb: "The mother said, 'I will die.' The daughter said, 'I will marry,' and in the meantime the house is full of dirt."

My mother shrugged. "Take him into the living room with everyone else. The generator is too loud in the kitchen."

Irakli Khorishvili, his wife, and the local alcoholics from the entrance were already seated in a parliament-like seating arrangement. They had saved the baize chair for our guest so he could feel like a king.

"Please sit here," we all said together in a medley of English, Russian, and Georgian.

Anthony sat down and stretched out his legs. His shoes were funny: red leather sports shoes.

"Why does he wear red?" Malkhazi asked in a low voice. "Is it in honor of communism?"

"It's Euro-fashion," Juliet said, as if she knew.

I turned on the TV. It was the comedy station. The comedian was weeping and saying, "No, don't force me to go to Kazbegi. The women there refuse to have sex before marriage. Waa waa."

"So stupid," Malkhazi said. Malkhazi's family is originally from Kazbegi.

I changed the channel to the news. An American soldier was passing out boots to the Georgian army. "We better not find these boots on the black market or you will be jeopardizing any future American-Georgian relations," the American soldier said to the camera. "American G.I. Joe," I said to Anthony. Now the news broadcaster, the young one whom all the Tbilisi girls used to swoon over (before he was later tragically killed in his hallway by some thugs), was saying, "Today, President Shevardnadze *again* vowed to give up corruption . . ." I stood up to turn up the volume, but Malkhazi waved me away and switched the channel to the exercise station. The aerobics leader shrilly yelled out in Russian, "Do not give up!"

My brother, Zuka, wearing his blood pressure pump around his neck, showed Anthony the new icon he had carved.

"Do you see this icon?" I asked Anthony. "Do you think it's beautiful?" I couldn't remember which saint it was though. "Our problem is that these days we can't remember how to pronounce the names of the saints correctly. In the village schools there were so many leaks in the buildings that the only thing we learned when it rained was how to wash our hair."

Anthony's brow furrowed further and I worried about his sense of humor.

Juliet lit the candles on the table while Zuka piled onto it plates of farmer cheese, tomato wedges, and green onions. A pan crisped the edges of the *khachapuri* my mother was making and the smell spread throughout the kitchen. I set out the jade cups and emptied five liters of white wine into three clay jugs.

At the table, thin ribbons of Sulguni cheese marinated in bowls of butter still browning from heat. Platters of eggplant, rolled in garlic and nuts, sat atop the wild turkey. In Georgia our buildings are always falling down—we pile plates on top of each other like a last hope. Irakli's wife had brought a humble mound of goose pate from the import store. Dishes of sweet carrots, roasted red peppers, stuffed grape leaves and olives vied for a place. I scooped some *pkhali* onto Anthony's plate. "*Pkhali!*" I pronounced for him. "Ground walnuts and boiled nettle leaves."

"*Fali?*" he asked, trying to articulate it.

"*Pkhali, pkhali,*" Malkhazi said, trying not very successfully to be helpful. There was a potato and beef stew, also from Irakli's wife; a chicken and tomato soup from another neighbor; a mutton pilaf; mashed liver; a beet salad layered with cream; fried forest mushrooms; and crepes flavored with pepper. Malkhazi had caught a trout from the river and had slit it open for the eggs. Someone else had brought a soup made of knucklebones. Banana liquor for the ladies, and vodka for the men at the far end of the table, who were quietly toasting themselves. Anthony picked up his fork. "This looks like some sort of Roman feast," he said, "that you see in those religious paintings."

"Tell him to eat," Malkhazi said in Georgian to Juliet.

"Tell him that if he doesn't eat we have no choice but to kill him," Zuka pronounced, also in Georgian, thankfully, looking to Malkhazi for approval.

I gave Anthony my grandfather's drinking horn and told him to hold it still while I filled it with wine.

Malkhazi was *tamada*, our designated toastmaster. After all the glasses had been filled, Malkhazi solemnly stood up. "Even though there is war, we always desire peace," he pronounced. "And this is not only peace between brothers, but peace between nations. The Armenian border guard may stand like this." Malkhazi crossed his ankles. "The Turkish border guard may stand like this." Malkhazi crossed his arms. "The Georgian border guard stands any way he wants to because he's a Georgian, but we are all Caucasian people and we understand the truth of nature."

When I tried to translate this toast to Anthony in English, it sounded sloppy, like someone stumbling over his shoelace, or as if the sentence was about to fall apart but was being held together only by a frayed string, or possibly by the same shoelace, or more like one of our mountain musicians from Ossetia trying to keep the beat of the song on his *chonguri* but irritated because the percussionist is off in the kitchen. I told Anthony, "Even if you cannot understand this toast, you cannot sip. It is necessary for you to drink to the bottom."

My mother brought from the kitchen a Georgian blood pudding fragrant with hazelnut oil, a recipe passed down through the Makashvili family for eight centuries. And then Zuka presented Anthony with three white cakes in the shape of lambs.

"How long will you stay in Georgia?" I asked Anthony.

"It's always impossible to know," Anthony said, balancing a strip of browned village cheese on top of the corn flour bread, and then dribbling wild plum sauce with garlic and the *khmeli suneli* spices on top of that. "Usually," Anthony said, trying to fit his corn bread building into his mouth, "British Petroleum gives a frantic call in the middle of the night and says, 'There's a problem. Please take the next flight over.'" A purple rivulet of plum sauce curled round his wrist. He looked for a napkin and Juliet got up to get a cloth one, which she had embroidered with yellow butterflies. "Thanks," he said, winking at her. "It's not inconvenient because I live so close to Heathrow. British Airways now has direct flights. This is delicious. Did you make this?" he asked Juliet.

"Tell him you don't cook anymore," Malkhazi said to Juliet.

"So I fly out to Tbilisi and they drive me over to Supsa, to the port up north," Anthony said. "It's always the same thing. I say, 'Yes, indeed there is a problem,' and then I fly home. I tell BP again and again, 'If you want the pipeline to withstand the pressure of the river you'll have to dig it three meters deeper.' They shake their heads and say, 'Three meters? That's expensive!'"

"Very expensive," solemnly declared Irakli Khorishvili, who had been listening in to our translations.

"I told them it would be much easier, of course, if they built the pipeline *over* the river, especially since this new pipeline will have to

"Juliet, tell him the women look bored because they know that women can live without men. But men cannot live without women. How can I, a Georgian man, live without women? Even if I am fighting a Turkish man and a woman throws her handkerchief on my sword then I must stop. Isn't that true, Juliet? She is the only one who calms me. We must obey the woman and we must fight for her, and we must win her, even if she doesn't want to be won."

But Juliet was no longer listening. She was taking her guitar off the wall.

"What was he hollering about?" Anthony asked me.

"I don't know," I said. "Ask her."

"It's just men's talk," Juliet told him. "If you could understand Georgian you would see how stupid it all is." She began to strum an old Adjarian gypsy song. After she drinks wine she is never without her instrument.

"What is she singing?" Anthony asked me, looking for a place to put down his drinking horn.

"Carefully! You must not set that down or it will spill," I said. "She is singing a song about a little stream."

Zuka began to dance the *Giorgoba*, an Ossetian folk dance he had been practicing. He kept yelling at Anthony in Georgian, "Why not come live with us? Why not? Don't be all alone!"

"If he wants to sleep here he will," Malkhazi said.

At the far end of the table the men were becoming louder, more obtuse.

"Turn off the generator," my mother yelled. "It's too loud in here."

"*GalmarJOS! GalmarJOS! GalmarJOS!*" the men were singing as the generator went quiet and the light went out.

"What are they singing about?" Anthony asked me.

"They are singing, 'Long live,'" I told him.

"Long live what?" Anthony asked.

"Just long live. I don't know. Long live their song."

He shook his head. "How is it possible? I don't understand how you all survive, or at least how you don't all pass out."

"It's called the Great Georgian Mystery," I told him. "Everyone wants to know the secret."

"My conclusion," Anthony continued, a little riled-up, "is that the only way a country like Georgia can exist is because God sustains it."

"Or because everyone is a criminal," I suggested.

"Of course," said Malkhazi, ignoring me, and commenting again in English. "God sustains every country," he said and then bit into a spoonful of butter.

"I believe that here, absolutely I do, but I can't believe it anyplace else, not when I'm in London."

I think that Anthony must have been getting a little drunk. It's true that when people think about the meaning of life, usually they are a little bit drunk. It is the time when they can become drug addicts so easily. So many times I have seen those Georgians go to the outskirts of Batumi where the narcotics grow up between the railroad ties. They think about why does the neighbor have a car and that kind of wife, and why do I have such idiotic children and this kind of wife? It's better to just drink some more and eat some salty fish. The human law and God's law are something quite different— perhaps they can never be reconciled. Maybe God just wants us to remember we are human by feeling a little sick from salty fish on the bus ride home.

I finally asked Anthony myself, in English, what I really wanted to know. "Your government is paying you a lot of money. Yes? Why else would you keep coming back here?"

"Slims," Juliet said. "He just answered that. He finds God here."

"No, it's a good question," Anthony said. "Maybe I come because it's a great challenge."

"Yes, the exertion of effort to obtain goals brings great happiness," I responded, quoting from my textbook imported from Iran on the free market economy. "But I believe it's much more possible to achieve goals in your country."

"But those goals are nothing," Anthony said. "You think it's a challenge to shop at discount stores?"

"Have you found your challenge here?" I asked him. "And can you share your challenge with me?"

"Well, sometimes here it is *too* much of a challenge," Anthony admitted.

"Yes, most people here have given up," I said.

"This is boring talk. Let's change the subject," Malkhazi said.

I raised my glass. "Let's drink from our hearts to peace between our two nations! *Galmarjos!*"

Though Malkhazi's plan was to kidnap the foreigner, I decided to prescribe to the more modern Georgian way to treat a guest: get him drunk, disarm him, and then ask him for a visa invitation.

"Nope, it would never work," Anthony told me. "To get a work visa you need a business organization to sponsor you. I'm a private contractor. The only kind of visa a private individual can get for you is a fiancé visa." And then he winked at me.

"I'm not gay!" I cried out. And then I realized he had been winking at Juliet.

"Well. Do *you* have a sister?" I asked him.

Anthony shook his head.

"A cousin?" I asked.

He shook his head again.

"Your country is very rich but poor in virility," I said.

I filled up the drinking horn again, handed it back to him, and said, "If you can't get me the visa, then at least you can allow me to poke a hole in the pipeline!" I pointed to our gas canister. "For heat, that only lasts for three days. That pipeline is going to run through my mother's village. I can pay you in roses. Our village is famous for its roses. We can't sell them anywhere anymore because of our transportation problem. But if you provide the petrol, I can arrange to send you a lifetime supply of roses."

Anthony stood up. He was still holding the drinking horn but it looked like he was ready to depart. Malkhazi yelled at Juliet. "Tell him he must drink to the drinking horn he is holding. It's older than his country!"

"Don't insult his country," Juliet said.

"I just meant he should not set it down. It's not time for him to leave."

"How about a mother? Do you have a mother?" I asked him. "Even Armenians have mothers. I can send *her* a lifetime supply of roses."

"Let me tell you something," Anthony said. "No one will ever invest in your country if your people continue to poke holes in the pipeline."

"I think you underestimate the power of the rose," I said.

Suddenly the electricity came on.

"Ah," everyone at the table said in unison, pointing to the lit-up chandelier.

"A sign," Malkhazi said.

At that moment, Shalva, Batumi's most popular policeman, kicked in the door with his boot. Behind him was a crew of cameramen from our local television station. While the cameramen filmed a close-up of Shalva's boot, Shalva told us in Georgian, "Sorry about the door." He then perused the table and finding Anthony awkwardly holding his drinking horn, ran to him and shouted in English, "Are you fine!" It was more of an announcement than a question.

Perhaps Shalva would have pretended to handcuff Malkhazi. The television cameras were already directed at him, but at that moment my grandfather forged through the door. "An Englishman?" my grandfather was shouting. "An Englishman in this home? I have this cherry liquor. See here? For three years it's been sitting on my shelf waiting for a special occasion."

Even though Shalva longed for his mighty deed of saving a foreign pipeline worker from a kidnapping to be written up in the newspaper, custom dictated that he listen to my grandfather's toast first.

"Why didn't anyone tell me we were going to have an English guest? I would have caught a fish," my grandfather said as he poured cherry liquor into tiny crystal glasses and distributed them around the table. "Oh, we're so lucky to have an English guest!" he said to Irakli. He raised his glass to Anthony. "This is to you," he said. "May everything be good for you. May you marry a good woman. May your life be full of happiness. This next toast is to your family, your brothers and sisters and parents. And to your ancestors. Let's never forget our ancestors. Christopher Columbus. You remember him? Why did he have to bring us the corn! Fuck you, Christopher Columbus! I hate working in these damn cornfields. Why couldn't he bring us cocoa or coffee beans or some more interesting crop? Oh, why didn't anyone tell me earlier that an Englishman was coming? I would have killed a sheep!"

5.

As we say in Georgia, "When the guest visits it is like the sunrise. When he leaves, it is sunset for his host."

"Oh, mamma mia," Malkhazi said, clutching his head. "I drank too much last night."

While walking to work, I kicked up squash-colored leaves into the pallid blue air. The shimmer of autumn light on the mountains behind Batumi was interrupted by miniscule tufts of smoke, likely caused by the explosions of people trying to construct some electricity. I glanced at the headlines in front of the Central Telephone Office: CASPIAN SEA STILL ONE OF WORLD'S BIGGEST OIL BLOCKS; WATER SHORTAGE IN RESERVOIR COINTUES TO HALT TURBINES; PIG DEATH IN ADJARIAN PROVINCE BLAMED ON TURKISH PORK SELLERS; PRESIDENT SHEVARDNADZE VOWS TO FIGHT CORRUPTION—AGAIN!; GEORGIAN HOSPITALITY STILL NUMBER ONE! There was a picture of Anthony holding a sheep horn.

Zurab, the newspaper seller, was discussing the market price of petrol. I bought a *Newsweek* from him—he wrapped it in brown paper, and I tucked it under my arm.

At the Maritime Ministry of Law I saw that the white paint still flaked off my side of our building despite the anti-salt solution I had brushed over the walls a few weeks ago. The Black Sea would soon corrode the paint down to the marble. The guards leaning against the counter at the front door filling in crosswords didn't look up when I stepped past them. They never prevented anyone from going into the building, only out. That's why we had to always accompany our visitors to the door.

"Three Georgians united make a world," I chanted to myself walking down the corridor to my office. But at work it was impossible to unite even two people. I could unite myself with neither my boss, his secretary, nor the Big Boss. Any reconciliation was always lost in some hullabaloo. In the hallway my boss, Mr. Fax, was shouting at his secretary. I must digress in order to explain that it's very impolite to say in public, "I need to go to the toilet." Instead, it's better to say, "I must go send a fax." My boss used this phrase so frequently that "Mr. Fax" had become his nickname. Also, he was unusually fond of his fax machine. The previous week the fax machine had been covered in dust, but now, in the corridor, that layer of dust was imprinted with someone's body, as if Mr. Fax himself had tried to cover it up with a big hug, to protect it, as if he had won it in a contest, as if it were a *new* fax machine. Maybe Mr. Fax didn't know that new fax machines were smaller. This one was still huge. Seeing me examining his fax machine—which was blinking "Toner is low" in English—Fax scowled. I looked away. I felt nervous looking too much at the fax machine for I feared that Mr. Fax might figure out some day that I stole his fax from Hillary Clinton. He looked at his watch. "It's already eleven-thirty," he said. "You are late again!"

"True," I told him. "But the state is more than six months late paying me my salary."

Fax ignored me. He received the same salary I did but he made much more money on the black market. Once when I put a tack on his chair he was so busy leaning over his fax machine, trying to extort money out of whomever he was talking to on the phone, that when he sat down he didn't even know what the problem was. He slowly realized he was uncomfortable because he was sitting on a tack. But while one hand scratched his sore behind, the other hand was extended, still waiting for a bribe. Whenever he was about to bilk someone, to receive remuneration for an overinflated invoice, I would walk into his private office and ask, very pleasantly, if I could borrow a book like *The Law of Sea Convention* from his library. Or, "By the way, what is the distance in kilometers from the port of Batumi to the Cape of Good Hope?" And then I would look at the invoice and divide it in half. He would smile in front of his customers, but I could see his clenched fist and his little brain mechanism thinking, "Foo! Foiled again!"

That's an expression I taught him from Sherlock Holmes. I am an avid fan of Sherlock Holmes, even though most of his stories were meddled with by the communist propagandists. For example, at the end of one Sherlock Holmes story, about the mysterious disappearance of the Ku Klux Klan in America, in came the censors proclaiming in brassy tones at the bottom of the page in true Soviet style the following footnote: "Unfortunately Sherlock Holmes was wrong. The KKK is alive and thriving in America. Victory to Soviet Georgia!" The Soviet propagandists also used to proclaim in the *Red Star Worker* that the American husband in his home sits with his feet on his fold-out sofa bed and says to his guest, "Come on in and get yourself a beer from the fridge. But only take one. I don't have much time," and then he looks at his watch. I told Mr. Fax that was only propaganda. I said, "How do we really know what an American acts like if we've never met a live one?"

Even though Mr. Fax knew my opinion of him, he couldn't do anything about it because I was the only person in Batumi who knew about my particular field of maritime law—how the oil ships were affecting the fish. I had spent many years assiduously researching the declining population of the Black Sea spiny dogfish. Originally, I had been attracted to this fish because its name reminded me of a sailor's scrubby insult. But then I learned to love it in a deeper way because it was a full-blooded, pedigreed, Georgian fish, recklessly swarming the reefs and rubble of the Black Sea, our fates inextricably twined, going extinct together. Part of my job consisted of mapping the population of the fish and rerouting oil ships to preserve their habitat.

Because of this, Mr. Fax would accuse me of being an environmental-ist. But I wasn't quite the same species of environmentalist as the in-trepid Greenpeace volunteer I read about who skulks on boats in the Northern Sea at whom the Russians unabashedly yell, "Hooligan!"

But anyway, Fax was holding today's newspaper, shaking it in my face. "I see here that you have met the new foreigner in town? Mr. Anthony?"

I nodded.

Fax lifted an eyebrow. "And what can you tell me about him?" he asked, his voice low and greasy, like under a car engine.

"What is there to know? He likes *tkemeli* on his cornbread. I think he likes my sister."

"This Anthony," said Mr. Fax, "says he is in Georgia to inspect the oil pipeline. But he has been seen near the port observing the oil inspections. And now he is photographing new building construction in Batumi. Yesterday, he was seen at the new kindergarten asking about who funded the project. And next week he is going to visit our office to photograph our customs regulations. How can one person have so many jobs? There is only one explanation."

"He is obviously an agent provocateur!" I said. "Sent to detect self-incriminating acts!"

"Not a spy," Mr. Fax said. "A judge. He is judging our country!"

"Oh," I considered. "That is an interesting perspective."

"The point is, if he is going to judge us, we need to renovate."

I never ceased to be surprised at the method by which Mr. Fax arrived at his conclusions. He developed this particular conclusion-forming method after reading the famous capitalist handbook *How to Win Friends & Influence People* by Dale Carnegie. He had since become a Dale Carnegie technician, perfect at imitating a Westerner, or at least how he supposed a Westerner acts: fawning, unctuous, sanctimonious.

"Perhaps we should show him some anticorruption strategies," I told Mr. Fax. "This might be the perfect time to set up our commu-nity electric meter. It could be a showcase."

At work I was trying to promote the use of mandatory community electric meters. The old ones were out of order and disregarded by every energy distribution company. I had told my boss that if we could get fifty families to share the meter and pay as a group, no one would ever betray their own neighbor, and we would always have reliable electricity. As it was, people would always steal from the government, but never from each other.

Fax looked dubious. "Why don't you work on that while I go to lunch? Make sure you keep an eye on the fax machine."

I always kept an eye on the fax machine. And I wasn't the only one. Whenever Fax was at lunch, Fax's acquaintances usually came to visit. Today, as usual, they drove up in a black Volga, Radio Fortuna blaring. The driver stayed in the car while Zaliko, our town's chief archaeologist, got out, strode over to the door, pulled his mountain hat down over his eyes, and asked if Fax was here.

"Don't worry. He's out," I said.

Zaliko leaned close. "Have I received any faxes?" he whispered.

I told him that he hadn't.

"Foo! I'm expecting a packet from the U. about government aid programs in Armenia. Our land is filled with one-point-seven-million-year-old giraffe skulls, but does *our* government care about funding this? They already have enough Mercedes for everyone in their family." He pronounced Mercedes the French way, with the accent on the last syllable. "What else do they need to spend their money on?"

"You think I know this?" I asked him. "Batumi doesn't even have a bowling club."

The archaeologists usually frequented the local Center for Democracy so they could use the long distance telephone there. But there were too many competing archaeologists at the Center for Democracy. Tempers would soar like the missiles Yeltsin used to launch into the air to blow away all the clouds for a sporting event. The archaeologist had to choose his friends wisely or he would be stepped on. Inevitably he got stepped on anyway, and then he had to pick himself up and learn to run with the others.

When Zaliko left, I typed in "Black Sea Fish" into Google. I only found another recipe for salted jellyfish.

That afternoon, after lunch, Fax called me to his office. On his desk lay the stack of Zaliko's faxes. "Look at this," he said. "It's so interesting. Last year the Americans gave a lot of foreign aid to Armenia! There is an NGO starting a company for, read here," he said and pointed, "'Sustainable Uses of the Armenian Boulder.'"

Fax turned to another sheet of paper, his finger stabbing the page like a blunt sword. "Here is a joint American marketing venture trying to popularize the use of ketchup in Armenia."

I leaned closer, disbelieving. "And here," he added. "A nongovernmental tourist organization in Armenia that is promoting the religious significance of Mount Ararat. And look at their family farmer loan program. Look at their budget. They've included a salary for a secretary for each cow."

"Ah," he continued, shuffling further through the pages, "here's one called 'Global Marketing of Traditional Armenian Bread.' Slims!" he said. "You've been studying English. Why don't you put it to some use for once. You need to write about how Georgian bread is better suited for export than Armenian bread."

"But what's the difference between Georgian and Armenian bread?" I asked.

"The difference is that Americans really like Armenians," said his secretary, as if she knew.

"It's not the bread that matters," Fax scowled, as if we were both some brand of donkey. "It's what you smuggle in the bread. How can we get ahead if we don't tap into this resource?"

"You're a bigger dreamer than me," I told him, "and you're not even my relative."

"Slims, you need to learn to wield your power, like those journalists in Moscow always threatening a political celebrity with a satire."

"That was more effective in the nineteenth century," I pointed out.

"The Americans only give foreign aid to the Abkhazians. I've heard they only like to help refugees," said his secretary.

"I'm not interested in the bread business, but how about water?" I said.

"Water? Yes Borjomi water," said Fax. "Beautiful water. Famous water. We can start a business."

Though Fax was talking about sweet Georgian water, his tone of voice was gruff—as if he were speaking from inside a very important volcano.

When it was almost time to go home, I heard Fax's offensive voice boom down the hall yelling for his secretary, Mzia, to bring some glasses for himself and Vakhtang, a minister from the Ministry of Finance.

When Mzia brought Fax the glasses, I went with her to peruse his bookcase for the Georgian history book *Swords Without Sheaths* in order to ascertain what kind of corruption Fax was planning for this evening.

Fax doled out wine for the minister, Mzia, himself, and poured me a glass as well. "This kind of wine is what we call the beauties from my village. Sweet and dense," Fax said and held up his glass and made a toast. It was the true story about how his wife always criticized him for being so obnoxious when he drank, so one day, when it was their son's birthday, he told her to prepare a feast. Of course she had to drink in her son's honor. She got drunk easily, even on rose petal cognac, and only wanted one glass, but Fax kept making toasts to their son so she couldn't desist. She drank, felt woozy, and went to bed. Then Fax broke all the plates in the house. When she woke up, she looked at all the broken dishes and asked what had happened. He said, "Terrible woman. You got so drunk last night that you broke all the plates. Now don't scold me when my friends force *me* to drink."

Vakhtang patted Fax's back. "*In vino veritas*," he said.

I put my glass down.

"Why didn't you drink?" he asked me.

"Your wine is too sweet," I said.

"Too sweet? Then just add some salt!" Fax said and cleared his throat. "Anyway, anyway, I have called you here to discuss how we are going to welcome Mr. Anthony to our office. We must present to him an image of modernity."

"How are we going to do that?" I asked.

Fax took off his jacket. He was wearing a pink shirt. "Imagine a Georgian *Santa Barbara*," he said.

"The TV serial?" I asked.

"If we just clean up our beaches a bit, from all this crap that floats up from Turkey . . . just imagine the kind of people we could attract to our beaches." Fax held up a photograph. "Look at this reception for British Petroleum at the Park Hyatt Hotel in Baku." The photo showed some dark-haired Russian women sitting on the hood of a sports car, wearing nothing but stilettos. He flicked them with his finger. "My actresses," he said. "They will sit in the lobby."

"Why don't you make a TV serial called *Sex in the Elevator*? That is more true to life." I was referring to the time he and his secretary got stuck in the elevator, after which time their relations have never been the same. Though, to be fair, since the elevators were always getting stuck, this was a very common phenomenon. "Actually, it could be a kind of documentary," I suggested.

"I suppose you would like to make a movie called *Communal Electric Meter*," Fax said.

Mzia, Fax, and Vakhtang all looked at me with pity. And then Fax called me a Bolshevik.

On my way home from work, I sat down at the Paradise Cafe, ordered a beer, and took out some more paper to write to Hillary. The beer was warm and strong and made me start to think philosophically. It's better to be philosophical while drinking, I told myself, even if some might consider it sophisticated, because it's still better than being like a Russian who shouts on the street, "Do you respect me?"

Dear Hillary, I began again.

Since the Soviet Union became broken, the Russians cannot forgive us. It's a complicated story, an ancient story of jealousy. We were the crown jewel of the Russian empire. Now Russia is feeling nostalgia for us, which is normal, except that it has become a dangerous type of Imperial

Nostalgia. You know, we already suffered a lot at the hand of the Arabs, Persians, Mongols, Seljuk and Ottoman Turks, but no power could ever separate Georgian peasants from their grapevines. In the valleys, the first question a guest will always ask his host will be: "I hope no misfortune has befallen your vine, has it?" Every foreign invader has attempted to destroy the vine. Even the Russians tried to make us grow watermelons instead of the vine! It seems a bad fate that God gave us such kind of neighbors.

    But forgive me. By now you may be tired of reading our war episodes. Hillary, I want to cuddle you and your mighty country.

In writing these letters, I admit, I had fallen a little in love with Hillary. Or perhaps I just needed a woman.

It was in the beginning of last summer that I almost got a wife. I had gone back to the village for the cattle breeding holiday. As I walked to our house from the bus stop, I could see girls giggling through the veil of the wooden banisters, the lattice carved with each family's signature design: hoopoe birds, apple seeds, jugs of wine, poppy petals. Some boys were washing clothes while others were playing tug-of-war with the clothesline. The littlest one was making a hammock out of string. Their mothers sat in the shade of their balcony awnings, fanning themselves.

"Slims!" one of the women called out to me. "I heard your mother has gone to the market to trade the bull for a cow!" Her companion, Nona, the postal worker, yelled out that she had read all the letters I had sent to my girlfriend Tamriko that month. In fact, they had *all* read my letters to Tamriko. "It's true," confirmed a third. But it didn't matter to me anymore what they thought. All the problems of Batumi felt as if they belonged only to a bad dream that the cold water from the well could wash away. It was summer and I was home in the village, sunshine and watermelon coming out of my limbs. I was even singing a song to myself, an old Adjarian folk song:

A falcon has flown out of its silk nest
But your love, girl, will never fall out of my heart.
It's raining
and the water washes through my white trousers
But girl, your love is deep in my heart.

I walked by the doctor who was making medicine from herbs and flowers, pounding them down in his boxwood mortar, made by our village's master mortar manufacturer. He scooped out a spoonful of his famous bee venom powder and held it out to me. "This will help you live a potent life," he said with a wink.

Next to him lived the bed-maker. He wasn't home. He was out plowing the popcorn fields. Shota, the artist who made Biblical scenes out of sheet metal, was his neighbor. He was very sorry, he called to me, that he had just sold all his corrugated landscapes to some rich tourists from Tbilisi.

I arrived home to join my cousin's birthday party now midway in progress. My uncles were midway intoxicated, as was the priest who had borrowed a guitar on which he was playing Django Reinhardt's "Minor Swing." My mother met me at the doorway and handed me a jar of cream to go trade for a bottle of shampoo—a birthday present for Giorgi, my five-year-old cousin. Giorgi's older sisters said they wanted to come. Instead, they dragged me out to the tomato plants, sat me on a log, and told me that they thought I should propose to Tamriko that day.

"Why else would your mother be trading her bull for a heifer?" they cried out.

All was colorful and emotional that day. Grapevines ran rampant over rusted iron balconies; velvet plums ripened into orange, red, and royal purple horse riding outfits. Wild sweet peas dangled this way and that, donning their little folk dancing hats. I remembered how in the village, deep depression in the morning is always cured by breakfast.

When I returned with the bottle of shampoo, Tamriko was near the front gate, wearing a white dress. I took off my shoes and sat down on them.

"Why are you sitting there?" she asked me.

I said it was obvious.

She stood next to me, looking suddenly shy. I told her I was waiting for my friend Zaza, who would bring me a fake passport so I could find a government job. I offered her a shoe to sit on. She again asked me why I was sitting there for so long. I looked at her closely and said, "It's simple." Then we threw little stones at each other, gray ones. She still stood so I said, "Why are you standing like a soldier, all stiff?" She didn't say, "I thought this is how wives should be. Attentive," and I didn't say the traditional man's marriage proposal of, "Follow me!" Nor did I propose the way our old Soviet textbooks advised, that if a man wanted to make a woman his wife he was to say, "Let's go to Siberia together and build a city!" Or even better, "Let's join a space program, go to Jupiter, and build a city there!" But Georgia is no longer affiliated with the Kazakh space station so such propositions are irrelevant these days. Instead, I asked her how many days she could go without food.

Three. Just like me.

And then I changed my mind. The village with its fruit and wine and sheet metal art, with its promise of possibility, looked poor and bleak again. I didn't have a job yet, at least not one that paid anything. What was once true was no longer so. I couldn't have her living in the village, standing by the side of the road selling cigarettes like the black-shrouded widows do. I said I needed to find work in order to support her. She said she could support herself with her singing. I said I couldn't depend upon the support of a woman. She said she couldn't depend upon the fickle emotions of a man.

"Besides," she said cruelly. "Gocha said he could get me a job working in his bank!"

"There's no money in the bank," I said.

"Slims Ahmed," she said. "You should know, you're not the only one who wants to marry me. Gocha wants to marry me too."

Georgians have huge hearts. When we love, it is like something crazy. But when we hate, it is something terrible. Whole mountain villages have been destroyed because someone's enormous heart became poisoned and started a nine-generation vendetta. If I were such a type of Georgian I would have grabbed a sword and killed Gocha, or at least pushed his head into the toilet. Instead, I just mutely and cowardly sat on my shoes and watched her walk down the road.

O the Georgian woman. At first she is a trembling bride like a baby calf in the market. But when she marries she stands in the milk room over a pot of boiling milk, her cheeks ruddy from the fire and plump from sweet buffalo cream, her heart filled with frivolity and gossip. She can sing about her love for her village, how she can't wait until summer when she will return to the mountain pastures of Beshumi to take part in the cattle festival, how she will make wreaths out of the vines of the white flowering potato plant for her husband's hair.

It is well known that we Georgians have the highest sperm count in the world; we have always prided ourselves on getting any girl we wanted. But it was obvious that Tamriko wanted a businessman. I was only a dreamer trying to hold her hand.

I wandered back out into the village, hoping to find happiness again. Women in the fields were harvesting huge purple cabbages, carrying them home as if they bore twins. The boys who had been washing clothes were now doing handstands, trying to imitate Jean-Claude Van Damme. Iza, the postal worker, still poking around with her cronies, called out to me, "You sure are walking around a lot."

I ambled down to the river, watched it gorge itself on foam. They say it's impossible to separate a Georgian soul from the land, but I couldn't find the land's soul anymore. I felt like the person from "Suliko"—the old Adjarian gypsy song my sister always played on the piano—the person looking for his soul, asking the bird, "Are you my soul? Have you seen my soul?" and asking the rose, "Are you my soul? Have you seen my soul?"

I wandered back past the plum orchard to my uncle's house feeling *naialagari*, feeling, as the word means in Georgian, "having just returned from the summer pasture in the mountains"—in other words, feeling unhinged. I stacked three chairs from the kindergarten on top of each other in order to sit at the right height and started cleaning grain. The machine was already half-full so I sat flicking the lever every few seconds to let the clean grain fall into the metal bucket. The rumble of the machine calmed me down.

And then I heard Tamriko's voice behind me, singing that song that used to tear me up, the song that the Georgians sang to their relatives on the other side of the border with Turkey when none of the border guards were looking. Was she trying to torture me now?

> *Why don't you turn your head?*
> *Maybe there are tears in your eyes*
> *Why are you plowing with tears in your eyes?*
> *I wish I were a silver bowl*
> *Filled with red wine*
> *Which you'd drink and feel satisfied*
> *Or I wish I were a silver thimble*
> *To protect your fingers*
> *Or a silver coin*
> *In your pocket*
> *I wish I were a sickle on your shoulder*
> *or a sorrow in your heart*

Songs used to give advice to the heartbroken and the misunderstood, but love, these days, doesn't resemble those old songs. So I continued to shovel piles of millet into the grain-cleaning machine, flicking the lever every time the grain got caught in the sprockets. She stopped singing and shouted, "Is that so interesting?"

I turned to her. "It's work," I said and stood up. She squinted her eyes at me—perhaps I was staggering a little from the birthday party *chacha*.

"You have lost control of your reins," she said.

"Ha!" I said. So she notices, I thought. The horse of my soul is leading me in a new direction. And where shall it be?

6.

Dear Hillary,

Do you believe in the Real love? If there is such a thing as Real love wouldn't I have died too when my father died? Hillary, what do you really feel towards him, your husband? I don't know anymore if Real love can be found in Real life but I suggest it is possible to find it in our Georgian films. If You don't know our famous Georgian films, do not feel bad! I will explain them to you.

At Batumi's Cinematography Club we watch under-appreciated Eastern European movies and appreciate them, or at least try to. My friend Malkhazi says that he would rather sit on a tack than watch these films because none of these films have a plot. But plot is for the West, for heroes who have obstacles that are possible to over-come. The films that we see convey pure idea instead. Usually these films are about men rushing through life never producing anything in their relationships with each other that resembles the harmony of Georgian music. The films are asking us, "Do you recognize yourself?"

In your American films, the story is not so complex:

the boy meets the girl and then he loses the girl because his strength is kind of weak and then he gets a little stronger (though still he is not a very strong boy) but he gets the girl again anyway, the one who he does not deserve. In our Georgian movies the boy sees the girl and he opens a bottle of beer for her with his teeth. Another man, maybe his fat boss, also sees the girl, and while staring at her, agog, he drops a hubcap on his foot. For the rest of the film both men engage in multifarious and innovative methods to kill each other: one drops the other from a crane, the other tries to bury the first in a big hole he dug with the bulldozer he borrowed from the state. Near the end of the film, when both men are fighting each other on top of the oil train car, about to get their heads decapitated by a tunnel, they forget about the girl, jump down onto an empty cargo flat, and embrace like long lost brothers. That is the Georgian way, as it should be. If you come here you can understand the truth of Georgian love and be happy.

"That's not the plot of *all* of our movies," Malkhazi said, when I showed him what I had written. "That's only *Serenade*."

In our Georgian movies there is always a character who is fixing the roof. He never actually fixes the roof. He just sits on top of the house, editorializing, or explaining the action. I told Malkhazi that I was writing an American letter and I didn't need a roofer in the letter.

"How will Hillary know what's happening then?" he asked. "She'll just be confused." So Malkhazi thought it was his duty to play two roles at once—one as my friend, and the other as the roofer, in order to insert editorial comments to Hillary.

"It's taking you a long time to write your letter to Hillary," Zuka said. He was carving an icon of Saint Eustace, the cobbler.

I pointed at the Georgian cookbook he had borrowed from the library, *All About Dough*, and said, "Well it took that author forty *years* to describe the nuances of Georgian cooking."

"Have you read that cookbook?" Malkhazi asked my sister. But Juliet said she didn't have time to read cookbooks anymore. She began to describe the grammar symposium she had been required to attend that afternoon at the university. "Nadia, my former classmate, stood before us, holding her pointer so stiffly. If she made any energetic movements this would displease the dean, who sat in the second row taking notes. Such sophistication, such as how Nadia manages her pointer, is supposed to prove that we are a Western nation, part of Europe, and not Eastern, not part of the slow drawl of Asia."

"I think the English teachers are so sophisticated because they do not drink enough alcohol," I suggested.

"Well, trying to imagine my colleagues in an intoxicated state is quite impossible."

Someone on the street called Malkhazi's name so he stepped out to the balcony.

"Besides," Juliet whispered to me, "I was thinking about other forms of communication, without words. I was thinking about when Anthony came to dinner and how he winked at me when I handed him a napkin. When I walked him down the stairs that evening he told me that I didn't seem like a typical Georgian woman, not so old-fashioned, not like those ladies at the university. He said they remind him of Nancy Reagan. It's true. They always use words like *gutter-snipe*. At the symposium today, when Nadia wrote an example on the chalkboard of the English stylistic device that she was demonstrating, 'The world is a bundle of hay, eeach tugs it a different way,' immediately all of my coworkers objected that she had put an extra 'e' in the word *each*. So I started thinking of each one of us. Anthony and I.I was thinking how a real Englishman was in our country, and how with him I could reinvent my personality. I could become a real classical bandit. I could become Juliette of the Shooting Range."

"That university really brings out the aristocrat in you," I remarked.

"Anyway, I have to publish something before the new semester starts or else the university will only give me the students who always eat sunflower seeds in class."

She was supposed to write about all the English women writers who had the name of George in the nineteenth century, but when Malkhazi came back inside he convinced her to translate our mountain poet, Vaja Pshavela (Fellow from Pshavela), into English instead, promising to help her. Since Malkhazi had lived in the mountains longer than the rest of us, he was more intimate with what they wanted to say. He used to climb through the gorges, up to their mist-obscured peaks, and—ensorcelled in the thoughts of the mountain—blend his thoughts and the mountain's thoughts until he didn't know the difference. Actually, when he got to the top, he didn't have any thoughts—the mountains are so steep, all thoughts fall off.

That evening I lay on the couch sated with my brother Zuka's famous vitamin borscht and stared at the wall. Juliet had recently wallpapered our flat with olive-colored wallpaper, stenciled in an Arabic design, resembling the floral chapter titles of one of her Victorian novels. She had labeled everything in English, taping English words to every noun in the house. H20 on the water container. SALT on the crystal bowl of it. DOOR, WINDOW, LAMP (NOT WORKING).

It reminded me of the setting of the old Soviet movies in the seventies, when the strong Soviet housewives used to label all of their household products with the periodic table. For it was a scientific decade, preceded by the decade of the '60s when the Soviet scientists studied John Kennedy's brain. "Well the head is open," they said, "might as well weigh the brain."

I overheard Malkhazi in the kitchen helping Juliet translate "The Withered Beech Tree." That's when I wondered if I was wrong that Georgian love didn't exist anymore because I could hear the love between them. The words leaned over and touched and then settled into a summer-sound murmur. "Everyone, including me," they were reciting, "loves high green mountains haloed in flowers. The smell of spring, fresh grass melting like breaking ice. Sinlessly, without harm, the young sprouts gaze up to the sun, to the world, hiding, but on that soft face . . ."

Malkhazi, in Georgian, protested. "No, no, I don't think that word works."

"Which word?"

"*Sinlessly*. Isn't there a better English word for the tender green grasses in the springtime, you know, the innocence of the little children when they are dancing around, moving their fingers like this, when they dare to dive deeply into summer?"

"I don't know," Juliet said. "I don't know that word."

"What's the point of English if you don't know that word?"

Yes, I considered, what's the point of English if no one listens to the word? I took out a fresh sheet of paper.

Dear Hillary, I began again,

I would like to point out the danger of losing trust in the documents of a minor nation. These documents are but a paper, a plea, and nothing is being done to realize them. Let us recollect the words of your famous American thinker and politician Fulbright that it is an injustice of life that children are killed in a war started by their fathers, and that fathers are killed in a war started by men who act like children. What about the claim in the United Nations assembly that women and children should be protected? For Abkhazians and Georgians, they bitterly grin at these laws. From the very beginning of the Abkhazian war, children witnessed these crimes. In Sukhumi, in school number 12, drunk Abkhazian soldiers played football with children's heads. The same took place when separatists killed 600 people and left their heads on the fence posts.

I didn't want to continue, didn't have the stomach for it.

When I was younger my friends in the village said I had a chicken heart. When Malkhazi heard them calling me that he said, "How a *chicken* heart? Haven't they seen the way you ride over the suspension bridge on your donkey?"

"I'd rather a chicken heart than a heart with no bottom. A bottomless heart never finds the end of pain."

"No, that's an untested heart," Malkhazi had said.

* * *

Since the power was out, I didn't bother going to work the next day. I stayed home instead and listened to jazz on Malkhazi's battery-powered radio. "The Maritime Ministry of Law can survive without me," I told my mother. "No one follows the law here anymore anyway, not even on the sea."

Outside, the late August storms swirled black water around us, like gasoline in rain puddles, but without the rainbows. These were sultry days, dreary as the dull aluminum forks at a Soviet cafeteria, or as a boot wading through gutters of turbid water.

In church, the icons continued to weep, like Father Mikhail had said, but to me it was obvious that the paint was undergoing some chemical reaction to the saturated air, which created condensation that dripped down like candle wax. When no one was looking I even licked it. It tasted salty, but I didn't believe in these tears.

When the torrents of rain pounded down the grapevines creeping up our iron balconies, most people took the weather personally and sulked at home, quoting lines from our twelfth-century epic poet, Rustaveli: "To fate, we owe this sea of woes that over us ceaseless flows." Only the drunk men on the street defied the dark rain, "You think you are the winner? No, I am the winner!"

I tried to think up something good to write to Hillary before crumpling up the half-written note in English: *Hillary, We are fine but little bit sad. Even after World War II we had more electricity than now. Now there is no heating, no water. All day long we are thinking about water, the price of bread. But I think it's our destiny to carry on.*

But how to carry on? Whenever I tried to hunker down to the ground and try to hear God's words, all He ever said was, "Why do you forget everything?" He didn't give us any good sort of advice.

At home, Malkhazi sulked that his plan hadn't worked out. He sat in the kitchen and brooded, leaning back in his chair uttering the name of Georgia, how much he wanted to go explore her regions in a car, as if she were his long-lost, unobtainable girlfriend—a sufferer on top of a hill taking care of the goat herd who knew how to chop firewood but also looked great in a dress, a girl who knew him better than he knew himself. "*Sakartvelo,*" he muttered—this is our country's real name—and looked protectively toward the mountains.

Sorry, Hillary, I just have nothing to say. The same gray colours here. I'm trying to cheer up myself but no use. Maybe you had better just come here and I think we'll find something interesting to do. The KGB archives are closed to us, unfortunately, but we can borrow a gun and go kill a sheep.

Eventually the radio's battery died, and I couldn't think of anything more to write to Hillary, because the only time I was inspired to write was when I listened to the radio—its music made me feel that I was an important hero in a movie, that I had reason to hope that my dream could come true.

I tried making a battery based on an article I found in the library called "Veggie Power – Making Batteries from Fruits and Vegetables." The article cautioned, "Do not eat the fruit or vegetables that have been used to make the batteries. A battery cell made with a potato provides a different current than a battery made with a lemon or an onion." Unfortunately, the writer of the article failed to mention that a current from a potato wasn't sufficient to run a radio.

The generator still had a little petrol left so I abandoned my letter and turned on the TV. "Today the Georgian people have forgotten about the bird flu and are more concerned with how to stay warm this winter," the news broadcaster was announcing. "The weather has let them down." I switched the channel. A news anchor was interviewing the American director of Sateli, the new multinational electric company in Tbilisi. "We love Georgia," the director said into a microphone in front of a crowd of women jeering at him. "We love the people here. The traditions. But the bottom line is, if they don't pay for it, we can't continue to supply them with electrical power." In the background a group of children were yelling for electricity. "*Shuki! Shuki! Shuki!*" they said, pounding the air with their fists. Light! Light! Light! "We can't afford to keep our presence here," the American director said, raising one eyebrow in concentration—he was famous for that gesture—"when ninety percent of the people are stealing electricity. You have, well, an overeducated population here. Bob, have you seen these devices they've rigged up to turn off the meters? I've never seen anything like it. But they need to know we will shut down the entire city if they don't pay their bill." In the far corner of the screen an old woman was shouting, "May God help you the way you are helping us!" Another was preparing to throw a cabbage at the American's head, but then, *your mother*! We ran out of petrol.

We coveted light. During Soviet Union times, we got used to getting it for free. Now the electric bill was more than our monthly salary, but the conspiracy theories still didn't cost anything. Some said the government turned off the electricity in the winter to force people to buy oil from them in order to heat their houses. Others said all of our electricity was being funneled out of Tbilisi and into the aluminum factory in the suburbs. Some joked that if there really was such a thing as Big Brother his little brother was let loose in the electricity factory. On again off again. Every time the light would come on, the refrigerators in the building would make a banging sound. We had a refrigerator rock band in the kitchen. Once I opened the window and yelled, "I want to think about other things besides electricity! Other things!" and no one responded until someone's window popped out—the glass shattering onto the street below. "That's it!" a woman's voice cried from below. "I'm moving back to Armenia!"

But some said we lived in troubled times and that the darkness brought us all together. For in the waiting came neighbors knocking on our door with matches and lanterns, sometimes carrying a pig's head leftover from a wedding with meat still unpicked. In the waiting I lent some tools—a hammer and a ladder—to another neighbor who was doing renovations. And in the waiting Juliet would come home from the university and pound out Adjarian gypsy tunes on the piano. In the waiting some green peas would sprout on the counter and surprise us a little, reminding us of things that grow, of the real life out in the field under the sun. In the waiting everything was mostly simple.

In fact, during those hard times it was difficult to find a place similar to Georgia in the world. We had our own special logic that was not based on individual gain. There is no individual happiness on earth, but we invented our own special calmness when we looked at the sea, or when we felt our will, or when we listened to the Louis Armstrong song "What a Wonderful World." It was even a kind of mortal rapture, the fullness of being, knowing that the next moment everything could stop working. The electrical blackouts kept us in a state of constantly remembering this. We constructed things without any special equipment, without any special effects. It was without institutions, without support of any kind. Of course it wasn't a masterpiece or anything. There were no commodities. Sometimes there was not even food. But it was life most direct. Since I had only known darkness, I sometimes wondered if it was true that we required the darkness to keep us all together because sometimes we just sat and waited in such a strange sort of happiness.

In a magazine I read an article about how in Czechoslovakia there was a new therapy program called dark therapy where a person goes and just sits in the dark. For five weeks he sits in the dark and paints. Maybe he paints things like animals or fish. He starts to see after a few days. It is a kind of inner seeing, not in the air, only in his brain. If you go and you are a little crazy, it is supposed to help you. If you go and you are normal, maybe it makes you a little bit crazy. In the magazine they showed some of the drawings that the man drew. I cannot say they were good drawings. The body was too long maybe. But that is because he was sitting in the dark. When you leave the dark room, the guide tells you how to go. First, in order to adjust to the light, you must wear sunglasses. I thought about how if we sit in the dark long enough to become crazy, we can just sit in the dark some more and then become normal again.

But mostly we raged against the darkness like Yeltsin against the weather and tried to do something about it. Malkhazi had once tried to make some light from scratch by building a windmill out of the remains of the abandoned tea factory. He spent months on it, but even he was surprised when it actually worked, generating enough power for eight-elevenths of his uncle's house in the village. None of us were all that surprised however, when, two days after he got his windmill to work, the government announced that windmills were illegal. Without electricity we were forced to turn to petrol. But now we had run out of that.

I made my way down the dark stairs into the dark courtyard in search of some oil coupons for the generator. I sat on an empty oil cistern in the yard, looked up at the cold stars coming through the sky like fax messages. I waited for someone I knew to walk by, but I just heard the complaints again.

From my little brother Zuka: "The electricity went out and I only got to watch half the movie." From my mother: "Why does only the *governor* get electricity?" From Juliet: "There's no light by which to read at home, so I prefer to stay at the university." From our neighbor, Sadzaglishvili: "My daughter's boyfriend is stuck in the ski lift, so we've lost our chauffeur."

A few years ago a Western aid organization came to town, like a circus troupe in a novel. They called their organization Al-Anon and opened an office in Batumi to help all the wives and sisters of alcoholics. They always said the same thing: "Let go. Let God," which was a very funny phrase. Al-Anon lasted for about three weeks before shutting down because they realized that we already live that way. Everyone lets God do everything.

What about individual problem solving? I asked myself. What about having faith in our efficacy? But how is it possible to think deeply about solving the problems of our country when instead we are always thinking about electricity? Always wondering: If I leave the house I may miss the hour of electricity, and then I will have lost my chance to fill up the water bucket. If I leave the tap open, will I return in time so that water doesn't overflow onto the floor and drip through the ceiling of the downstairs neighbors? Should I take a vacation to the ski resort on Mt. Kazbegi even though I might get stuck in the chairlift when the electricity goes out? Since there was never an electricity schedule we had to plan our day from moment to moment, and never more advanced than that.

I raised my head and announced to the Great Toastmaster in the sky, "I'm tired of thinking about electricity. It's a very boring subject. I will try to put forth individual effort. And if that doesn't work out, then I will just give up for good, and toast Your name."

7.

ON THE BUS TO WORK THE NEXT MORNING, I SKIMMED THROUGH THE packet of my favorite English verbs: to strive, to aspire, to achieve, to succeed. Outside my office I glanced at the newspaper kiosk. FIGHTING RESUMES IN PANKISI GORGE; PRESIDENT SHEVARDNADZE VOWS TO GIVE UP CORRUPTION—AGAIN; ENVIRONMENTALISTS STILL OPPOSE BCT PIPELINE; MIKHEIL SAAKASHVILI, NEW WESTERN-EDUCATED DEMOCRAT, GIVES SHEVARDNADZE A FRIGHT.

I leaned closer and read the last article. According to opinion polls this new Saakashvili was the second most popular person in Georgia. Last year he had accused the state security minister and police chief of corrupt business deals. Now he was telling parliamentary members that they needed to keep itemized accounts of where they had bought their Armani suits and Mercedes and explain how they could send their children to Swiss schools. The current government had scoffed at him, had called him a Bolshevik. Wow, he is similar to me, I thought.

In the lobby, the *panduris* were humming and twanging softly. A group of Adjarian workers were amusing themselves by drinking and singing Ilya Chavchavadze songs in honor of the Georgian warriors whose deeds once awed the world.

"Three Georgians united make a world," I chanted to myself

down the corridor. At the end of the hall Fax greeted me with a little bow. "Slims—Anthony, the foreigner, will be our guest today. I will need you to help watch over him."

At one o'clock, when Anthony arrived, Fax had changed into his pink shirt. He heaved a box of apples onto the center of the conference table and began his charade of acting like a very important man. He sat down in the only chair in the room while Anthony remained standing before him. Vakhtang stared at Fax behind his plume of cigarette smoke, bemused, until, spotting me, he harked at me to get the guest a chair.

When I returned with the chair, Anthony was explaining to Fax, "I'm a geologist, not a shipping agent."

"You are a pipeline specialist," Fax said. Ha ha. Wink. Wink. Hands rubbing together like a nervous girl flirting. "A highly coveted position in Georgia. If you look on the list of jobs we are willing to give immigrant residency status to, pipeline specialist is one of them. Now, tell me, do you know Hillary?"

"Who's Hillary?" Anthony asked.

"Hillary Clinton."

"I'm afraid I don't."

"Too bad. I've been waiting for a fax from her." Mr. Fax said. "Would you like a cigarette?"

"Thank you."

"You have children?" Fax asked.

"No," Anthony said. He looked a little worn out and I started worrying Fax was going to take advantage of him. I tried borrowing Malkhazi's crystal gazer power to silently root Anthony on. I imagined in his heart a mini cheerleader waving her pompoms, which were the colors of his national flag.

"No children?" Vakhtang asked, eyeing Anthony skeptically. He pointed his two index fingers at each other and touched them. "Plus. Minus. If you have two pluses, it doesn't work out. What did you study at the university?"

"Geology," he said.

"Yay, geology," I tried to imagine the little cheerleader crying out.

"Ah, so biology is not your strong subject," Vakhtang continued. "You have a girlfriend?"

"Um, ha ha," laughed Anthony. "I don't need a lifetime supply of roses."

"Yes, you do," I thought. "For the little cheerleader in your heart."

"Ah, yes," Fax said. "Our friend is a business man. He is not interested in roses."

"Perhaps he prefers apples," Vakhtang said and dug into the box of apples. He gave one to Fax. Fax studied it.

"It's firm. It's pink. It's a beautiful apple," Fax said to Vakhtang. "And we have an entire shipping container full of them."

"Don't eat it. It was grown near the Armenian nuclear power plant," I told Anthony. "Fax bought the cargo of apples from Armenia because they looked good on the video. But now he can't transport them anywhere. Transportation is our national problem."

Fax scrutinized me. Even though Mr. Fax was trying to be a capitalist, he had the unfortunate fate of looking like a communist—yellow skin from smoking filter-less cigarettes down to his fingers, the ash long like the criminals' cigarettes in the illustrations of one of my Sherlock Holmes books, his spectacles like magnifying glasses that so exaggerated his watery eyes—heaven help anyone whom he chooses to fix them upon. "You are like a little kindergartener," he said. "So cute with your little jokes."

I heard a man selling watermelon outside. "Would you like some watermelon?" I asked Anthony. "Our watermelon has no radiation." I ran outside to get one.

"Ripe as a fine woman," the watermelon seller said.

"I don't want a wife. I want a watermelon," I said and hefted it inside.

"Is it a good one?" Fax asked.

I cut it open. "Well, it's red," I said and handed Anthony a huge slice.

Anthony took a bite and watermelon juice ran down his chin. "Georgia has the sweetest watermelons I've ever had," he said. "I'd like to take back some of these seeds to plant."

"Do you have a cow?" Mr. Fax asked.

"Beg your pardon?"

"You need good cow compost for this kind of watermelon," Vakhtang contributed.

"Okay, cow compost," Anthony said, writing it in his notebook.

"Do you really want to know how?" I asked him. I told him I had some watermelon seeds from Kakheti if he wanted them, and that it's better to burn the place where you will plant the seeds in order to get rid of the roots. "Plant them indoors in cellophane first. That way when you plant them outdoors you trick them because you can cut the plastic with a knife so carefully, without disturbing them, without them knowing."

"Tricky. Tricky," Mr. Fax said.

"Stop watering the watermelons when they are big and the leaves dry up," I said.

"Then you wait. You wait for the watermelons to sweeten," said Vakhtang.

"Eat some more watermelon, please," Mr. Fax said. "Now, let's talk about apples."

But Fax's secretary peered her head around the doorframe and told Fax that the shipping captain from Odessa had arrived.

"Why don't you take Anthony into my office? Treat him with some wine from my village," Fax told me.

In the hall Anthony stopped to photograph the hat rack piled with sailor caps. I told him, "My boss is going to try to sell all those Ukrainians a Georgian flag so they can maneuver their ships in and out of customs more easily." I pointed at the bookcases. "He is also trying to renovate."

In Fax's office I opened the cupboard, saw the bottle of wine from his village and a bottle of brandy. I chose the brandy and poured some of it into a cup.

"Now, tell me, do you think our law firm looks like modern civilization?"

"Modern enough."

I noticed that Anthony wasn't drinking his alcohol. "This will help you understand us better," I said, pushing the brandy closer to him. "Go on. Drink it. I am afraid I have not been a good enough host," I said. "I wish I could offer you more."

Anthony laughed. "You served me a huge feast, sold your house, whatever the joke was."

"No, really we should have welcomed you with an orchestra."

Anthony laughed.

"It's been done before. Really. If only I could go to England."

"I believe you wouldn't like it. We aren't as hospitable there."

"No, I meant that then I could be your *host* there." I turned on the computer and waited for it to warm up. "My website isn't attracting very many clients," I told him. I opened the page (www.black-seatrading.org.ge). "Do you have any aesthetic suggestions for me? I am trying to appeal to business investors." I showed him what we were advertising:

GEORGIAN FLAGS
MATERIAL: Polyester
FLAGPOLE MATERIAL: Plastic
STYLE: Flying
USAGE: Advertising and Customs Patrol

Also: "We have immediate supply of Greenleaf tea. Georgia's finest elite. Full bodied malt flavor, (bright and bubble varieties). We have large quantities."

Also: "At this time we can provide airplane scrap metal from L-29 piece by piece. Minimum units: one. Maximum units per week: seven."

He looked at the two pictures of oil tankers, at the Georgian and American flag entwined, and the caption that read. "Bridging Nations." He read the quote on the bottom, "We feed our horses on wolves' meat."

"Georgians are quite taken with this warrior mentality," Anthony said. "This manly-man complex."

"What?" I said. "This is not about warriors. Don't you know it's impossible to feed horses on wolves' meat? They eat grain. But we have to do what is impossible. Our society is so corrupt that the only hope is to go against the current. We need to find foreign investors for our country but no business wants to risk coming to Georgia because it won't benefit them financially, at least not right now when the leaders take all the money. But investors must invest out of love, for the love of our history and traditions."

I saw a strange, sarcastic look on his face. "Perhaps you ought to join the rest of the world. Try swimming *with* the current," he said.

"As our former president Gamsakhurdia once said, 'Only dead fish swim with the current.'"

Anthony cleared his throat and scooted his chair closer to the heater.

"I should have gotten a degree in air quality control," I said. "It would have been more useful than knowing about fish. I can haul this heating unit over to your hotel if you like, along with those bookcases in the hall. In exchange, you can teach me about long-term business practices, about the free market economy."

"I don't need a heater," he said testily. "Or a bookcase. But what I can tell you is that if you really want people to invest in your country, first of all you've got to get rid of your mafioso-style habits."

I looked at him in surprise. "Mafia? You think we roll our enemies around in pickle barrels? You think we have connections to Saudi Arabia and carry around a suitcase with twenty million US dollars in cash? You think we say to each other, 'I have the most *beautiful* house in Beverly Hills but you can buy the one next door' and then burn down the house for the fire insurance?"

"Well, the ones in power, take your dictator of your little province of Adjaria here. I think he's kind of sheisty."

"Ah, yes," I said. "Of course. But. Do you think he cares what you think?"

"He may not care what I think. But what about the long-term? Is it really in his long-term business interests to lose his foreign investors?"

"You think he cares about long-term? Long-term he will be sitting on the beach laughing at you."

"I still think that it is necessary to set a precedent that it's possible to achieve progress through legal means."

"Well then," I said. "Teach me how!"

"You can start." He took a sip of his brandy. "You can start by telling those men in your villages to stop poking holes in the pipeline."

"Ah, I see. You think it's only men. It's also the women. And the archaeologists. In order to fund their research. They think, 'If the pipeline is going to run through our archeological sites and old graves and property, then we have a right to some of the oil. It's the capitalist way.'"

Anthony snorted.

"Please tell me, with complete truthfulness. Do you think we have a chance at success?" I asked. "Or should I just give up and praise God's name?"

"You have a chance here if you can help me stop those folks in your villages from poking holes in the pipeline."

I surveyed him and lit a cigarette. "The people in the village are real mountain people," I said. "They are very, you know, rude. They aren't used to foreigners, and so who knows what they might do to you?"

"I don't think you understand that if they keep sabotaging the pipeline the military is going to be sent in."

I couldn't help laughing. "Our little villages are so important?" I asked. "I'll take you there and you can tell the archaeologists yourself to stop poking holes in the pipeline."

He took another sip of brandy and asked for a cigarette. "I never used to smoke," he said. "I seem to be in some sort of culture shock. I've lost my iron will. I spent the whole morning just staring," he said. "Feeling like some sort of Hamlet. Like those men outside. Those men just yelling in the parking lot."

"Which men?" I asked.

"Out there, in front of the fruit stall."

"Them? Actually, they are not just yelling," I said. "They're watching out for each other."

"Well, what are they yelling about?"

"Well that one, the security guard? He used to be a famous Soviet actor. There is a monument to him in Kutaisi. He just said, 'Hey, brother! The price of flour is cheaper over there.' That one relaxing in the beer truck? He used to be an opera singer. He just shouted to the woman standing at the bus stop that the bus doesn't stop there anymore. And that one leading a goat used to be a famous mathematician at the Agricultural Institute. He is yelling at the little boy not to smoke."

"I feel languid," he said. "Like I can't move."

"It's blood pressure," I said. "Because of the weather. You need to drink a cup of coffee."

"I don't think it's about blood pressure," he insisted. "Before I came here I had my astrocartography chart done. My astrologer said that Georgia was a dangerous place for me, that I would be dealing with forces beyond my control—sex, death, the oil industry—that frankly, I shouldn't come here unless I was participating in a sporting event."

"Your astrologer needs to go hit himself with a big stick," I said.

"But perhaps he was right. I feel that fight-or-flight instinct here," Anthony said.

"You have traveled all around the world doing your geological surveys. Haven't you accustomed yourself to that feeling?

"Yes, but other places I felt like fighting. Here, the flight instinct dominates."

"Yes, I see that."

He was only seeing the darkness here, not the light and relief that darkness brings.

When I walked home, the new bishop was speaking in front of his handmade church he had just completed. Tamriko was there, listening in. I hadn't seen Tamriko since the summer. I'd heard she'd gone to a resort in Borjomi with Gocha. She was wearing a yellow housedress, and the usual halo of her hair was flattened against her face by what looked like the heat of exertion.

The bishop was making the following announcement: "I have told you before, it is a sin to trade your cow for some furniture."

Tamriko objected. "Of course it's a sin to barter your honor for gold," she yelled out, "but where's the sin in bartering cream for a sack of cornmeal?" The problem is that the new bishop worked for the government and it was bad for the government's economy to barter—that practice didn't support a sustainable taxation system.

When she saw me she pointed at my pants and said, "Nice trousers. New shoes?" The bishop had recently tried to object to these kinds of conversations during his sermon. He said, "When you are in a church, or standing outside of one, you should speak more quietly. Practice reverence." But we are Georgians. We don't know how to speak quietly.

The bishop was now reading from the Bible, from the book of Isaiah. "Those who wait upon the Lord will renew their strength." He looked up from his book and told us, "This is a story written by a desert people—not in a subtropical climate—but do we not have the same desert climate in our hearts now?" He bent his head back to the book. "They shall mount up with wings like eagles. They shall run and not be weary. They shall walk and not faint."

The only problem is that these days usually Georgian women don't have a second wind. When they walk up a hill, "Whoo!" they say, fanning themselves, and must sit down for a little rest.

"Slims, can you help me carry some buckets?" Tamriko asked. "The water is out." I wondered if her opinion of men was that they were only useful in order to haul things. But in the beer factory district neighbors always help neighbors haul up buckets. Guests help hosts haul buckets. Press the elevator button. Hard. Press it again in an exaggerated fashion, as if you are on stage and the audience is far away.

"The problem is the new import store," Tamriko said on the stair landing. "Whenever their electricity goes out it affects the fourth, sixth, and eighth floors. When are they going to fix it?"

That was the question. The answer was that no one knew how. That was the problem.

"We don't know anything about these *industrial* problems," Tamriko said as we hauled another bucket up the stairs. "We are an agricultural country. Slims, we don't remember, but my mother says that Russians always did the industrial work. In Rustavi, at the metallurgical plant, they had to call in people from the Urals who knew about these things. We are deeply connected with the *land*. We are perfect at watching over the vineyards." She began to sing:

Blossoming vineyard
So tiny, so kind
planted in paradise
We are a vineyard country
As long as you live
we live also.

"Do you remember when I sang that song at the chess championship?" she asked.

"Yes," I said. "It was beautiful."

"Well the government doesn't have any more money to sponsor another concert. So what can I do now? Go to Moscow? They are so terrible to Georgians there. Also, I've heard that in Moscow these days you must always be on time. How grotesque!"

In her kitchen, Tamriko fanned her face dry and lit a cigarette— only, it wasn't a cigarette, but a garlic stem.

"To keep away toothaches," she said, blowing garlic smoke out the window. She clipped the ash off with some scissors. "Drink this," she said and handed me a glass of fermented mushroom tea. "Herbalife recommends it."

All day long, in order to counter the baleful effects of radiation, controversially regarded to bring summertime hallucinations, Tamriko and her mother, Guliko, the kindergarten director, sipped these shots of fermenting mushroom tea at room temperature. The jars of mushrooms overcrowded her kitchen counters like an American PTA meeting. The mushrooms, even though they were fermenting, continued to reproduce. She thought all the neighbors coveted the biggest one. She called it Our Mother.

"Did I tell you that Shalva came yesterday to tow our car?" she said. "I yelled at him, 'You have no right to tow that car.' I even ran outside and threatened him until he ran away. Imagine! The policeman running away with me running after him." She went to the sink and began washing cucumbers with the water from one of the buckets. "Sometimes I think . . . what now?" Her attention was distracted by something out the window.

I looked outside and saw a truck pulling a house down the street with a seatbelt. A pedestrian, tired of the slow wait, stepped over the strap.

"They always love to tow something," she said as she sliced the cucumbers.

As I watched her with the cucumbers I couldn't help admiring her hips. I tried to distract myself by remembering what was common between us, to try to share one consciousness with her like I do with my friends when we stay up all night playing Monopoly until everyone owns everything and we turn it into a giant Monopoly commune. But my eyes roamed back to her hips. As we say in Georgia, "Whoever *I* love is the most beautiful." But she was no longer mine. "Tamriko," I said, "I should leave."

"But you must try these cucumbers," she said. "I brought them from a village near Borjomi. Oh, close the window. It's starting to rain again." She set down the knife and surveyed me. "Why do you always wear black? And you ought to wear a different hat, you know. Your hat reminds me of a revolutionary. Revolutionaries do not make very good mates."

"Well, what kind of man does make a good mate?" I asked.

"It's better to have one of those Robin Hood complexes," she said. "It's very romantic. Though it's something quite different from that movie with Errol Flynn. You Georgian men are so emotional. Imagine if you took all that energy and used it for something useful, like stealing something." Suddenly the light came on. "Oh! You see? What I'm saying is true! Can you plug in the refrigerator?"

"Okay," I said, reaching down to plug it in. "Can I read you something I've written in English? I'm asking Hillary Clinton for some help for us.

After I read to her everything I had written, she stood up, walked to the stove, leaned over it, and tasted something in the pot. "Strange," she said. "I feel ill."

"What's wrong?"

"I'll be fine," she said, fanning herself with her hand. "I feel a little faint. It's the changing of the seasons."

"I hope it's not anything I said."

"Well no," she said. "Actually, yes. It is. Slims, it's depressing what you write about Georgia." She slumped down into a chair. "But perhaps it's important to face the truth. We must."

I sat uncomfortably. The last thing I wanted to do was depress people. "But is this the truth? That is my question," I said.

"All I know is that I'm Georgian. That gives me some strength when I wake up worried in the middle of the night. My mother only receives fifteen lari a month for a pension. She feels guilty that she doesn't pay for our food. I tell her that fifteen lari buys all our bread but still she sulks on her couch. And she fell yesterday and had to go to the hospital. Oh, don't listen to me. These kinds of complaints are something for confession. Usually I try to think of others. But sometimes I wonder, who are my true friends? But who am I to complain? The neighbor's son has a heart disease and the operation will cost a thousand dollars. Maybe you *should* go there. I have heard that in America they are very charitable. They have donation societies and people put money in a box at the airport." She handed me the plate of cucumber slices. "Anyway, don't worry. Try these. Did you hear that this new bishop had a dream? He says that when Jesus returns, the first place He is coming back to is Georgia, up in the mountains near Kazbegi. He marked the spot with a Georgian flag. When that happens, people will start marrying again."

"We have to wait until Jesus comes back to start marrying again?" I asked.

She shrugged.

"I should go," I said. But the cucumbers *were* so fresh. I reached for a cucumber and knocked the knife onto the floor.

"*Opa!*" Tamriko said. "If a knife is dropped a man is coming, if it's a fork . . . no. No. A spoon. Oh, I don't know. If it's a knife though, a man is coming."

"Maybe it's Jesus," I said, picking up the knife and handing it back to her.

8.

THE NEXT TIME THE ELECTRICITY WENT OUT THE ONLY PERSON WHO
wasn't complaining was Malkhazi. He said, "Good thing we have
such a powerful car battery. It provides good enough light to shave
by." Shalva had decided to give Malkhazi his car after all. "He just
got back from Frankfurt where he bought a new car," Malkhazi explained. "He drove it through Austria, Italy, and Turkey. He avoided
Bulgaria because he got beaten up there once before. You know, Slims,
one car can usually feed a family of four for a year. But Shalva is very
resourceful. He even knows how to make fruit roll up on his cutting
board. When I was visiting him he kept having to go out to the balcony to check on the chicken sausages that he was smoking. He even
has a business certificate framed on his wall."

Malkhazi now spent all of his time in the courtyard under the
fig tree fixing up his new car and listening interminably on the tape
player to *alternateev* music that some foreign sailors had given him
at the port: Nina Simone, Ray Charles, Tulku. Practically overnight,
Malkhazi, the Disco King, had become DJ Ethno-musicologist.

I spent time a lot of time in the car too. It was like our own
spiritual hut. "I don't know what else to write to Hillary," I admitted
to Malkhazi one evening, when he had just finished painting it. "I

really think I would be a good candidate to teach about peace and security in our world. I need to go there and give Georgia a better reputation. Do you know all our foreign shipping clients don't feel secure here?"

"How can they not feel secure here? We are a friendly people."

"I did an online survey at work. I asked them to rate their feelings of security in Georgia between one and ten. They rated it, on average, negative five."

"Foo. If you really want Hillary to invite you to America you should change your name. It's a Muslim name. Hillary is going to think you're a terrorist."

"Why don't you change *your* name?" I asked him. "Your name means little, nimble man. But you're big and slow."

"Read to me what you have written to her so far," Malkhazi said. "Maybe I can give you some advice."

He listened while I read and was silent when I finished. Finally, he said, "You didn't tell her about David the Builder. Let's make a toast to David the Builder."

"Be quiet," Guliko, the kindergarten director, called from her balcony above.

"I'm sick of your Georgian heroes!"

I rolled up my window. "I could never marry Tamriko because then Guliko would be my mother-in-law!"

"Hmm," Malkhazi said as if he were really weighing the pros and cons of that possibility. "Well, since she's not your mother-in-law yet, and is unlikely to become your mother-in-law unless you do something about it, you should write about our twelfth-century battles. Tell Hillary that fifty percent of our Georgian traditions consist of explaining how it is possible for men and women to have a relationship, and fifty percent are about our battles."

So I wrote to Hillary about David the Builder, how he was a great Georgian dictator in the twelfth century; how under David the Builder, five thousand Georgians fought against fifty thousand Persians; how he called Georgians together in the name of Christ. It was a great inspiration, but even though he built a lot, he thought he didn't build enough, so because of this, he wanted people to trample on his grave in Gelati. "But Malkhazi," I said. "In the seventeenth century, when Tbilisi was being pillaged for the fortieth time, our people lying in the carnage, this person's limb going in one direction, that person's head in another, who was thinking about David the Builder? Besides, this is a modern business letter," I said.

"What is this *modern*?" Malkhazi said. "The communists destroyed our traditions. The true Georgian can only be found in the twelfth century, in our Golden Age."

"But twelfth-century characters were always weeping in the forest," I said. "I'm tired of people weeping for Georgia. Even the icons in the churches are allegedly weeping for Georgia."

"That's because they always weep before an invasion. That is why I must prepare my sword to fight the enemy." He rolled down the window and shouted up to the balcony. "Juliet, let's go get a cutlet." But Juliet didn't have any time for us. The English teachers were having a scientific competition on the verb "to be."

We hadn't had any electricity for nine days and I was a little worried about Anthony. I felt sorry for him, imagining him hauling buckets of water up the stairs by himself, without any company. I told Malkhazi, "We should give that British guy some help."

He started the car and we headed to the Paradise Hotel, where Anthony was staying.

But when we got onto King Parnavaz Street, Malkhazi shouted, "Your mother!" A policeman was waving us over with his glowing red stick. Malkhazi drove to the side of the road. He grabbed his documents from under his sun visor, stepped heavily out of the car, and tried to explain to glowing red stick man that he was a good friend of Shalva's, that this was Shalva's former car, and that is why, even though his turn signal was out of order, he shouldn't be written a ticket. Of course the policeman agreed with Malkhazi that he shouldn't write a ticket because who would benefit from that—certainly not the policeman who hadn't been paid his salary in ten months. A crowd of other policemen skulked around him.

Malkhazi watched the policeman shift his weight from one foot to the other while standing in the middle of the road, examining Malkhazi's documents by the flame of a cigarette lighter.

Malkhazi walked to my side of the car and reached his hand in the glove compartment. "Here, do you want this document too?" Malkhazi offered the cop, suddenly cheerful. He gave the policeman a page of English grammar. "How about this one?" He handed him a university exam question written on a 3x5 sheet of paper. "And this one?" He gave him his library card. And then, even though Malkhazi was technically too young for such certification, he proffered a pass called *Victims of Soviet Repression* that permitted him free entrance into any museum.

Another policeman, perhaps tired of the hesitancy of the first, and ready to find a more lucrative client, tiptoed behind the one trying to sort through all of Malkhazi's documents and said to him, "Why do you insist on *all* of his documents when you don't even know how to read?" Then, with a wink, he waved Malkhazi on.

Malkhazi laughed hilariously as we drove down the road. "Did you hear him?" he cried.

I shook my head. "In America, you could never get away with that."

"Are you telling me that if a police stopped me in America and I said, 'I am George Bush's relative,' they wouldn't let me go?"

"According to my law book, no."

He shook his head and clicked his tongue. "Why do you want to learn about such a system?"

The Paradise Hotel was in the district called "I'm Kind" (it's kinder than it looks) and was an old relic from the times of the Soviet Union. We parked in the parking lot and walked toward the building. "How many hours of water do you think he has a day?" Malkhazi asked.

"Maybe three?" I said, looking for the entrance.

"That's good enough," he said and shrugged.

"At least the courtyard always has water," I said, pointing to a spigot.

We climbed the stairs, avoiding the rebar.

At his door we called out to him. While we waited, Malkhazi bent some wires back in the wall that were hanging above the doorway.

When Anthony opened the door he was standing in the dark.

"Give him some matches," Malkhazi said to me.

I lit my lighter. "What are you doing in the dark?" I asked.

"I don't mind it, really," he said. "I think better."

He hadn't bothered to brush his hair. It stuck up like a field of rough straw.

"Are you becoming a Hamlet?" I asked.

Malkhazi was examining the telephone that sat on a little table by the door.

"Doesn't your telephone work?" I asked Anthony. "I've tried to call you."

By the light of flaming newspapers we examined his living environment. Malkhazi looked around the kitchen. "If he wants hot water, it looks like he has to use this heating prong," Malkhazi reported to me. He opened a cabinet. It was empty. "If he needs anything, tell him to make a list."

Malkhazi opened the refrigerator. "Ah! Ketchup!" he said. "Tell him if he wants to eat anything, my friend Vakhtang's wife lives downstairs. Manana. He can just knock on her window."

"My refrigerator is empty because I unplugged it," explained Anthony. "It makes too much noise every time the power goes out."

Malkhazi was opening the window. "Manana!" he called. He cupped his hand and called again. "Manana! Hmm. She is not home."

"How long have you been without electricity?" I asked him.

"About two weeks."

"Why didn't you *say* something?" I cried. "I gave you my *telephone* number."

"I thought it was normal."

"It *is* normal," I said. "In Africa. You are staying in the same building as the mayor. Everyone in his region should have electricity. Obviously, someone has been stealing yours. Anthony, if you are too filled with pride to ask for help, you will starve here. Do you have some tools?"

"What for?"

"We will steal your electricity back for you. It's the one thing we know how to do very well. And Malkhazi can make you a second line, and a third line. I cannot guarantee that they will always work, and you must be careful and not electrocute yourself when you switch over."

"I prefer the legal method."

"Yes, there's always that," I said. "But next summer will arrive before you get any result. By then it will be hot and you won't need any electricity. You can go sit by the sea. Or in the Paradise Cafe that has air conditioning in the basement, and a very good violin player, always playing French songs. Why not do it the easier way? Don't you know the story about the Svani man? He was driving his walrus backward and the tusks were digging in the ground. 'Turn it over,' someone said. 'Oh, it's easier now,' he said."

"That is ridiculous," he said. "What about the electricity company? Can't they restore it for me?"

"Who?" I asked.

"The people who, you know, govern the electricity."

"Who does that?"

"Don't you people know? Don't you ever think about taking charge of your life? It's insane! How can a country like Georgia go on existing?"

"We wonder that too," I said.

He sat in a contemplative mood and I started worrying that the Hamlet complex might be returning to him. "Can I offer you some tarragon lemonade?" he asked.

"No, thank you," Malkhazi said. I could tell he was a little offended that Anthony was declining his help to fix his electricity.

He poured two cupfuls from a green bottle on the table but I saw the fizz had all vanished.

"This guy really confounds me," Malkhazi said in Georgian. "He probably wouldn't even steal money to feed a houseful of widows. What's the matter with him? Maybe he's hungry."

"He might not want to eat anything," I told Malkhazi in Georgian. "I think he's really in a cultural shock."

"What should we do?" Malkhazi asked.

There was only one solution. Take him to the finger puppet theater.

Bankers were there with their families, sitting in the front, yelling "Bravo!" and impatiently clapping their hands. Niko, Batumi's finger puppet director, had taken out a loan for his finger puppet show. When the bankers had called back on Tuesday night and asked Niko when he was going to pay back the money, he said he could repay them in tickets. Now, the bankers' sons squirmed in their fathers' laps waiting for the spectacle to begin.

A finger, a professional finger, dressed up in the latest Italian fashion trends, slinked down the miniature fashion runway. Women fingers, bedecked in gauze and old lace, danced a traditional finger folk dance from Ossetia. The folk music, loud and accordion-filled, inspired the fingers to jump twice their height. The banker children were laughing hysterically. The finger toy soldiers wore little feathered hats. A finger martial artist and a finger bionic man fought in slow motion. The bankers continued to yell, "Bravo!" And then came the erotic dance. So riveted were the fathers that they forgot to cover the eyes of their children. A whole naked hand pulled off the glove of another, one finger at a time. For once the audience's attention was focused on something other than their own miserable and heavy hearts. Instead of the hot daily tears of frustration, cool tears of relief flooded down cheeks.

"And now the real show begins," I told Anthony.

The plot was as follows: Some of Tbilisi's parliamentary members built a time machine and flew back into the 1930s. They ran into a finger puppet of Stalin on the street. Just as Stalin was about to shoot their heads off, the electricity that fueled the time machine went out. (That was part of the performance.) Without electricity the time machine defaulted back to modern day Georgia. The finger puppet parliamentarians got out of the time machine, slammed the door, and said, "Give me this year without electricity. It's better than the years of the Big Man." In truth, it was a rerun. We'd all seen this one before on television. And we all knew the moral: the electricity went out and they were saved.

9.

WHEN I WAS WALKING HOME FROM WORK THE NEXT DAY I PASSED THE
new pizza restaurant. The usual boys who work at the Internet cafe
were sitting at the tables outside. They had gloomy countenances,
stooped shoulders, and were thin from thinking too much. But at another table I saw Tamriko, sitting alone. She was looking very tender
and beautiful today, and her lips, for some reason, reminded me of
the rubies in Queen Tamar's ruby necklace, the one in the State Art
Museum. I looked around for Gocha but the only boys were the ones
from the Internet cafe. They were now trying out one pose with a cigarette and then another. I noticed Zuka had joined them. I nodded to
him but my eyes returned to Tamriko, and then to her lips.

I ordered an ice cream coffee for her. During Soviet times, coffee
used to be a capitalist drink. Mothers-in-law would complain to each
another, "Oh, poor me. I have such a terrible daughter-in-law."

"Why? Is she a whore?" the other would ask.

"No, worse. She drinks coffee."

But during Soviet times Tamriko and I used to stand in line at
the cafe where the poets would secretly recite poetry to each other
and the KGB stood around supervising. We would order a cup of coffee, drink it, then get back in line, drink another cup, and another,
until we felt fantastic.

When the Soviet Union collapsed, we still drank coffee, but instead of reciting poetry, Tamriko was always talking about how Georgia was changing, wondering if she should learn English with an American accent or a British one. "Why aren't you talking about our relationship, and how to improve it?" I asked her once. As far as I knew, she still drank coffee. Yet when the ice cream coffee came Tamriko said, "Give this to Juliet. She's meeting me here."

"Why? Are you fasting?" I asked.

"No, I'm on a diet and I can't imagine eating, not me," she said, so apparently modest was she. But look behind a pillar, or a leafy plant, and Tamriko was always smoking a cigarette. "The Georgian woman smokes like a ship," the French poet writes in graffiti on the French buses. But the Georgian woman also knows how to flutter her handkerchief to turn a man into a slave so that all he desires is to carry her up the stairs.

Tamriko was now pulling the hot peppers off her pizza and putting them on my plate. "I am thinking of getting a virginity restoration operation," she said. "It costs four hundred dollars."

"Hello, Middle Ages," I said.

"Gocha is a modern boy like you, Slims. He likes partying, soccer, and computer games, but he won't marry someone if she's not a virgin. He's the one who suggested it."

"If you marry, it's a pity," I told her. "If you don't marry, it's a pity."

At the next table Zuka had lit a cigarette. Readjusted his pose.

"Look at me," Tamriko said, sharpening her lip liner with a razorblade. "I used to be so beautiful but not very wise. So many men wanted to marry me. But these days the good men refuse to marry. But Slims, a woman needs a man. A man is a mountain. A woman needs the shade of a mountain."

"Or at least the shade of a little hill," Juliet said, sitting down.

I scraped some mayonnaise off my pizza and put it on Tamriko's plate. "These days maybe it's better not to marry," I said. "Besides, you already had a husband," I reminded her, because she had married ten years ago when Georgia was all helter-skelter and young men and women were running off together in an ineffectual attempt to create stability. But then her husband sailed away on the Black Sea. I mean, it was his job. When he returned and was cleaning out the chicken coop, Tamriko told him, "I don't want to be like a woman in a fairy tale, always waiting for you to return." So they divorced five years ago. But then Tamriko became a hypochondriac and thought she was going to get that disease that women develop when they don't have a man, that a woman must have love and express that love because that is her nature.

There is a poem about the Georgian woman, if I can remember it correctly. It is about how they pray to God, how they have a sweet part, how the enemy threatens them. It goes:

> *Georgian woman!*
> *Don't give away your soul,*
> *and don't let the enemy break you*
> *you want to retain completeness,*
> *oh woman, Georgian woman*

Oh whatever! I can't remember it.

There is another poem, not so good, but still, it makes its point, called "The Georgian Man."

> *I am a man*
> *I have a son*
> *He gives me hope*

But I didn't have a son yet, and my life was speeding by, unapplied. Sitting here with Tamriko seemed to exaggerate that point. Usually, whenever I was about to sink into a depression that I was a man without a wife, I would remember the old Georgian saying, "If a wife is so great, why doesn't God have one?" and feel a little better. But this time, remembering that didn't make me feel any better.

Juliet interrupted my thoughts. "Slims," she said. "Do you think Anthony is a homosexual?"

"No," I said. "I think he's a petrosexual. He only caresabout oil."

"Ah, yes," Tamriko said. "How can we understand these modern sexualities these days?"

"The only way a Georgian man knows how to make love to a woman is to buy her things, cans of Pringles potato chips," Juliet said. "Or orange Fantas. That is the problem."

"The problem is the word *love*," I said, "which sometimes means something stupid, and sometimes means the purpose of life. My love for a friend, or for a woman, or for this country, is something all very different. How can I compare one kind of love that sustains me, and another that destroys me?"

"It is the same as the word *head*," Juliet said. "My head is something quite different from an Iranian refugee's, or even an English person's head. An English person's head is very magnanimous and free, simply because it is other and quite beyond mine; whereas my head is there to keep the rain from coming into my throat."

I stared at her. Sometimes she said some extraordinary things.

"Have you noticed, Slims," Juliet continued, "that Malkhazi is always disappearing somewhere. He says he's gone to sell cucumbers, but really I think he's involved in some kind of black business."

"They always blame the poor cucumber!" Tamriko said.

"Maybe it's better for you to forget about Malkhazi," I said.

"But what is the alternative?" Tamriko said. "You don't want to get the climax disease. A married woman never experiences the mood swings of menopause. What about the finger puppet director?"

"Niko? He only has one small room above his finger puppet theater."

"What about the documentary filmmaker?" I asked.

"The one who was always trying to woo me with his films about ancient Svani door locks?" Juliet asked. "He thinks I'm already too far gone with the climax disease. I'm not sure I even want to marry a Georgian anymore. In England they don't believe in this disease. They are more independent. They live privately, make appointments, call before they visit. The women don't sit home all day in their black dresses grinding coffee, hoping a neighbor will turn up. Nor do they gape from their balconies trying to find something funny. They don't have men pilfering my books or scolding me for not cooking cheese bread more often, or always pointing out the advantages of the code of Hammurabi. The point is, if I married a foreigner, then I could think about other things. Besides love. Georgian love is too difficult," she said.

"Well, that's a very modern thing to do," Tamriko said, curling off shavings of lip liner again. "But," she said and looked up at Juliet, "are they fertile?"

"They take a lot of vitamins," Juliet said. "Westerners take vitamins under constant fear of death."

I had always thought that Juliet would marry Malkhazi, ever since he first moved to Batumi and started courting her. I had always assumed that Malkhazi would become my brother-in-law, that they would have a village wedding with potato flower wreaths, or maybe he would kidnap her and take her to a tower in the mountains in order to save money on a costly wedding—then you don't have to feed the whole town, only the closest relatives. But Malkhazi didn't want a regular job, he wanted a job that would make him feel like a king and I was no longer sure if he was the right man for my sister.

"It's better to find a man when you are young," Tamriko said. "It is the condition of the world that as men grow older they lose their ability to express their feelings. They say, 'I love you, gorgeous,' and they kiss you but they don't express their tenderness or vulnerability anymore."

I wondered if that's how Gocha treated her.

When Tamriko left Juliet turned to me. "Slims, why did you stop courting Tamriko?"

I stopped chewing. To explain it I could have quoted to her the words to the song she had sung at the chess championship. "Our love was strong but so short. We were not suited for each other. We were not like the sun and the rain," but that wasn't true. Instead, I told her, "One shouldn't marry one's neighbor. That's like marrying your sister." It was a good excuse. If a man marries his neighbor then the whole neighborhood calls that man "brother-in-law."

Juliet shook her head. "The tall one wouldn't bend, the short one wouldn't stretch, and the kiss was lost."

10.

IT WAS THE MIDDLE OF NOVEMBER AND TUFTS OF EARLY, GREASY SNOW
dulled the life on the street. I had just attended a conference at the
university sponsored by a local NGO. I went because Anthony had
volunteered to give a talk about how to how to acquire scholarships
to study abroad. But I didn't learn much because as he was expounding on the importance of web access for students at the university,
some local vigilantes joined in. They sat in the back and refused to
speak English, which they referred to as "the language of barbarians,"
and would only speak the "language of Don Quixote." Overpowered
by Spanish, Anthony ended the session early and said, "Well, maybe
next time we can accomplish more."

I had recognized the Spanish-speaking contingency as acquaintances of Malkhazi's and asked them if they had seen him recently but
they hadn't. Malkhazi had disappeared for two weeks and a rumor
was spreading that he had joined a Robin Hood gang in the countryside, the ones holding up trains protesting the upcoming election of
President Shevardnadze. But Malkhazi didn't care about politics. Anyway, he had disappeared before, quoting, when he returned, a Mexi-
can saying he had heard on a documentary, "Man must go to the
mountains because it is important." Every time Malkhazi disappeared
I would worry that he had gone to avenge his father, and that he had

gone to the Turkish border, eight kilometers away, to shoot a Turkish border guard. But he also knew the Turks didn't understand about our nine-generation vendettas and to shoot at them would be like a little man provoking the power of Godzilla.

I only had a little over a month left to complete the application for Hillary Clinton's competition. I tried to think of something especially unique to write, something that would distinguish me from the rest and show her that my hand was raised higher than every other post-Soviet person also vying for this opportunity. I walked home after work avoiding the patches of dark ice in the road. Evening was pending and the overcast sky made it difficult to see more than a few meters in front of me. The only sounds were the clops of a stray donkey and a farmer yelling at it, also throwing his hat at it.

When I got home the electricity was still out. My mother had gone with Zuka to the hydroelectric dam for a holiday. Juliet was reading by candlelight.

"Juliet," Malkhazi called from the street. "Come here! Juliet," he called again more loudly. "We have had a victory!"

"I'm sure he hasn't taken part in a military skirmish," Juliet said, as if she wished that he had. "He has probably just stolen some gasoline out of a neighbor's car."

I leaned out the window and looked down at him; his torso was hanging out of his car. He sounded like a little boy who says, "Mama, mama, give me some honey."

"Slims, tell Juliet to come. You too! Let's go for a drive."

"You come here!" Juliet yelled back.

Malkhazi, apparently not wanting to obey the commands of a woman, changed his tactic. "Stay there," he demanded, pointing his finger at her. "Don't go out!"

When Malkhazi got to the door he was breathing heavily, carrying a crystal chandelier. "Why haven't you turned on the light?" he asked. "They've turned on the lights because of the elections. Look out the window."

I looked out the window and saw that everyone else's lights were on.

"Here, I brought you this," he said and set the chandelier on the table. "It's from Czechoslovakia. May the light always shine on your head. Oh, look at your hands," Malkhazi said, feeling Juliet's fingers. "So cold. You must allow me to fill up your water buckets for you. Oh, I almost forgot!" he said and stamped back down the stairs.

"How could he fill up the water buckets?" Juliet said. "He's never here."

"Here, Slims, I found us some fuel," he said when he returned. He set down a blue metal canister labeled USA.

And out of a basket in his other hand he took a bouquet of plastic flowers and a pink hand towel. "I traded some wine with a British sailor for them," he said.

"They use plastic flowers on their ships?" I asked.

"Sit down," he ordered us both. "I'll make some coffee."

I was surprised he even knew how to make coffee. "I don't drink coffee," he usually said, as if coffee were only a woman's drink. I always thought he would rather starve or eat a raw fish head than cook anything. But there he was, standing over the stove as if he had been making coffee his whole life, as if he were some kind of coffee preparing master, like some of the women of our town who have their own secrets of preparing it and are more popular than famous poets.

He opened the can of sugar and scooped some into the pot.

"Oh, not so much sugar," Juliet said. "I wish to live a long time."

"You've stopped eating sugar?" Malkhazi asked.

Juliet shrugged.

"You don't like foam right?" he asked her. He poured the coffee into three black cups with golden dragon's tails, but having miscalculated the measurements, he gave me all the foam.

I swirled my cup around trying to find some coffee. Couldn't find any. Malkhazi gave me his cup and said, "I don't drink coffee anyway."

"Now, sit down," Malkhazi said. "Sasha and I have a plan."

"Who's Sasha?" I asked.

"An Armenian. He works at the port."

"What kind of plan?" Juliet asked him. "Something illegal?"

"Would you object so much?"

"Would that make a difference?"

"The man is not a wall," he said. "He is moveable."

"But at least the wall supports the roof," I added.

"Juliet, Slims, my dears," Malkhazi was now saying. "Tell me. What is illegal? Besides, if there are a hundred pieces of gold and no one is counting them because they are already rich, and I take one little gold piece, then they are happy and we are happy. It's no problem."

"Why do you have to do illegal activities?" Juliet said.

"It's not an illegal activity! Okay, I'll tell you. I'm an inspector."

"Like in Sherlock Holmes?" I asked.

"No. At the port. On the ships. Gocha got me a job there, working for his family. You can call me Inspector Number Twelve. Twelve for the twelfth century," he said, taking out a metal badge from the pocket of his jean jacket and pointing at the number twelve.

"That's where you've been? I thought you had gone to the mountains to sell cucumbers," Juliet said.

"It looks like you haven't shaved the whole time," I said.

"The sea is filled with ships. I don't have time."

"Oh, it's that kind of job," I said. "Now you are going to be hustling all the time and won't have time for anything else. You don't have to have this job, you know. We can get by without it."

"Sure, by selling Zuka's icons and with Juliet's English students and you, with whatever you do, and your salary that only comes sometimes."

"But what kind of life is there at an oil terminal? Besides, oil is killing all the fish."

"Write to Hillary about it. You could start it like this: Once there was a man from Georgia who finally got a job. We Georgians don't have to do anything we don't want to do. We don't do *anything* and still we are Georgians. This man . . ."

"Inspector Number Twelve," I repeated to myself and stared out the window, through the palm trees, at the steady surf of the sea.

Malkhazi was now working for Gocha, the banker. Now I really had to get out of this town.

"I went to the interview in Baku," Malkhazi was saying. "I said I knew Excel or Nexel, whatever they call it, and all the other computer programs and that I know how to speak English. But when I came back to Batumi, the first thing I told Gocha's uncle was, 'I don't like to pretend. I will tell you now I don't know these computer programs of Excel and Nexel.' But I told him that I can learn them. And I told him that my English is not very good. Also that I don't believe in the Internet. We have lived without it for ten thousand years so why do we need it now? Also, computers bombard us with radioactivity. And they ruin women's eyes. But Gocha's uncle knows I'm from the mountains, related to a Svan, and that Svani families have nine-generation vendettas. So he told me, 'These programs are not difficult to learn.'"

"What do you *inspect*?" I asked.

"Oil and gas. We also have another department, the Agricultural and Minerals Inspection Division, but I don't know anything about minerals."

"You need to drink a lot of milk then," I said. "Because of the fumes."

"Slims, don't you understand?" he asked. "We don't *only* inspect oil and gas. Last week I inspected my first ship. It arrived from Poland filled with bananas. The workers in the port confiscated twenty boxes worth. We said we had to test them. So we ate them. We took pictures and faxed the pictures to the Polish shipping agent. We thought he would be angry because we had stolen so many boxes of bananas, but instead he wrote back a telegram that said, 'HA HA HA.' I inspect everything like a true Georgian," he laughed. "Even tarragon fizzy water! And last night I delivered eight boxes of bananas to the village! I told them I would bring more food so they don't have to take it from those Jehovah's Witnesses."

"Did they even know what a banana was?" Juliet asked.

"No! They tried to boil them like potatoes."

"Forget about the banana! What about how oil is causing global warming?" I said.

"Foo. If that were really true do you think I would work for such a company? I would sell my gold ring to support us. No, I can't. It belonged to my father. But I would sell our stove. No, I am not only working for the money. I just want to work. Otherwise I can't sleep at night." He picked up a tomato from a glass bowl on the table and turned to Juliet, "Do you really like the color red? Is it because Anthony wears red shoes?"

Juliet swirled around the grounds in the bottom of the cup, turned it over onto the saucer, and tossed back her head. "How am I going to learn to be an independent woman if I'm always being interrogated by you?" she asked Malkhazi.

"Why are you trying to be independent? What is the meaning? You want to live alone in the mountains like Vaja Pshavela's wife? Even she was not happy sitting all day under the beech tree with only the little tender green grasses."

"Well I have my own announcement to make," she said. "I've decided that I don't wish to marry a Georgian anymore," she said. "I would rather marry a foreigner. They are much more polite."

"Foo," Malkhazi said. "You mean someone like Anthony?" He spat on his boot and then decided to polish it.

Juliet turned the cup in her saucer right side up and looked into it.

"Not only women can read coffee grounds," Malkhazi said while taking her cup from her. "Ah!" he said peering into the cup, "I see darkness, loneliness. But then there is light. And here, a man, on a horse, or maybe that is you, running off to marry. Perhaps he has kidnapped you in order to save money on a costly wedding, and then you will live a beautiful life and everything will be good and there will be nothing bad."

Juliet opened the window and pulled in the platter she had set on the ledge to cool. It contained the pig's head Irakli had brought earlier. "Have some?" she asked Malkhazi.

He was sitting on the edge of his seat as if ready to run off somewhere.

Juliet excavated some meat off the skull with a fork but some of it was hard to get at so she started using her fingers. "Slims?" she offered. I reached in too. The meat was fatty. Juliet got up to get a napkin and the fork fell on the floor.

"*Opa!*" she said and leaned down to pick it up

"You see?" Malkhazi said. "You are forgetting what a Georgian woman is!"

"Because I dropped a fork?"

"No, because you must allow the man to pick up your fork!"

I regarded him and then started to laugh. Sometimes he really was a rustic.

"And a man from, for example, England, wouldn't pick up a woman's fork?" Juliet asked.

"Try it!" Malkhazi said. "Next time you are eating with Anthony drop your fork."

"When would I eat with him? I hardly know him." Juliet poured herself some water from the pitcher.

"You did it again!" Malkhazi said and punched his thigh.

"What!" Juliet said.

"You poured your own water. You should have asked me to."

"I'm not going to ask you to pour my glass of water."

"Don't ask. Just make a move with your glass so I know you are thirsty."

Malkhazi watched her from across the table with a kind of ardent adoration.

"Why do you always treat me this way?" Juliet asked.

"Why? What do you mean why? Do you think I want anything from you? My role is to serve you."

"Nothing else?"

"I think you know what I want," he said. To me, at that moment, it seemed his eyes were full of lust.

I picked up my glass, intending to hit him on the head with it.

Malkhazi turned to me, annoyed. "I think she knows that I want her to join me on a ship, with all of my best friends and sail on the sea. I don't know what *you* are thinking," he said. "Listen to me, Juliet. I will tell you a secret that Slims doesn't know. Now look. You have been reading so many English novels maybe you have forgotten this, but the true Georgian man sometimes helps with the housework. In the evening, just look outside and you can see the husbands hanging the laundry."

I looked outside the window. So did Juliet.

"You can't *see* them. Otherwise, the next day, the whole town would be gossiping, saying, 'Oh, did you see Irakli washing the carpets?'"

There was a little knock on the door. "Maybe that's Irakli now," Malkhazi said, walking to the door.

"Don't open the door!" Juliet cried out. "It's the man coming to collect the money for the electricity!"

"Or possibly. Is that Anthony?" Malkhazi asked. "No one knocks except him."

And it was. The little home movie this was turning into could now be entitled *Imbroglio: Complicated Situation.*

"Why did he come here? Has he come here before?" Malkhazi whispered to Juliet over by the door.

"He says his TV only gets MTV," she said.

"And you believe that? He only says that because he wants to see you."

"He doesn't have any friends here," Juliet explained.

"Why are you telling me that?"

"To explain why I spend time with him."

"Oh, okay. I was worried you were going to ask *me* to be his friend."

"Sit down, Anthony," Malkhazi commanded after Anthony had taken off his jacket. "I'll make you some coffee."

"Please, sit down," Juliet said to Anthony. "Would you like some cream torte? My neighbor has been making this cake for the past eight years. It's mostly cream."

"Would you like some walnut liquor?" I asked him.

Malkhazi brought more coffee and Juliet brought some slices of cake that had too many layers to count. "This doesn't have very much sugar," she said. She watched closely as Anthony took a bite. Juliet herself took a bite. And then I watched her slowly, slowly slide her fork off the table. When a fork is dropped it's nothing to worry about—visitors will come over, man or woman, and we should be in a good mood about it, everything's fine; besides, it's a holiday whenever anybody visits. But the important thing really is to pick up the fork for your friend. But Anthony, not coming from an ancient civilization, really did remain aloof to the fork.

"When a fork is dropped a woman is arriving," Malkhazi told Anthony picking up her fork. "She is coming but she is not going. She does not leave Georgia."

"When a fork is dropped, it's time to get a clean fork!" Anthony said.

"Oh," Juliet said. "This cake is very impolite!"

"Beg your pardon?" asked Anthony.

"The taste," Juliet said. "Of this cake. It is very impolite."

"Oh no. It tastes fine," said Anthony.

"I hate it when you do this!" Malkhazi said, brandishing the fork. It scintillated under the chandelier. "Every time you speak English you turn into some kind of British woman. Our culture is being invaded by these foreigners and you sit and quote English people!" Malkhazi said. "It's time that I prepare my sword to fight the enemy!"

"Well," Anthony said, standing up. "Thanks for the cake. I really just stopped by."

"I thought you believed in the Georgian martial art of fighting without weapons," Juliet said. "Besides, these days they don't fight with swords, my dear. They push a button."

"I don't have that button," Malkhazi said. "Watch what will happen. These foreigners will come, buy up all our property, and impose their ideals of political correctness on us."

"Doesn't he have other interests besides fighting?" Anthony asked me.

"Well, right now he is busy making a fire," I said.

"Making a fire?"

"You know, expressing his unhappy emotions. In Georgian we say making a fire. But he's not really as violent as you think," I said.

"We fight because when our swords clash they sparkle and give us some light."

"Besides fighting," Malkhazi said, interrupting me, "we have love. But this love is dying out."

"Actually, even when we kiss we are fighting," I told Anthony.

"Oof!" Juliet was saying. "Sacred Georgian traditions."

"You are not a true Georgian," Malkhazi told Juliet and punched his thigh again. In Georgia, if you love someone, often you want to beat something.

"You see?" Juliet said, turning to Anthony. "How can you even have a conversation with him? I'd rather have a conversation with the cat. Come here little kitty. Malkhazi hates everyone you know."

"I don't hate *any*one. But I have said it before and I will say it again that I will kill anyone who takes our land or destroys our traditions."

"Like I said," Anthony said. "I really just stopped by . . ."

Juliet was speaking to Malkhazi in Georgian now. "This poor Englishman. He's going to think we're all people from the mountains with your kind of values."

"No, he knows it's just me."

"You talk about sacred Georgian traditions that still exist in the village," Juliet said, "but you refuse to work in the fields. I would have been happy living in the village. You're just like this new generation, always having to do something, never happy with this life you were given. You're ambitious or something!"

To be called ambitious in Georgian is almost as bad as being called a *davcliavdebuli*, a plumhead. I worried that I too had started becoming ambitious.

Anthony sat there and, to his credit, had a stoic look. The crystal chandelier tinkled delicately about his head. "The people are sort of heavy here," he remarked to me.

"What are you talking about?" Malkhazi asked him.

"The traditions. They seem to hold people in chains."

"What people are you talking to?" he asked him.

"I don't have to talk to anyone. I observe it."

"You are observing a different Georgian than I know," he told him.

"Everyone is afraid of the devil here."

Malkhazi and Juliet stared at him. "Only unmarried women are afraid of the devil," Malkhazi said. He turned back to Juliet. "Look, Juliet. I want you to be free," he said in Georgian. "I don't know how this has happened but I only care about your happiness. Georgia used to be blessed but God has forgotten about us now. If you have to move across the ocean with a strange man, I will still love you from that distance. Plan your life as you like, will you? Real *kurdi* never marry anyway." He threw his big, black jacket over his shoulders, said, "I'm off to meet a very influential man," and then he disappeared.

Juliet settled into the couch with Anthony. In Georgia, if someone proves to you their love, then you don't need it anymore.

11.

A FEW DAYS AFTER OUR PRESIDENTIAL ELECTIONS THE RESULTS WERE tallied and we discovered that Old Shevy had won again. "I think we need to ask for Hillary's help on this," I told Malkhazi. "Or else Shevardnadze is going to be the president for our entire lifetime."

"America is not a country to give advice about elections!" Malkhazi said. "We could have had ten elections in the same time it took for them to decide who won in Florida and still we could have elected the person for whom nobody voted." Malkhazi rolled down the window and lit a cigarette. But then he stubbed it out in the ashtray because my mother was crossing King Parnavaz Street.

"Deyda!" we both yelled. She waved back.

I was driving with Malkhazi up to Poti to help him check the seals on an oil train that was going to be unloaded at the port.

"It doesn't matter to *me* who becomes president," I said. "I have no relations with either of the candidates. I was hoping that guy Saakashvili would run."

"You mean the car bomber?" Malkhazi asked.

"No, the guy who studied anticorruption techniques in America. The human rights activist. He would have made a good president."

Conspiratorial theories were running rampant through the

countryside. They said that due to the fact that Shevardnadze ignored the pleas of the villagers for most of the year, hoarding everything for himself, keeping the money in his own pocket, he had to make amends to the villagers on Election Day. Therefore, he sent his own smoothly outfitted representatives, laden with tomatoes, knocking on the doors of all the houses in every village. Ben Hur, my cousin, informed me of this. He said that Shevardnadze's representatives came knocking on the door of his pinewood hut with the ballot box in hand, singing like roadside vendors, "Tomatoes for true Georgians." Then they told Ben Hur, "Those who cannot go to the ballot box, the ballot box comes to them, to those who are true Georgians." The representative and the one holding the ballot box, looking so polite and patriarchal, took a few breaths of mountain air, stomped their feet, and waited for my cousin to sign. They coughed into their pink fists, polished their boots with new snow, and headed to the neighbors. "Thank you for participating in the New Democracy," they called back.

Shevardnadze had many city sycophants working for him that day, bringing the ballot boxes and bags of tomatoes to villages. 99.9 percent of the population voted for Shevardnadze. But I am dubious about this percentage.

We drove along the Black Sea passing dirty foam and swaying palms. Little lights had been artistically arranged around the telephone poles and tangled electric wires to resemble King David on a horse. They were blinking to celebrate the Christmas season, illuminating little bits of snow clinging to the tree branches. Maybe I had exaggerated the lack of electricity. Maybe we had it more often than not.

We were driving into the mountains, above Batumi, and passed Stalin's old lemonarium. Sadly, no lemons grew there any longer. They used to be very famous lemons.

Malkhazi shoved the soundtrack of *Braveheart*, which some Romanians had given him at the port, into the tape player. I heard clashing and a low bass thumping. "It is the new sound for this century," he said. "In this music you can feel Georgians preparing our swords for battle."

"But in the movie *Braveheart* even the nobles betrayed people," I said.

Staring pensively at the road Malkhazi said, "The Romanians gave me this tape because it's the sound of independence. They understand how we had to fight for our independence. They understand Georgians. But I had been having a hard time understanding the Filipinos. For one thing, they don't eat anything, they only drink tea all the time. But the biggest problem is that the Filipinos are so afraid of Georgia that they don't even understand a joke. While they were loading the oil onto their ship I said to one of them as a joke, 'Ah, I see you're hiding fifty tons of oil in that tank to keep for yourself!' If anyone looked into this tank he could *easily* see that it was dry and that I was only joking. But this sailor actually climbed down into the tank to check! When he saw that it was dry—of course it was dry, anyone could see that—he climbed out and started jumping up and down. When he jumped he was a little bit taller. He yelled in English, 'You are liar. Mafioso! Mafioso!'"

"Oy!" I said and turned up the volume of *Braveheart*. "Let's listen to this music. I don't like to hear about our mafiosi reputation. It's very offensive."

"It's a big problem. Maybe Georgia has a bad reputation because the world doesn't know the story of Sapar. He stole Almaskhiti's dappled horse out of love for Zia-Khanoum because higher than the law is the woman. It's okay to steal if it's out of love. But anyway, that's not the end of the story," Malkhazi said.

"This is a long story."

"So last night in the cafe one of the Filipino sailors ran up to me and said, 'Can you tell me where I can find a good woman?' I told him we were not that kind of country. 'Come on, man! Don't you have a club?' he asked. It's a problem because the only place they can go for relaxation is the cafe in the port. He invited me for a beer. I declined his offer but invited *him* for a beer instead. And do you know what? No longer was he a scared Filipino sailor, afraid of everything. I realized that we are exactly the same."

"How is that?" I asked.

"He told me that at home in his village in the Philippines where he lives, by the sea, he had to make an announcement, an *announcement* over the garbage truck loudspeakers, saying that he no longer would go to any more weddings. He told everyone in his neighborhood, 'I am a modern workingman and a workingman only has a few days off. I don't want to waste them at weddings.'"

"What about funerals?" I asked.

"Of course he must go to funerals," Malkhazi said. "But I agreed with him that weddings are a problem. I have had to be the toastmaster of fourteen weddings already. I get so tired of all the eating and drinking and all the butter I have to eat beforehand. Nobody ever considers that maybe I'd like to lose a little weight. Wouldn't that be funny, Slims, for me to make such an announcement that I wouldn't attend any more weddings? It would be like a foreign comedy. 'Comedy, comedy,' people would say."

It was evening when we finally got near Poti. "*Sheni deyda*!" Malkhazi suddenly swore. "They never pull me over when it's just me. You must attract them or something." A policeman, standing on the side of the road, was flagging us down. "Watch this," Malkhazi said and pulled over. He didn't even get out of the car. The policeman had to approach the window. Malkhazi rolled it down and said, "I am Inspector Makashvili." And then he adjusted his rearview mirror.

"Ah, Inspector Makashvili," replied the policeman. "Are you related to the Makashvili of Hashuri? No? How about the Makashvili of Hulo? No?" the policeman asked, seeking some connection.

The policeman checked Malkhazi's documents again, and then catching sight of Malkhazi's badge, glinting from a passing headlight, said, "Enjoy your journey."

Since the Mingrelian region had less electricity than ours it was easy for some people to skulk along in the dark night tapping holes into the railcars without being seen. That night, after Malkhazi had checked the seals on the top of the train cars and we were walking back along the track we caught an old man stealing a bucketful of acetate. When he saw us the old man fell on his knees before Malkhazi.

"Get up," Malkhazi said. "This time you have made a mistake. This is not gasoline but a chemical to make jet fuel. What are you going to do with it?"

"My wife needs it to clean the paint off her nails," the man told him.

"Whatever," Malkhazi said and let him keep his pilfered profit. My cousin was not hard-hearted.

Malkhazi kept insisting that he wasn't corrupt, that as inspector, he only tested the quality of oil for the foreign shipping agents—any kind of oil: crude oil, jet fuel, gasoline. Sometimes even olive oil. "Don't worry," he told my mother a few evenings later, when he brought a jar of it home. "We don't put the olive oil in the same containers we put the gasoline." He also monitored the quantities of oil pumped in and out of the great storage tanks, located on the north side of Batumi, near the refinery and the oil pipeline museum. Thick hoses lying on the bottom of the sea connected the storage tanks to the foreign cargo ships. Foreign shipping companies would pay this ZGZ Oil Inspections, this "global corporation," to ensure that the Georgian government was not pilfering more than fifty tons of oil per ship for customs taxes. Fifty tons was permissible, not more than that.

Malkhazi would first determine the amount of oil in the storage tanks on the land to ensure that the amount that the head families of Batumi discharged was the same amount that they *claimed* to have discharged, rounding off to the nearest ton. Then Malkhazi would measure the volume of oil on the ship to make it look like the oil discharged from the port's storage tanks was the same amount that was in the ship, and that the fork in the hose lying at the bottom of the sea hadn't stolen some of it. The fact that they had stolen quite a bit of it wasn't a contradiction to Malkhazi. He justified it by insisting that the foreign ships belonged to richer countries and needed it less. Then he would print out these documents of quantity and quality, ensuring the level of sweetness and lightness of the crude oil: seventy-two copies of the same document for the captain (Malkhazi called him "the master") to sign. Printing out seventy-two documents doesn't sound very daunting but it took a long time when the electricity kept going out and when the outdated computer, donated by a nongovernmental organization, didn't work very efficiently, and Malkhazi had to ask Sasha, the Armenian guard at the port, to keep pressing the print button.

Malkhazi used to love ships—had taken to calling them *vessels*—but now that the Black Sea had started filling with them, he was beginning to tire of them. He would come home and fall asleep immediately. When Malkhazi and I got home one evening, before he fell asleep, I told him that maybe he should break away from his job, become a true Georgian hero, and fight corruption. "Besides," I said. "I need a plot. In the West, the characters in their novels always go through some sort of positive change."

"Don't you know the story about the man who is playing his *chonguri*?" Malkhazi asked. "All day long he only plays one note. His wife says, 'Husband, why do you only play one note while everyone else plays different ones?' He says, 'They are playing different notes because they are searching for the one I've already found.' That is like Georgia. In Georgia, we don't need to change because we are perfect as we are. God gave us His land . . . oh, I'm too tired right now to finish that story."

"You need to get more sleep then," I said. "I'm tired of making excuses to other people about why you always miss their birthday parties."

"But how can I avoid it? I must always take care of the foreign sailors. The guest comes from God. It is my duty as a Georgian."

The only time the plot of our life advances forward is on a holiday, when we turn our life upside down, and we can be our opposite selves, living in a carnival or a liminal world. On Christmas Eve was the festival parade, where the bishop and his groupies walked down the streets, singing church songs, holding icons and the church banner high in the air. It read, "Stop regarding the universe as a gigantic machine hurtling through time and space to its final destination." They looked like true magicians bringing the good news. Anyone who wants to can join in the parade and see the candles casting a yellow light in the blue windows of every house. When Malkhazi and I were younger we never missed the procession in the village, but even on Christmas Eve that year, Malkhazi was so busy working on the ships that he didn't come home.

On TV the government was broadcasting *Lazarus*, the old Georgian classic. It is a story of ancient love. My mother and I watched it together but at the end I felt depressed because I wondered if that kind of love still exists. So my mother brought out the bottle. In Georgian, porridge is called *papa* and papa is called *mama* and mama is called *deyda* so we ate *papa* while Deyda poured us a martini. Then she set before me a bowl of melted ice cream. "Holiday food," she said. I wondered if it would feel more like a holiday if I had a wife. I wondered if Tamriko was at church. So I walked over to the church, through the crowds of people. At first I looked for her but then I tried to concentrate, instead, on the icon of the Mother Mary, to feel Her a little. I know She is painted a little differently than She actually looked in real life, but this is art—our only means to find Her is through exaggeration. She tried to show Herself to me through the paint, I think, because while I was standing there, staring at the chipped paint of Jesus, I saw Her wink at me, at me wearing my Sherlock Holmes hat, and my tears started to flow out. When you look through these kinds of eyes you see the best truth because the world welds together, and all separateness is blurred. This made me believe that maybe I had some love left, arching out into the void, creating forms to be met by the tentacles of another, and all was not lost.

I whispered to her: "May everything be good and nothing bad. May the fishermen catch many good fish, may Swiss chocolate factories discover our hazelnuts, may the soil always be fertile, may our cups always be full."

Those were enough prayers. I should have stopped there. As we say in Georgia, if you give a blind man eyes, he will ask for eyebrows. I became greedy like an Armenian and added, "May I make it to America."

Then Zaliko the archaeologist came driving by, shouting at the bishop to give him some petrol, and everyone began shouting like politicians trying to jail each other, and everything vanished as if I were not standing there, as if I were not talking to Her. I realized that my only hope was that the bright emerald beauty of this world could be protected from them—all those who are yelling—and from me, when I yell.

Even though Malkhazi had worked on Christmas, on New Year's Day he had to take the day off because he had been asked by our neighbor's wife to be the man with the "happy feet." It's also called the man with the "gold footies." Since he was one of the few with a job, she thought he was the best one to bless her home and bring some luck by stepping over her threshold with a basket of wine, sweets, and boiled pork.

When Malkhazi came home from that important duty, he was dressed up in New Year's clothes, wearing a new woolen vest that an Indian sailor had given him. My mother brought to the table *khachapuri* and Chicken Kiev, which is named after the capital of the Ukraine, but, like in all matters culinary, Georgians are superior at its preparation. Malkhazi looked at her gratefully. "Ah, Deyda," he said and sighed. "This is my favorite time of the day. All together like this with this food."

He poked his fork into the chicken and melted butter squirted out onto his new vest. He wiped it off with a napkin. I noticed that Juliet was trying to avoid all the butter on her plate. I folded my *khachapuri* in half the same way I had seen boys eating pizza in an American movie. Zuka imitated me and then begged Malkhazi to tell him another shipping story.

"Yes," Juliet. "Do tell us another one of your tales of corruption on the high seas."

"Juliet," Malkhazi said, "Is that what Anthony is telling you? That I am corrupt? He is a good guy, but . . . he resembles a smoked fish, a little emotionally unresponsive. He doesn't understand what we do."

"And what *do* you do?" she asked.

"I work with him. But last week in Poti, he kept creeping around with his notebook, inspecting the operations, while the rest of us were trying to play ping-pong. 'Yeap, yeap,' he kept saying. What is this English *yeap*? At first he was telling me all these rules like, 'the surveyor must wear a helmet.' But when he realized he was only talking to the air he tried to become my friend by saying, 'Oh, I didn't know you did it like *that*,' when I was taking the measurements."

Malkhazi tore a piece of bread and dipped it in the pool of butter on Juliet's plate. "Here," he said and put it in her mouth. "You must eat this. It's the best part. Anyway, as usual, the actual figures on the ship were different from the figures on the land. There was a forty-eight-ton discrepancy that I had to correct. But Anthony? Oof! I tried to protect him from knowing about how I have to correct the figures because he is such a nervous man already. Every time I ask him to hold the measuring stick, his hands are so sweaty that when he gives it back to me it's wet. When he saw me change the numbers on the computer he said to himself, 'Where am I? This is unbelievable!' I tried to calm him down. I told him the difference in figures was probably a miscalculation, that our Georgian calculators don't always work correctly. Mostly, I was concerned about his health. Why should he care so much about corruption when he should be paying more attention to his health? The way he was breathing, I was afraid he might have a cardiovascular arrest. But then he asked, 'What if these sailors tell their captain that you've manipulated the numbers?' 'Why would they do that?' I asked him. 'They're Filipino and he's Greek.' 'Ah,' he said. 'In my country we call this the mafia.' 'No, not mafia,' I reminded him, 'government.' 'Beg your pardon,' he said. Why does everyone think I am mafioso? I'm just a simple guy. I only ask for the proper documents. A few days ago I *helped* the master of an Italian ship. The port had stolen one hundred and seventy tons of oil so I called them and said, 'You'd better pump back at least one hundred and fifty tons.'"

"Maybe they think you're mafiosi because you always cross yourself whenever you drive past a church," I suggested.

"But I don't go to confession! I don't approve of this new Father Michael and his big Mercedes. He is even trying to befriend me. He gave me his mobile phone number in case I ever wanted to confess anything. I told him, 'I have nothing to confess. I don't steal oil on Easter or the day before. And if I was ever walking on church property and I saw a diamond on the ground I wouldn't pick it up.'"

"If you are going to be a mafioso, you can't speak like you are out of a Dickens novel," Juliet said. "Do you know you speak English with a Victorian accent?"

"That's probably because I have to spend so much time with Anthony. Remember, Slims, how we took him to the finger puppet theater? Well, on the ship Anthony decided to perform his own anticorruption finger puppet show. One of his fingers was a customs official at the border of Turkey, and his other finger was a Georgian robber trying to smuggle out a painting that he stole when the electricity went out in the State Art Museum."

"Ha!" I said.

"But then his fingers started swearing at each other in English, as if he was trying to be gruff sailors. Foreigners, especially the sailors, think that to be one of us they have to swear. But I never swear in Georgian, it sounds too terrible, only in Italian. Italians are very rude-mouthed people. Once when I asked a sailor how to say in Italian, "Please give me an oil sample," he told me instead how to say, 'Please give me your sister.' Please excuse me, ladies. I don't mean to offend you."

"Would you stop doing that?" my mother asked. Malkhazi was flipping his mobile phone around in his hand like a hyperactive person. "Eat some more."

"Anyway, the more I see those *other* ships, the prouder I am to be Georgian. Every ship is a representation of its country. They speak their own language, obey their own customs. Step onto a Georgian-manned ship they will always give you something to eat. And everyone knows how to do everything. But today, I was on an American ship. 'Ah! The American ship!' everyone was saying. 'So clean and computerized.' But the one thing I didn't understand was why everything was fenced in with all kinds of restrictions? It was as if they were afraid to talk to a person, as if they didn't know the law of the human. The ship didn't even have a captain. It was run by computer. We had to have breakfast, God save us, on the Romanian ship. Their borscht was strange and they gave us only one piece of bread each. We had to eat our borscht with cookies!" Malkhazi's phone started to ring its new Nina Simone ringtone.

"Oh no, not again," said my mother.

He flipped open his phone. "I'm listening," he said. "I'll be there right away." He flipped his phone shut and said to my mother, "Another Turkish ship has arrived, and they don't know how to balance the weight again."

"At least take some *khachapuri*," my mother called after him.

"At least drink milk, to save you from the gas fumes," I said.

"Hopefully, I'll be right back," he said, and with his cigarette lighter lit the icon lamp.

He left us sitting around the glow of the icon.

"And have you been writing to Hillary about these oil shipping stories?" Juliet asked.

I thought about the application, how it was due at the end of the week. "America cares about oil above all things—tangible or otherwise—so I think she will be interested to know what happens on America's oil ships," I said.

"Why are you writing about *oil*?" Juliet asked. "Why don't you write about our wild strawberries or our cheese making techniques, or how to make pig sausages? Why don't you write about how the more sweets we have at the New Year the sweeter the year will be. Or what about our Georgian dances, hot like the sun and swift like mountain rivers?"

"I am writing about that. But I also think the oil industry is part of our fate," I said.

"But if you are writing about our fate, it is already written," Juliet said.

* * *

Ugh, but I was tired of discussions of oil ships and oil pipelines. I was tired of seeing fish dying in leaking rainbows of oil. I was tired, most of all, of my pointless essays to Hillary with little italicized words trying to call attention to the problems of my country.

In order to see the world most correctly, in the most modern fashion, perhaps it is best to see it as temporary, provisional—like our provisional, interregnum oligarch government. Or the provisional, temporary energy solution. Thousands upon thousands of barrels have been transported over our sea, over all seas. But the oil industry has nothing to do with the true law of the sea or the law of the human. Over the past century, in the Black Sea alone, one hundred and fifty ships have already collided, spilling their oil into our sea.

I didn't want to write letters with little letters anymore. I wanted to write with big letters, on billboards, and post them like Mr. Fax's fake flags on foreign ships for the rest of the world to see, flags that said, "PEOPLE OF THE INDUSTRIALIZED WORLD. WE INVITE YOU TO WAKE UP."

So I wrote to Hillary about the Black Sea—about the history of all 420,300 square kilometers of it; how we usually think of the Black Sea as benevolent; how the currents are only wind-driven ripples running counterclockwise. How the salinity is only half the salt of a regular ocean, a low-sodium potato chip. I described how the Turks named it *Kara Deniz*, Sea of Black, because of the tempests in the middle that arise unpredictably. Yet, it's known to the Greeks as Hospitable Sea since it nurtures enough fish for all the people bordering it. And six million of their guests. Fifty thousand oil tankers a year carry in their holding tanks the hydrogen/carbon crude oil compound across the watery expanses, navigating through fogs and the hostile and congested straits of Bosporus to the rest of the world, bringing petrified sunlight to refine; to generate electricity; lubricate industries; to make rubbers, chemicals, plastics, detergents. And what about us, on the subterranean shores, over here, in the darkness, in the shadows of their industries? While they build their skyscrapers above ground, into their heaven, we build our skyscrapers down below, hundreds of feet. We build whole cities downward, into the sea, to benefit *them*, Hillary's people, to keep their lights on.

And then I wrote to Hillary about that which was on the surface of my heart, the most accessible part, and, most importantly, about the Black Sea spiny dogfish. I wrote:

Europe and the United States generally exports raw-materials and semi-manufactured goods to Asia e.g. fish, textiles and paper. This means that Far East mostly exports finished products back to Europe and America e.g. clothing and fish sticks. Isn't it a better idea to process the fish on the same continent? It would be a great business to start a Black Sea spiny dogfish packaging business

Up until now I did not consider myself a businessman, at least not in the sense Mr. Fax was. I was not actually serious, as I wrote in my letter, about starting a spiny dogfish packaging business. Besides, no one in Georgia would want to do that kind of work anyway. I was trying to point out the value of the fish for its own sake, not as an item of consumption. I wanted to depict the fish as a sort of role model, how it had learned to adjust to modern influences, how it could be a symbol of inspiration for the globalized world and even help promote Georgian tourism. But like many other Georgian words, my ideas didn't translate very well into English. So I added a paragraph about all of its uses when it was dead. It had a lot of omega-3 fatty acids. I had read that Americans love omega-3s.

The morning I submitted my application to Hillary, my mother made one of her American-style cakes. I told her, "You are not supposed to be able to *bribe* the Center for Democracy." But when I arrived, I saw cakes already piled up at the entrance: huge, chocolate layer cakes; cakes with fresh cream, decorated with mulberries and kiwis, with graham cracker layers as round as moons; cakes sprinkled with imported coconut, meringue mushrooms, and banana slices.

"But only three people *participated* in this competition from Batumi!" I insisted to Geloti, the guard.

"They must be bribes for something else then," he reassured me.

Into the application I tucked all the letters I had written to Hillary, so they would think I had some connections. And then I waited. I was used to waiting.

12.

IN LATE JANUARY THE RAINS WERE ESPECIALLY HEAVY AND FLOODED THE roads. Malkhazi's car had almost been swept into the sea when he was delivering purloined grain to the village. He came home drenched and complaining that nobody knew how to steer their cars and keep the sea from washing them away. A few cars had been drowned in the sea.

The mail carrier hand-delivered a letter to me. "It's from America!" he said. He apologized that it had gotten wet. "There's no money in it," he said. "I already checked." Standing in the doorway I tore open the envelope and read the paper inside.

Dear Slims Ahmed,

Thank you for writing the honorable Hillary Clinton. She appreciates learning of different points of view. She and her team thank you for your input. As you know Hillary Clinton is a woman of formidable intelligence and strong opinions. Always welcoming challenges, she comes from a tradition of discipline and pragmatism. Even though she is a high-energy woman, she rarely has time to answer each letter individually. In your case, she has made an exception. The following is a personal message from her:

"Thanks for the kind and inspiring letter. I know times are tough but knowing there are folks like you and your husband gives me confidence things will keep getting better. We urge you to contact the White House if you still require assistance with a federal agency."

The signature was electronically typed. I could tell because the rain had seeped into that part and the ink didn't run.

Malkhazi was in the kitchen playing poker with Zuka. "I'll bet two candles that she's going to have twins," Malkhazi said referring to one of our neighbors who was pregnant.

Zuka added three candles. "Triplets!" he said. Having babies seemed to be our only hope.

The lights came on. "Ah! You see?" cried Zuka. "It's true! I'd better go tell her!"

When Zuka left, I descended into gloom. It was a very familiar feeling. We like to exalt this feeling and call it being human. Was America really so impersonal? Was this the result of all my striving? Malkhazi said, "Be happy. At least today we have electricity." Usually I would be, but this time I still felt dark inside. He suggested we go to Cafe Soviet Nostalgia, reminding me that Tamriko worked there and she made the best *kingkali*, and this thought cheered me up a little. I thought about how I had promised the Great Toastmaster that if my individual effort didn't work out I would just give up and toast his name.

On the way Malkhazi wanted to stop at the Paradise Hotel and pick up Anthony.

"You don't even like that guy," I said.

"I have an idea of how he might be able to help us out."

"What sort of idea?" I asked, my gloomy mood lit up with sparks of irritation.

"In March is a ship auction. They will be auctioning off Turkish ships very cheaply. If we can get him to invest in a ship, then we can sell oil to him."

"Oil is killing all the fish! And causing this global warming."

"You already told me that. And telling it to me again does not make it more true. It's just a cheap game that those Western scientists are playing."

"Well you already told *me* that."

Anthony was waiting for us in front of the Paradise Hotel. He was wearing a tie and sports jacket and smoking a cigarette. Anthony tried to open the door to the backseat but it was locked. I leaned back to unlock it but Malkhazi told me not to. He rolled down his window. "Finish your cigarette first," he told Anthony. While we waited for him to finish, Malkhazi asked me for a light. When I lit a match, Malkhazi took the matchbox instead, pulled out a match, and began chewing on it, rolling it back and forth in his mouth. "I'm trying to quit smoking," he said.

He leaned over and unlocked the passenger door behind him after Anthony had finished his cigarette and told him to get in on that side.

The Cafe Soviet Nostalgia was so crowded that we had to wait in a long line outside, in which Malkhazi smoked the rest of my Parliament cigarettes.

"I only smoke when I have to stand in a line," he explained to Anthony.

The lobby's cucumber green paint and token palm tree did successfully evoke a Soviet feeling. A taciturn woman sat under the palm like a foldable chair. "Is there a table?" I asked.

"There are no tables!" she said, not looking up from her crossword.

We were at an impasse.

"I know you *say* there are no tables, but we're asking you if there are any empty tables!" Malkhazi boomed. Soviet-style open sesame.

Maternally she smiled, and let us pass.

Tamriko, swaddled in a frumpy green dress, clumped over to us in square heels. "What do you want?" she asked. A Georgian woman would never normally welcome us that way, but Tamriko was paid to say it that way because this was Soviet nostalgia. But when she saw me, she kissed me double on the cheeks and said, "Hi, my prince." Prince was a very formal greeting. She used to call me the word for darling in Georgian that is untranslatable. Maybe it could be translated as *organs* or *intestines*, but not quite.

We sat at a table under a rose-petaled chandelier. Heavy green curtains billowed along the walls. Stalwart men in military uniforms, displaying metal collections on their chests, sat along the drapes, under the ruffles. I wondered if they knew that this was a Soviet nostalgia cafe, and not a Soviet continuity cafe.

Tamriko brought us three steel plates, each containing a cutlet, a bowl of over-boiled buckwheat, a dirty glass of cherry compote, and a spoon. As she walked away, her green hips shimmered like non-absorbent Soviet plastic napkins.

Malkhazi blew on a pair of sunglasses. "I spent my entire salary on these," he said, wiping the lenses with a napkin. When he and I were younger and unemployed we used to go to cafes and order hot water, put on sunglasses, and say, "This is how the people from the region of Raja drink coffee," because the dark glasses make the water look dark and the people of Raja were so poor they couldn't afford coffee. This would usually lead to the lament of, "Raja, oh Raja, beautiful region in the mountains, and visited by who these days?"

Now I wondered if Malkhazi even thought about mountains anymore. The room was lit only by dim lanterns, but Malkhazi had put on his sunglasses. They looked like little mirrors. Even though Malkhazi lacked the extravagant wealth of the nouveau Georgians, he was still trying to copy their style.

"Give them here," I said. They had a little logo on the side that said, POLICE. "Did you mean for this to be here?" I asked him.

"Foo! I'm not wearing sunglasses that say 'police.' You keep them," he said.

"I don't want them," I said and pushed them toward Anthony. He didn't notice them because he was intently staring at the group from the older generation sitting at the table next to us, already intoxicated, crooning in three part harmonies a song about Stalin.

One singer's Soviet-red lipstick had smudged her teeth. She

leaned her head against the blonde head of another woman. They looked like a photograph from the Soviet coffee table book—which, when you think about it should have been a tea table book—about Georgia when the combines still worked, the tea leaves still grew tall, and the women still wore heels during the harvests.

Against my will, these old Soviet songs filled me with a complicated emotion. Trying to shrug it off, I had no greater emotion to replace it with. I drank down the cherry compote. The cold, half-filled glass reminded me of the time when we used to drink Soviet-style Kool-Aid for breakfast. It was my job every morning to fill up the yellow pitcher with the pink powder and then with water from the tap. We didn't have water shortages. If I had just woken up feeling hungover from a nightmare, I would tell that to the running water and watch it swirl down the drain. This is only if it were a bad dream, like if we were fighting the Turks with our swords and I was watching the rivers fill up with blood, or if I dreamed of a man from the region of Hulo. (They are very ugly people up there.) If it was a good dream though, I would tell it to the water filling the pitcher and watch as everyone drank it, my good cherry-colored dream making them strong with the color of Kool-Aid. I would look up at the overbearing sky and wink to the Great Toastmaster who resided there. Back then, even the morning weather was politically aligned. The sky, gray and swollen, contained a feeling of anticipation, the very capaciousness of it reminding us that we were part of something grander than ourselves, part of the new man, *Homo Sovieticus*, living lives of experiment and anticipation. "Victory to Soviet Georgia!" were the bullhorned words the garbage trucks pumped out onto the streets at dawn. Lunacy! And yet this patchwork quilt of Soviet dreams and Soviet promises was the fabric of my childhood. I looked over at Malkhazi—he was spitting out the splinters of a match.

I noticed that the spoon with which I was eating my buckwheat had been stamped with the symbol from the 1980 Moscow Olympics. "Remember how we used to have to iron our school uniforms every day with only one crease?" I asked Malkhazi

He nodded.

"Now I forget how to iron. Juliet irons for me."

Malkhazi pulled at his shirt, "We have Turkish shirts now. They don't wrinkle."

I looked around at everyone singing with vodka-flavored dissonance, thinking about how we were sitting in this Soviet nostalgic cafe with dirty green curtains and getting drunk on disillusionment. The great watermelon had fallen out from under our armpit, as we say.

At another table I recognized Zaliko, the archaeologist. He was sneering at false American promises, how they tempted us with their capitalism—said they would help us, but what have they done? Who have they helped but themselves? "George Bush wants to use our airport as a base for his attacks on Iraq. And Shevardnadze will allow it."

I yelled over to them, "Shevardnadze is allowing him to use the airport because he hopes that George Bush will fix the potholes on the runway."

I started to tell Malkhazi an old Khrushchev joke but he was yelling to the bevy of singers, "Shut up with your Stalin song."

Tamriko came back and asked what we wanted to drink.

"Do you prefer yours or ours?" I asked Anthony. "Your orange Fanta or our fizzy tarragon water?"

"I'd prefer beer," Anthony said.

"He wants beer," I said, "but I'd prefer to drink you," I told her.

Tamriko turned away quickly and when she brought the drinks she wouldn't look at me and I felt ashamed. I turned to Anthony and said loudly enough for Tamriko to hear, "We usually don't toast with beer but in any case we must drink at least three toasts for the three different names for God."

"But if everyone loves each other like you seem to here, we don't really need God," Anthony said.

"Well, we don't love each other as much as we *should*." But Tamriko was no longer within hearing distance. "Anyway, first we must drink to Upali," I told Anthony, "the god who owns everything. Then to Xmerti, the divine presence of the moment, and then to Matsxovary, the god who blesses you, not only during your life, but after your life also."

"Why only three toasts?" Malkhazi asked, pouring wine into our glasses and beer into Anthony's. "Maybe he wants more."

"Three is enough," Anthony said.

"Ah, but you must, after you listen to this toast," I said. "For the fourth toast we will toast to friendship between England and Georgia," I said. "Eh? You see? You must drink to that."

Tamriko set her steaming dumplings before us. She was famous for her lamb *kingkali*, making them the old-fashioned way, so that they looked like an old woman with twenty-one wrinkles. It's impossible to eat only one of them.

I raised my glass to Tamriko, but she walked away and then Malkhazi started toasting to women. Anthony turned to me. "There are no women here at the table to flatter right now. Shouldn't the guy chill out?"

Malkhazi murmured in Georgian, "If that's how he is, I will do an untraditional toast then. Ask him what should I toast to." He took from his jacket pocket a Coke bottle filled with vodka he'd distilled from cantaloupes. "Malkhazi said he will toast to whatever you like," I told Anthony.

"The pipeline is almost completed," Anthony said. "Let's make a toast to that."

"It will run through our village," I said. "We will be rich." I raised my glass. "Many fish will die."

"And I will lose my job on the ships," Malkhazi said.

"Not likely," Anthony said. "There will always be shipping needs."

"But possibly."

"Alright, never mind then," Anthony said. "Let's toast to the Armenians. They helped us a lot with the pipeline."

"The Armenians?" Malkhazi asked Anthony in English. "For what?"

"Because they are your neighbors. How is your country going to progress unless you learn some national diplomacy?"

"Why are foreign people so interested in Armenians?" Malkhazi asked me. "Why should I toast to people who took our land?"

"And our lake," I added.

"Wouldn't he also be offended if the Armenians said that *his* written language looks like someone threw spaghetti on the wall?" Malkhazi said in Georgian.

"Don't listen to him. We have friends who are Armenian. But when we talk about him we say, 'He's Armenian, but he's okay.'"

"My friend Sasha is Armenian," Malkhazi said. "And I have a cousin whose mother is Armenian."

"And do you like your cousin?" Anthony asked in the tone of a teacher in first form.

"Yes, he is my best cousin," Malkhazi said. "But his mother is the Armenian and she is the strange one."

"When God made the people," I explained to Anthony, "He gathered the clay together and made a man and said 'Amen.' The devil also wanted to make a human. So he gathered some rocks together and made a man and said, 'Armen.' That is why we have Armenians."

Malkhazi sighed. "The Georgian man must always obey the guest so, for him, I will make a toast to the Armenians." He picked up his glass and put it down again. "Just don't tell anyone, okay?" he asked me. After he drank he looked around to see if anyone had seen him but the only witnesses were the members of the party next to us, who were already drunk as could be assumed from the song one man was now singing: "I prefer the lips of the wine jug to the lips of the woman."

"You are right, of course, Anthony," Malkhazi said. "It's wrong to hate Armenians. We are very bad people for it. In fact, we may be the worst in the world. But why do you care so much about it?"

"Because I'm trying to understand," Anthony said. "Every culture has happiness and joy. But in Georgia I only feel pain."

"Ah, now you understand Georgia," Malkhazi said and patted his back. "Your turn to drink."

"You see," Anthony said, "I don't have such a complex about it. I can toast to anything. It's not such a big deal."

"He thinks he is so uncomplex," Malkhazi said to me and then turned to Anthony. "Okay. Let's make a toast to our local dictator," he said.

"But he is totally corrupt!" Anthony said.

"But why do you *care* about corruption so much? Do you say to your children, 'Watch out, you better be good and obey me or the corruption man who is hiding in the closet will get you,' and move your fingers like this?" Malkhazi wiggled his fingers around his ears. "It's no problem for us. He's taken all he needs. If anyone replaced him that person would take everything else. Why don't you try to understand him?"

"I have no interest in understanding him. I think he is a corrupt despot."

"I have to agree," I said.

Malkhazi laughed and said, "But look at how much we have ordered! And no one is eating it." He heaped food onto Anthony's plate, while he himself took only bread—the end pieces.

"Anthony," Malkhazi said while eating his bread. "Have you seen the Turkish ships in the harbor?"

"Mmm," Anthony said.

"They are very old. Very cheap. They will be auctioned in March in Sarpi. I have a very good business idea for you. I can help you export oil to your country at a very good price. Very cheap."

"I'm a geologist. I'm not interested in getting involved in selling oil for a corrupt country."

"Back to corruption already?" Malkhazi said and threw up his hands. He turned to me and said in Georgian, "He's not very bright, is he? Do you think he's some kind of imbecile?" To Anthony he said, "But do you know how much oil I can provide for you?"

Just then the electricity came on.

"Ah," Malkhazi and I both said at once. "A sign!"

Malkhazi ordered another bottle.

"Malkhazi," Anthony said, "No other countries will invest here because it's impossible to even drive safely on your roads without worrying about getting held up by bandits."

Malkhazi seemed to consider this deeply, resting his palms on the table and staring at the back of his hands. Finally, he raised his head and said, "Thank you for opening my mind."

I stared at him in surprise. To open Malkhazi's mind to an English person's point of view was something that happened very seldom. Anthony must have been thinking something similar. "Are you serious?" he asked.

"I know you want what's best for Georgia," Malkhazi said simply. "Now, enough of this complaining. Let's sing. Sing us a song about your mother."

"I don't know any songs about mothers," Anthony said.

"But every country has a song to their mothers, even the Armenians. Who shall we sing for then? I know, let's sing to the soldiers. Ours and yours. Together they are fighting the terrorists in Iraq."

"No, not terrorists," Anthony said. "I believe they will be fighting for oil."

Malkhazi laughed. "Well in any case we both will have soldiers fighting together for some reason that we don't know about."

Malkhazi began to sing:

Though we don't talk about it
we all will die
This is why I sing.

I knew this song so I joined in:

Mothers love their sons
But sons don't talk about their mothers
I will die

Ach! I can't remember it now. It's better after you have been drinking. I called Tamriko to come sing with us so I could remember the song better:

The village is obscured by mist, the color of night
What is our life?
It can fly like a bird
Our life is nothing

Mothers love sons
but sons never remember mothers
When I die
I want my wife to cry for me
I want my village to always be happy and nice
I, underground, am dead
Who can cry for us?
What is left of our house if it turns into a flower.

's better to die early and ate all the salad. It was only a joke.
ll. I added on top of that my shoehorn, a shine brush, and a
npty can of shoe polish. My mother knitted up the holes in my
and gave me a roll of tape I could use to remove the lint from
ousers. Zuka carved a tiny icon of Queen Tamar, a miniature
of the one in the Tbilisi State Museum that he insisted I carry
d with me. Juliet gave me a book of English sayings. I glanced
h them. *Fish or cut bait. The road you leave on you must return
hrew it on top.

hated goodbyes. Besides, I told them, it was only for six weeks.
amriko refused to see me but wrote me a letter instead that
Goodbye. Not just see you later, but goodbye forever." Why
ye forever? I thought, irritated. Besides, if I do move there
oring everyone over. Or at least come home for the summer.
what everyone else does. Then she included in her note
eorgian words for real life. As if I would forget them?
ვეღი—the birds that bring rain. ყელიანი ფეხსაცმელი—
that curl up at the toe. სარწყელებები—hidden mineral
s with life-extending waters. მანნა—the white flakes that fell
heaven and sustained people until they could grow better food
th. მზე—the sun that is connected to women. მთვარე—the
that rules men. ია—the type of violet that grows on stone.
the beehive that makes life sweet. მაყვალი—blackberry bram-
ენი—mother bread. ობილეთ—the mustache of a mountain
წარბი—eyebrow, the two coming into one across the forehead,
every Persian girl in the mountains seeks in a husband,
ო—the frog and the sound the frog makes when it has lost its
I wanted to write back to her, "They have the sun and the
in America, and blackberries too. But why do you write about
ebrow? Is that why you like Gocha so dearly? Because of his
w?"

ut no, I couldn't write that. In Georgia, our Caucasus Moun-
nly allow certain thoughts to be spoken. Our poets, long ago,
those sentences when they searched through nature for them
eir words are still enough for us to live by. If I tried to write

13.

THE MAKASHVILIS ARE FAMOUS FOR THEIR DREAMS, BUT EVERYONE,
even Natasha, the Russian woman who worked at Batumi's Central
Telephone Office, knew that the Makashvilis did not necessarily make
their dreams come true. Usually, whenever I came in to use the telephone, she would look at me with a peevish expression. When I could
only hear static or her Russian *I love you, Sergei!* mafia music through
the receiver, she shrugged. She never deviated from her condescending
expression even though the strands of pale straw on the chair she sat
on sometimes snapped. Not looking up from filing her nails, she
would tell me to pay later. I only ever once saw her show a glint of
arousal, when one day her boss lumbered in, reached into the pocket
of his Western-style jeans, and asked her to take care of his gun. I had
told them both, "I think you have watched too many Fellini films at
the cinematography club."

But on January 31, at the Maritime Ministry of Law, I received
a fax from the American embassy addressed to me. Fortunately, it was
lunchtime and Mr. Fax was away. I stuffed it into my pocket and
found an unoccupied office where I could read it. The fax said that
the American embassy had received my application, they had read all
my letters to Hillary, and were inviting me participate in an internship
in the US for six weeks. The fax explained that I was going to study

with other students from selected post-Soviet countries, to live with an American family, and to learn the managerial skills of a fish packaging plant in San Francisco.

Had there been some kind of mistake? I thought Hillary had already responded to me. Wait a minute, I wondered. Does Hillary Clinton even exist? But San Francisco! But packaging? Who wants to package fish? Only Turkish people package things. Their boxes of chocolates are so shiny you can watch them like television sets, like a Ricky Martin music video.

I wanted to make sure this fax was true so that's why I went to the Batumi Central Post Office to use the telephone and call the consular official while Natasha stared at me the whole time with her snobby expression. When he confirmed it was true I thanked him profusely for considering me for a visa. "Thank you. Thank you," I told him. "I am so happy to see your beautiful country. Rocky Mountains. Las Vegas. I am so, so happy." While I walked home from the telephone office clutching this document, I wondered if I should send him a cheese pie. I would include a note to the consular that said, "I write this with my heart on my cuff." No, I would write, "I write this with my heart in my chest." But I was afraid to send a cheese pie. I considered that maybe he wasn't allowed to open packages. He might think it was an explosive device.

When I reached my flat, I circled the block a few times until I started to attract the attention of the usual fellowship of alcoholics; I had to figure out how to tell Malkhazi that I would be going to America.

Malkhazi was sitting at the table eating bread and margarine. I handed him my letter. Malkhazi put it on the table and continued eating his hunk of bread over it. I swept the bread crumbs off it and he picked it up, turned it over, and said, "You know my English is not so good. What does it say?" So I read it out loud, translating it into Georgian. He put his slab of bread down, leaned back in his chair so that two of the legs came off the floor, and clutched at a tuft of his cropped hair. I wondered if the shock of a dream coming true disrupted his idea of what it meant to be a Makashvili. I told him

that we are Makashvilis, we are dreamers, we [...] Our name is not dependent on the places whe[re...] live, or shall have to live forevermore—like t[...] dwell in Mookhraneli, or the Mitaishvilis wh[...] Eastern churches. Nor are we related to the Ko[...] name comes from the expression meaning the [...] in a corner, which is why the Konchulias liv[...] name is not beholden to a place.

However I tried to explain this to Malk[hazi...] to care, as if starting a business had never bee[n...] childish notion, a fickle longing. In a dim viol[...] the kitchen, breaking the handles off the cupb[...]

"What are you doing? You just fixed t[...] braided him, coming into our flat with an a[...] the garden.

"What?" he said. "It's only cheap furnitu[re...] for all of us." He bounded down the stairs [...] used in the village when he had been gambling [...] river and suddenly remembered it was time t[o...] field near the school.

After Malkhazi had left the house in the sul[...] see, I took out the suitcase. It was probably [...] felt so restless—I had to do something, like [...] dashboard in a car going up a hill knowing i[...] help the car go faster, but the impatience lea[...] I put my gray and blue plaid Sherlock Holm[...] in the bottom of my bag. I added a book o[...] Georgian artist Pirosmani. I stowed my Geig[er...] pocket. Provision, I thought, remembering t[...] to such sensitivity that it bleeped even when [...] a restaurant, I had held it over some salted to[...] friends backed away. They pushed away the[ir...] their chairs and lit up cigarettes, said they w[...]

13.

THE MAKASHVILIS ARE FAMOUS FOR THEIR DREAMS, BUT EVERYONE, even Natasha, the Russian woman who worked at Batumi's Central Telephone Office, knew that the Makashvilis did not necessarily make their dreams come true. Usually, whenever I came in to use the telephone, she would look at me with a peevish expression. When I could only hear static or her Russian *I love you, Sergei!* mafia music through the receiver, she shrugged. She never deviated from her condescending expression even though the strands of pale straw on the chair she sat on sometimes snapped. Not looking up from filing her nails, she would tell me to pay later. I only ever once saw her show a glint of arousal, when one day her boss lumbered in, reached into the pocket of his Western-style jeans, and asked her to take care of his gun. I had told them both, "I think you have watched too many Fellini films at the cinematography club."

But on January 31, at the Maritime Ministry of Law, I received a fax from the American embassy addressed to me. Fortunately, it was lunchtime and Mr. Fax was away. I stuffed it into my pocket and found an unoccupied office where I could read it. The fax said that the American embassy had received my application, they had read all my letters to Hillary, and were inviting me participate in an internship in the US for six weeks. The fax explained that I was going to study with other students from selected post-Soviet countries, to live with an American family, and to learn the managerial skills of a fish packaging plant in San Francisco.

Had there been some kind of mistake? I thought Hillary had already responded to me. Wait a minute, I wondered. Does Hillary Clinton even exist? But San Francisco! But packaging? Who wants to package fish? Only Turkish people package things. Their boxes of chocolates are so shiny you can watch them like television sets, like a Ricky Martin music video.

I wanted to make sure this fax was true so that's why I went to the Batumi Central Post Office to use the telephone and call the consular official while Natasha stared at me the whole time with her snobby expression. When he confirmed it was true I thanked him profusely for considering me for a visa. "Thank you. Thank you," I told him. "I am so happy to see your beautiful country. Rocky Mountains. Las Vegas. I am so, so happy." While I walked home from the telephone office clutching this document, I wondered if I should send him a cheese pie. I would include a note to the consular that said, "I write this with my heart on my cuff." No, I would write, "I write this with my heart in my chest." But I was afraid to send a cheese pie. I considered that maybe he wasn't allowed to open packages. He might think it was an explosive device.

When I reached my flat, I circled the block a few times until I started to attract the attention of the usual fellowship of alcoholics; I had to figure out how to tell Malkhazi that I would be going to America.

Malkhazi was sitting at the table eating bread and margarine. I handed him my letter. Malkhazi put it on the table and continued eating his hunk of bread over it. I swept the bread crumbs off it and he picked it up, turned it over, and said, "You know my English is not so good. What does it say?" So I read it out loud, translating it into Georgian. He put his slab of bread down, leaned back in his chair so that two of the legs came off the floor, and clutched at a tuft of his cropped hair. I wondered if the shock of a dream coming true disrupted his idea of what it meant to be a Makashvili. I told him that we are Makashvilis, we are dreamers, we can do what we want. Our name is not dependent on the places where we live, or used to live, or shall have to live forevermore—like the Mookhranelis who dwell in Mookhraneli, or the Mitaishvilis who live in-between the Eastern churches. Nor are we related to the Konchulia family whose name comes from the expression meaning the people who are living in a corner, which is why the Konchulias live in a corner. But our name is not beholden to a place.

However I tried to explain this to Malkhazi, he pretended not to care, as if starting a business had never been a dream of *his*, just a childish notion, a fickle longing. In a dim violence he mulled around the kitchen, breaking the handles off the cupboards.

"What are you doing? You just fixed those," my mother upbraided him, coming into our flat with an armful of potatoes from the garden.

"What?" he said. "It's only cheap furniture. It's too small in here for all of us." He bounded down the stairs with the same stride he used in the village when he had been gambling with his friends by the river and suddenly remembered it was time to collect the cow in the field near the school.

After Malkhazi had left the house in the sulk he didn't want me to see, I took out the suitcase. It was probably too early to pack but I felt so restless—I had to do something, like when you push on the dashboard in a car going up a hill knowing it's not actually going to help the car go faster, but the impatience leaves you no other choice. I put my gray and blue plaid Sherlock Holmes hat with the earflaps in the bottom of my bag. I added a book of paintings by the great Georgian artist Pirosmani. I stowed my Geiger counter in a zippered pocket. Provision, I thought, remembering the time I had adjusted it to such sensitivity that it bleeped even when a jellyfish sloshed by. At a restaurant, I had held it over some salted tomato wedges and all my friends backed away. They pushed away their plates, leaned back in their chairs and lit up cigarettes, said they weren't hungry anymore. I said it's better to die early and ate all the salad. It was only a joke. But still. I added on top of that my shoehorn, a shine brush, and a half empty can of shoe polish. My mother knitted up the holes in my socks and gave me a roll of tape I could use to remove the lint from my trousers. Zuka carved a tiny icon of Queen Tamar, a miniature replica of the one in the Tbilisi State Museum that he insisted I carry around with me. Juliet gave me a book of English sayings. I glanced through them. *Fish or cut bait. The road you leave on you must return on.* I threw it on top.

I hated goodbyes. Besides, I told them, it was only for six weeks.

Tamriko refused to see me but wrote me a letter instead that said, "Goodbye. Not just see you later, but goodbye forever." Why goodbye forever? I thought, irritated. Besides, if I do move there I can bring everyone over. Or at least come home for the summer. That's what everyone else does. Then she included in her note the Georgian words for real life. As if I would forget them? ფრინვეღი—the birds that bring rain. ყეღიანი ფეხსაცმეღი—shoes that curl up at the toe. სარწყუღებები—hidden mineral springs with life-extending waters. მანნა—the white flakes that fell from heaven and sustained people until they could grow better food on earth. მზე—the sun that is connected to women. მთვარე—the moon that rules men. ია—the type of violet that grows on stone. სკა—the beehive that makes life sweet. მაყვაღი—blackberry bramble. პური—mother bread. ისიღეთ—the mustache of a mountain man. წარბი—eyebrow, the two coming into one across the forehead, which every Persian girl in the mountains seeks in a husband, ბაყაყი—the frog and the sound the frog makes when it has lost its village. I wanted to write back to her, "They have the sun and the moon in America, and blackberries too. But why do you write about the eyebrow? Is that why you like Gocha so dearly? Because of his unibrow?"

But no, I couldn't write that. In Georgia, our Caucasus Mountains only allow certain thoughts to be spoken. Our poets, long ago, found those sentences when they searched through nature for them and their words are still enough for us to live by. If I tried to write another kind of sentence not given to me by the pathos of the mountain, if I tried to write a sentence that might offend the woman, for example, my pen mark would slip into a curlicue.

Mr. Fax was furious. "You stole my fax!" he said. He spoke in a kind of eructation, as if he were *still* speaking from the bottom of his volcano, but now realizing he might not ever get out. "That application to attend the business seminar was meant for me!" He counted on his fingers. "Last August? I was wondering why that application never came."

"I will not allow you to leave your place of employment for six weeks!" he added, after I refused to sell his antique plates and silver crosses for him in America. But I hadn't been paid my governmental salary in over eight months, so he couldn't keep me at the job, because at this pay rate we were practically a volunteer organization. "Don't Cry for Me Argentina," I whistled and then I invited Fax for a beer to celebrate, but he was insulted that I didn't invite him for a whiskey.

That evening I went to find Malkhazi. He was sitting in the cafe near the port. Even though the weather was chilly, the sailors were lifting mugs of cold beer to their chapped lips. But Malkhazi drank only hot water, in between cleaving hazelnuts with a hammer. He kicked a white plastic chair out from under the table over to me. I offered him a cigarette. Some Turkish sailors across from us were doing strange tricks with their lighters, but Malkhazi paid no attention.

"Slims," he said, scooting his chair closer to mine. "Let's speak from the soul." He was going to get village heavy. "I know we've been trying to leave Georgia ever since . . . I can't remember. It's been our dream, sometimes our only hope." He nodded to someone a few tables away. "But what about Nino's aunt? Remember her?"

"No."

"She was working at the Interclub at the port, before independence, and she fell in love with a foreign sailor and defected to

Yugoslavia. She wasn't allowed to return for ten years and she became so homesick she turned into a nun. When she finally returned all she could do was kiss the ground. I saw her in the market today. She was still kissing the ground."

I rolled my eyes.

"I've seen people leave," he said. "And when they return they're crazy."

"Already, my mentality is not normal here," I said, glancing at the Turkish sailors drinking Fanta, a drink I couldn't afford, through polka-dotted straws. "What's here for me anymore?"

Malkhazi sighed. "I've never told you this before. Do you know it was your grandfather in the village who saved me? He's never gone to school but he knows everything about how people should live. Before, I always thought Georgia was a goddamned country, but when I was living in the village he taught me what it means to be a real Georgian. He sees lightness everywhere. You know how he loves everyone? Of course he is easy to take advantage of because of this, but he told me that humans created the darkness, the devil, that actually everywhere is light. But you understand that I cannot tell this to anyone else or they will think that I am disrespecting their religion?"

"My grandfather told you this? Well, if everywhere is light, then there is light in America too," I said.

Later that night Malkhazi fixed the handles that he had broken off the cabinets and took out our batch of walnut liquor. It was so potent it had dissolved the walnut shells marinating in it, rendering it good for the kidneys. Malkhazi poured us each a cupful. Raising his glass, he said, "Every day that you're gone, I'll kiss the ground for you. I mean, I won't roll around on it, but I'll look at it and do it in my head."

But now I wonder if I even cared if he kissed the ground for me. My thoughts before leaving Georgia had been restless, impudent, a Georgian man thrashing under the confines of a seat belt.

After dinner Malkhazi handed me a bundle of *churchella*, our sticks of grape candy, made from boiled grape juice and nuts—our traditional traveling food that we bring with us when we are fighting a war, staving off the Scythians, Mongols, Turks, Persians, Cherkezi, Ghlighvis, Didos, Kists, or Lekis. Our Georgian Snickers.

"It's from the village," Malkhazi said. "It will remind you of home, of your roots, and will pull you back. 'Bitter roots yield sweeter fruits,'" he said, quoting Davit Gurmanishvili.

"I don't have room in my suitcase," I said. But the real reason I didn't want to bring *churchella* was because I remembered how when my friend Vano had brought them to America he hung them over the doorknob of his hotel room. The cleaning service called the police who accused him of possessing dynamite. Instead of recalling this story for him, I said, "I do not intend to be pulled back to this little town, to my roots. The main thing I need are some new boots."

"At least take my boots," Malkhazi said and flung them at me from the boot rack near the door. Oh, I had been tempted: his high quality, Russian-made, sturdy, leather, mountain man boots. But on the heel were the stamp *USSR*. No, I didn't need an Achilles heel. So I bought my own boots from the new Italian shoe store on Mayakovskaya Street with some of the scholarship funds I had been given.

I still had my doubts about whether it would be possible to actually open a fish packaging factory in Georgia. That would really require a lot of investors and most investors, as my survey at work had indicated, were afraid of investing in Georgia. But I was touched by the optimistic spirit of America and wanted to live up to their belief in me.

When I said goodbye to Anthony and told him that I would no longer need his assistance in acquiring a visa he asked me if I was sad to be leaving Georgia.

"Am I sad to be leaving?" I asked him. "That is very strange question. No Georgian would ask that question."

"Oh, right. Because your culture is too masculine?" he asked. "You don't go in for the feelings?"

"No, because we have too *many* feelings," I said. Anyway, I told him that I would bring him back some cans of coconut milk because he'd been so busy working on the pipeline that he hadn't had any time to go to the American embassy's supply store in Tbilisi.

* * *

Just before leaving Georgia our dictator summoned me for a meeting. I had never before been invited to anything by the local dictator. Sometimes a touring opera singer was allowed to talk to the dictator's wife, or to sing to his Viennese goatherd, but even that was uncommon.

After passing the soldiers guarding his lawn, which was longer than the Norwegian tanker that had recently docked in Batumi, I met him at the entrance to his residence. I was surprised that I was taller than he was. He told me to sit down in his sitting room, which looked like a court—a king's court, not a court of law. He had a tight and mean face but he looked oddly insignificant in such a large golden chair, all the golden light from the chandeliers reflecting off his balding head. He spoke quietly. That was a shock. How can a quiet man be a Georgian leader? It's not normal.

In a winsome voice he reminded me that developmentally and industrially—though not spiritually of course—we were behind the West. He made all kinds of allusions with his eyes—that I couldn't understand very well—to the gilded photographs of his aristocratic ancestors on the wall; talked about how soon he hoped to make a recovery for Georgia, soon *he* hoped to make a recovery, not the *other* one; and he indicated with his head where the *other* one, President Shevardnadze, had an office, down the road.

He then gave me French perfumes, a plastic model of his proposed Super-Hyper market building project, a calendar with photographs illustrating before-and-after images of the old style Georgian homes on the blocks surrounding his residences (the after photos seemed to be in the future, because the houses were much cleaner and larger than they were now), a revivalist party T-shirt with the emblem of his political party on the front, and an envelope containing one hundred dollars. "Remember it as a gesture from a father figure," he said avuncularly.

I was moved, though I couldn't help thinking, "Oh, here is two months of the salary that the state owes me. Now you only owe me six months more."

* * *

After that, everything fell into place with the speed of a solid fuel booster rocket.

The director of Tbilisi's branch of the Center for Democracy ushered me into the front of the line at the American embassy in Tbilisi, charging past the people who had been camping outside the gates for five days. I tried to keep up with her. When we got to the front of the line, the consular was calling my name. "Slims Achmed Makashvili. Is he here?"

In front of the American consular I had to sustain the imported facial countenance of "poker face." I told her that I loved my glorious country of Georgia but that I wanted to learn about the American policeman, to be able to promote democracy and capitalism in Georgia through the fish packaging business. I took out a piece of paper and showed her the logo of two sheep horns I had designed for a car hood, in case Georgia ever manufactured a new kind of automobile. I didn't tell her that I had no intention of returning, not when I had the chance to live in a place where I could get paid for that which we must do for free at home.

At the airport I marched down the boarding ramp and onto the plane, the air pressure sucking at my ears; sat down in my assigned seat; ripped open the plastic package of earphones; and listened to channel seven, the airplane's rave station. Now I really felt like I was a character in a movie on an important mission.

While flying over the ocean I switched the knob on the music dial to the "atmosphere" station and heard ocean waves. I plunged over them as if I were a gull skimming the surface for the silver flash of fish. The deep sound of a man's voice: "Just feel how calm and relaxed you are . . . you have tranquilized your mind, your emotions, and have begun," the swoosh of waves, "with those three deep breaths, to feel calm and relaxed." I ripped off my earphones and heard a disturbance in the back of the plane. A clan of Georgian businessmen stood up to smoke, opening overhead compartments, taking out greasy cloths of food. The flight attendant was politely requesting them to extinguish their cigarettes, sit back in their seats, that the plane was experiencing turbulence. I reassured her that everything would be okay and tried to give her the *churchella* that I discovered my mother had secretly stowed in my bag.

"What is it, a candle?" the British flight attendant asked, holding the long, bumpy stick of *churchella* up to the light of the window.

"A candle, yes, a candle," I said and gave her the whole bundle. I never wanted to look at anything that even looked like a candle again.

As I walked off the transcontinental flight, my belly full of trans-fatty acids from the airplane meal, I quoted quietly to myself our poet Joseph Tbileli's words, "I leave the home that was to me a joy as well as misery." Although, *he* was writing about his uncle Giorgi Saakadze, the Georgian military leader in the seventeenth century who, after trying to improve the social conditions of the peasants, emigrated to Persia. My situation, admittedly, was a little different.

And then, like a child falling into a long lost God, I joined the hearty breed of Americans. All at once I was blinded by the electricity. Western electricity illuminated a different world, a calmer kingdom. American land was diluted, as if on the periphery of a microscope, not under the focus. The streets were practically empty. Those who walked them wore baseball caps, oblivious to Euro-fashions. Like caricatures from a Soviet propaganda cartoon they walked to their cars, consulting their Palm Pilots, checking for their next appointments. "Oh! The parking meter has run out," one says, and sees a parking ticket on the windshield, then hears the ding-ding sound when he opens the car door, then wonders what restaurant to go to for dinner.

But I write ahead of myself. I hadn't yet witnessed the frustration of a parking ticket because I arrived in San Francisco at night.

In the passport control line, when I stooped to shine my shoes, I heard a customs official say to a man in front of me who couldn't understand English very well, "These are not allowed. And ignorance is no excuse," when he confiscated the man's paper bag full of fruit.

I was grateful that someone was going to meet me in San Francisco, so that I could get accustomed to these American habits before venturing onto the slipperiness of the American businessman's mob. I had heard that American businessmen like to psychoanalyze each other. They ask, "What is your favorite animal?" in order to try to understand what kind of person you are. I had decided that if someone asked me I would say a mouse because mice are very tricky. Once it took me five days to catch one.

Flocks of businessmen in the greeting hall held up signs with English names on them. And then I saw "SLIMS ACHMED MAKASHVILI" held by a man with yellow mountain-style hair, dressed in the traditional American folk-dance costume: a farmer-style shirt, jeans, and sandals.

When I approached him he thrust out his hand in that effusive American manner and said, "Slims? Slims. Good to meet you. I'm Merrick. You speak English, right?"

I nodded.

"Great. Is this all you brought?" he asked, looking for more luggage while he heaved my blue canvas suitcase over his shoulder. "You're a light traveler. That's great. This way," he said, as we melded into the crowd. "I took BART, the train, down here. I have a pickup but my sister's boyfriend is borrowing it. Anyway, I thought you might like to get acquainted with our public transportation system." We stepped onto a descending escalator. We walked through red neon-lit underground corridors that reminded me of American action films of the 1980s, or Russian action films of the 1990s. "I read your paper on the dogfish, how you use the liver for omega-3s, how the meat contains necessary vitamins, and you use the skin for sandpaper. Even fertilizer! Talk about sustainability! After reading your essay, I felt like we had something in common, you know, our common love for the sea. Two planets in the universe converging. Though, these days they're calling the universe the omniverse. Anyway, there's no such thing as a coincidence. That's what I believe. But sorry, I don't want to sound all *woo woo* hippy-dippy, 2012. It's just that I harvest seaweed off the coast, up north, in Mendocino County. Have you heard of it? I mean the area. Have you heard of the area? A lot of people know it for its bud. Do your people eat seaweed? I dry it, package it, sell it to health food stores. I'll take you up one day."

I worried all of a sudden that my English skills were very low, because I could not understand very much of what he had just said. I understood each word individually but not when he put them all together. I watched the doors open and close at all the stops letting on and off only a few passengers. So much electricity for only five people on the train. On the wall was a poster of a baseball team. Underneath the photograph were the words, SIT LOW, PAY LESS DOUGH.

"I also run a roofing business called Precision Roofing," Merrick said.

"You have your own business?"

"It's major stress. I always worry that one of my customers is going to say to me, 'You said that you do a precise job, but this job is not precise!' There's a lot in a name, how we label something. I had this dream recently where I changed the name of my business to Merrick's Good Enough Roofing. People should be happy with good enough. Of course I didn't change the name because in reality who's going to hire someone only good enough? But this dream was a blessing from the universe, the omniverse I mean, because it relieved some of that anxiety. I did decide to give up driving my truck everywhere and now I ride my bike to a job site and haul my roofing equipment in a cart behind. I have some anxiety, though, that the chemicals used in the roofing materials aren't very eco. I wear this gas mask but no matter how tightly I adjust it, I can still smell the fumes from all that tar, and I'm thinking, man, this is going into the atmosphere. Some people are a little put off when I ride up on my bike. They expect some big guy with a truck. Isn't that weird that people only trust you as a roofer if you have a big truck? So I start a job by driving up in my truck, get to know the guy, and then gradually start using my bike once I've delivered all the roofing to the site. I would have picked you up in my truck but yeah, my sister's boyfriend is borrowing it."

We got off the train on Market Street, a wide boulevard with brick tessellated sidewalks, newspapers fighting their way through the valleys of the tallest buildings I had ever seen.

"This is the financial district," Merrick said. "But it's kind of funky at night."

We got on a bus, Merrick talking the whole time. "I'm thinking of getting out of roofing altogether because lately I've been feeling like I'm working for the man. I'd rather work for mankind. I have a friend who sells imported clothes from Thailand off his bicycle, he calls it a Thai-cycle. Get it?"

As I listened to Merrick I stared outside the window. All the streets were illuminated like the day before our presidential elections. When we got off the bus I tried to pay close attention to what Merrick was saying as he pointed out the street sign. "From this little hill you can see the towers of the Golden Gate, when it's not so foggy. If you walk in that direction you'll hit Geary. If you start to get homesick, you can speak Russian there. Buy Russian products."

"We only get homesick in our own country," I said.

We walked toward his house. "It's the gray one there. But I have to warn you about one thing. I have a homeless guy living with me for a little while. I met him on the bus a couple of months ago. I got to talking with him, and he told me his whole life story, about how he grew up somewhere in the south. Georgia I think. Ha ha. Like you." Merrick unlocked the metal gate. Behind were some brick stairs leading up to his door. I picked up my bag that Merrick had set down. "And his house burned down, something like that, he's looking for his wife, or his kid, I forget, but he's trying to find a job, but he can't get himself cleaned up enough to find one. So I thought, man, I've felt like that before. So I invited him home and told him he could stay with me for a while. I had an extra bedroom because my girlfriend just moved out. There's only one minor problem: he watches TV all day. I'm pretty busy during the day so I don't know what programs he watches. Do you watch much TV?"

"The news."

As he fumbled with the keys to his door at the top of the stairs, he spoke a little more quietly. "I ordered one of those assemble-at-home dollhouse furniture kits to give him something to do, try to get him up on his feet. Oh shit, wrong key. You order these pieces from a catalog and then they pay you to put them together, to make little dollhouse rocking chairs or wardrobes, there's even a DVD player, but I worked it out, oh I think this is the right key—they all look the same—and even if you're working as fast as you can, you're making like forty cents an hour." He opened the door and whispered, "I spent a few nights assembling the pieces with him but I ended up doing all the work because his fingers are so stiff. Have you heard of fat finger syndrome? You can hang your jacket in this closet. I can't kick him out because every day he's like, 'Jesus took pity on me through you, praise the Lord.' That's why there are dollhouse furniture pieces all over the floor. Watch out for them." He put his finger to his lip, "I think Charlie's sleeping. I told him he had to sleep in the living room on the couch."

We tiptoed through the dark, down a hall.

"You're probably exhausted right now. There's the bathroom. You can sleep here." He pushed open a door.

When he turned on the light, I saw a guitar on a blue plastic stand in the corner. A green blanket covered the bed next to the window. "I burnt some sage to sort of cleanse the room. Sleep in however late you need to, all day if you want. You don't have to start the seminars until Monday. Oh, here are some matches if you want to burn some more sage. Or if you want to light some candles."

"Please no candles. I do not like candles."

"Suit yourself." He shut the door behind him.

I lay down on the bed, still in my clothes, and contemplated the low ceiling that resembled Russian farmer cheese. Then I got up; hung up my clothes, my trousers, suit jacket, and tie in the closet; put the roll of tape and every other thing I owned on the half empty bookshelf, glancing at the books. *The Renaissance Guitar. The Surfer's Encyclopedia. Building Bridges for Those Who Burn Them. Rise Up Singing. Raising Sheep the Modern Way. The Modern American Language Bible.* I opened the Bible and read, "And then

Jesus invited us over for a snack." Interesting. I had never read the Bible before in English.

Merrick hadn't updated the month of the calendar on the wall. January had a photograph of a sunset over the sea. I opened the window, leaned my head out, and looked down into a yard overgrown with greenery. The fog was too thick to see beyond that. Moisture curled off the leaves, the names of which I did not know. I put my head back inside and closed the window. I lay on the bed and considered the ceiling again.

Even though I had dreamed of traveling to the West ever since I had procured my coveted Western civilization law textbook, I had thought that in America I would still be in the same movie of my life, but with better lighting.

When I left that Georgian medieval matinee, I didn't know that I would enter a new movie altogether, one in which I didn't know any of the characters.

I took out a piece of paper. "Dear Tamriko," I wrote. But I didn't know how to continue so I quoted some lines of poetry from Shota Rustaveli:

Forgive me that I went from thee and thy command did not obey.
No power had I to do thy will: enthralled, from thee I stole away.

I fell asleep with the light on.

14.

I WOKE UP LISTENING TO THE SLOP OF THE SEA. THE ELECTRICITY WAS
on. I should use, I thought, this opportunity to fill up a water bucket.
I opened my eyes and then remembered where I was. For the first time
in my life, I felt homesick for the sea.

Merrick cooked pancakes for breakfast. "I hope you're hungry,"
he said.

I nodded.

"Wait until you taste these. I buy the mix down at Whole
Foods. Actually, we call it 'Whole Paycheck,' but it's the only place
where I can find blue corn flour pancake mix. I like to add bananas
and walnuts. Blueberries too for the antioxidants. Oh," Merrick
said, opening the freezer, "I guess I'm out of blueberries. Charlie,"
Merrick called from the kitchen, "I'd like to introduce you to Slims.
He's from Georgia, not the state, the country. It's part of Russia,
right?"

"No. Not part of Russia," I said.

Charlie came into the kitchen patting down his hair. I shook
his hand.

"Charlie, if you eat stuff, that's fine with me," Merrick said,
rummaging through the refrigerator. "You just need to tell me so that
I can replace it. You'll have a pancake with us, won't you?"

"I'd rather have some bacon," he said.

I looked inside the refrigerator. There were about a dozen bottles of beer labeled LOST COAST ALE. Maybe the Soviet propagandists were right about Americans and their beer. That was the dominating item. But the refrigerator was also filled with all kinds of vegetables: red peppers, cucumbers, and bunches of coriander—the types of vegetables we only eat in the spring and summer.

I thought about the time one winter when Tamriko had run out of vegetables and I had brought her some jars of tomatoes and eggplant, but she refused them. She had said that according to the Herbalife company eating vegetables in the wintertime is equivalent to stealing from the earth. Instead, she fed herself on strawberry jam and pickle juice. She slurped her vitamins from condiments. I tried to explain this to Merrick.

"She drank pickle juice? Like as a salad? Like in a bowl?"

"Well, from a spoon," I said.

Merrick cracked some eggs into a bowl. "I hope you like my food. I'm not really into condiments but I have some mustard I think. I'm introducing Charlie to a new way of eating, actually to a whole new sustainable lifestyle," he said. "Charlie doesn't get out of the city much. I took him to a sustainable building conference up in Hopland where we designed a hut out of straw bales." Merrick looked up from his pancake batter to make sure Charlie wasn't still in the room and whispered, "When we were there Charlie said, 'What? You all make a house out of straw? What kind of house is that?'"

"Yes, that is a little strange," I said. "We usually use wood, or concrete, or stones."

"No, I'm not saying it's *normal* building material. It's sustainable technology. It's so well insulated you can heat it with a candle."

"Yes, people in our villages do such things," I said.

"But don't you create alternative power in Georgia? Isn't it a movement?"

"It's illegal," I said. "The government controls the electricity, turns it off most of the time, so that we must buy their oil to heat our houses. The villages almost always have homemade electricity though.

So I guess they're alternative." The frying pan splattered oil on my neck. "Is it usual for men to cook?"

"Sure," he said. "When my girlfriend lived here, or I guess she's my ex-girlfriend now, I did all the cooking."

"Why did she leave?"

"It just didn't work out. Have you heard the saying, 'I'd rather be single than married to a psycho?'"

"No."

He told me about how she would always become emotional, and how when he tried to cheer her up, she would say, "Don't try to fix this. I just need to feel like this." Perhaps Americans don't like to fix things because everything works properly all the time? Anyway, in America, it seemed, women were just as emotional, but they wanted to have long conversations about it a lot. It's the opposite in Georgia. The men are always wanting to talk about relationships and the women say, "I'm tired of talking about relationships."

"Here, try them now while they're hot," he said, scooting a pancake onto my plate. "Charlie!" he called. "Come and eat." When Charlie came into the kitchen, he sat down in a metal chair across from me and started eating, so I did too.

"Charlie, do you cook?" I asked.

"Sure," he said.

"So, this is the American weekend," I said, biting into the pancake. "I have heard about the American weekend."

Merrick turned on the radio. "Do you like jazz?"

"Sure," I said, trying to imitate his language.

The American man passes his time on a Sunday with a big breakfast, listening to jazz and then playing folk songs on his guitar. It appears to be a prodigious activity. Bob Dylan, the Beatles, and particularly songs about peace.

After Charlie and I had "stoked" ourselves with pancakes, Merrick said, "Slims, in your room there's a book called *Rise Up Singing*. Could you get it for me? And Charlie, could you fold up your bed? I want to vacuum." I got the book. Charlie folded up his bed back into a sofa and Merrick vacuumed up the dollhouse furniture pieces around it.

"Have a seat, Slims. Be at home here," said Merrick. "I'll bet you never heard these before," he said flipping through his much marked-up spiral-bound book.

We sang "Yellow Submarine," "I Am Changing My Name to Chrysler," and "Waltzing Matilda," and then Merrick cried out, "Here's one for you, Slims, turn the page, it's called, 'When I First Came to This Land.'" He began to sing, "When I first came to this land, I was not a wealthy man, so I got myself a farm and I did what I could. And I called my farm 'Muscle in My Arm.' But the land was sweet and good and I did what I could."

I debated whether to sing for Merrick a similar Georgian song by Raphael Eristavi, which goes:

Dust am I to dust I cling
I was born a rustic.
My life is one eternal strife
and endless toil and endless woe
till life is gone I plow, I sow, I labor . . . on.
With muscles strained,
in all kinds of weather,
I can hardly live on what I earn.
And I remain tired and hungry.
The owners of the land keep tormenting me.
Even the little ant is my foe.
For the people in the town,
for the priests,
for the villages, like I pig,
I sweat and plow and sow.

But then I decided I wouldn't.

"Here's one for you, Charlie," Merrick cried out, "you'll remember this one, come on now, 'I ain't got no home, I'm just rambling round, Just a wand'rin worker, I go from town to town. The po-lice make it hard wherever I may go, and I ain't got no home in this world anymo'." Merrick stopped playing. "But you got a home here, right bro?"

The doorbell rang. It was Merrick's father. "Dad," Merrick said. "Didn't we agree that you would call before you visited?"

"Yes, but I wanted to meet your new guest." When he saw me he put his hands together as if to pray. He made a little bow, as if he were a Japanese person. "We deeply respect your traditions," he said. He looked at Merrick. "Can he understand me? Maybe I should speak more slowly." He turned to me and bowed again. "We. Honor. You. Our culture has lost its way. We live in a spiritually bankrupt society. We hope that you can teach us the old ways. We can get you a horse."

"What?" I asked.

"Perhaps. You. Have. Not. Ridden. In. A. Car. Before."

"Dad!" Merrick said. "He took the airplane here. He's heard of a car before."

"Quiet, son. Haven't you heard of Ishi, the last Native American? He stepped aboard a train but who knows what was going on in his soul? We don't want to turn this fellow into a jaded American. What sorts of activities have you arranged for him?"

Pluck. Pluck. Merrick plucked his three-stringed guitar. There they were. The father, the son, the homeless man, all singing songs for me. They couldn't sing very well, hadn't mastered the harmony, but they were trying so hard. They had such hope, such mighty idealism, such open expressions. "I haven't had this much fun in fifteen years," I told Merrick. "I think your family is not pessimistic."

"Actually, my dad is fairly pessimistic. He's always worried about global warming. Any time I go to a baseball game he says, 'You better enjoy it now. There won't be any baseball in the future.'"

Later, I pulled the lint off my trousers with the tape I had brought. I polished my shoes with a sock. I put on my sunglasses and slicked back my hair with some water. I told Merrick, "I am ready to see the town."

As we walked down the street, I took off my sunglasses because the sky was overcast. A few blocks down some workers wearing helmets and matching orange jackets with reflector tape on them were excavating the sidewalk to insert some pipe. They had been provided with a lot of equipment: huge cables; cranes working, purring; humming machinery. "Usually the only cables we have left in Georgia are seat belts," I said. "Your machinery makes me feel like a dignified man. It is helping me see things from a vertical position." I tried to stand up straighter.

On the street of Geary was a Georgian bakery. I was very surprised. "I am shocked that you have such a shop devoted to the old world," I said.

"The old world? Right. You're a man of the old world. Would you like to go inside?"

"But why? I already know what the old world smells like. It is like old leather furniture. Your country has a new smell. Besides, what excuse would I give to make their acquaintance?"

"Just to talk?"

"But why? We don't meet in other countries just to say hello. They might become suspicious and think I'm a junkie."

But no Georgians worked there—only happy Chinese people, and I did not feel comfortable asking them for a job. They sold *khachapuri* for four dollars each. "I think that price is a little too high," I told them. "In Georgia they only cost twenty cents." But they also sold beautiful and cheap slices of cakes called Mother-in-Law, Napoleon, Princess, Madonna, and Tbilisi.

I bought a Mother-in-Law, took the cake outside, and sat down on the curb. "I have heard that in America it is okay to just sit on the curb and eat cake," I told Merrick. "We will share this cake," I said and took from my pocket a fork.

"You brought your own fork?" he asked. It is easy to shock Americans, even in their own country.

Another funny incident: Radio Shack. Merrick wanted to buy some special AAA batteries for a project he was working on. I scrutinized the cords, wires, and tiny adapters sold in perfect packages with clear directions. "It's so easy to understand these directions," I told Merrick. "In Georgia, our writers use words from the sixteenth century in order to sound sophisticated."

A customer walked up to the counter, and waiting for the clerk, rang the little service bell. She kept dinging it, annoyed. I called Merrick over to the surge protector section, which was located next to the service counter. "Come here!" I said. "Quickly! Watch!"

"What? What?" Merrick said.

"Quiet," I said. "Just listen."

The clerk had come out from the back and was saying, "Sorry for making you wait," he said. "Phone call."

"Oh, excuse me, I'm wondering if you could help me. I have a problem with my answering machine. Maybe you could look at it?"

"Isn't that funny?" I nudged Merrick.

"What's funny about that?"

"It's beautiful. So many words! In Georgia we only say, 'Fix this!'"

Outside, we crossed the street at the crosswalk. A car coming toward us stopped. I waved at the driver. "They are so polite," I said to Merrick.

"Not really. It's the law."

"In Georgia it's the law too, but no one follows the law. Tell me, seriously, how do you get everyone to follow the law here?"

"Not *everyone* follows the law here," he said.

That wasn't a good answer because it was obvious that Americans followed the law well enough to keep their electricity running. I pointed up at the dozens of power lines strapping the city together. "In Georgia the copper contained in those wires is worth about five dollars a kilo at the current exchange rate. If this were Georgia those wires would have been clipped a long time ago."

"That's hard to believe," he said.

"Believe it. I'm not joking. A few winters ago half of our power lines were cut and sold to Turkey. But here, I have heard that even if utility companies try to raise their prices they first have to pass many regulations. They can't just raise them whenever they feel like it like in our country. It's a beautiful system."

"Yeah," said Merrick, "I guess we're used to it."

"But it's important to think about it, to pay attention to it.

America looks how Georgia used to look. And then in one night, kaput. Now, in Georgia, we only talk about, you know, mysticism and delirium."

That evening I lay in bed, staring at the ceiling again, and wondered if I could stay here. Find a job here. Send money home. I threw away the lines I had written to Tamriko and took out another piece of paper to write to my family.

Everything is fine here. Don't worry about me. My host is a good guy. In the shops everyone smiles so happily. That is the best part. And the streetcars move in and out with electricity all the time like they used to in our country and it is so regular that it is easy to be calm. California also lost electricity last summer and it was called "national disaster." Imagine. I am trying to have an adventure but Americans are such quiet and polite people. They donate rooms in their houses to people with meager salaries and are studying to make houses out of straw. I am living with a Democrat. I do not know the exact meaning yet. I begin business seminars tomorrow. Merrick says they are all Republicans there.

15.

MERRICK WOKE ME UP EARLY IN THE MORNING. "SLIMS," HE SAID, rapping on the door. "If we're late my sister is going to kill me."

Susan, Merrick's sister, was in charge of the business seminar. Her organization had run out of host families, which was why I was staying with her brother. Brother and sister did not resemble each other at all. She was the one who looked, how else can I say? Official. But elegant. The backlight through the window shone a cinematic highlight on her hair, the color of good quality Russian chocolate. But the overall atmosphere around her made you feel as if you were watching a documentary on a Turkish-made TV. The reds were too bright and smeared outside the lines. Maybe she looked like this because her lipstick had smudged, creating the impression that she was always rushing-rushing and didn't have time to look at herself too closely. She wore a maroon "power suit," as she described it, and her smeared lips were in sync with her suit, and drew me to them because they contained the authority of knowing what they were saying. I admired her nostalgically and a little tenderly. She reminded me of a younger Hillary Clinton. I tried to imagine her in one of our Soviet spas. I wondered if she liked to rub her body with the cubes of salt that Merrick kept near his bathtub. Despite the ample curves in her maroon suit, she acted like a businessman. I was sure she went to the building under the computer center for business lunches and didn't attend any womanly cooperative craft society.

As is the American custom, she first gave us an *outline* of her life by clicking her computer mouse in what she explained was a program called PowerPoint, a type of software that would be *advantageous* for us to learn. "It looks more professional," she said, "to have bullet points. Though it's usually men who tend to be more impressed."

She said in her *former life* she used to work with the World Bank when they were funding the construction of nuclear reactors in Eastern Europe. But one day when she was walking to work she saw her reflection in the black glass of a savings and loans building and said to herself, "Who is that woman wearing those professional looking shoes?" So she quit her job with the World Bank and decided go into foreign policy for nongovernmental organizations. "And yet," she said, "I must admit I've never lost my *competitive edge*. I want to teach you all about the free market economy. If you learn about policy making, you can make the policy. Not many people realize this. There are always organizations vying for diminishing funds, but not many know the appropriate means to obtain them. Though the exorbitant budget cuts by the current administration have compromised our resources, the US still has a vested interest in financially supporting programs for the development of democracy in post-Soviet republics."

I hadn't sat in a lecture hall as a student in seven years, though I did occasionally *deliver* lectures at Rustaveli State University on maritime law. But it was always my bad habit that whenever I sat in a lecture, the military instructor before my eyes became a little bee, engaged in an activity that had nothing to do with me. Such were our instructors. I could barely endure the last month of the university, having to sit and listen to the military lecturer tell us that if one Georgian was facing y amount of soldiers, he should be able to defeat them; that if we were being attacked from the rear, we must turn around. "Let us practice outside now," he would shout.

Of course it's okay for our poets to sit drinking under the almond blossoms thinking philosophical thoughts. But when *I* sat under the almond trees outside the university, on my shoes to keep dry, nursing a bottle of homemade *chacha*, the military lecturer would come over and yell at me, "Slims, you are supposed to be marching around with the others. We are on a reconnaissance mission. Already they are nearing the Turkish Boys' School."

"Don't you have any respect for the great philosophers?" I had yelled at him.

"What sort of Georgian are you?" he had said. I almost had to join the Georgian military for my wanton remark.

Susan also resembled a bee, but watching her, the life of a bee took on an entirely different meaning. I remember learning how in order to communicate to the others the bee does a little dance and points at the honey with his behind. I felt that by listening to Susan I could find America's honey. "We already know that current leaders in positions of power in your countries," Susan was saying, "have no viable examples of a free market economy, of democracy, of adaptive techniques other than the staid echoes of communism. Over the next six weeks, we will therefore mentor you in sustainable business practices and aid you in your search for partners, potential donors and investors. We will work side-by-side with you to study the achievements of the businesses in your own countries and help you make informed choices about new marketing concepts to help promote awareness of your products and services. The first two weeks will be your induction period and the last four weeks you will participate in your internships. As I said, this effort will require courage, creativity, and extraordinary willpower. Let's go around the room now and introduce ourselves. I want to hear your positions."

We were all a little reticent, especially after that speech. I had been looking forward to coming to the American heaven, but now I was also beginning to understand that there is a lot of pressure in paradise.

"What's she talking about?" asked the Russian man sitting next to me. I wondered if his understanding of English was poor.

"Just follow her example," I said. "She's really happy, like an optimist."

"Like Puff Daddy," he said.

We sat in a circle, or rather a square, on plushy leather couches. Sergei—the man sitting next to me, slumping in his chair—was of the melancholy type. He wore the traditional mafioso outfit: black leather jacket, sweatpants, flip-flops, and in his mouth he chewed a toothpick.

"Sergei," Susan said, looking at her clipboard. "Can you tell us where you're from?"

He was from the Urals. His mother was a Russian factory worker but his father was a Tatar—he was quick to qualify. "My biggest concern is for our water right now. It is filled with all kinds of metals. When I fill up my bathtub the water is the color of forest honey, the black honey that comes from the trees, not the clear honey from flowers."

"Sergei here is always thinking about our nature," interrupted the man sitting next to him, and slapping him on the back. "Allow me to introduce myself." He stood up and addressed Susan, ignoring the rest of us. "My name is Mikhail, or Misha you may call me." Swankily dressed in a white shirt, tie, and gray sports coat, with a mobile phone attached to his hip, even his lanky body type was fashionable in a *new* Russian sort of way. "And I, we"—he stooped to rap Sergei on the shoulder again—"want to tell you that in Russia now there are good people and there are bad people." Sergei, beside him, nodded slowly. "Believe us," continued Misha, "believe us, really. It's a fact. Maybe you see these Russian immigrants in your cities in their tracksuits talking loudly and smoking Marlboros by the swimming pool. And we sympathize with your condition. That is why Sergei is the only company I can truly trust. Do you agree, it is only possible to trust the company you were born with?" He looked around the room. "Okay, we are all in agreement. It is a fact. That is why Sergei and I can know that we, ourselves, can establish a new tradition among the travel agents. I know you think that our travel agents are corrupt. And yes, your thinking is correct. Our travel agents take bribes from innocent people. But we are striving for something other than that. Sergei and I want to study about the American travel agents. We have formed a sort of covenant and no longer will we be accepting bribes." I gazed at them dreamily. This was something quite interesting. "Here is our phone number." He handed our instructor his business card. "If you ever come to Russia and if you have any problems with your travel arrangements you can call us. With the glory of God you won't have any problems. But if you do, you can call us."

"Thank you, Misha," Susan said, taking the card.

"Don't say thank you now," he said and shuddered. "Only say thank you when you mean it. But by the glory of God you won't ever need it."

I was about to stand up in order to invite her to Batumi, but apparently we were going around the room in the other direction. The girl sitting next to Misha, wearing many little barrettes lined up like railroad ties in her multicolored hair, came from a small town in Russia, from Neftograd. "The name of our town literally means Oilville," she, Lena, said. "I'm sure you can imagine what our problem is. We are a very rich republic, but the wealth is not divided equally and many people are resisting this."

Papa must have paid Lena's passage here, I thought. He probably works for one of those ubiquitous companies that manufacture some sort of tube. "My concern is that it snowed in my city in July," she said. "And it snowed *last* year in July. This is not our usual weather pattern. But who is hearing of this? Also, I am very interested in women's rights, women's businesses. I would like to start my own clothing line or at least learn how to create a catalog like this." She took a stack of mail-order catalogs out of a shopping bag labeled "Krasnyi Vostok," Red East, Siberia's most popular brand of beer.

The man sitting next to me was from Kazakhstan. He was introducing himself now. I couldn't see what he looked like very well because his baseball hat covered half his face. He whispered to me in Russian, "Can you translate for me?"

"He doesn't feel comfortable speaking in English," I said, "so I will translate for him."

"That's all right, I can understand a little Russian," Susan said in Russian.

"No," Lena said, flinching at Susan's heavily accented Russian, "I'd prefer it if he translated," and she pointed at me.

"Okay," Susan said and shrugged. "It's better if we speak English anyway."

His name was Chemistry.

"Your name is Chemistry?" Susan asked in surprise. "But that is a very unusual name."

"It's a Soviet name," I said. During Soviet Union times it was normal to name your son after science.

Chemistry told me, and I started to translate, that his mother knit camel hair socks for the passengers on the Trans-Turk railway, but he worked as a DJ in his small town on the steppe. "Tell her how it's a problem because I can only get access to the same twenty cassettes, and people are bored because they hear the same music. But maybe that's not important," Chemistry said quickly. "I am truly concerned about our potato crop. In Kazakhstan we are no longer allowed to grow any potatoes because of a beetle epidemic. These days potatoes are so expensive because they must be grown secretly. Those who grow them are like mafiosi chasing each other down the road always asking the same question, 'What is the price of potatoes?' Even truck drivers are afraid to transport them."

When my turn came I said, "My name is Slims Achmed Makashvili. I am from Batumi. It is very interesting and humbling to sit here. As for my problems, we have many problems in Georgia, but the biggest one for me is, well really what I'm wondering is how you get people to follow the law here? Of course if your family is hungry, it's necessary to steal something. But we just need to bring up *one* generation where the children do not look to criminals as role models."

"Well, I see you all come from a variety of backgrounds," Susan said. "I hope that we can all benefit from each other's experiences. I have some books to pass around that may help you in this effort at democratization." She passed half a pile of books to one side of the room and the other half to our side. I rummaged through our side's stack: *The 7 Habits of Highly Effective People, Eleanor Roosevelt's Guide to Leadership for Women, Capitalism: A Primer for the Roadside Vendor.*

I was relieved to see that Dale Carnegie's book wasn't included. "You are free to borrow these books," she said. "But the method by which you will learn the most is through your own initiative, by phoning people, asking questions. It's all about the telephone call."

"We encourage you all to acquire cell phones," she continued. "Our institute will be able to provide you with a reasonably priced telephone plan." When the board was covered with Susan's life outline and there was no room left for her to complete her illustration of a telephone receiver with her green felt pen, I ripped a piece of paper out of my notebook to erase the board for her, but she picked up a cloth eraser and did it herself.

In the afternoon we had a guest lecturer, a Mr. Tetley, like the tea. He was American but he looked a little like Anthony, which meant that he also looked a little like George Bush. As he wrote on the board, he spoke aloud the words he wrote.

"If . . . you . . . don't . . . know . . . where . . . you're . . . going . . . that's . . . where . . . you'll . . . end . . . up. Nowhere!" Then he passed around photocopies of a million dollar bill. So we could hold it. "Does everyone have a pen?" he asked. "Take a few minutes and write down all the goals you have in your life on this bill. Income level. Family. House. What is it that you want? While you write, I'll play this Bob Marley song on the CD player."

"*Wake up and live y'all wake up and live. Wake up and live now,*" the lyrics repeated as we wrote.

After a little while, Mr. Tetley turned down the volume. "Mr. Makashvili," he said, squinting to read my name tag. "Read to me one of your goals?"

"I'd like a lot of money," I said.

"Okay, and what do you need that money for?"

"I'd like to buy a car?"

"What kind of car?"

"A BMW 525."

"Yes, I have one of those. Light blue. Now imagine. How are you going to feel when you sit in that bucket seat?"

Everyone oohed.

"I feel good," I said.

"Yeah, I'm right there with you. If you're feeling half as good as I am as I anticipate you sitting in that bucket seat, you're halfway there. I had a goal to lose body fat and gain muscle. It hasn't exactly worked out for me yet. But it has worked a little. I was 189 six months ago and now I'm 182."

Chemistry leaned over and asked me how to spell wife. "Is this right?" he asked. "I want to good wife."

"Yes, that's right," I said. "Take out the *to*."

Mr. Tetley was now telling us about a man who made a plan to sell something called pixels. "If you fail to plan, you're planning to fail."

Chemistry slid his paper over to me. "Is this right?" he asked. I read, "I want to the another house."

"Yes, that's good," I said.

"He sold pixels on eBay," Mr. Tetley said. "He made a million dollars in five months. And four months later he made four million. Money generates money. People bought entire Internet neighborhoods."

Chemistry scooted over his paper again. "I want to good pay. I want to good vacation. I want to good car."

"That's enough. That's enough goals! Now why don't you listen to the guy?" I shoved his paper away.

"Now what is an affirmation? An affirmation is a way to get out of a rut," continued Mr. Tetley. "The best way to get out of a rut is to make a new rut. An affirmation is a positive feedback loop that rewires your brain chemistry. Often an inspiration will come to you. Have any of you heard of feng shui? The most energetic part of the house is the southwest corner. So look to the southwest and the affirmation will arise. If your goal is to own a party planning business, that is a good goal. You might want to take steps. Work for someone who knows the business. First off, I am going to hand out these affirmations on these pieces of paper that I have found to be extremely helpful. I'll read it out loud and then we can read it together. Does everyone have one? Let's read the first line together. I AM PROSPEROUS. It's the most powerful aspiration you can have if you want to change your life. Yes, Chemistry, if you could continue passing those around. Make sure everyone gets one. Now together. Everyone. I. AM. PROSPEROUS. Wait. There's a trick here. What's the most important word?"

"I," someone said.

"That's right. Actually, *I AM*. This is really important. I want all of your eyeballs on me. Again. I. Am. Prosperous. I. Am. Prosperous."

"Not yet," said Chemistry to himself.

"No!" I whispered to him. "The point is that you are prosperous right now! Right now!" He grinned at me as if he understood.

"I AM PROSPEROUS," Mr. Tetley said in capital letters. "My innate, natural, original self is prosperous."

"Excuse me," I said.

"Yes, Mr. Makashvili?"

"Please explain the meaning of original self?"

"I mean the thing that you want the most is your essential self. For example. You want that car."

"I changed my mind," I said.

"Okay, so what does your original self want?"

"I want a business. But if I was my original self I do not think I would need a business."

"Another way of thinking of it is this way. What is the most important thing for you at the time of your death, Mr. Makashvili?"

"At the time of my death? I don't want to die in the poison oak. But that is out of my control."

"No. Now this is a difficult thing for most people to understand. Somewhere you decided what kind of death you wanted. Just like you have created this moment right now. To learn from. Everyone is an expression of creativity itself because we have created this moment right now."

"Can we listen to that song again? Time to wake up?" Chemistry asked.

"Well, first look at your goals on your million dollar bill. Do you have any million-dollar ideas? Find the one that motivates you. That's what you're going to put energy into. Here's a grid. Pass that around. On this grid you can put down the steps to reach your goals. Let's try a fun exercise. Imagine what you will be doing in ten years. Don't forget about your other goals. I'm sorry. Are there any leftover goal sheets? This young lady is missing one."

Chemistry showed me the square where you write the affirmation for that goal. It was empty. "What here?" he asked. I pointed to the heater. "You're supposed to look in the southwest direction. Wait until something arises. Look for a need. Find a need that should be filled."

As the first week progressed I didn't know how to tell Merrick, and especially not Susan, that I had no intention of opening a fish packaging factory in Georgia, that I was more interested in learning how to get people to follow the law in Georgia.

Chemistry wanted to learn marketing strategies for packaging his mother's camel hair socks to make them appealing to the passengers on the Trans-Turk railroad. "The problem is that in one hundred and ten degree weather no one wants any socks," he said. He needed a logo that would remind people of the wintertime. Sergei wanted to sell the bee pollen venom from the apiary he had built in the forest behind his house. Misha wanted to work with the new boxcar construction company opening in Tikhvin, Russia, to open a tourist line.

"That's a wonderful idea," Susan told Misha.

"As for me," I told Susan, "it will be difficult to come up with a feasible business plan because my boss already has a monopoly on the sea, flying his fake flags. As far as business pursuits, maritime law is a dead end venture for me. Especially because no one follows the law in Georgia, on the land or the sea."

"The law of the sea? You mean for the fish?" Misha asked, trying to make a joke.

"You obviously don't understand the law of the sea," I told him, "because you are a Russian and a man of the river."

On the first day in the cafeteria's buffet line, Misha wouldn't talk to me because he said I spoke Russian with a Polish accent. I told him that I didn't even want to speak Russian, that Russian people are nothing like Georgian people. A few days later, though, when he realized that I was from Batumi, on the Black Sea, he remembered what a *romantic* place Batumi was, and from that day on he only wanted to tell me about when his cousin Piotr visited there in the summer once. After that Misha always sat next to me and was my role-playing business partner when we role-played business deal simulations. He was A-Man and I was B-Man:

A: I'm so happy to meet with you today. I think we can create a win/win.

B: Let's thank our financial counselor, first, for coming all the way from Concord.

A: When will we wrap up our quarter profits?

B: Oh, look at the time!

And because it is important to eat, I added, "Buffet time!"

Misha complained to Susan about me. "Listen to this guy. He is not taking this seriously." He began to taunt me. "In your country, do your business deals consist of *meh meh*?"

"*Meh, meh*?" I asked.

"Because you sell so many sheep to Qatar?"

"Just because we sell sheep to Qatar doesn't mean we speak sheep language!"

Susan heard us talking and thought we were being serious. But we were only joking. In Georgia we say of our Russian friends, "He's a Russian, but he's okay," and then we kiss their cheeks and it irritates them because they don't like to kiss as much as Georgians.

When I got home after the business seminars, all I could do was lie down on the bed and stare at the farmer cheese pattern on the ceiling. I had made it to America, yes, but under the false pretext of claiming

I wanted to learn how to package fish. I thought about other businesses I could start instead. I could open my own carpet cleaning business, haul vacuums around in a van, expand it into an extended family of vacuums, an extended family of vans. Or I could take a salesman training course and sell those eye massagers—the ones that look like what Merrick wears to keep out tar fumes when he's on the roof—that I'd heard Russians buy on TV.

In the back of my mind, though, I couldn't forget about my friend Vano. He had worked for a SWAT team in Georgia, but now he worked for a concrete company in Michigan. He said he could get me a job there. It was not an option that filled me with happy feelings. It was a last resort.

In the living room Charlie was sitting on the green reclining chair and flwip, flwipping through Merrick's ninety-eight television stations. Lying back in the warm, well-lighted house, trying to improve my English skills, I listened to the modern sound of America: "As the CEO of our firm, I reevaluated our whole business strategy. I had to tell our lenders, 'You will never get between us and our customers,' and as I said, that lender became one of our better partners. You need to be able to send out enough volume and that really requires capital. That quarter we raised over a hundred million dollars. Most of it we spent on marketing and advertising. That's equal to one percent of all mortgages of the United States."

"Bob, did you say one percent?"

"That's right. We always thought the challenge would be to sign up the banks. You need to get lenders to come in and change the value of business. If you look at the history of economics in our country, Jeff, you'll see we did not have huge centralized call centers."

"Extremely profitable. Look at the financial history."

"It's a history of innovation, Jeff. How else do you keep yourself in a competitive position? We went through a period of very vigorous competition and what we realized was this: we were going to have to empower consumers. The history of the market is not about ruthless competition. The history of the market is about innovative lending models. There's always some resistance but at the end of the day the businesses we deal with are entrepreneurs. You have a pool of consumers who love to shop and compare. We provide the content. At the end of the day, what will they say? That mortgages and financial services have been democratized. The information advantage shifted to the level of where the playing field leveled out . . ." Flwip.

"Do you feel like you need a nap in the daytime? Have you considered that your mattress might be the problem?" Flwip

"Giving you the shiniest, silkiest, sexiest hair you've ever had. Allows you to easily curl or straighten, and its extra long swivel cord allows you easy mobility . . ." Flwip.

"Hello, I'm Paul. I'm here to introduce you to a remarkable new product. I'm not here today just to represent my pharmaceutical corporation. I'm here to show you these pictures of actual people who have tried our new antiaging topical cream. My wife swears by it. I swear by it. You say, 'Of course you swear by it. It's your line . . .'" Flwip.

"Toughest guy pounding Harrison. I say if you don't want to hit and be hit then don't show up today. We've got the most physical NFL teams in the league. These teams understand that it's still about imposing your will on others. Defense. Blocking. Tackling. But today on the field I have not seen the physical domination I expected . . ." Flwip.

"The greatest national product of America is its good heart . . ." Flwip.

"I agree, Maureen. What we're seeing is fashion for every price option. Some of this stuff you can do for yourself if you're handy with the sewing machine. You can even make this outfit . . ."

"Oh isn't that cute!"

". . . for your little dog." Flwip.

"Ooh. And what's this?"

"That's our arugula pesto. Keep in mind that the problem with pesto is that people add too much of it. What I love about these products is that our package comes with its own wooden utensil . . ." Flwip.

I was beginning to understand that so much electricity allowed for a lot of televisual experiential diversities.

I got up from the TV and looked on Merrick's computer to see if there was some sort of Georgian community in San Francisco, but I couldn't find one. The last Georgian/American Commerce Meeting was held on March 23, 1996.

In the kitchen Charlie made us both an avocado and cheddar cheese sandwich. It was too slimy. "Let's make an omelet," I said.

"Merrick said I should eat more vegetables," Charlie said.

"In my country eggs are considered vegetables."

After we ate our omelets, I helped Charlie put together his dollhouse pieces. We made a miniature billiard table.

The next day Mr. Tetley brought what he called an "om machine" to our seminar. He asked us to help move the conference table aside so we could stretch out. "Slims," Mr. Tetley said, "why don't you stand where you have more room? Stretch your arms out. That's right. Is everybody here? Everybody-ish? Today, for our introductions, let's try something new. We get stuck in patterns of who we think we are. So instead of that let's tell each other what body of water we are identifying with. I'll start. I am Roger Tetley. Remember, when you say your name, emphasize the I AM. Today I am identifying with Clear Lake, a calm and clear lake that I recently explored in a kayak. Susan? How about you?"

Susan and Mr. Tetley had both changed into exercise clothes, or what Susan called a leisure suit. "I am Susan," she said. "Today I am identifying with a shallow puddle with big red boots stomping up and down in it."

Everyone laughed but me. How could someone change their personality so quickly?

"Slims?" Mr. Tetley said.

"Yes?" I said.

"What body of water do you identify with?" Misha yelled from the back.

"Truthfully, I wasn't identifying with any body of water today," I said.

Misha made sounds of annoyance. "But usually, I think about the Black Sea," I said. People seemed to be satisfied with my answer.

After everyone had identified themselves with a body of water—Misha, of course, had identified with a river, the Dnieper River—Mr. Tetley said, "We will now try to feel the water of our own bodies by om-ming." Taking a deep breath he reached his arms toward the ceiling. "Since our bodies are mostly comprised of water, this is a technique to get in touch with the liquid currents of our bodies. It's called being 'in the flow.' When you're in the flow, you're heading toward prosperity. You will find that if you practice this every day, your health and your intimate relationships will improve. Not to mention your pocketbook. We're all here for that." He sat down next to his machine, turned it on, and instructed everyone else to sit down on the floor too. "With this next exercise," he said, "we will create a feeling of unity and one-heartedness between us. Take a deep breath in on this note." Mr. Tetley pulled out the bellows. "And exhale with the word *om* on this note."

I think I breathe more slowly than Mr. Tetley because he was pushing those bellows in and out a little too fast, speeding up our breathing so that soon I was hyperventilating. I was trying to watch his breath, to create one-consciousness and one-heart, but Sergei, behind me, stopped om-ming and began chanting, "Wah wah wah . . . wah, wah, wah." Mr. Tetley halted. "Stop," he said. "Everyone stop. Some of you may not understand the point of this team-building exercise, but once you start working for a corporation, having to deal with the demands of some power hungry, cocaine-addicted CEO, you will realize the benefits of om-ming together as a group."

Sergei, in the back, said, "I like to chant individually."

After lunch Mr. Tetley changed back into his gray suit. Now was the scheduled time for individual consulting. When it was my turn we sat at the conference table with a bottle of water between us. "On their list of exports," Mr. Tetley began, "many countries boast of plastics or rubber products. Steel. Redwood. Pig iron. I see here, Slims, that you are interested in packaging fish. Let's expand our vision a little. What products, besides fish, and oil transport, of course—we can't forget about that—is Georgia best known for?"

"Georgia is best known for its liquids," I said. "Wines and waters. Brandy. Perfumes. Tangerine juice. Besides fish, I think the best business for me would be to get involved in exporting Borjomi water, especially because it comes from the park behind my village. That would be the logical thing. I mean thinking purely pragmatically. Purely business. Do you agree?"

"Borjomi?" Mr. Tetley asked. "I'm not sure what that is."

"But you know the word *KGB*," I said. "How can you not know *Borjomi*?" I pointed to the bottle of water between us to give him a little hint. "It was the Coca-Cola of the Soviet Union, the drink of choice for the Soviet elite. Mineral water. Borjomi. It's the same word. Just this year, so far, the Georgian Glass and Mineral Water Company has earned fifty million dollars in revenue, that's ten percent of our exports. I heard that French financiers have invested twenty-five million dollars. I think I could do it for less. The biggest problem is the shipping expense." I lowered my voice so Misha couldn't hear. "And there are many counterfeiters in Moscow who just add salt and baking soda to their tap water and say, 'This is real Borjomi.' I am sure that seventy percent of Borjomi water is Moscow tap water. But it doesn't have the magical qualities in it and people can taste that."

"Magical qualities?" Mr. Tetley asked.

"Now you are telling me that you don't know about the magical qualities of Georgian water?" I asked, incredulous again. "But even our street bards sing about the famous fizzy water in Tbilisi and how it gives you a long life! You can add tarragon flavor, chocolate, orange, or even a chocolate-orange combination. There are always so many people at the Borjomi Cafe who want to try that water that people go just to watch who has the patience to stand in that kind of line." I tapped my pen on the table. "There are some logistical problems we must take into consideration, though. We must export the water to Russia, through Abkhazia and Chechnya and there, I'm sure you know, everyone is always shooting each other. I know that a percentage of Borjomi water is always stolen by customs officials. I've heard it's not a high percentage, though. They steal a lot more from other businesses in the region."

"But the climate over there is starting to improve, yes?" Mr. Tetley asked. "In fact, business can only get better, I think. Anyhow. What I've learned is that the real challenge in doing business in former Soviet republics is getting rid of the old way of doing business. I was consulting with a company in Kazakhstan a few years back. A rubber plant. Anyhow, in order to make this company viable, not only did we have to retrain the managers, but we had to cut back on all those services and benefits that Soviet-style companies used to offer to their employees."

"Like what?" I asked.

"Business cannot support kindergartens. Nor can they sustain sanatoriums, hospitals, or summer camps. You've got to get rid of those burdens and focus on the product."

"I think your capitalism is about as effective in Georgia as a private hobby, like stamp collecting," I said.

But Mr. Tetley was really tenacious; he wouldn't give up. "What other products do you have besides Borjomi?" he asked.

"Hazelnuts," I said. "But I already sold ours in the market. I couldn't get a high price."

"Ah, that is where you must change your thinking. Why didn't you wait until there was higher demand for them? Then you could charge more."

"But then they would have dried out and weighed less," I said.

Even though I knew that all week long Americans look forward to Friday—"TGIF! TGIF!" the radio announcers always said—when Friday finally came, I was exhausted. As we say in Georgia, "The cat which did not reach the sausage said: 'Anyhow, it's Friday.'" Along the marina the gulls were pecking at paper bags. Little children, like everywhere, were digging for gold on the beach. I had the opportunity to become a businessman. Slims Achmed: a man with a capitalist plan.

When I used to drink homemade *chacha* with Malkhazi under the combines, or sing peace songs at Soviet pioneer camps, I never imagined that I would one day be in America, encouraged to come up with a business plan.

At home I made a tuna fish sandwich and sat on the sofa, staring at the TV, which presented a documentary about a man who made fifty thousand dollars a month while sitting at his kitchen table in his underwear. But I was interested in neither nudism nor "telecommuting," so I switched the program to Oprah. She was talking about how to make friends with yourself.

Merrick's father stopped by, saw me watching TV, and told Merrick that he should be arranging more cultural activities for me. "He comes from an ancient culture," his father said. "You need to show him that we have some traditions here too."

"It might be a very good cultural experience for me to study the law here," I suggested to Merrick.

But instead, Merrick took me hula hooping. "This is the one day of the week when I really need my truck, in order to carry the hula hoops," he said. "But my sister's boyfriend is still borrowing my truck. Do you mind carrying some hula hoops for me?"

"In Georgia we like to carry swords these days," I said. "I feel insecure not carrying something."

We walked down Geary to the gas station where Merrick had organized a peace vigil ever since the American war with Iraq had started. "We meet here, in front of the gas station," Merrick said. "You see Slims, we can't stop the war in Iraq but nobody can stop us from protesting every third Friday of the month. Our little peace group has become a San Francisco tradition," he said, propping up some "political art," as he called it, that he had made out of pieces of cardboard. "The Marin newspaper even wrote an article and called us 'Hoop for Peace.' I don't like labels, but I like to think of ourselves as concerned citizens and people who love America."

Merrick began to rock his hips back and forth, suspending his hula hoop over his hips. Behind him was the 3-D cardboard gas pump he had set up, actual size. It showed the current numbers of soldiers who had been killed in Iraq. Tonight, the number was 602. Merrick said that last month it had been 204.

Like his sister, Merrick was a *multitasker*. While he was hula hooping, he spurted fake blood out of one of his homemade oil derricks. Then he worked the levers on his infrared, remote control toy tank he had bought last Christmas season for twenty dollars. "I discovered this thing was manufactured by Halliburton. It gives me great joy to use their own propaganda against them," he said and fired off six plastic missiles from the front of the USA Freedom Force M-1 Tank at a 4x4 driving by while a computerized voice said, "Enemies crushed."

"You understand the technology on this thing?" Merrick asked. "The batteries alone would have cost almost ten dollars on the shelf. They were included. This tank was subsidized by taxpayers' money!"

Some men dressed in uniforms had started to congregate. "Uh-oh," I said, pointing at the soldiers.

"They're forest rangers," Merrick said. "Most of them have never been politically active before in their lives. But they always come out for this."

As I learned how to hula hoop that evening, Merrick, from inside his hula hoop, lectured to passing pedestrians about the dangers happening to our environment, about black oak sudden death syndrome that was killing all the oak trees, and about the glassy winged sharpshooter—an insect that all the vineyard owners in the North were terrified would demolish their seventeen-million-gallon-a-year wine producing region.

I preferred not to hula hoop, but filled with *cultural experiences*, my life became so busy, like a workaholic's. I did not even have time to philosophize about how America was not how I expected, not like a picture by Edward Hopper: a long road at sunset, red dirt, and in the middle of the dirt, a short gas pump.

16.

Deyda, Malkhazi, Juliet, Zuka and everyone else in the neighborhood,

I am in the library now reading books about Admiralty Law, Evolution and Science of Mankind. Also I have been studying about environmental law and met with the professor who teaches it.

My emotional content is a little low because I must expend so much effort to understand the people here. All the time in the cafeteria's buffet line the Americans use the following expression: "You're in my space." It is a difficult concept. The only way to translate this in Georgian I think is, "You invaded my dominion."

And today something really strange happened. I went to the store to buy beer. So many different kinds of brands! So I choose one named after my favorite Czechoslovakian metal band and went to sit on the steps. I sat there. Such a nice afternoon. I lit my cigarette and cracked open the beer. But what was this? It tasted like a hospital! Malkhazi, have you heard of this strange kind of beer? It was called root beer. I looked in my dictionary and a root means a carrot.

Well . . . why not?

Anyway, a few days ago I had another course with Mr. Tetley, the motivational speaker. He was giving us good advice on global marketing, about emblems and brands. I drew for him my sheep horn design for a Georgian car hood and he was very impressed.

But the most interesting thing happened yesterday, which I would like to tell you about. My host Merrick took me to a place called Corte Madera mall, which is a big crowded shopping center with a JC Penney's where I bought a new jacket. Also an Armani tie (handmade in Italy) because we are supposed to look professional. Gocha's silk shirt will not be able to compete with my new image. My host Merrick told me, "Slims, if you want to buy a jacket that's okay but the reason we are here is for a different reason. We are here for guerilla activity. We stood outside JC Penney's in the parking lot and sang a song that went like this. I will try to get it correct: "Buy nothing today / Consider that you might have and be enough / Invest yourself in the ones that you love / Instead of amassing more stuff." The police came. They said it is illegal to stop people from shopping and told everyone to stop singing. The police really have a lot of power here. I suggested to Merrick that perhaps the police would like a popsicle but he said that wasn't a good suggestion.

In Georgia we think the Gurians from our village are funny but people here are even more funny. I read on a military blog about an anticommunist public convention here in America. At the convention, people made speeches like, "The communist is a criminal and we must stop him." They said that Russian martial arts and Georgian Chidaoba must be banned. Remember Zuka how you were taking Chidaoba classes to learn how to fight without weapons? They were even saying humorous stuff like Chidaoba instructors are secret KGB agents. Some high schoolers couldn't lift a Chidaoba instructor during a class so they accused him of having scientific crystal-gazer power created by Soviet scientists during 1950s! They don't need to worry so much! We cannot go back to the USSR. We are not the Beatles!

When I showed Merrick the website about people who are afraid of Chidaoba he told me that only people who have a lot of time to waste write comments on those sites. I had been in the US for almost two weeks so far and I didn't want to waste my time so I joined Charlie on the couch. He was watching the Larry King show while Merrick played the guitar. The lighting design on the wall behind Larry distracted me so much it was hard to pay attention to what he was saying.

Larry was talking about something serious, about deploying very expensive missiles over an Afghan cave. All his advisers were there with him. Senators and other congress people, everyone nodding their heads gravely. "But how can anyone take this seriously," I asked Merrick, "with those festival lights, like a New Year's tree, in the background?" Merrick didn't answer but only continued playing folk songs on his guitar. "They take it seriously," I explained to him, "only because they all know it was the work of the most expensive interior designer." Merrick still didn't look up from his guitar. "It's important to notice these things," I insisted to him. "A designer charged a lot of money to make everyone believe him. But now the Larry King show is like a satire. Our Georgian news is very serious," I said seriously. "There's a time for news and a time for satire. It's important to know the difference."

"You're only seeing the outside of it. You need to stay here longer and then you will see a deeper level."

"How a deeper level?" I asked.

To find this deeper level, I closed my eyes and pretended I was blind.

* * *

The next Sunday, the day I had free, I went into a restaurant near the marina—the Cable Car Bistro. It specialized in clam chowder in a carved-out bowl of bread. It resembled our *Adjaruli khachapuri*— cheese in a bread boat. I think all cities next to the sea must make their food into boat shapes. The waiter approached a man who was looking over the menu. He waited for him to order. The man finally said, "I think I'll just have a beer." It was so funny. America has such fantastic characters. "I think I'll just have a beer," became my favorite phrase. But to the waiter I said, "I think I'll just have a water."

When I got home I told Merrick about the Cable Car Bistro. He was busy dipping a chopstick in cans of orange and brown paint, and daubing it on a section of PVC piping. "I think I'll just have a beer," I said and laughed.

"Slims, why is that funny?" he asked.

"Because, you know. No one would say that in my country. We can't just drink *beer*. Beer is a capitalist drink, you know. You can drink it all night and still not reveal your true feelings, still have something sneaky in mind. If a Georgian saw me just drinking beer he would think it was some kind of comedy, that I was drinking beer because I was no longer Georgian, and that would be a tragedy, and where there is tragedy there is humor."

"That is interesting," Merrick said. He was concentrating hard on something he was building.

"I'm going to make some macaroni. Do you want some?" I asked.

"Sure."

"What are you building there?" I asked.

"A didgeridoo," he said. "This design is called a walkabout pattern. I'm trying to get my power back. I lose my power around my sister."

"Around Susan?" I asked. "I do not understand your meaning."

"It's not that I compare myself to her, that I feel bad that she has the big house and not me, because I don't want that, don't want the swimming pool and the life insurance policy, or even her boyfriend's vintage Crown Victoria with the push button gears. I've grown beyond all that kind of envy because that wasn't the life I chose. I mean I *thought* I was beyond all that. Today I went over to her house to pick up my truck. And, in her garage I saw her boyfriend's Shop-Vac. That thing can suck up anything! I realized, when I was standing there, that I do really envy her boyfriend's Shop-Vac. With that thing I'd be able to suck up all these dollhouse pieces that are ground into my carpet. But fine. If her boyfriend wants to own the most expensive Shop-Vac on the market, just for the prestige factor, that's fine with me. The thing that really gets to me though is that there is so much support for my sister's dream in this country. This country works for her. She's not trying to stir up a revolution to overthrow the corporations. When people are worried about their mortgages all the time, they are less likely to stir up a revolution. If people are too stressed with thinking of how to pay their health insurance, who has time for a revolution?"

"But why do you want a revolution?" I asked. "Revolutions aren't usually successful."

"I'm talking about an inner revolution," he said, putting his chopstick down. "But you can't even find that here. One of my roofing clients just told me that down at the Zen center today the *monk* gets up there and says, 'The miracle of life is childbirth. To witness it is to take part in your own spiritual evolution.' Which is true. Which is fine. Which is beautiful. Granted, I give you that. But even he is looking to overwhelm people with childcare expenses. Couldn't the nuclear family be more *optional*? I mean, most people aren't listening to some Buddhist monk anyway. They stay home on Sunday mornings to paint their trim instead. At my sister's house today she was standing there arguing with her boyfriend because he didn't like the color of paint she had chosen for the dining room. She had ripped off the little doggie wallpaper she had put up and was repainting it. She says to her boyfriend, 'The people in my seminar'—she was talking about you guys—'probably only have one color of paint to work with. They would be *delighted* with Malibu beige.' So I'm thinking, 'Oh, my sister is changing. She's waking up a little, recognizing other people's needs.' So I tell her, since she's always so stressed out, 'You know, you should try meditating.' But then she says to me, 'Merrick, I heard there was *scandal* down at the Zen center.' That's her response. But she's right. This roofing client of mine, thirty-five years she was there. Was the gardener. Didn't develop any worldly skills. And now they won't give her the retirement plan she was contracted for. She goes to litigation but she gets so mad and yells, 'I won't take your blood money!' Which is funny because she's talking to a Zen community. Now she regrets her reactionary response. But what does it all matter when we're destroying the planet? By the way, Slims, have you heard that people are drilling for oil? I mean, in your *car*? You think you're safe with a lock on your gas cap but they've started to drill right into the metal of your car. Here. In America! Because of gas prices. A thousand dollar repair job. So anyway, it's not that I feel myself inferior because I haven't achieved the dream. It's that I feel myself despairing because I haven't achieved *my* dream. Here I am in this entrepreneurial country, though these days with the dot-coms they're calling it *info-preneurial*. Creepy, isn't it? I mean I have my roofing business which I take some pride in, but in the back of my mind I'm always feeling like I'm doing something wrong, that something's a little off. I want community. I want a tribe. So what do I resort to? A homeless man and a foreigner. No offense. I really like your company. But I mean I'm thirty-four years old and nearing the grave. I'm no longer a bundle of potential but a bundle of bad decisions. I'm tired of banging my head against the wall asking the question, 'Who am I? Where did I go wrong?' Or, is this just the normal human condition? Sometimes I feel like I'm just treading water, over and over, and not getting anywhere."

"How long have you been treading water?" I asked.

"For years, it feels like," he said.

"That's a good skill. You won't drown. You'll be able to wait for the coastguard."

He looked at me and laughed. "It's not funny. I mean it is. Yeah. I've even started watching old people in the street. Some are all hunched over, can barely walk. Others, the same age, have this swing in their step and are whistling. I want to ask them, 'What is *your* story?' Anyway. So I'm trying to recreate a new story for myself, in this walkabout pattern, like the aboriginals do, on this pipe here."

"Do you know the story about the man who is playing his *chonguri?*" I asked him.

"No," Merrick said.

"All day long he only plays one note. His wife asks him why he doesn't play music like everyone else and he says that it sounds like music but actually everyone else is simply searching for the note that he found. It looks like you are searching for your right note."

"Exactly, Slims."

"But maybe it's better to just make music," I said. "Most people in Georgia think they've found the right note, that we don't need to change because we are fine as we are. But then they are only yelling their note loudly, always thinking their opinion is the right one."

Despite this advice, I could understand Merrick's point of view because in America I was also was not fine as I was. I did not feel at home. They say it takes a year for the angel of the place to spread her wings and reveal herself to you; I had hoped the process would be quicker. But Merrick had been here his whole life and he still was not at home so I told him, "Sometimes I feel confused too. At home I have two personalities. One is my personality that comes from the city and its high culture. Always I have to polish my shoes and try to speak in an aristocratic way. The other is my village personality of 'homeless-ness, horror movies, drink vodka, lalalala.' But anyway, it's boring to always talk about our problems so much. It's better to just tell jokes." I told him the joke about a man from Svanetia, a mountain man, who was driving on a mountain road and, being drunk, he drove off the cliff and hit his head when his car collided with a boulder. At the hospital the doctors operated. They opened up his head. But his head was empty except for a string. One doctor asked, "What is this string?" The other doctor cut it and the Svani's ears fell off.

Merrick started laughing.

"Don't laugh so hard," I said, "or tomorrow you will be crying. At least, that's what my grandmother always said."

But he looked depressed all of a sudden. I tried to remember more advice from my grandmother. "Never feel alone, then the real life begins," I said. But I wasn't really sure about that advice. My grandmother was the milkmaid heroine of the Soviet Union and her main company was cows.

"No, I don't feel lonely," he said. "Sometimes, I just don't feel useful."

"You think the Svani mountain man without a brain, and now without ears, is useful? But everyone in his town still loves him." But I was running out of advice. "Nothing looks beautiful on an empty stomach," I declared. "It's better if we eat something. So do you want some macaroni?"

While we ate I wondered if America needed to change its dream. All the time on TV the politicians said, "Everyone has the right to the American dream." The house. The car. The laundry room. A whole row in the supermarket of laundry detergent. But is this a very good dream? In his head, the man, like everywhere, is always wanting things, but here he thinks he should be slurping the entire world up. Every morning, wake up, drink coffee, go to work, slurp up some world, and then have a weekend. And people must leave their families at such a young age! Only thirty-four? In Georgia we stay with our families until forty or fifty.

Every day in Georgia we are eating and drinking with our families. But in the U.S., I felt like a fish on the factory floor. My gills opening, closing, trying to breathe, developing strange complexes because everyone had to be very ambitious and not have the normal human connections, urgently trying to create their own happy bubble. In Georgia if you called out on the street, "Hey you! Ambitious!" you would get a punch in the head. I wondered if it was possible that the American dream had become old-fashioned. Perhaps I should have chosen the European dream instead, or even the Venezuelan dream.

I had actually been looking forward to my job at the fish packaging factory, which was to start the following week. We had had two weeks of the American doctrinization program and now it was time for the internship. It was located over in Oakland near the Honda dealership and I would have to commute. I was looking forward to becoming a commuter. And at the factory, at least I could just work and not think. At least I had that. But after the very first day there, I felt a heavy soreness in my heart. On my way home I stopped at the employment agency and then went to the corner store and bought the *San Francisco Chronicle* and the *San Jose Mercury News*.

When I got home Merrick said. "Buddy, I think you're addicted. Sometimes I find the news a real downer. I hope you're going to recycle all that paper."

"I bought these newspapers for you so that you don't spill your walkabout paint all over the floor. Actually, that's not the truth," I admitted. "The truth is that I do not want to package fish. I have to come up with a new idea. Maybe these newspapers will help me think of something."

"But I thought you were really into the Black Sea spiny dogfish."

"I don't have a problem with the fish, but I have a problem with the packaging. After today, I am not sure I can go back."

"What was so wrong with it?" Merrick asked.

"Do you know what happens there?" I cried. "They send us the leftover pieces of the fish, frozen blocks of it, two feet by one foot. They don't even use cod. They use pollock for cheaper sticks. I told them, 'Cod tastes better!' They said, 'What does it matter? Everyone dips it in ketchup.' Then they cut the blocks into little fingers. They add a layer of water and a layer of flour and a layer of batter and a layer of crumb. They call it the three-pass system. When they dip it in the hot fat, all the water turns to fat and then they package it, freeze it, and send it to the shops. I do not like this factory farming."

"Right?" Merrick said. "But Slims, what you're describing doesn't only happen at fish factories. The whole system is breaking down, but no one has time to mention it."

"Actually, the fish factory is in quite good condition. The point is they want me to stand at an assembly line and make two hundred fish fingers a minute. I don't mind about the work. But there is no love going into the food."

"Right," Merrick said. "I know what you mean. Well, what did you want to be when you were a kid?"

"When I was a child? I wanted to be a nature scientist because there was one man at my school who drew pictures of big fish. I forget the word. What is this word that means a big fish with milk?"

"A whale? Whale milk?"

"Maybe. Let me look in my dictionary." I looked in the pocket dictionary I carried around until I found the word "Ah. Mammal. Mammal? Like *mama*? That is a good word! It is like a word for homeless people. Not like high-level word—corporation. Separation. Disappear. It is like words in my language. It is like an Eastern word a little bit. Mammal. Mammal. Like Bible. Bibble. Mammal. It feels good in the mouth. Anyway, so today, after work I stopped at the employment office. I looked at the Opportunity Knox and the government employment job board. So many employment opportunities! It doesn't make sense to limit myself anymore to packaging fish. I never realized in America you could get a job as an insect catcher. There was even a job working for the Gorilla Foundation. Emotionally, at this point in my life, I would love to work for the Gorilla Foundation."

"Whatever you do, don't work for a nonprofit," Merrick said. "There was an article last week about how the majority of them can't even pay their rent anymore. Slims, you gotta realize that this is a major urban community and what runs it is money. As soon as those people from, say, Kentucky realize how much money is to be made here, they are going to start flooding the market. If you're gonna live in California you've got to be making at least fifty thousand a year. You're worth that but you're not going to be able to make that as an insect catcher. These young guys starting these dot-com companies are making so much they don't even know the worth of it. They throw thirty million here on a tract house on two acres, grow some grapes, and then buy old whiskey barrels because the barrels are cheap, and then they've got this whiske-tasting wine that nobody will drink. Listen, the thing you've got to get into is the techpub."

"What is that? Some kind of beer house?"

"No. It's tech publishing. I mean face it. You gotta work for the rest of your life, right? So you might as well do what you're good at. I read your essay about the dogfish, but with a class or two you could write about modems. Keyboards. Software. There's some people in Fremont—true ritzy neighborhood—and there's this sign that says GOATS FOR SALE. It looks like it was written by a five-year-old—all the letters backward and shit. You KNOW they are just that rich. They probably owned all that land and are just holding out with their five acres and their goats. Their goats are real cheap too. Fifty dollars. A hundred dollars."

"Are they milking goats?"

"I don't know about that."

"How about sheep? Are people selling off their sheep?" I asked.

"I haven't seen very many sheep around," Merrick said.

When I opened the newspaper I read an article about how farmers in England were selling off all their sheep, exporting them to other countries, in order to move to the city to work in technology fields. Misha continued to joke about how Georgia's main export was sheep to Qatar, but maybe this is a very modern thing to do. What if *I* exported sheep from Georgia? This way I could export them alive, like the old story of Jason and the Golden Fleece, without any packaging.

17.

"SO WHAT DO YOU DO WITH YOUR HOST FAMILY?" I ASKED MISHA ON Monday morning.

"We travel to the wine country. We drink wine," he said, twisting his mustache. "We go to restaurants, very *fine* restaurants. And you?" he asked.

"We sing Leonard Cohen songs," I said.

He tapped his forehead with his middle finger as if trying to draw memory to the surface, "Cohen, Cohen, ah yes, he was a minister of something."

"No, not a minister. Just a poet."

"But the name Cohen comes from Cogan, like Khan, as in Genghis Khan. Yes, Cohen's family were Tatars, like me. It is a fact," he said jabbing his finger at me. "What are the words to the songs?"

"I can't remember the words," I said.

"You sing all weekend but you can't remember the words?"

"Misha," I said. "I know you didn't really go to fancy restaurants. What did you really do?"

"I observed the local travel agency," he said. "I studied their techniques. And you?"

"I took a rest from the fish factory and studied the techniques of the police instead. They were very interesting." I had noticed that usually you can't see the police; they are invisible. But if someone starts to speed, goes through a red light, or if he is missing his front license plate then the highway troopers appear and give that person a ticket. If in the grocery store the large bin of almonds falls down on an old woman's head, spilling almonds all across the aisle, a policeman and a fire truck come at once in order to put a Band-Aid onto her head. The policeman first talks to one person and then to the other person and everyone stands there, not even shouting at each other or throwing the metal part of a seat belt at each other. He, but sometimes the policeman is even a woman, writes down all their information, and then another policeman arrives and sometimes still another, all driving different police cars, all flashing their lights.

So much money spent on policemen and their flashing lights but it seemed to me that the postal workers were dying out. They didn't even have their own sirens to deliver the mail. Maybe because everyone had started using e-mail.

Even back in Georgia Juliet had started using e-mail. That afternoon I got the following e-mail from her:

Dear Slims,

I know you have had problems too with love in your life. Is America changing you? Can you tell me, darling, what the men in America are like?

Was America changing me, I wondered, or was I becoming more of myself?

> *It is written in our civics textbooks at the university, "The Georgian man must not be greedy or an egoist, a miscreant or a villain. He must not equivocate or perform espionage. He must be sweet, kind, and gentle." But I am certain that there are only thirty percent of those kind left. The Georgian man was much more fulfilled when he was running through the forest with his sword, staving off the*

Scythians, shouting at the women to go hide themselves in a cave and guard the wine.

Malkhazi used to be so gallant, driving me up to the top of a cliff overlooking a rugged view of the sea. He would take off his worn sweater as we stood together in the cold, though of course I would notice that the sweater was unraveling at the elbow and feel obliged to repair it for him. On some days I really believed that he was there to protect me. But then struggle, hard labor, too much hard labor, the unrelenting daily shackles of survival: haggling, conniving with policemen, and probably his mandatory hubris are crushing him down.

But oh, his car: he treats it so tenderly. His car is his only means of expression. He shifts its gears in sync with his gloomy thoughts. If I have trouble closing the door he says, "Just kick it shut." But when I kicked it he got offended and said, "I didn't mean it. What kind of person kicks a car door!" Yet, when he drives he treats his car like a horse and he, a boy in a village violently lashing it to get to the next house around the curve where a bowl of home-made chacha *waits for him. God help any pedestrian trying to cross the street when he's driving—she must jump to the center divide.*

He loves to wave to the policeman, to slap some pocket change into his hand, or yell some humorous remark to the neighbor while I am trying to talk to him about something significant. If modern music blasts through his speaker system like, "You and me baby ain't nothing but mammals, so let's do it like they do it on the Discovery Channel," he will throw up his hands and quickly change the station while cursing the Americans and their stupid music. Life itself offends him because it's not tough enough to meet his challenge, to overpower his capacity to endure.

So proud is he of being able to give me a ride in his

*car that when we arrived at the destination he forgot to
open the door for me and said instead, "Now, get out!"
He refused to come inside and eat some pickled watermelon.*

*"Watermelon?" he said, as if he doesn't understand
the word anymore, as if a man wouldn't even use that
word.*

*When he is with a group of his friends, they stand in
a huddle as if helping to preserve themselves. No longer
does he sit politely, deferentially, at the dinner table in the
company of guests. He has no time. He excuses himself
with, "I won't join in the conversation but I'll pay for
everything." He doesn't like to talk anymore, especially if
anyone wants him to. He forgets about flowers, about
cheese, about his date with me and a can of Pringles on a
dark street. He rolls his eyes and says, "I don't have time."
If I object he puts his hand to his head and with a beaten-
down voice says, "I'm tired," so that suddenly I want to
console him, but he says it in a way that makes me suspect
that maybe he is tired of me. If I suggest this possibility he
looks up shocked; suddenly awake, suspicious, "You don't
understand me?"*

*When I asked him, "What has happened between
us?" he said, "Too many questions. Once questions begin,
friendship ends."*

*The only time he smiles anymore is when he's talking
to a policeman or sea captain, making a joke, calling his
bluff, or when he talks to Anthony, joking with him about
how now he has more access than Anthony to coconut
milk.*

*He says that he works this hard because it is his duty
to me. He even told me that he would support me so that
I can do more important things, like nurture my soul. He
actually does have feelings because he is a human, but he
can't find them anymore. He covers them up because they*

serve him no purpose. He only appreciates something after he has lost it. Then he is filled with regret. And only then does he hunch over a bowl of wine. But he's so big these days it's difficult for him to get drunk. I write this because it's not only Malkhazi who acts like this but Gocha too and Gocha is worse. I worry about Tamriko. I think she misses you.

I crumpled up the letter. What was happening to Malkhazi? Was there no place free of the corrupting influence of day labor? Maybe it was better to just have a normal life, a family, a house and avoid this all this modern drama about new boyfriends and girlfriends and who has the most access to coconut milk?

When Merrick got home he saw I was depressed about my family. Maybe for this reason he presented me with a present wrapped in white butcher paper. "You helped me out so I want to help you out," he said. I unwrapped it. It was a book called *The New Century Hymnal.*

"Thanks, Merrick," I said. "It is beautiful. Does this have all the songs we've been singing?"

"Yeah, but let me tell you the history behind how I got this thing. Earlier in the year I started going to this church. It wasn't like a regular church. It was led by this defrocked minister. Actually, I loved telling people, 'Yes, at my church . . .' and watch their expressions. 'You go to church?' they asked, because they couldn't really imagine me being a churchgoer. The rumor even spread. 'At my church . . .' I would say and someone else would say, 'Yeah, I *heard* you went to church.' Anyway, the minister once gave a sermon about how he'd been climbing a hill at Zion National Park and how he didn't think he'd make it up. He was really out of shape and he had run out of water. So he started singing a hymn. He belted out that hymn and at the end of the day made it up the mountain. After that, any time I was having a bad day I'd start to sing a hymn and usually it really helps. So today I went to the church office and said, 'Do you sell the hymnals?' and the woman there said, 'No. Absolutely not. We don't sell the hymnals.' She yelled to the back office. 'Do we sell the hymnals?' 'No. We don't sell the hymnals,' they yelled back. I told her how every time I was having a hard time I would sing a hymn, and how my friend here was having a hard time too so I wanted to get one for him. 'Aww,' she said. 'Did you hear that?' she yelled to the back office. 'Aww. We'll find you a hymnal,' and she started going through the bookcase. 'No, I didn't mean the big one. I already ordered the big one off of Amazon,' I told her. 'I meant the homemade one, the church's personal one, where you changed all the he's to she's.' 'Oh sure!' she said. 'You can just take one.' I think she thought at first I was just a stranger walking in off the street wanting to buy a hymnal. Like I was a journalist or something and was going to write about the church in some devious way according to its hymns. Anyway, so this is for you, Slims. You gotta just leave the hymnal sitting around when people come over. We'll tell people the hymnal is the new piercing. We're hard core to have a hymnal. Hell, yeah!"

"Wow," I said. "Thank you. It has a nice style to it."

"Anyway, after I picked up the book today I went to this ceremony in Oakland at my friend's house. My friend was also inspired by the teachings of a defrocked minister, though a different one, who argues against the idea that God is working in the innermost individual soul. He thinks that God manifests himself in community instead. So my friend has started hosting these cosmic techno trance rituals at his house."

"Actually, I don't really understand what you mean," I said.

"You see, in the West, we tend to divide the world into isolationist individual reality versus collective reality. But this minister, he does this thing called a techno cosmic mass dance that mixes techno, dance, and live music. He says that the West has lost all our rituals, which is why we need to recreate them through liturgy. He says that Saint Augustine in the fourth century really ruined us with this idea of individual salvation, that individual rumination is a Western plague, that really this life is not about original fall and redemption but about original blessing."

"Yes, we think the same in Georgia," I said. "God gave us the land He was saving for Himself. We had a lot of saints visiting our country in the fourth century, but it's a good thing that particular one—what was his name, Saint Augustine?—didn't visit."

"Right? The problem is that my friend's cosmic trance dance ceremony today didn't go so well. He created this earthen pyramid in his backyard because the word *pyramid* means 'burning heart.' He built a fire in it to make a sweat lodge and then started invoking the spirit of the Mayan gods while his girlfriend chanted to the four directions, and the animal communicator made woofing sounds. But during the ceremony, I started to feel kind of self-conscious that the animal communicator was going to pick up on my bad vibes because the woofing sounds were getting obnoxious. I had to imagine positive energy going in her direction, but my walls were going up. The whole thing felt enforced and just off, you know? Now I'm not so sure of the best way to make a ritual."

"But what was the main idea of it? Isn't a ritual a reminder of what matters most to you? For example, how you feel after you get a letter from someone you have loved for a long time. It doesn't have to be so exotic. Ritual could be pouring wine into another's glass. But you have to know beforehand that this is the plan. Everyone has to know all the rules and pass down the rules like in my country. It's not a performance, or an imposition by someone else."

So the next weekend Merrick decided to host a techno cosmic trance dance at his house, and he informed everyone in advance that they would be making didgeridoos.

Everyone from our course came, even Susan. I was developing a cold and so Merrick kept forcing me to drink grapefruit juice and goldenseal extract. "I don't want you to get sick," he said. But I think the herbal remedy was very strong because I began to hallucinate in the same way I did when I was a kid and had accidentally swallowed some gasoline when I was trying to siphon it into the combine. The men in the field at the time patted my back and gave me some milk to drink. I am sorry to say this, but my farts smelled like gasoline for two days.

When Lena and some of her friends arrived they took over the kitchen.

Merrick went back to the living room and covered the floor with newspapers. "Good thing you bought so many of these, Slims." He set new containers of red and orange paint on top of the paper. We had bought PVC piping at Home Depot earlier in the day and now several of Merrick's friends from the antiwar protest and a few of the forest rangers were banging on the floor with it. The sound made my head ache a little so I went back into the kitchen with the girls.

"Don't you want to make a didgeridoo?" I asked them. Lena suggested that we go bowling instead but her friend started mixing vodka and cranberry juice. "I'll have mine straight," I said.

As usual, the girls in the kitchen only wanted to talk about politics and geology. They mixed it together as if it were the same word, and not just because they were drinking. It was advantageous for them to know about politics, especially for Lena, whose father had a powerful position in oil-ville. I imagined that every geopolitical class in her university was filled with such new Russians, sitting in the back of the class and calculating the worth of natural resources with their calculators in the same way they did at lunchtime when they converted the prices of dollars to rubles in their French perfume catalogs.

"So, what *exactly* does your father do?" I asked Lena after I had made a toast to our parents.

"I told you, he provides tubes for companies," she said.

"But what *kind* of tubes?"

"I don't exactly know what he does," she admitted.

"Ah ha!" I said. "But you have a car."

"Of course," she said and then pirouetted with her pink drink. "You should come visit us. We have parties in Nizhny all the time. You should come to our parties. Bring your friends. We have a Mercedes, actually. We could drive to Lake Baikal. Or we could drive anywhere."

"My uncle's been to Russia," I said. "He bought a wine factory in Siberia but then the government closed the borders so we couldn't export any grapes to the factory. We had to abandon it."

"We could drive to that factory," Lena said.

From America, everything seemed possible. From America it looked like Russia was engaged in her own perpetual cosmic trance dance.

More of Merrick's friends had arrived but no one was providing any organization. There was no toastmaster, no order, no "we." Everyone sipped their drinks individually and no one there really knew how to make the shy ladies comfortable.

Misha and Sergei were over by the window daring each other to drink more. They alternated between staring at the girls and peering between the window slats like men from my village do when they're watching out for the combine mechanic during harvesttime.

Merrick was looking through the images in a book on aboriginal dream designs. He squatted down beside Susan, showing her a caption. She was wearing hiking boots and drilling holes into the PVC piping. Sergei was staring at her while Misha said, "I'm taking the language proficiency test, the TOEFL, next week so at least I will have something to show for this time spent here. Lena had joined them and was telling Sergei, "I like a man who is capable. We Russians are not American women."

Merrick pounded the floor next to Sergei with his PVC pipe. "Slims, buddy, sit down here. Aren't you going to work on one too?"

I watched the anarchy build into chaos. But when I closed my eyes and listened, the sound was somehow euphonious.

"Slims," Lena called to me and then said in Russian, "How do I say in English, give me a cigarette?" I knew she knew how to say it in English but she was hinting at me to give her one.

"Slims, where are you going?" Merrick said.

"I'm just going to get some cigarettes."

"Cigarettes! It's bad for your health, Slims."

"So is living," said Sergei. "Take off your jacket, Slims. I have cigarettes."

Lena sauntered over to him and he gave her one. Sergei caught Susan's eye across the room, extended his arm, and shook a cigarette out for her, but she turned away.

Susan was now making her own didgeridoo, daubing on orange

and white walkabout patterns with a chopstick. Was she, too, trying to reinvent her life? America seemed to be all about endings and new beginnings. But the beginning of Georgia happened too long ago for us to remember. And we never make a toast to endings. All the time we sing, "Always we are and always we will be."

I went outside with Misha and Lena. Lena was pointing to the first star that had just emerged. "Make a wish," she said to me. The full moon hazed under our smoke. "It's better to make a wish to the moon," I said. "In Georgia we say, 'If the moon helps me I will scoff at the stars.'"

"What is the meaning?" Lena asked.

But I couldn't discuss the meaning because Sergei came out and asked me, "Is it true that a man from the Caucasus can seduce any woman?"

"A man from the Caucasus has the highest sperm count of any man in the world," Misha said. "Fact. Our scientific conclusion is that they want to take over the world."

I rolled my eyes at Lena and went back inside. Sergei and Lena followed me. Lena, as if making a final announcement, snapped open the gold clasps of her purse and procured a CD. When she put it in the CD player the song bolted out, "Ya loobloo tebya Sergei," the same song that Natasha, the Russian woman who works at Batumi's telephone office, always listens to, and everyone started dancing, swinging their hair around, and banging their polka-dotted PVC piping on the floor.

The only one not dancing was Chemistry. I went and stood by him. "I used to like parties, all the eating, drinking, but then my brain changed I think, and got a different formation," I said.

He nodded, as if the same thing had happened to him.

"By the way, do you know the film director Rashid Nugmanov?" I asked him. "He is from the Kazakh New Wave movement."

"The Kazakh New Wave?" asked Susan, joining our conversation. "What is that, exactly?"

"If you do not know about the Kazakh New Wave directors, do

not worry, that is normal," I said to Susan. To Chemistry I said, "Have you seen the film *The Needle*? It's my favorite film."

"Of course," said Chemistry. "I have seen that film ten times."

"It's about a girl who is a drug addict," I told Susan. "Her boyfriend takes her to a mud hut in the Karakorum desert to help her recover. When she is better and looking lovely, wearing a white dress, she says to her boyfriend, who is playing with a scorpion, 'I am going to the sea for a swim.' So they walk to the Aral Sea but the Aral Sea has shriveled and there are only old cargo ships left scattered here and there on the cracked earth. The beach is now thirty miles away. So the couple plays on an abandoned ship, swinging happily on the chains. It describes perfectly the end of civilization. America has not seen the end of civilization yet, has not yet had to say when all has fallen down, 'We're here. We remain here still.' I'm sorry to say this, but you are not a very modern country."

But then I thought about America and their love for new beginnings. Maybe, because of this love, they would be okay.

18.

THE NEXT DAY, I WAS READY TO PRESENT MY PROPOSAL TO MR. TETLEY.
I had watched enough television to know the proper language. Also,
after observing Merrick's cosmic trance dance I realized that maybe
people just needed to be reminded of the rules of nature.

Dear Mr. Tetley,

I am ill today in your country.

That part was true. I had caught a cold.

> *It is nothing. Do not worry. Just a small cold. I am
> never sick in my village, however, because we always drink
> the milk of the sheep.*

That part was a lie. But, as I had learned, it is okay to lie in a
commercial. In truth, in my village I drank the milk of a *goat*. But the
difference between sheep and goats is very small.

> *Some people in Georgia say that mountain people are
> a little crazy because they don't have access to the medicine*

that the sea generates. They say if you buy a house in the mountains you must ask, "How are the neighbors? Are they normal or are they crazy?" But they forget that the mountain sheep also has all the medicine anybody requires. Sheep milk contains all the necessary vitamins to stay spiritually and physically healthy and live a long life.

Mr. Tetley, I looked on the Internet for statistical information about sheep's milk. That is how I know now America is running out of the sheep. "Sheep numbers are at their lowest in the US, about ten (10) million," an expert says.

Ten million is less than one sheep per thirty of your people! Every healthy person requires at least one sheep to maintain proper health. For example, in the state of Georgia, according to US census, there are only 1,300 sheep kept on 106 farms. Clearly, this is not enough. The sheep was man's best friend much before the dog, even before the Caucasian sheepdog. Also, how will you make drinking vessels without the horn of a sheep? Also, the sheep is not as stupid as many people think. We know it cannot recognize its owners from an upside down position, but is it really in a sheep's best interest to be upside down? And besides, the owner can't recognize his own sheep either if the sheep is upside down.

If we start to apply sheep-marketing techniques over the Internet, we can see how our monthly income can grow. A sheep changed my life and it could change yours. This is an unscripted testimony.

Mr. Tetley was dubious about my idea of importing Georgian sheep. "Sheep?" he asked. "What about those Georgian liquids you mentioned? Or the airplane parts you showed me on your website?"

"The Russian mafia already has a monopoly on all the liquids. It hasn't occurred to them yet that America could have a sheep deficit."

"But Slims, it's not very realistic. How would you get them over here?"

"The same way we get them to Qatar. By boat. My cousin works in shipping." I had looked up customs taxes for sheep on the internet but could only find a long sermon about the Lord leading His people into the holy land. "Please understand," I told both Mr. Tetley and Susan. "I am not some kind of holy shepherd. I do not especially like sheep. The Turks sent in their sheep to our country so that they would pull up the grass by the roots and turn our land into a desert. I am talking purely business here."

"What would Americans use them for? The wool?" Susan asked.

"The cheese. The vitamins."

"Who knows anything about sheep cheese?" Mr. Tetley asked.

"You don't know about sheep cheese?" Susan asked him. "Surely you've heard of Roquefort. Pecorino Romano. Manchego?" she asked.

Mr. Tetley turned to me. "Have you considered leather goods?"

"Everyone knows that the Russians already have a monopoly on leather goods."

"Well, most *Americans* don't know that," Mr. Tetley said.

"If you want to raise sheep in America, why don't you find some Georgians here who already have sheep?" Susan asked.

"If I wanted to *raise* sheep, I would stay home!"

"But what about the fisheries industry? That's what you have experience in," Mr. Tetley said.

"You think I am some kind of Zorba the Greek?"

"The real question to consider is where you would find buyers for these sheep," Susan asked.

"I already considered that. Off the Internet."

I had added sheep to my website using the same template I had used to sell flags, airplane parts, and green tea. I showed Mr. Tetley and Susan the results:

PRODUCT TYPE: Livestock
WEIGHT: 40 kg

BRAND NAME: Georgian sheep
BREED: Colchis and Tushetian
PORT ARRIVING FROM: Batumi
MINIMUM ORDER: 1000 units
SUPPLY ABILITY: 150,000 per week
STYLE: Alive (NOT PACKAGED)
ADD TO SHOPPING CART

"How would you get the sheep to your client if you did manage to get the sheep to this continent?" Mr. Tetley asked.

"I will herd them."

"Herd them? Why not ship them in a truck or a train?"

"That would not be an enjoyable experience for the sheep! Besides, that is a waste of very valuable resources."

"Slims, you can't herd sheep across the country," Mr. Tetley said. "What about the interstates? You'd need some kind of permit."

"I will herd them through your great national parks."

"I don't believe people are allowed to herd sheep through parklands anymore," Susan said.

"I'll find a way," I said. I had seen a documentary about a man who herded sheep through Montana. The whole movie was silent except for when the man called his mama and started crying that some of the sheep had escaped down the mountain. My heart really went out to that man. But that movie must have been made a while ago because when I decided to do more research about herding sheep across America I found some discouraging news about something called the Grizzly Bear Protection Act that had just been passed. It was true: no one was allowed to herd sheep through Montana anymore.

That afternoon, Mr. Tetley wanted to have a meeting with me. "Slims. I am concerned. You came here on the pretext that you were interested in learning fish packaging. If you have stopped attending the internship, I'm going to have to be frank with you, we are going to have to send you back to Georgia. It's part of the contract."

"That just takes the cake!" I said, using the new idiom I had learned recently. "I thought America was a free country! All the time people on TV are yelling, 'Those terrorists want to take our freedom, our way of life.' But how are you free if you can't herd sheep across your own land? It could be a wonderful movement. Sheep Across America! It could bring people together. People could work cooperatively. I've been wondering and wondering how you get people to follow the law here. I have been watching and observing and now I finally know. You get the people to follow the law here because of something very terrible. People follow the law here because everyone here has an *inner* policeman."

I collected my belongings and stomped out of the building into the fog. When I got home Susan was in the kitchen discussing something with Merrick. I was worried that she had already come to send me away but she had just brought her boyfriend's Shop-Vac for Merrick to borrow. "Check it out, Slims," Merrick said. "Look how clean the carpet is! It only took like one second." They were drinking vodka and toasting to the Shop-Vac and the carpet. "Can I make you one, Slims?" Merrick asked.

"Sure," I said.

Merrick poured some vodka into a metal canister and shook it up with ice. He extracted a green olive from a jar and washed the olive under the tap in the sink. I usually don't drink vodka, but with that gesture he looked like an elegant person making an elegant drink. He handed the drink to me. I raised my glass and said, "It is good in America that the sister takes care of her brother, bringing this Shop-Vac. But what should be the duty of the brother for the sister? Should we always return to them? Should we always protect them?"

"There is no way my sister would let me protect her," Merrick said.

I thought of how Juliet was always complaining about being over-protected. Maybe it was time for me to grow up, to move away from my family, to individuate like an American.

I left my drink on the counter because it's okay to do that in America, and went to my room, looking for my passport. I found the page with the visa and went back to the kitchen. "See my picture?" I said to Merrick. "Do I look like an intimidating Georgian gangster?"

"A gangster? Not really."

"I know," I said. "How about now?" I said and put my grandfather's revolutionary hat on.

Susan squinted. "Kind of."

I poured more vodka into my glass. "This is to sisters who like their freedom."

Merrick was now spreading newspapers over the carpet. I think he wanted to finish up his PVC pipe project. Susan had gone into the other room to talk on the phone.

I looked at the expiration date on my visa again. I looked at his car keys on the counter. "Do you have a pen I could borrow?" I asked him.

"Sure," he said and gave me one from his shirt pocket.

"My friend Vano said he could get me a job in Detroit working in concrete. Do you think it is possible for me to just change the date on my visa and stay here longer?"

"You can't do that," Merrick said.

"Why?"

"You can't just change a date. They have computer records." I saw that he, too, had an inner policeman. "Slims, Susan told me about the visa issue. We can figure something else out. Maybe you can work with me as a roofer."

"In Georgian films the roofer is always up on the house making editorial comments! He's so irritating. I don't want to be a roofer."

I took the cap off the pen. I wrote on my hand. "It's the wrong color. Do you have a black one?"

"Susan!" Merrick called to her. "Your Georgian here is trying to change the date on his visa with a pen."

I waved my hands. "It was a joke. A joke. You Americans can never understand a joke."

"What?" Susan said while coming into the kitchen.

"Oh, never mind. He said he was joking."

"So do you want to use the Shop-Vac for the leaves on the roof?" she asked.

While they were heaving the Shop-Vac up to the roof, I grabbed Susan's car keys from the counter.

It might have been the influence of the vodka—I should have just had a beer—but I prefer to think it was the influence of the wide-sky euphoria of the American landscape. I left Charlie sleeping on the sofa, and I left the didgeridoo with its last dabs to the walkabout patterns of Merrick's new life, and I walked down the stairs swiveling Susan's boyfriend's car keys around my wrist.

"Where are you going, Slims?" Merrick called after me.

"Cigarettes!" I said. I was not *stealing* the Crown Victoria. I was borrowing it. After all, Susan's boyfriend had borrowed Merrick's truck for over a month. And I had to get to my friend Vano in Detroit before Mr. Tetley or Susan stopped me and forced me to go back to Georgia or the fish factory. I taped Zuka's icon of Queen Tamar—my mojo—to the dashboard in order to not feel isolated, anticipating the vast prairie land of America.

When I started my drive it was too dark to see very well, so I can't describe that part, except by brief compendium: darkness and taillights. I drove by braille, navigating according to the reflectors in the center divide.

For seven hours, I drove past farmlands, over bridges, and into corporate lands whose economy, like my own, I had heard was dependent upon the nut. I drove through gristled, raw, granite mountains and past snow, rock, and sky before arriving at the dirty and famous gambling towns of Nevada. I stopped in Reno and lost thirty-five dollars in seven minutes.

Leaving Reno I slid along highway turf, which was as smooth as an oil slick on the surface of the Black Sea, or perhaps the Texas steppe. I rolled down the window and the air smelled of tar and broken buses. Lanes of red taillights amassed in front of me, the traffic flexing and releasing its grip. I drove the American highway, my arm out the window, careening around the curves like a spring let loose in a cartoon that kept making the sound *boing boing*. This was America going 130 kilometers an hour—if only those Georgian minibus drivers could see me now! Malkhazi! I want to show you this. The way you were bragging in Beshumi at your favorite tea stop about keeping the needle shaking at 100 kilometers an hour! The highway system of

America! It's like the beloved American woodsman poet Robert Frost: many paths diverging all over the place, except here all of them are taken. I started to imagine myself as an anthropologist of American culture, a Georgian folk hero, belonging to the city of Detroit, the mayor giving me the key. I could invite Zaliko and his archaeologist friends could come over and we could dig up the city and make historical proclamations about it.

Nevada, when I squinted my eyes, looked like the Ural Mountains—the flat expanse of dry, dull earth on the outskirts of a factory mining town where it is impossible to tell the difference between the flats people live in and their summer vacation houses across the street, and where there are always explosions on the horizon; whether it's a thunderstorm or someone mining in a mountain, who knows?

Road signs, green with white reflector letters, told me that Independence Pass was up ahead but no service was available. Which was fine, because I had no need of any services—at least not just then.

An hour later, I stopped at a mini-mart for oranges, bananas, bottles of water, and also to buy an audiocassette sung by a trucker—the latter in order to get the proper feeling. I heard the villagers talking about fishing equipment and storm weather. Seeing them leaning against the counter like that, I realized I didn't need to be in a hurry anymore, and bought a powdered sweetie roll and cup of coffee.

Back in the car I listened to the song by the trucker. It sounded to me like an ode to beer. But the words of the song made me feel sad because he was all alone in his truck. It reminded me of the way I used to feel as a boy in the village when I would stare up at balconies, of the first time I saw Tamriko as a young girl, her head wrapped in a black shawl lowering her eyes at me, laughing behind her hands as the white lace curtains blew through the open window. I suddenly felt a deep illogical love for my country, as for a troubled, rebel child whom Georgian mothers sigh over at night but love the most. As we say in Georgia, a mother will understand what her dumb child says. I turned off the music.

The regions I had come upon were so remote. I was really far away from anything! Snow decorated the scrub brushes and little hills. The vast blue sky grained-up when I stared at it too hard. The entire country of Georgia could fit between each farmhouse, though they were more like small shacks. I never imagined how many Americans lived in tin huts and mobile homes, town after town of them. The mountains started to get violent and scuffed around the edges as if kicked by the boot of an angry farmer. Mile after mile of nothing but spare branch, scattered snow, and foothill.

There was no way to describe all this land to my friends in Georgia. So why try? As I drove I looked at the icon of Queen Tamar on my dashboard, at her ruby necklace. I looked at the landscape, or the lack of a landscape, if the absence of something can provoke so much reflection, which I guess it can, like the absence of electricity. Out here I could just stop, settle down. I could conjure up some fake documents and get a job fixing electricity. I could buy my own car—some kind of old, half-broken thing, which would still be cleaner and more reliable than a brand new Russian car. There were no soldiers checking passports here, no police cars. In fact, whenever *I* got on the road everyone slowed down because I think they thought the Crown Victoria, with its big antenna to access many radio stations, was an unmarked police car. I wanted to remind them that this was really an *old* car, with its push button gears, that police cars were new with lots of flashing lights. But maybe the new police cars were only in major metropolitan areas. Maybe the government had forgotten about this place. Who could possibly care if I ended up here? Well, of course my family would care—but the government, like our government, seemed to have skipped over the area.

In Wyoming gas cost $1.28 a gallon—half the price of Californian gas. There were no dividing lines in the middle of the road trying to direct me; I felt gradually more at home. Was my love for my homeland losing its adhesiveness, like the Velcro gloves Merrick gave me but that lost their sticking power after tumbling around too many times in the dryer? I imagined the possibilities of settling down in a cold, flat town, roaming the streets feeling an existential feeling. Begone claustrophobia from tight spaces and too much Turkish furniture! Yes, this is who I had become.

Listening to the Christian radio station, I heard about a bowling ball rosary in Wisconsin. I stopped in a small town and went to a cafe that had thirty types of coffee. I bought a newspaper and read the Help Wanted section. There weren't many jobs but one said, "Part-time to teach beginning adult students AC/DC basic electricity. Six hours weekly (two three-hour sessions on Tuesday/Thursday evenings) during Fall 2003 semester. Students are apprentices in Stationary Engineers' Union. Examples of curriculum include Ohm's law, magnetism, power metering, A/C single phase generation, A/C three phase generation, transformer operation and principles, single and three phase motors. Applicant must have minimum six years experience in Basic Electricity."

Another option, I told myself, and put the ad in my pocket.

Driving through the prairie lands I came upon an aircraft supermarket. I could sell my airplane parts here! My gas gauge was low, so I looked for another mini-mart but for many miles I saw nothing.

But there! Truly? I had passed the sign for Buffalo Bill's ranch. My ancestry! Was this really the place where my great, great grandfather from Guria came, where he introduced the tradition of trick riding? I detoured off the highway and soon I was rumbling down a dirt road. My gas gauge was on empty. But what did that matter? I was about to enter the village of my great, great grandfather. But I drove over a hole and the car got stuck.

I got out of the car, looked around, and checked my tires. I put my hands in my pockets to warm them. I turned around three hundred and sixty degrees. Here is the real life, I told myself. Under this wide, cold, blue sky, in the middle of the prairie, stuck in a hole and out of gas.

In the nineteenth century, Nikoloz Baratashvili wrote from the top of a mountain:

> *O sky! O sky! Thou hast engraved thy image on my heart forever! Thy radiance conceals this fleeting world of woes!*

The radiance of the vast sky could forever solve all my woes, even the problem of my transport being stuck in a hole. A car would surely stop soon. But when one passed and didn't stop and then no cars passed at all, and then another one passed that again didn't stop, I started to feel a little confounded. I wished I had filled the glove box with candy as we do in Georgia. Every half hour we push the button that opens the compartment and yell, "Time for a snack!" In Georgia, it's important to be a good host even in your car. The sky was darkening with clouds. Mr. Tetley was right. It would have been impossible to herd sheep across this place. The stalks of grass were so dried out and hollow, no nutrition. Now all I could remember was the old sheepherder's song:

> *My friends are late*
> *They are not seen anywhere yet*
> *They are all my mates in the field*
> *They are walking and playing somewhere far away*
> *Gambling away enemies like tigers*
> *And me hiding here in my flock*
> *They go to fight and I sit like a woman*
> *Among the sheep*
> *But God, you know it's not my fault*
> *Everything happens involuntarily*
> *I have lots of work to do here*
> *Please let me see my friends*
> *Maybe they've turned their backs to me.*

I was standing there in the field when the storms came. Another car drove by and this time I tried to stop it by standing in the middle of the road but it swerved to avoid me and kept going.

I got back in the car to try to get warm. I stared at the dashboard, at my icon of Queen Tamar, regarding her. Staring at her ruby necklace reminded me of Tamriko's lips. I sat there a long time and stared at them. Suddenly the ruby color got into my blood and reminded me of who I was! I, Slims Achmed, cynical of my corrupt politicians, renowned re-teller of Khrushchev jokes, suddenly remembered the spirit and honor of the twelfth century.

Ah bollocks! I thought to myself, Malkhazi was right.

Malkhazi had told me many times to take a pilgrimage to Queen Tamar's ruby necklace in the Tbilisi State Museum. He had been telling me to go ever since he left the mountains and came to live with us in the city, when he looked around at our modern influences and declared that we had a problem. He told me to go every time I lost my temper at Mr. Fax and was ready to offend him with a newly minted insult and every time I joked about how our classical poet, Rustaveli, must have smoked too much marijuana in the backcountry.

How can I explain it? How can a ruby necklace remind an average modern citizen of anything, except for the need to possess it? Therefore, what can I do in Georgia but show a guest the view and wait for his approval, show him the physical world and wait for the contours of the mountains to tell him their own stories. It is up to the guest to recognize them. All I can do is point at the mountains, at the solid rocks, at the archaeologists digging under them, at the world which looks upside down and crooked but lo—only to the guest.

What other choice do we have but to point at the real world and claim it is enough?

This is what I tried to explain to the policeman when he pulled over but since in America I was the guest, I asked him "How do you not feel confused on this wide earth?"

He checked my passport, my visa, my registration. "This is a stolen car," he said. "Perhaps you won't feel as confused in your own country." And so I was deported.

19.

I WAS FEELING AN IMPENDING SENSE OF DREAD AT HAVING TO GO BACK.
More like doom. But this feeling of doom, annoyingly, was a very familiar feeling.

I had told Merrick in the library, "I can bring this knowledge of Western law back home, back to the Black Sea. I will initiate a conference. I will perform guerrilla activity on the oil pipeline in my village. I will show my people a new Democratic way. I have a purpose and a goal. I will become distinguishable from the rest!" But a sixth sense was already warning me that the bosses in Batumi would merely laugh at me and scoff.

In order to avoid this lugubrious hunch that I had a condemned fate, I smoothed out my new suit jacket that I had bought at JC Penney's, felt my passport in the inside pocket, and my new sixty-nine dollar Seiko watch that I had bought in Chinatown.

In the airport, the whiplash of people hurrying to their planes felt like an air conditioning unit in my heart. Then I realized that in America my heart had been irreparably torn in two, as if unable to reconcile the disparate cultures of East and West. When my boots had been walking down the sidewalks of America, I had sung the Jim Morrison lyrics that Merrick had taught me, "Break on through to the other side." And now I needed a way to break on through back.

But this is an airport, I consoled myself. Everything is in-between in an airport. Too soon to believe in fatal resignation to modern isolation, this self-sufficiency in a single seat. As if to rebel against this sense of isolation, I slung both legs over the top of the metal bar that separated each seat and slept, hungrily slept. Two more hours passed, and then another one. In a dream I ran to my plane. I plunked down my passport and the British official called over another uniformed man and said, "This man did not know how to hand me his passport politely."

I heard the rowdy sounds of the Georgian language: histrionic eulogies and proclamations. My familiars! I opened my eyes and recognized my countrymen over by the wall smoking in front of the NO SMOKING sign.

On the airplane I fell asleep up with a sweaty cheek against the plastic window, hoping that the next time I woke up, this unreconciled, unriddable thing in me would be resolved.

We flew over Hungary, Romania, the Black Sea, over the snowy peaks of the Caucasus, the emerald swath of forest valleys, and then to the eastern side of Georgia—dun-colored like a Mongolian endurance horse. We circled Rustavi, with her stacks of dilapidated Soviet block apartments looking like bar codes, and I saw not a single flickering city light in the early dawn: still without electricity. And then the British Airways flight touched down onto the potholed runway of the Tbilisi airport, and the Georgian men in the back of the plane hallelujahed. What a bunch of ignoramuses, I thought.

I looked outside the little airplane window and saw icicles on the wing. Georgian baggage workers in orange vests and earmuffs were flinging suitcases out of the luggage compartment and laughing, not offended, but merely quizzical at the red-faced man, probably the unfortunate boss, who was scolding them and pointing at the baggage cart which they obviously hadn't hooked up correctly. I started feeling like myself again. At least we could be ourselves here.

From my heart!
From my soul!
Georgia, you are . . .
My home!

It's a poem. Well, in Georgian it rhymes.

In the airport, I tucked in my shirt and pressed the collar of my jacket around my neck. It was so cold when I stepped outside onto the curb, and the same temperature inside the taxi, which was the same temperature as my heart. "Don't freeze!" I demanded of my heart. "Everything is going to be okay!"

The driver wore a woolen hat pulled over his ears and kept chafing his bare hands together, blowing on them while he waited for his Lada to warm up. He drove with his hands high on the steering wheel, a cigarette between his lips, filling the car with smoke from cigarettes made at the Armenian Marlboro factory. He turned to me, squinting through the smoke, and asked where I had returned from.

"America," I said.

He gaped at me, as if I was no less than—to borrow my favorite Chekhov expression—a twenty-two-carat psychopath. He took the cigarette out of his mouth and said, "But why did you come *back*? In winter? Our electricity problem is worse this winter than last."

"I came back because I *love* my mother country!" I told him. "And how about you?"

He became like a stone. "I love my country too!"

I didn't tell him that I *couldn't* stay in America—how if I had, then I would be a Georgian in hiding, a renegade, evading the immigration and naturalization officials, the Department of Homeland Security, ineligible for social security, a 401K, even a dental plan.

"I came back home because American Coca-Cola is nothing like ours," I told him. "When I tasted theirs it was a shock to my system."

He extended great effort to try to see through the windshield. His windshield wipers didn't work—he had to use his arm.

"It didn't have that chemical taste," I continued.

"America?" he asked, wiping his arm on his pants.

"Their Coca-Cola."

He managed to get the windshield wipers working again. "But what did you *achieve* in America?" he asked.

"Psychological promotion," I said.

"You went to a psychiatrist?" he asked and then drove over a pothole; we both hit our heads on the roof.

"No, no one uses them anymore. They all take the pharmaceuticals," I said.

"They no longer need the *psychiatrist*?" he asked.

"No, they need the psychiatrist to prescribe the pharmaceuticals."

"Let me explain to you how *I* understand it. A wife goes to the psychiatrist and says," he added a lilt to his voice, "'Oh, my husband isn't paying any *attention* to me anymore.' So the psychiatrist says, 'I can recommend for you a new brand of makeup.'"

"That's an interesting perspective," I said. "Let me explain it. A person goes to the psychiatrist because in America some people wake up in the morning feeling depressed and don't know the reason."

"How can they not know the reason?"

"Well, anyhow, sometimes they don't. Too many choices. They get easily confused."

"There are two solutions for that."

"What's that?"

"Don't go to sleep, or don't wake up," he said. After a time: "Do you think I could get a good job as a psychiatrist in America?"

"Why not?"

We drove along the banks of the Kura River and I looked to the far side at the dilapidated houses leaning over the cliff. Before I had left Georgia I had looked at those houses and thought I could be a prince, or at least his shepherd, if I lived in such a house. They have fireplaces where I could stretch out my legs and dry my socks. Now they looked like decaying layer cakes with the icing sliding down. In the other direction, on top of Mount Mtatsminda, loomed the huge Soviet monument of Mother Georgia, hovering over the red, green, and orange tiled roofs—one hand holding a cup of wine to welcome a guest, and the other hand wielding a sword. She had looked so permanent before but now she looked like she was made of aluminum foil.

"Schwarzenegger," the driver said, contracting his muscles on the steering wheel, "Did you meet him? Shevardnadze wants to name a mountain after him. 'Mount Schwarzenegger' he will call it."

I left my luggage at the train station and told the driver to drop me off outside the Central Tbilisi Telephone Office. Swaddled-up Georgians waiting to use the telephone booths gossiped or talked about their problems. I bought a card for my new mobile phone and walked out through the heavy doors back onto the street, loud with fur-clad Tbilisi women hurrying in all directions amidst the chaos of black Mercedes flaunting their German horns and the unmonitored mufflers of Russian cars still alive twenty years after their expiration dates. I looked up at the crumbling concrete buildings of the city, so cold and damp. The last remnants of Western residue still clung to me like cream on the top of new yoghurt. Indecisive, unable to move, I wasn't sure if I was ready to go back to my old life.

My little brother Zuka said he'd meet me in Tbilisi on Rustaveli Avenue. And there he was singing on the street with his guitar: "I'm just a musician from Batumi singing for my neighbors who have no electricity." And walking by Zuka were also others I knew. Tbilisi is a small city and on the street it is possible to recognize many people: the hundred-year-old Soviet ballerina, the talk show host whose huge yellow sunglasses make him look like a bug, the documentarians who make films about ancient door locks. Look in front of the bank. The security guard was once a famous bison breeder.

I clasped Zuka's leather-jacketed shoulder. Zuka packed up his guitar and said, "Let's go." I put my hands in my pockets and felt the little red ball with an @ on it that Susan had passed around on the last day of our training session. She suggested that we squeeze it whenever we felt the modern American emotion of stress. "Isn't it fun?" she had said. I took it out of my pocket and watched the pink and purple swirls but quickly jammed it back in my coat when I saw Zuka staring at me. Walking past my reflection in the windows of the Bata shoe store, I remembered the Western-style importance of promoting the image of self-confidence, and took my hands out of my pockets, tried to stand up straighter. But with my little brother at my side, I looked so hulky. There was Zuka, strutting the street in his black trousers and rabbit fur earmuffs and a new gold bracelet on his wrist that he said was a gift from Malkhazi, and I, also in black trousers, stretched a little tighter—I had gained weight in America—wearing my airplane-rumpled new JC Penney's sports coat. But already, I was looking Georgian again. Even if I were wearing a Chevron cap, I still wouldn't look like an American. Maybe if I tried to master President Bush's furrowed brow expression . . . I furrowed my brow.

"What's wrong?" Zuka said.

"Nothing."

"What's wrong?"

"Can you tell me?" I asked. "Have there always been so many Marlboro cigarette advertisements here?"

"What are you saying? It's an advertisement for a *horse*," he joked.

On the Tbilisi-Batumi Express train—stenciled with palm trees on the outside to remind everyone to take a nostalgic holiday to the sea— the whistle blew. It slowly pulled out of the station. Ancient Soviet machinery once again proved its durability. The conductor even came in and showed us how to switch on the light. "Ah? Ah?" he said, so apparently proud was he of his train where the lights worked.

I leaned my head out of the window and the cold wind blew in my face and through my hair. We passed the abandoned train cars that the Chechen refugees were camped under. A man dragged a tree branch to a tarp while his son followed, hacking it to smaller pieces. We passed Msketa, our ancient church on the hill, and I put out my cigarette and went back to my compartment. Some farmer had crammed two bushels of mandarins under the seat. He sat on the bottom sleeper looking out the window.

"Friend," I said. "Are these your mandarin oranges? I need a place to put my feet."

I rubbed some dirty steam off my side of the window to see what he was looking at. Outside, all of the factories in the dismal suburban town had been stripped of their metal walls, leaving only the lathing. Shards of rusting metal scraped the sky; stray goats grazed on dandelion stalks.

"Nothing left but the silent insult of rust," I said.

Zuka came into our car with a bottle of Old Tbilisi. In the other hand he held a cup. Zuka gave the cup to the farmer, who cradled it in his hands. The man's hands shook as he leaned down and smelled the wine I poured. "To independence!" he said ironically, drank and returned the empty cup to me.

"America is a boring heaven," I said. "But we are an exciting hell."

He looked skeptical. I slapped his back. "It's all good, friend."

I filled the cup again and toasted to Georgia. Georgian wine: petrol leaking through a weather-damaged steel pipe, pine mulch on the forest floor, emanations of the fish market, apple trees in October. The smell is reminiscent of a strangling on the back of the neck in a despot's unforgiving thumb grasp. The fragrance pleads for memory.

When I picked up my cup of wine and looked out the window I could feel my grandfather leaning over me, holding onto my collar. I felt implicated, as if I'd stolen this wine, like the villager in the Georgian movie *The Wine Thief*, because my love for this land was subversive and so illogical. It felt audacious and perhaps altogether wrong to be toasting it as we witnessed its perdition.

We traveled out of the rusty suburbs and into the orchards, their bare branches percolating with tiny green buds.

I heard Zuka's voice in the hall arguing about whether the man who was recently named "Business Man of the Year"—the man from our neighborhood who had invented and marketed a new kind of beer, fourteen percent alcohol instead of our usual twelve—deserved that title.

"But this beer has the same alcohol content as wine," a man argued. It's true that no other product had been created in Georgia this year, argued Zuka, but were we Georgians going to reward a beer maker when we have always made wine? Zuka was beginning to sound like Malkhazi.

Someone in the next compartment had brought a radio. The volume, adjusted to its highest caliber, blared the song "I Will Survive," drowning out Zuka's conversation in the hall. I was still humming to the tune of "Oh, Oh, Oh, I will survive," when he returned to the compartment.

"You like that music?" Zuka said. "I thought only people from the village listen to that kind of music." Actually, Zuka was not sounding like Malkhazi. Malkhazi would never say something like that. I felt bad that I felt closer to my friend than to my own brother. But Zuka was becoming his own little person. He had brought bedsheets from the conductor—clean but still damp. We spread the sheets on our sleepers and I poured another cup of wine for the farmer.

"May the sun always shine on your head," I said.

"This train is slower than a cow," Zuka said.

"Friend," the farmer called from below. "Do you know if Gogiashvili still lives in the same house in Batumi?"

"How am I supposed to know Gogiashvili?" I said.

"Do you want to sleep now?" he said.

I turned off the light and rolled over so I could watch the moon traveling with us along the tops of the wet grasses.

20.

SOMEONE WOKE ME UP IN THE MORNING WITH A FLASHLIGHT IN MY face. I turned over and fell asleep again until I smelled eggs frying in the conductor's cabin. Outside the window I watched pigs rooting into an alder. The name of the town had been written on a board and nailed to the tree.

"Are we only in Hashuri?" I asked. But no one was in the compartment. I looked at my watch—past nine. We should have been in Batumi by now. Passengers had alighted the train and were smoking, sitting on wet benches stained with eucalyptus leaves. Zuka came back carrying a stack of bread.

"I bought some honey but gave it to him," Zuka said, motioning out the window.

Our train mate was outside, sitting on a bench, holding the cup of honey and staring at the ground. I went outside and lit a cigarette, asked about why we had stopped, but no one knew. I knocked on the conductor's cabin to ask why we were waiting so long and the conductor said, in between mouthfuls of egg, that some bandits were holding up the train. And then he added that he was out of hot water so if I wanted some tea to go to the kiosk outside.

I went back outside and kept my mouth closed so the bandits, wherever they were, wouldn't see my gold tooth.

We arrived in Batumi early in the afternoon. Passing the botanical gardens I saw the leaves of the palms had been tied up with string. I told Zuka, "In America the blues of the sky are deeper, but our greens are more vivid."

I remembered a song that Merrick had taught me. It went, "My country's skies are bluer than the ocean and sunlight beams on cloverleaf and pie, but other lands have sunlight too, and clover and skies are everywhere as blue as mine." This was really true.

Even though spring had just barely begun, the Batumi shrubs had a halo around them, and I thought of the little green sprouts in the poem by Vaja Pshavela. I had been gone for only six weeks, but it felt like I had been gone for ten years from the sea and salty air, from Our City of the Chipped Paint Lady.

Malkhazi was waiting for us at the station. He had gained weight too. Even his soul was heavy looking, and he looked like a Soviet bureaucrat in his new uniform, as if paying allegiance to the Mercedes he was standing in front of. "It's not mine. It's my company's car," he explained.

We got in. Zuka tried to joke with him. "Have you heard of the Svani mountain man who is driving a Mercedes and he keeps running people over? The police reprimand him. They ask, 'Why do you keep running over people?' He says, 'You see that symbol on the hood? Isn't that a target sign?'"

"Foo!" Malkhazi said. "What was wrong with that guy?"

"What's wrong with *you*?" I asked.

"It's nothing. It's pressure. They are pressing down on me. But you're home. I don't want to talk about my problems."

When we got home Malkhazi stayed in the driver's seat and kept the car running. Malkhazi, rather Mr. Inspector, tooted the horn and my mother stuck her head out the window, wrapping the white lace curtain around her head like a scarf, as if she were a *tavsapartsakrali*, some sort of extremely religious person. "Slims!" she cried. She brought her hands to her face, imitating the sign of eating. "Come eat!" she called. "You too, Malkhazi!"

Malkhazi told us to get out.

"Aren't you coming up?" I asked.

He shook his head.

"I haven't seen you in two months."

"Nobody has. Now get out," he said. "I'll meet you later."

I got out of the car. As usual, the elevator was broken. Zuka heaved my bag up the stairs and we went inside.

When my mother saw me she pushed me into a chair, ladled out some bean soup into a bowl, and crumbled some *chaadi* on top. She cut squares of briny farmer cheese, put them on a plate. Did I want a fried egg? How about a boiled potato? More soup?"

"No. Please, no," I said spooning the beans into my mouth.

"I should have more to offer you but we're fasting for lent. Zuka!" she called. "Go buy some potato chips for Slims. Just a small package. And some tarragon lemonade." My mother took money from her purse and counted out the change.

Zuka ran off and I went over to the heater to warm myself.

"I thought you were coming back a week later," she said. "Everyone's been asking about you. They all want to talk to you about their business plans. How about some vodka?" She poured me half a glass, sat back down, and pressed her fingers into her temples. "They're working Zuka too hard at the furniture factory. A fifteen-year-old! He's not strong enough. And Juliet says she is always at the university but I think she's sneaking around with that English fellow."

Zuka returned with the potato chips and my mother told him, "This is for Slims."

"No please," I said to Zuka. "Have some."

"Slims is offering you some, Zuka. Take it. Go outside and play now."

Zuka rolled his eyes at me and left.

She rubbed her eyes. "Malkhazi never comes home anymore. *Vaimay*! I have an appointment with the bishop. Oh Slims. Slimiko," she said. "I didn't want Zuka to hear this but the whole town is in a crisis." She began to talk so fast I didn't know what she was saying.

"Calm down," I said. "Tell me slowly."

She had gone to church that morning and the bishop had issued a warning about a man named Mr. Moon from Korea. His workers were passing out dough to pedestrians, telling them to take it home and bake it because it contained magical qualities and would bless their homes. "But beware!" the bishop had said. "This bread is infused with the blood of sacrificed animals. If you eat it, you and your household will come under its spell!" One woman in the church had shrieked, "Oh no! What have I done!" The bishop chastised her in front of everyone, saying, "We tell children not to take food from strangers or eat off the street, and you, a grown woman, have baked the bread of a stranger!"

"And then," said my mother, "he told her to go to her soul father to be punished and purified. O! I've been telling Malkhazi not to eat food off the street. Oh, Slims, what if he eats this bread of Mr. Moon?"

"Please don't worry about that," I told her.

She put her hand on my head before leaving to meet with the bishop, and grabbed the umbrella on her way out the door.

It was sprinkling outside. I stood at the window and watched my mother chase the chickens and ducks into their pen before realizing that the green rug under my feet was soaking up water. I tried to tape up a crack in the window. Then I bent over a dead wire protruding from the wall and stared at the clock that said ten after two before remembering that the clock didn't work.

I didn't feel like talking to the neighbors about an American business plan. I was tired of business plans. Besides, how could I explain things like how someone at the San Francisco airport was *paid* to pull the suitcases upright at the baggage claim belt to make them easier to grasp, more convenient, and that in America they use candles for *fun*.

I headed for the kiosk in the basement of the post office to read the news about Georgia. I glanced at the headlines: RUSSIA'S OIL RESERVES COULD PROVE TO BE THREE TIMES HIGHER THAN PREVIOUSLY THOUGHT; GEORGIA'S GREEN TEAM TRY TO STOP BTC PIPELINE FROM RUNNING THROUGH BORJOMI.

Zurab, the newspaper seller, was talking to Zaliko about the high price of petrol. When they saw me Zaliko threw up his hands and cried out, "Ah, Slims, tell me, what is the price of petrol in America?"

"It's always fluctuating," I said.

"But their money doesn't fluctuate!" Zurab said, as if that explained something.

When his gesticulating hands came to rest he wrapped my *Newsweek* magazine in a piece of brown paper and bound it with a string, now talking with someone new about the rising cost of cornmeal.

I didn't feel like going to Seaside Boulevard and seeing anybody I knew, so I brought the brown packet to the park that surrounds the lake near the university. Here, New Georgians walk their exotic dogs, grandmothers push their bundled-up grandchildren in strollers, and someone is always fishing from behind a bush so that undoubtedly you trip on his line and he shows himself long enough to give you a condescending look. I sat on a bench under a magnolia tree, untied the string, and opened up the pages of the magazine.

I used to depend upon this act of reading articles in the park to make me feel like a character from one of my sister's Dickens novels, a Mr. Pickwick. It prevented me from sinking too deeply into the darkness of a Georgian man's world on those days that were especially difficult, though I now considered that perhaps those dark days were necessary in order to appreciate the days that had light. In any case, I wasn't able to concentrate very well. Irakli, my neighbor, walked by and, seeing me, sat down and began snapping and spitting out the shells of his sunflower seeds. I showed him an article in *Newsweek* about how George Bush claimed he had been called by God to fight in Iraq. "Look for yourself what is happening over there!" I said. He whistled in astonishment.

But he was more attracted to the ad on the opposite side of the page: a housewife standing next to her shiny white refrigerator.

"What a lucky refrigerator," Irakli said, "to have the embrace of such a woman."

Irakli's wife came and sat with us with her little daughter. She glanced at what we were looking at and said, "That is an advertisement for a *refrigerator* and not meant to be sexy."

I was going a little out of my mind. I tried to explain to myself that I was still suffering from a cultural shock. Why is it that cultural shock is more extreme upon returning to the familiar than upon visiting a strange place? Is it because something inside has changed and now all the old familiar things must be introduced to this new person? I had missed home greatly, but the idea that I was perhaps stuck here forever gave me nothing to look forward to for the future. And reading these magazines did not help me feel like a Mr. Pickwick. I looked up at the Tamada in the sky and quoted Rustaveli, "Alas! O world, what troubles thee? Why dost thou whirl us round and round?"

I decided to visit the Center for Democracy thinking that there I could perhaps find a portal between the worlds I was trying to reconcile within me. But when I crossed King Parnavaz Street to get there a policeman blew his whistle at me. I marched straight toward him intending to kick him in the shin, like Irakli had when he returned from Afghanistan, but instead, I broke down. I told him how I had just gotten back from America and how crazy I felt. "I feel like some sort of insane person with a bad brain," I said. The policeman looked at me with sympathetic eyes but didn't suggest I kick him. He only said, "But how is their Coca-Cola? Is it really different from ours?"

I didn't know where the Center for Democracy got their money, only that the restoration of the building was funded by our local dictator. The building itself was appropriated for him by his brother-in-law, much to the chagrin of the people who happened to be living in the east wing at the time. Near the entrance, the smooth bronze heads of fashionable New Georgian patriarchs had been soldered over the roughly hewn edges of recently decapitated Soviet leaders. As I advanced across the street, toward one of the corduroyed columns, I saw the security guard talking to some girls. I approached them, nonchalantly, intending to follow them into the building, but when one of the girls removed her hood I realized it was Tamriko. I didn't want to encounter her and Gocha so I stopped and bought some sunflower seeds from an old Abkhazian woman on the sidewalk while I waited for Tamriko to leave.

After the girls left, I walked up to the security guard, who was now standing alone, polishing his shoes. "Is Anthony the British guy here?" I asked. I thought maybe Anthony could be my Western soul brother, could help me adjust to being back here a little. He pointed down the hall and I handed him my newspaper cone full of sunflower seeds.

I'd never been inside the Center for Democracy before. I'd heard from my neighbor, Sadzaglishvili, that the building was heated with a 150-square-meter fireplace, lit by crystal chandeliers from Czechoslovakia, and connected to an electrical line that always worked. But look at those marble floors! A thousand hectares of it to cool the enormous rooms, without need of an air conditioning unit. No wonder people wanted to spend time here.

I walked down a series of unmarked doors in a long corridor. Behind one door people were engaged in a meeting so official that they didn't even notice me. I opened another and saw some young men slouched on the leather furniture, smoking, and drinking beers. I recognized them as acquaintances of Gocha's, but not close ones. Gocha would probably call out to them on the street the more formal "Prince!" rather than "Friend!" One was playing patience on the computer. Another was on the phone. Seeing me standing in the doorway, he said into the phone, "Hold on, Zuri."

I asked if he knew where Anthony was.

"Anthony? He's not here. But you can wait." He pointed to a place on the couch.

After waiting a while I ventured to ask the one playing patience if *he* knew where Anthony was.

He looked up from the computer. "By the seaside," he said. "I think he's with your sister in fact," and gestured toward the window.

"You mean his *mother*," the other snickered.

"No, really, his sister. Don't you recognize him? He's a Makashvili."

I looked at the window, at the metal bars protecting it. I looked at the locked metal cabinets. They were most likely filled with fax machines. I imagined for a second attaching one end of a metal chain to the bars on the window, the other end to Malkhazi's new Mercedes, and in this way tearing away the metal bars and stealing all the fax machines.

The one called Ruslom looked up at me and said, "I remember you from university. You used to write little stories, trying to imitate Dumbadze. I heard from Gocha that you were trying to get a job with an American telecom business."

"That was a while ago," I said. "Actually, I just returned from the States."

"Really?" they said, suddenly interested.

"So besides telecom, what other kinds of businesses are Americans interested in?" Ruslom said.

"Ecotourism," I said. "Tell me, do you think we should go the way of tourism or the way of agriculture?"

Ruslom pointed to a picture of our local dictator on the wall and said, "It's up to him." Then he leaned over and asked me to help him fasten his gold bracelet.

Since Anthony wasn't showing up I decided look for him by the seaside. As I walked I considered asking Zuka to lend me a tape of his industrial music, a recording someone had given him of the Azeri oil derricks pumping on the Caspian Sea. I could write to Hillary, "This is the sound of democracy in the Caucasus right now. It sounds like the end of the world." That would be the most authentic way. To express my country in music is the Georgian way.

Dear Hillary,

Your version of Democracy and our version are quite different. Our version means if the leader says something we say, "Yes, you are right."

By the way, I just read that US Troops, GI Joes, are recently deployed in Georgia, fighting against terrorism : -), training Georgian "commandos" ; -) called Special Op-

eration Caspian Guard, and US is spending 64 million dollars for their training. But do you have any idea who they are fighting against? Perhaps a villager to get access to his potato field to bury an oil pipeline? New government says we are approaching new democracy :-) but we just have to wait.

I have some good news to report to you though. You will be happy to know that your own local Center for Democracy in Batumi enlarged their office after they evicted some families who were living in the east wing. They now also have purchased a modern air conditioning unit which will be useful in the summer. New Georgians have recently made a lot of money. I think you do not need to be afraid of Georgian mafiosi because Georgian mafiosi act just like Americans—the same easy confidence, and how you say happy-go-lucky. They don't really look like in your Al Pacino movies. The only problem is that they don't know what to spend their money on. One Rolex for this suit. A different Rolex for another suit.

In other news: thousands of pigs died in my village last month. It was probably a conspiracy by the Turkish pork sellers because our scientists say that Georgian pigs have the best quality of meat. It won't be a good kingkali year because there's no pork to put in the noodle. But don't be so sad, Hillary. It's nothing.

Why this terseness? Why was I so angry at Hillary? Our problems weren't really her fault. Maybe I was just angry at myself.

At the seaside I sat down. The water smelled like lemon rinds. I looked around for some small flat rocks to skip into the water but I only found big round ones. The surf splashed up onto my shoes and I saw that the sea was still layered with a thin emulsion of oil.

I felt a tap on my shoulder, turned, and saw Tamriko. She was wearing long black pants with the silver disco cuffs that flared out and platform shoes that were fashionable for women in those days.

O the Georgian woman! She makes me feel as if I am on a holiday. Even if at first she is a silly ridiculous girl, she will eventually become a woman. She is such a longtime sufferer that nothing offends her anymore—eternal and loving mother, fashionable beauty, always holding her head so high after retouching her temples with glitter.

"Why are you sitting on the beach all by yourself?" she asked.

I patted the ground for her to sit on beside me. "I'd give you my shoes to sit on but they are wet," I said.

She sat down.

I tried to think of something cheerful to say but all I could tell her about was an article I had just read. "I read in the news today that the water from our sea is more polluted than the Indian Ocean. I can't understand how we are still alive," I said. I picked up a stone to toss but then put it down. "Maybe I didn't study the right kind of knowledge at the university," I said. "And I definitely didn't take advantage of my time in America."

"Forget about the university. And forget about America. Why this foul mood? Why do you blame yourself?"

"That's the problem with Georgia. No one takes any responsibility. They blame it on everyone else."

"If you worry so much you'll get cancer. Come on. Let's go for a walk," she said pulling me up. "Look at that little girl over there, standing in the water with her mother. What greater happiness is there than that?"

"Have you read that Isaac Asimov story about the man on the moon who waits all year for the space shuttle? Sometimes I feel like I'm that, stuck on the moon." We continued to walk. "Look around," I said, "all those people staring, always so amazed at things."

We passed the public bathrooms, Gocha's peewee golf course, a beach sign that read: IT IS YOUR NOBLE DUTY TO RESCUE ANYONE WHO IS DROWNING.

"Ah, there's Zaliko!" I said and nodded to Batumi's head archaeologist walking past us. He nodded back.

"Look at these people!" I said after he had passed. "Why is he smiling?"

"What's *happened* to you?" she said.

"Don't laugh at me. Here, take a cigarette. Smoke! Do *something*!"

"Everything is going to be okay," she said.

And then the sea splattered more water. More oil.

"Yeah, why worry about polluted *water*," I said, "when we could be worrying about venereal diseases."

"Perhaps you already have one now?" she asked. "Is that why you are in a bad mood?"

"That's impossible," I told her. "Where could I find the time? But maybe you do?"

"That's impossible," she said, turned, and walked away.

"Oh, right!" I said. "That's because you had a virginity restoration operation."

What had happened to me? I had never been so rude to a woman.

21.

I WAS BECOMING GLUM—GLUMMER AND GLUMMER—AND ALREADY FOR-getting my English too. The sky pushed its oppressive weight down on my head. Even the corridor to our flat seemed dimmer.

Juliet welcomed me home by playing the American national anthem on the piano. But then she started complaining about Malkhazi.

Next door, through the walls, I could hear Tamriko ardently pounding wedding marches on her piano.

"So is she getting married?" I asked Juliet.

"How should I know?" she said. "I'm not a fortune-teller. But actually, to be a fortune-teller would be a good career. Sit at home. Tell a fortune for ten lari. If ten people a day came that would be a hundred lari. Imagine if a hundred people came!"

There is a joke about a Georgian who goes to a Bulgarian fortune-teller. The fortune-teller says, "It will be difficult in your country for two years."

"And then?" asks the Georgian.

"And then you will get used to it."

I had to get used to this regime of nothing working again; it would take at least two weeks, I predicted—the same amount of time it takes an American tourist, after traveling to an exotic country, to arm himself against American commercials again—at least according to Merrick. When he returned from Costa Rica, his life looked vivid and quiet at first but then for two weeks he was bombarded by the "violence of advertising," he called it. "But once I reached the saturation level, I no longer noticed them," he had told me. So now I had to make my own cultural adjustment to this not-working world.

"Another Spanish soccer player was kidnapped today by bandits," announced the news broadcaster on TV that night, but I couldn't hear more than that because the antenna fell off.

When Malkhazi came home that evening I asked him what had been happening on the ships. He looked at me wearily, like the little green leaves of a transplanted beet plant, trying to grow in its pot on the window ledge, but then the sun doesn't have enough strength to muscle it up. "It's work. It's life," he said.

"But what makes you continue this life?" I asked.

Malkhazi leaned back in the chair. "What makes me continue? Well . . . these days I look forward to the ships coming because they have electricity and then I can shave with hot water." Malkhazi stood up, went to the cabinet, and took out a bottle of vodka. He cracked the seal with a knife. "Just a little, Slims. Choot choot," he said, pouring me some vodka into a jade cup. "It will make your thoughts more tender."

His phone rang. "Allo?" he answered it. "Okay, I'll be right there." He hung up, turned to me, and said, "I have to go back to the Turkish ship."

That evening I lay on the couch with a belly full of Zuka's vitamin borscht. I stared out at a few clouds whose shadows underneath were darker than the washed-out pale blue above. The Sadzaglishvilis' white sheets blocked part of the view, swaying on the clothesline. I heard Guliko yelling up from the street to anyone who would listen, "Why do you throw your garbage out the window? I am not going to mention any names but they know who they are who throw their garbage out the window and don't just bring it down to the truck when it comes."

"I feel like I've lost my dream," I told Juliet.

"So your dream is gone," she said. "Don't worry. Twenty thousand more will come. Do you know what? God created the world for you. Doing this he had in mind to make you happy, to make you pleased with the world's beautifulness. While you say to him, 'I want to close my eyes. I don't want to go on. I'm tired of doing one and the same thing. I've suffered too much, because I don't always get those things that I want easily.' But my darling brother, please remember, it's somehow fine when we don't get those things we want because otherwise we wouldn't appreciate the things we have and we wouldn't keep our eyes to the true brightness of nature."

That night when I heard the oil trains in backyard whine along the tracks like a screeching woman, I asked Zuka, who was sleeping in the bed across the room, "How did I sleep through this before?"

"Just say, 'Tonight I will sleep and nothing will disturb me,'" Zuka said and turned over in his own bed.

When the last train had passed and the dark town swelled with silence, I heard the rain pattering outside. A little drop of water phlumped on my pillow. I remembered what Susan had said about how to keep a healthy psychology, that the best way to be happy is to be grateful, to think about people who are less fortunate than we are. So I thought about the Chechens.

Just as I was falling asleep, Zuka muttered, "The Armenians fix their leaks. We just put buckets under them."

I was about to fall asleep again but then I pondered Zuka's remark. We Georgians are proud of the fact that we don't waste our time fixing leaks, that we have more profound things to think about. No one can stop a Georgian man from grinning when something has newly fallen down, as if it's his proof that everything collapses. Herein lies a key to the Georgian heart, and, as Malkhazi is fond of saying, "Every heart has a key."

Unavoidably, this nonworkingness started to change me, and the only thing I could do was sit on a chair, wave a white flag, surrender, and not dare to move, afraid that the chair might collapse when I sat down in it to read before going to bed. It didn't collapse. But when I woke up in the middle of the night and leaned over the bed to get a glass of water, the bed frame—the pressboard part—fell on my wrist.

I didn't want to complain though. While I was rocking back and forth with my arm close to my chest, Zuka woke up and whispered from across the room, "What's the matter?"

"It's nothing," I said. "The bed fell on my wrist."

Why do I mention all of this now? So that I can get it out of the way, get used to it, and go on with the story.

The next day when I arrived at work I discovered that Fax's secretary had now become the economic director of maritime law consulting. She and Mr. Fax were probably having a *ménage à trois* with the fax machine. "Three Georgians united make a world," I joked to myself walking down the corridor. But when I got to my office, the door was blocked—it was crammed with Turkish cabinets. Apparently, the Maritime Ministry of Law was being renovated. Fax was behind the door and he greeted me with a little bow. "Slims, since you have been to America perhaps you could elucidate us on how to arrange the furniture according to more modern standards." Ho ho! Things were looking up for me.

"It must look organized," I said.

So Fax commanded the workers playing their musical instruments in the lobby to line up all the desks into rows in the conference room.

I surveyed the result. "But not quite in this fashion." I suggested that they should put a bookshelf in the toilet room because foreigners like to read in there. One worker was offended and stood up to hit me, but his friend who was taking notes calmed him down.

"How about a cup holder?" another asked. "Don't they like to drink coffee when they go to the toilet?"

After lunch, Fax lost his temper because his coffee cup holder was missing. "What happened to my coffee cup holder?" he raged at his new secretary.

"I didn't do anything with your coffee cup holder," she said, indignant.

"It used to be right here on the computer," Fax insisted. "It was the perfect size for a little cup of coffee."

"Oh, you mean this?" I asked and pushed a button.

"Oh, there it is," he said.

"That's the computer's disc drive," I said.

But I forgave his stupidity because he was under a lot of stress; he was already shouting at his new secretary. Oh! If you could have seen him when he was speaking, you felt as if a hamburger was talking to you, as if he kept a hundred marbles in his mouth and was in the middle of spitting them out. You had to make some sudden move in order to save your life and escape with only minor bruises.

At lunch, when Mr. Fax was out, a man from the village of Zalikos came in to use the copy machine. I didn't know what he wanted at first until he pulled a piece of paper out of his pocket, unfolded it, and asked if we had a Georgian copy machine. "No, Georgia doesn't make copy machines. We have one that was made in America though," I told him.

"No, no, that won't work," he said. "This document is in Georgian, not in English."

At the end of the day, everyone received their salary of fifty dollars for the month, except me, since I had been away. I tried to protest that they still owed me for the previous year but Fax just shrugged. One of the security guards tried to make me feel better by joking about his own paycheck. "I'm rich!" he said. Another added, "Now I can retire."

"I only have twenty tetri," I told the bus driver.

"Pay what you can," he said.

At home, the electricity was on and light yellowed up the stairwell. Neighbors opened their doors as I passed. "Oh, so that's what you're looking like these days," one of them said. My mother had mended a torn shirt of mine and it lay freshly pressed over a chair. Zuka had fixed the iron. Then he fixed the gas balloon. I felt a certain pang that Zuka seemed to be following in Malkhazi's footsteps. He had started reading stories about criminals—he had no other role models—and with a swaggering confidence he ran his cigarette lighter over the entire metal canister to prove it wouldn't blow up. "Don't you try this," he said to the neighbor children, who were eating the last of the American candy I had brought, the sparkly wrappers all over the floor.

"Zuka is really turning into a man," I observed to my mother. But I didn't tell her how by fixing the iron and by fixing the gas balloon, he had retaught me something important: that even if things break down, we only need to fix them again. When I visited the neighbors after dinner, the family had bought a new water heater. "It works?" I asked.

"Yes, it works well. It's Japanese," they said.

"Maybe we should poke a hole in it so we have something to fix," I found myself saying.

22.

Ten days had passed since Malkhazi had left for the Turkish ship and he still hadn't returned. Spring had started bubbling forth like a shaken-up green bottle of fizzy tarragon water. It (the spring) was waking up, gushing out, borrowing everyone's vitality to help it in its waking, and because of this the whole town wilted. If you drank a cup of coffee though, you'd be fine.

When I was walking home along the boulevard I passed Gocha's new disco café. All the tables had thatched umbrellas over them. Gocha was sitting at one of them and I watched him from a distance. He was wearing an imported Hawaiian shirt and sipping a cocktail from a coconut. The girls who worked in his cafe would walk over to him, look down at him sleepily, and then rewrap their sarongs over their bathing suits. Bored, he got up and colluded with the man behind the circular bar. I really couldn't understand what Tamriko saw in him.

At home, through the walls, I could still hear Tamriko playing the bridal march on the piano. All of the town seemed to have heard this wedding music pouring out of her fourth-floor window. It is rumored that if you are surrounded by wedding music, you are about to marry, and Tamriko seemed to be trying to get married by sheer force of song, thrum, and whistle power. At the shop, where I went to buy bread, I heard the shopkeeper say to her with a wink, "I hear wedding bells around you. Someone must be getting married soon." She winked back and smiled, almost as if she were a trembling bride, like a little baby calf separated for the first time from its mother at the Saturday animal bazaar. She was like a girl who rarely speaks above a whisper to her new mother-in-law and calls her husband "Sir!" in his mountain home. But let us not forget that as she gets older, of course, she has the loudest voice and the sharpest tongue, which can provoke any brother-in-law to shoot her by accident.

I had not been able to locate Anthony. Evidently, he had become an important man of the town and had more important people than me to talk to. But Juliet, who seemed to travel in the same circles as he did, had invited Anthony over for dinner. I wanted to impress upon him how modern I had become but Tamriko's piano playing coming through the walls as we sat at the table kept distracting me. Anthony stared quizzically at the rococo wallpaper. "I almost feel like a colonialist," he said. "Especially sitting in a formal dining room such as this. Would you like some more wine?" he asked Juliet. Perhaps the formal atmosphere created by the wallpaper affected him because he added, "My dear?"

We were eating spaghetti with canned peas, the closest resemblance to an English meal Juliet could muster, I guess. I scooped up a pea with my fork, and then another pea, and listened to Anthony talk about how BP was planning to use an untested pipeline sealant that was cheaper than the usual brand. "If you can't get them to dig the pipeline three meters deeper, you are not going to get them to buy a more expensive sealant either," I said.

Anthony shook his head, shifted around in his seat, took out a cigarette from his shirt pocket, and asked permission to smoke.

I pushed the seashell that we used as an ashtray toward him.

Anthony stared quizzically at the wallpaper. He cleared his throat. "Can I ask you why that picture on the wall is hanging upside down?"

"Which one?" I asked.

"That one. The little Russian church in the snow."

"Oh," Juliet said. "I put it like that to remind myself to turn my suffering upside down. And to remember that God's kingdom here on earth is upside down. Also, you live in the twenty-first century, yes? We live in the twelfth. Opposite. You see?"

"Ah," he said.

I poured him some walnut liquor from my homemade batch, but before I could make a toast he took a sip. Every time there is a silence at the Georgian table another baby is born in Armenia. Armenia already had enough people and didn't need any more to join their army and fight against us, so I was about to make a toast to peace to break the silence but Juliet began speaking. "They speak of death as if it were something natural. Foreign insurance agents speak of certain possibilities and the eventuality that something might happen to you."

"Beg your pardon?" Anthony asked.

"It's a quote. From someone named G. Mikes. It's in our English language reader. Haven't you heard it?"

"Afraid not." He bent his head to his shoulder and looked at the picture of the Russian church in the snow again, considering it from his sideways position. "Have you ever noticed how sexually free the Russians are?"

"Would you like to speak in Russian?" she asked.

When he spoke in Russian the few words that he knew, "oil, gasoline, no problem, hurry up," Juliet stood up and almost hurried over to his lap. I went into the kitchen. The sexual tension out there was becoming too much for me. Probably the neighbors were watching through the window, saying, "So when are they going to begin?" When I came back the electricity had gone out.

"The electricity went out," Anthony said. "It must be a sign." He had lit a candle.

"It's only a sign when the electricity comes *on*," I said. Juliet's chair was now on his side of the table. They were both peering at the Russian church in the snow. I could not understand where he got the idea of Russia being sexually free by looking at that painting.

"Perhaps, you would like me to play a song on the piano for

you?" Juliet asked him. I didn't know how to read his look. Was he pleading her to, or pleading her not to?

"But perhaps after listening to our music you will become depressed?" I asked. "Always singing, 'Always we are. Always we will be.'"

"I can play for you a gypsy song. Have you heard "Suliko"? It's about a person looking for her soul," Juliet said.

"You don't have to," he said. "Besides, the person next door is providing us with enough music." When he slipped his shoes off his feet I went back into the kitchen.

"Is it true what they say about Georgian traditions?" I heard him say through the wall that I was holding my ear against.

"About upside down? That's not a tradition. That's just a way of seeing."

"That Georgian women don't believe in sex before marriage?" he asked.

I didn't hear her answer but I heard him say, "Do you want to get out of here and go have a strong drink?"

"Wait a minute. Wait a minute," I said coming back into sitting room. But they had already left. In the film *Bella Mafiosa* the brothers insist the man *marries* their sister before they sleep together. Afterwards, the couple divorce. When the man wants to sleep with her again, her brothers insist that he marry her again.

So the next day after work, in order to explain some things to him, I asked Anthony to meet me at the cafe near the institute. I borrowed Zuka's guitar and headed over there. If there is anything important happening in Batumi, it is happening at this cafe, where the beautiful girls eat *chizi bizi*, spiced eggs with ground beef, and many groups of boys hover around them. *Chizi bizi!* My mouth began to salivate.

Anthony was sitting at a table looking out the window, though he kept having to wipe away the condensation with his sleeve. "The spring is beautiful here, yes?" I asked him. "Batumi's nature is different than elsewhere in Georgia," I said. "The rocks, the cedar and cypress trees, and even the women too. The tall, dark beauties are from Tbilisi.

They belong to the windy climate, to the frost and fresh air. The air is heavier here in Batumi so we are shorter. Mountain sun is different from beach sun. It produces a different color of brown on the skin."

He looked at me curiously and then I remembered that Westerners like to get directly to the point so I said, "You understand in Georgia, before we get married, we have no relations with a woman? I have heard that Americans have sex three times a year. Once with a stranger and twice with a relative, but this is not information I care to think about. I am not sure about you though, because I do not know the statistics for English people. I am looking for a good husband for my sister."

Anthony pushed back his chair and gave me a strange look.

"If you like, I will teach you the words to woo a woman," I said.

"Who says I want to woo a woman?" he asked.

"Life is short. What else is there to do?" I asked. Strumming Zuka's guitar I said, "Just imagine the situation. Two people are talking. A man and a woman. The first person sings, 'If you were so beautiful, little violet, why did I not notice you before?' The proper response is, 'Because my heart was not yet open for love.' Maybe in your country you say 'open for business' but in Georgia it's better to say love."

"But I'm not interested in wooing a woman right now. I have other things I have to deal with."

"Let's try another song," I said. "To get you in the mood."

I met a gardener
who woke me up with sweet words
lullabying me on his lap.

"Wait," Anthony said. "Who is singing this?"

"A man," I said. "It is very important for men to sing."

"A gardener puts a grown man on his lap?" Anthony asked. "Does this take place on a farm?"

"It's a *metaphor*!" I said. "But maybe if you cannot understand our language, you cannot understand this song."

"You are a very proud people," he commented.

I put the guitar down. "Do you think we are too proud?"

"Maybe not too proud, but, as I said, I think the people are sort of heavy here."

"Yes, maybe we are too heavy. We always have some problem. That is why I am looking for a less heavy man for my sister. Do you know how difficult it is for her to be a Georgian woman? Can you understand her fate here? There is a song about it. Have you heard this one?"

They will take her in her wedding dress
They will take off her dress
And put her beside her husband in the bed
But once she oversleeps
And her father-in-law sees her
He will wake her up
Her mother-in-law will make her work beside her
When her husband sees her tears
Instead of consoling her
He'll curse her
And make her leave the house
She'll slam the door
The main thing is
Hard times are coming.

"You know," Anthony reflected, "women in my country don't even know how to knit anymore. Would you say that, as a rule, women here really like to sew?"

"I don't really know about that," I said, "but you are changing the subject. I will give you another example of courtship." I thought of the time Tamriko and I were on a train, an old Soviet train, and we were making toasts in the springtime to all the plum blossoms exploding like firecrackers out the window. We were coming home from a conference in Tbilisi and I looked over at her across the seat and said, "This is a train compartment for a couple, yes? But look at the space between the beds." She had smiled a little so I moved closer and said, "It is an old Soviet train and I think they did not believe in love then." Now that I think about it, that was a stupid thing to say. Even Soviet people believed in love. Maybe they believed in love more than anybody else. But we all thought at the time that to bring people closer you needed to have common enemies, and the Soviets were our enemies. Actually, we still think that to bring people together you need common enemies.

Anthony was staring at me but I didn't want to tell him that story. "Okay, I will give you an example. If a Georgian woman says something intelligent, you whisper to her, "If you were closer I would kiss you."

"Why? Why would you say that?" he asked in a confounded sort of way. "If she is close enough to whisper, why not just kiss her?"

"Because she will know that you are quoting something from the old times that we say at the table, that when the *tamada*, the toastmaster, says something great we say, 'If you were closer I would kiss you,' because he is usually at the far side of the table. Try it. You will see that it works."

I don't know if he tried it, but it seemed to me that after that he and Juliet started to become closer. Good for them, of course, but I still didn't know how to get closer to Tamriko.

A few nights later when Malkhazi got home, he paced back and forth in the kitchen—his face alternately cradled in his hands and then looking up at me.

"I am a slave to the woman," Malkhazi said, his face in his hands again. "Only her words can calm me. Only *her* words."

Zuka was helping me fix a heater I had hauled over from my office. We both looked up at him.

"I have read Juliet's book of English quotes," Malkhazi announced. "I do not agree with most of them except for one. It says, 'There is no greater wretchedness than to love someone with all your heart who you know is not worthy of your love.'"

"Have you *ever* met a woman who is worthy of your love?" I asked.

"You have heard me say it before and I will say it again: man cannot live without the woman. Without the woman a man is nothing but a string bean. Tonight I went to a restaurant with Juliet. I made a toast to her. I gave her the highest compliment. I told her that she is as noble as Queen Tamar. But then she became bashful, like a young girl asking for more compliments. I became confused and didn't know what she wanted of me. So I explained to her that I can't marry her until I can support her, but that I would be able to soon. I didn't ask her logistical questions like how many days she could go without food. Instead, I made a toast to the harmony of the soul. I told her that that's why I never go to the cinematography club because all these European movies point out the weaknesses of humans and not the harmony. Why not watch movies that point out the strengths of characters? But where are those movies? No Georgians are making movies. Only Armenians. So I made a toast to honorable women. And to movies in the future with honorable women. And I told her it doesn't matter if she doesn't do the cleaning and the cooking, because she doesn't like such things. The only thing that matters is if she does the honorable thing. And then the electricity came on for one second and I said, 'Ah. You see? My words are true.' But she said, 'You want me to just live in a tower and weep for the sadness of Georgia?' Before I could tell her that's not what I meant, the damn waiter needed my help fixing the stove in the kitchen. When I got back to the table Juliet looked so sad. 'Why are you so sad?' I asked her. 'Because it's difficult to be a Georgian woman.' 'Be happy,' I said. 'At least the electricity is on.'"

"But maybe she doesn't care about being supported," I said. "Especially in some black market business selling oil."

"But Slims, how else can I live in these times? Go back to the village and grow corn? Go into animal husbandry? I was thinking about it last year. I read that book about the cattle business, but then I would be alone all the time, herding the animals over the mountains. I'd rather work on the land growing potatoes, but nothing is growing these days. The villagers just work on the earth and nothing comes up. No, it is better for a man to have power and to feel nostalgic for a lost love than for a man to follow a woman, lose his life power, and then go into despair. That isn't good for the woman either."

Malkhazi's was a provincial mentality, but a practical one. But I was feeling that I was both losing my life power and I hadn't even followed a woman.

23.

As spring ripened into summer, Tamriko's piano playing stopped. The bishop visited everyone's homes, carving crosses into the walls. I was hoping that the newly carved crosses would provide the kind of renewal that exists in America. But after the bishop visited our flat, I could no longer sleep. I was wide-awake in the middle of the night, when I heard steps outside the door. "Juliet!" I heard someone call.

Juliet was sleeping, so I opened the door. "Anthony!" I said. "Don't you usually knock?"

"Is Juliet here?" Anthony called again, almost in a fever. A love fever? "I need to learn some new words," he said.

Had he finally come to learn the Georgian words for love, for marriage? I wondered. But when Juliet came into the kitchen rubbing her eyes he asked her, "Will you teach me the Georgian words for *plastic polyethylene protective coating*?" He was pacing up and down.

"Condom?" she asked.

He stopped pacing and looked at her. "If only," he said. I was starting to feel a little embarrassed.

"The British people at my company aren't listening to me. I need to explain this sealant issue in Georgian to those who are actually going to be impacted. Let me explain. Our pipelines come pre-coated, with polyethylene, to protect them from corrosion. They come in twelve-meter-long sections. The ends of each section have no coating—they have to be bare metal in order to be welded together—but of course they also need to be protected from corrosion. It was recommended that we cover the exposed ends with an epoxy-based product known as SP-2888. It's the highest scoring product on the market. But epoxy-based paints don't stick well to polyethylene—there's a question about its adhesion properties and the coatings haven't been adequately tested. Ideally, we'd have a pipe and a joint coated in the same material, but BP does allow for some leeway. The problem is we haven't really known what could happen. We've known that this new coating could cause stress corrosion cracks, could cause pipelines to rupture." He pulled from his pocket a strip of metal piping. "A pipeline is only as strong as its weakest link. I told them this. I showed them a piece of pipe, like this one, and said 'You think you've got coating?'" He tapped it and pieces of paint flickered to the floor. "That's their coating. I told them I think BP might be making a serious engineering mistake, but they said the cracks were caused by us, the installers—that we didn't apply the paint during the correct weather conditions. They had told us to heat the pipes before and after we applied it. So we did this and then buried the pipe. We thought that would take care of it, but there has been some leakage."

I stared at him. "And you tell *us* not to poke holes in the pipeline?" I asked him. "Will it leak into the water?"

"I won't lie to you. It's possible."

"Part of that pipeline goes through Borjomi Park, where they bottle the water. So this pipeline could destroy our only export?" I said. "And what about the river in our village? Will it leak into that too?"

"I thought you said you cared about our nature," Juliet said. "When we were walking by the sea the other day you said you wanted to learn the words for *real life*."

"Juliet, we've done some good things to help Georgia. We provided a grant to the Bakuriani and Tbilisi botanical gardens to help preserve some of your rare and endangered plant species. We removed the asbestos from a school in Samshvilde."

"Samshvilde is an Armenian village," I said.

"In Rustavi we laid thirteen hundred meters of steel pipe for an irrigation system for one of your Svani villages there, the one that was displaced after the earthquake. Look, the point is I've told BP about it but they're not listening to me. In fact, they are threatening to fire me."

"I thought you said that English people were not corrupt," Juliet said. "Maybe no part of the world is free of corruption. Maybe the whole world has turned to *jandabashi*."

"*Jandabashi*?" he asked. "Juliet, you haven't taught me that word."

"*Jandabashi* means hell," I said.

"Listen to me," he said. "I don't know what I can do about the sealant right now but there's a way to divert the pipeline, at least to keep it from going through your village. We just have to claim that it was built on an archaeological site."

Which is why the next day I drove Anthony in Malkhazi's red Lada to the village to meet with the archaeologists. We drove out of town, past the row of elms painted white on their trunks, our ancient version of insecticide, and clambered up the potholed highway, trying to avoid the black Mercedes of a New Georgian whose driving habits said, "I own the road, the right side *and* the left side." I looked over at Anthony, who was looking out the window at the wilderness. I took a handkerchief from my pocket, leaned over him, and polished the window for him.

"What is the meaning of that?" He was pointing at a giant, homemade billboard of a painted cow standing next to a sofa.

"It's an advertisement to trade your cow for some furniture," I said.

When we passed a billboard announcing in big red letters the kidnapping of a Spanish soccer player I said, "Don't worry. It's a joke."

"Kidnapping is no laughing matter," he said.

"Don't look at the road then," I told him. "It's not beautiful. Look at the mountains instead."

I turned a corner a little too fast and saw a policeman who had been hiding around the bend. He pointed his orange baton at me and I had to pull over. I pulled my documents out from the sun visor and got out. "You already took my driver's license," I told him. "What else do you want?"

"Have you been drinking?" he asked.

I shook my head.

"Why is your passenger wearing a seatbelt then?"

I got back in the car. "Anthony, please take off your seatbelt. Otherwise, the police will think I've been drinking."

But then I had another problem. Anthony refused to ride with me without a seatbelt. "What is the problem? I'm a good driver." But still he wouldn't take off his seatbelt.

We drove in silence, I irritated and he, well, I don't know what he was thinking.

When we got close to my village I turned off the main highway and onto a dirt road. "Now we are entering the time before Christ," I told him. "Perhaps you would like to see one of our famous fortresses. Tourists like to see this place."

I knew the fortress where Jesus's shirt was buried was past the waterfall, but when we got there, the road was blocked by three big guys with their arms crossed over their chests, looking like statues of ancient kings. "This is the border," they growled. "You can't go beyond this place."

"The border is farther down the road," I said.

"Don't cross this place if you like your life. Beyond here is a war zone," they said. But they were only joking because they were fishing and didn't want to move their cars out of the road.

We parked behind them and got out. Anthony walked around the old fortress, peeking under the old sheets of corrugated metal that had been haphazardly thrown across the ditches to cover up all the ancient civilizations. Anthony sat down on a stone and stared at the ground, looking sad all of a sudden.

"What's the matter with you?" I asked him.

"You had pipes in Georgia before they were even invented in the rest of the world. And now we're helping *you*?"

"Don't be sad," I told him. "You're not helping us *that* much."

It was late in the day that we drove up the road that unraveled up the mountain. The mountains towered on both sides of us, lost in their thoughts, the mist shrouding their peaks in revelations that I tried to remember.

We rumbled past the old familiar dwellings my cousins had built into the hillside, made almost entirely of windows, glittering in the sundown. Long ago my grandparents had planked together pine and cedar to construct these houses. When the Soviet Union arrived and was about to take all their money, they spent it all on beds and goose down quilts. When the government asked what all the extra beds were for they said, "Our guests." Since then, my uncle and my grandfather have always been waiting for a guest.

I was a little worried what kind of mood my grandfather would be in, though. He usually loved guests but he hated them if he had nothing to feed them. He was sitting at the picnic table in the yard with the village chairman. Both of them were shirtless and were drinking from a barrel of homemade *chacha*.

"Is that Lenin tattooed on his chest?" Anthony asked.

"Lenin and Stalin," I said.

"He must have been really devoted to them."

"It seems that way, though actually he tattooed them there so that if he ever went to prison they wouldn't be able to shoot him in the chest. If they start fighting, don't interfere," I warned Anthony.

"How are you today?" I called to my grandfather from the gate.

"Bad. I'm dying. And we already drank all the wine this year."

"What's the matter with him?" Anthony asked.

"He says he's dying, but he always says that," I reassured Anthony.

In the house my aunt and uncle were arguing, but when she saw Anthony she stopped all her yelling and dragged a bed out to the balcony. Pointing at it, she commanded, "Repose!" It was the only word in English she knew.

My aunt removed her old guitar from the wall. She had won it in a Soviet singing contest and it was made from good cherrywood—but all the ivory was missing. She set to work peeling apples and then fed Anthony the slices from her hands. "Should I play him a song?" she asked.

"Don't disturb the guest," my grandfather yelled from the strawberry patch below. "Maybe he doesn't want to hear your songs."

My aunt began to play anyway.

Duduba my instrument
You are the remedy
for my soul
You, the medicine of all burnt souls
When I listen to you, sweet duduba
I can't hide my love
my eyes fill with tears
and sad thoughts come to my mind
My heart trembles
My feelings come to my throat
and the bowl of silence explodes
my blood becomes warmer listening to you
and flows through my body
My sweet-talking instrument
Why are you so good?
You are the guide of my life.

When she finished I told my aunt that we were eating with the anthropologists but she pushed Anthony and me into her kitchen and wrestled us onto the little chairs that she had borrowed from the kindergarten. "Tell him to eat some more fruit. Tell him the real reason you come back to the village is to help with your digestion because you eat so much macaroni in the city."

In a cabinet she found a hoarded plastic bottle of Odessa wine and poured us cupfuls so that we could toast to her household.

The post of the Georgian archaeologist, historically, has always been a coveted position—the handkerchief tied so dapperly around the neck inspired envy in even the most modest of men. In the village it was clear that the archaeologists didn't want to spend all their time at the Center for Democracy competing for funds from nongovernmental organizations, or at the Maritime Ministry of Law stealing faxes. Here in the village they were more comfortable in their natural habitat. They had taken over an old government building located between what used to be the library and the village's parliament building, both of them overgrown with grapevines and wild roses stretching all over the walls, in every direction, even over the aluminum statue of Stalin waving flirtatiously at us.

A group of women, already waiting for us, pushed the unruly grapevines aside on the balcony and waved like the mustached one. The dogs and chickens were yelping and clucking, and the archaeologists were making the noises that archaeologists make.

"*Galmarjos! Galmarjos!*" Zaliko was yelling, running down the stairs and hurrying toward us in the same way he hurries toward Mr. Fax's fax machine.

"This is my friend," I told Anthony, patting the back of Zaliko's rotund shape. "He discovered the one-and-a-half-million-year-old remains of a giraffe in Eastern Georgia."

"And this is our river," Zaliko said, pointing to a muddy conduit. "That river marks the end of the Ottoman Empire. Over there was the Persian Empire." We looked across the river at some branches sticking out of the gelid mud.

We clumped up the shaky wooden stairs to a table on the balcony laden with fragrant dishes: chicken in walnut sauce, potato stew with chunks of marinated buffalo, mixed vegetable medleys with a layer of bronze oil on top, beet salads already turning the cream purple, tomato salads sliced with peppers and herbs, coriander chutneys, red peppers stuffed with rice and olives, mutton *pilov*. The third layer of plates was a pastry of noodle and cheese. The food on the table wasn't just food but pure philosophy. And now the women were bringing hot, fried corn porridge stuffed with sulguni cheese.

But there at the far end of the table I saw Gocha. How had he gotten here? He turned to Anthony and smiled at him with his white dental smile, as if they belonged to the same bowling club.

That evening sitting at the Institute of Archaeology when Zaliko was giving the first toast to peace, every time I glanced at Gocha I could feel my lip involuntarily curl up as if I had just eaten a pickle. But then I remembered one of the English quotes from Juliet's book of famous sayings: "The opposite of love is not hatred but indifference." So I was able to forget about him.

"And to friendship between our two countries," continued Zaliko.

And then a toast to our Georgian land. I had purposely left my drinking horn at home because whenever I drink Georgian wine I start to forget about my ambitions. It is a very bad habit—especially at a meeting of archaeologists where one is hoping to intervene and stop the pipeline from creating any more destruction. Zaliko raised his glass and turned to Anthony, "This wine comes from our nature. The only problem is that the men don't have jobs here. And the Jehovah's Witnesses are invading us. But that is another problem not for this evening."

"What is Zaliko getting at?" I heard Gocha say to someone else. "We are from the city, not the village."

How impolite, I thought. Once and for all I will crash a chair over his head tonight.

"The problem," I told Gocha, "is that he's not a train signal. You can't just stop him with a lever."

The archaeologists now began to express their pleasure that finally a foreigner was showing interest in Georgian archaeology.

"Do they know that I'm not an archaeologist?" Anthony whispered to me.

But then to my dismay, Gocha began to toast the pipeline, explaining how it had funded their most recent archaeological excavation. And then suddenly they were all toasting to the past, present, and future excavations. A toast to the corn that grew on top of the graves of the excavation, for archaeology in general, and to the health of all archaeologists.

The wine from my village was a glacier indolently melting into a green, swollen river. It was softened sunlight, the mother of autumn. I raised my glass and told Anthony, "Real men only drink white wine."

More toasts to all the dead people who ever worked in archaeology, and then Zaliko talked about the time his car had gotten stuck in the mud and, upon removing the tire, he'd discovered an ancient pottery cup still in one piece. "Slims!" Zaliko cried, "Tell Anthony to lift his cup. Tell him I found that cup under my tire. It's fifteen hundred years old."

And then toasts to the shovels and picks and brushes, and to the cars that carried the archaeologists. Momentarily, I forgot about why we were there and stood up and toasted to the community electric meter that we might one day build in our village. Little cups of coffee were brought and young men pumped out more wine from amphoras in the earth, while their little brothers watched the procedure, and their grandfathers gathered round, supervising.

The children observed Anthony from a distance. "You see how well-behaved these children are?" I asked him. "They wait until we have finished eating to eat their own meal. They are very bright too. The kids in the town know only cards and backgammon." But Anthony wasn't listening. He was raising his glass and asking for more wine. He was really taking his fate into his own hands! Standing up he sounded like a priest. "We have gathered here today to move your country forward, to move past nepotism. With the proper regulations we can manage to divert the pipeline from going through your village. Since it's built on an archaeological site . . ."

Zaliko suddenly stood up and said, "I commend you in your efforts but as you know, in our country the man proposes and the government disposes. For years we have asked the government to fund our archaeological projects. Only the international companies responsible for the pipeline have provided the funds for our work to continue."

At this the men began performing unique drinking feats, clutching four glasses above their heads, a finger in each, the apricot-colored wine waterfalling into each glass like melted gold until the final one gushed into their throats.

"Evolutionism is communist propaganda!" Gocha suddenly blurted out. "How could we come from apes?"

"Here's to Gocha! What a philosopher," everyone cheered in unison. "The next toast is to Gocha."

Anthony, by now, evidently had given up hope of talking about how he might be able to divert the pipeline, at least at this table, and asked if he might go to bed. I wondered if there was any way this pipeline was going to be diverted.

But it was four a.m. already and all was becoming hilarity. One man sang to his wife, "I loved you with a great passion. I would have swum across the seas for you. My love was a great fire beneath me. And then one day I woke up and my love had disappeared. I'm so confounded. I don't know where it went." Everyone laughed and she threw her napkin at him.

I left the table at seven, when the sun was starting to rise. The women had left long ago but stayed up talking of others, as women do, avoiding the cigarette butts thrown off the balcony by the men. By nine most of the archaeologists were up again, smiling and greeting each other, clasping hands, the *tamada* bowing as he greeted everyone in a deep voice, "Victory this morning!" Washing their hands and faces in the faucet outside, they very soberly offered each other fresh vodka. A dutiful feeling pervaded, as if they had just climbed back up a ski slope together after the chairlift broke—the ruddiness of faces, the glow of friendship that one only encounters in the hunting stories of Turgenev. And then the toasting started again. "Good God! What is there left to toast?" Anthony asked, emerging from the room he had slept in.

In the early morning spirit of Georgian brotherhood, I was even ready to forgive Gocha. After all, in our Georgian films, brother embraces brother and forgets about the woman. But when I went to kiss him on the cheek, he tried to act like an American and turned his head away, so I punched him in the face.

24.

Later in the day I put Anthony on a bus back to Batumi and walked through the tawny fields past our village's twelfth-century church, which was being renovated. The reconstruction dust was settling on the scaffolding, and the afternoon light shining through the thin shafts of the church windows reminded me of the lines of Grigol Orbeliani: "For morn will break, and sunshine's beam will make the shades of darkness flee." Or in other words, "Don't poke out your eyes today because the sun might shine tomorrow."

I ambled through the village, then into the weald and the uncultivated country, the radio in my head resting at the station of birdsong. I heard the roosters and hens, the mules, the whole animal citizenry. In the plum orchard I sat on the picnic bench I had built when I was fourteen and looked at the gloaming river through the budding, wispy branches. Little boys were trying to catch fish in the fading light. One who reminded me of Zuka when he was younger was yelling something ardently to his friends as they plunged sticks through the muddy river, yelling at each other when the mud suckled their galoshes, and asking for help to be yanked out. They walked upriver to another fishing hole, and then I walked back past the church.

I sat down on the stone slabs of the church steps, watched the sun blabbing out light through the pine trees, and remembered parts of a poem by Irakli Abashidze:

Georgia's beauty leaves me speechless,
All her wonders make me breathless!
I know why the oak-tree towers
Over timid little flowers,
Why my heart weeps with the willow,
Or rejoices with the swallow.
What the ocean dreams when sleeping
melodies that love composes,
Subtle thoughts that man discloses.
Strength of eloquence avoids me.
To describe her is beyond me.
Words are mute and phrases helpless,
All attempts of speech are hopeless . . .
I must die,
In vain my yearning,
I must die,
Thus longing, burning.

Inside the church, a hushed pall fell over the atmosphere. Candles flickered. I stared at an icon, the one of Mary holding the Christ. I apologized to Her that I hadn't been listening to Her very well and I suggested to Her that if She yelled a little louder I could hear Her better. I apologized that I hadn't been to church that often lately and that I still wanted to base my life on Her even if sometimes it seemed that She just wanted me to watch the oxen go by on the road in a calm mood. And if She wanted me to do something other than that then She should really let me know, you know? I told Her She was still in my heart even when I was alone in my flat with Juliet's new weird seventies furniture design and Victorian green wallpaper.

I'd been away from the village too long. I didn't need to be inside a church but should have been holding a hoe under the warm sun heading to the other side of the half-plowed cornfield where my bowl of wine was waiting for me under the shadow of an old beech tree. I should be stepping sturdily forward, I thought to myself, with my chest toward the ground, my heart clinging to the earth like an ear shell clings to the wet, black rock in the sea.

I walked to the field near the school, found my aunt's cow, and started leading her home, moved by how green the fields were. But when I got to the edge of the field I saw on top of the hill that a long line of broken mud cut across the upper meadow. And, in the distance, along the sides of the windswept yellow mountain ridges, huge black metal pipes jutted out. I hadn't realized that the pipes would cut up the eastern mountain like a giant paper shredder. To avoid the mud I tried to take a shortcut through the school yard, but a Georgian G.I. Joe—"Colonel Giorgi," he called himself—dressed in a desert fatigue uniform and aviator sunglasses forged toward me from the forest below. Pointing an automatic weapon at me, he demanded to see my passport.

"What's the problem?" I asked.

"We can't be too careful these days," he said. "Our greatest danger is a terrorist attack on the pipeline."

"From whom?" I asked. He said he couldn't be specific.

I dropped off the cow at my aunt and uncle's house and went to the village center to catch up on the news. My old kindergarten friends Gela and Zviko, dressed in leather jackets and wool caps, were huddled around a roadside kiosk, drinking beer, and watching the British Petroleum trucks rumble down the road.

"There is little else to do here anymore other than watch the days slide by," my friend Gela said. "My wife complains that I haven't brought any meat home. But I haven't felt in the mood to hunt."

"The mountains are changing so fast it's like watching TV," Zviko said.

"They promised they would give us work, but so far they've hired maybe five people in the past two months," Gela said. "They told us there would be employment for seventy but I think that figure was overblown."

"They promised to pay money for our land but no one has seen any of it," Zviko said.

"They paid, but the government took it all," Gela said. "They say that at least they are helping our local economy by purchasing our food, furniture, and water, but I don't know who they are purchasing it from."

"And stationery. They *have* bought paper." Zviko said he was planning to move. The storage room for his pickled vegetables had a crack a quarter-meter wide. "It's because of all these heavy construction trucks. It's dangerous," he said. "No one can live like this. Remember when the mountains on the other side of the village slid down because they had worked the ground too hard, and they had to move into the tea packaging factory? This is worse."

"We told BP they ruined our land. And all they said was, 'It's not our fault,'" Gela said.

Our village life was changing. I wanted to talk to the old monk in our village about it, so I hiked downriver to his hut. He and I often had good talks over a bottle of his own Ojaleshi, made from the grape cultivated on the Western mountain slopes. As I walked I could see a few scattered oak and walnut trees still dotting up between open grazing lands. Most of the trees had been chopped down. Across the river, bulldozers were churning up rock and topsoil.

The old monk's hut, lined with planks of pine wallpaper, hung over the edge of the river. The water roared below but we could still hear the sound of bulldozers in the distance.

He served me a plate mounded with fried mountain potatoes and an oily bowl of cow bone soup. As we talked I helped him sculpt little loaves of bread, Jesus's flesh, on his dining room table. The table had tiny grooves in it, as if it had been carved with a spoon, and little bits of dough stayed embedded within them. His black beard nearly touched the dough he kneaded, which was stressful, but his stern look calmed me. His look told me that in the real scheme of things dough in the beard doesn't really matter.

Barrels of homemade wine insulated the walls. He poured me some amber liquid, a brew he had made himself, soaking it in a special wood that gave it the flavor of cedar. Since he'd been in the mountains for so long and away from modern city influences, he still believed in miracles. He told me that when the bishop blesses houses in the spring, carving crosses into the wall, and the glue drips down, it is important to distinguish these glue drippings from the real tears of the icons. "In the evenings, twice a year, an icon will weep," he said.

"But is that really true?" I asked.

"I'm afraid," he said, "they always weep before an invasion."

"Russia has too many problems to invade us," I said. "Also, whenever they send over one of their missiles, it always crashes in the wrong place without even going off. Their navigational systems are defunct. Or, perhaps you are referring to these pipelines."

He kept on kneading.

After another bottle of wine and more kneading of dough until it began to feel like a woman in my hands, I began to feel emotional. "My being is bound up with the land," I told him.

"Some are called to the priesthood. Others are called back to the land," was all he said.

In sweat, grief releases. The next morning, I took a hoe out to the cornfields. I started to work on the earth singing the old songs. I heard the morning cry of the rooster. The song of chickens sometimes gives me a sad and lonely feeling, so I worked the field harder, back and forth between the old beech trees. As I worked I thought about the things that most mattered to me. I decided that the next day I would return to Batumi and go and face Tamriko. But first I would go visit my father.

I climbed halfway up the mountain to the cemetery and sat in the little yard surrounding my father's grave. I picked out the twigs and leaves and smoothed the dirt. At the edge of the cemetery I bought some violets from a woman dressed in black standing at the entrance. I was surprised anyone was selling flowers today, but she said there was a funeral procession on its way. She told me about an old woman who had lived near the river. She had gone outside in her bare feet and caught a cold and died—she had been known to be a little crazy. She had lived in the village for as long as I could remember. I walked up to my father's grave, dumped out the old water from the plastic pitcher, and changed the flowers. Superimposed on my father's stone marker was the photograph of him dressed up in a traditional Adjarian folk dance outfit, looking jubilant as he held a bottle of wine on a tray, askew, as if he were ready to clap to the music on the piano behind him. Next to his head was a little picture of his minibus. Death couldn't be that bad, I thought, because it was peaceful here and the birds were singing.

I wandered through the rest of the cemetery. There was my school director. In another place were my very good friend's parents. I used to eat dinner at their house all the time. Ah! I knew all these people. And there—a man's family had built him his own balcony into the hillside so he could enjoy the fresh air.

A father and his son carried flowers and candles to attend to a grave. I heard the man tell his son, "This is my uncle's grave. But look how no one has been here to clean it in a couple of weeks. He has a son and a daughter. They both have cars. They just drive around all day. Shame on them."

The funeral procession was coming over the bridge. The imam, who lived in the Muslim village on the other side, used to sing the call to prayer on top of a barnyard ladder, but recently his village had gathered enough money together to build a mosque. They had painted a mural on the outside of it, facing the river, for the Christians in our village to enjoy.

When I was a kid I used to bring this imam coffee on my donkey. He taught me the sunrise prayers, told me they were morning toasts. He encouraged me to give up pork, and only to drink on Georgian holidays. But *you* try giving up alcohol if you are a Georgian boy growing up in the village.

The Christian priest from our village and the Muslim imam from the other village are actually old friends, but they were now shouting abuses at each other. The imam must have seen the funeral procession heading to the Christian cemetery, so he had stomped over the river—

the suspension bridge was still shaking like jelled bone marrow. "What are you doing?" he cried, confronting the priest. "That woman was a Muslim!"

"In this life she became a Christian!"

"But her father was a Muslim!"

"But her father appeared to her in a vision, holding a cross on the side of the road, and ordered her to convert."

The imam stood there, arms crossed, blowing steam from his mouth, his wool jacket buttoned up to his throat and his face crinkling and uncrinkling. "Only people who come from disturbed families convert!" the imam said, turned on his heel, and marched back across the bridge. But just before he got across, he turned again and saw me, squatting near my father's grave. "Slims Achmed!" he shouted. "I don't care what your belief system is. But don't change your name. Be proud of your Muslim name."

The Estonian family who live in our village hate our loud weeping. They say, as if to hint to us a better way, "*We* weep quietly in our hearts." But everyone in the funeral procession was weeping loudly, with smeared faces, walking around as if they all had a huge scrape on their hearts.

People were placing strong drinks, some sweets, cigarettes, and a great mound of bank notes into the coffin, so that she could buy whatever she needed, whenever, wherever she needed it. Armenians don't put money in. They just provide clothes and a towel.

I overheard someone from the Estonian family say to another, "They'll get drunk and take their cars and drive like mad, and to hell with the corpse. And then the music choir's going to have to deal with the body." But no one had hired a choir. They must have been thinking of those days when we used to have the big brass bands. Now the brass bands were disappearing.

A deep thirst for water brought me down off the hillside.

In the courtyard, my aunt ran out, tripping on her purple robe. "Come quickly," she said. "We're on TV."

There was our little village. "There's Zviko," my grandfather said. "He should have polished his boots."

"The Bush administration has dismissed concerns about the pipeline's effect on the environment and local economies," the newscaster was saying.

Now a spokesman for BP was being interviewed. "Imagine being in a place where no one has ever sold or exchanged property," he said. "That means you can have four thousand different standards for property sales. It's not an ideal situation. It really sets up an atmosphere of mistrust between people and the company."

But intervening was a young Georgian representative, the new Western-educated politician I had heard about, this new Saakashvili, my role model. He was talking with the pipeline representative. He knew how to use very bad language. He knew what to call the current leadership. He promised the villagers that they would get compensated for any damages.

According to the opinion polls, the TV reporter reported, Saakashvili, this new United Democrat, was supposed to win our upcoming presidential election. A state budget in the pockets of the president and his family had proved too much for us.

But Saakashvili was someone I could finally believe in. He was young, had gone to a university in America and believed in Western law. He even had a Dutch wife who could sing Georgian songs. Mr. Fax hated him because he was trying to rid the country of corruption. If Fax hated him then he was the man for me.

My aunt brought us coffee. My grandfather and I both drank it to the sludge at the bottom. Even though only very old women know how to read the silt of the coffee in the bottom of a cup, we both peered into ours, looking for a sign from the Great Toastmaster. "It's looks like the politicians are going to start using bullets again," I said.

On the bus back to Batumi the next morning, while looking out the window at the buckwheat fields, I could hear the speaker system above my head playing a new Georgian pop song filled with the spite of youth. I listened more closely and realized it wasn't spite—it was helpful advice. They were singing, "Get out! Get out you, out from under Shevardnadze. Do all you can! He's been president for our whole generation. Is he the only one you'll know your whole life? Aren't you bored with him yet?" In fact, a whole youth movement against She-vardnadze had begun in Tbilisi. They called themselves Enough!

The situation reminded me of the old joke. Shevardnadze is sit-ting at home. He asks his grandson, "What would you like to be when you grow up?" The little boy says, "I want to be president." Shevard-nadze says, "Think of something else. There can't be two presidents."

Everyone was talking about Saakashvili. When I got home to the beer factory district, Guliko, Tamriko's mother, called to me from her window, "Slims! I haven't had any coffee yet because I haven't had anyone to drink it with me." I climbed the stairs to her flat, hop-ing Tamriko was home, but Guliko said she was out. She sat me down, put a piece of torte in front of me, and started complaining.

"Yesterday," she said, "I heard a conversation in the courtyard between your brother Zuka and another boy. You know that irritating one with the dalmatian who is always yelling to his mother, 'Natasha! Natasha!' Anyway, I heard them say that this new Saakashvili wants to overthrow Shevardnadze. 'It's so extreme!' they shouted. *Vaimay!* All these young people *love* this extreme disease. But I'm afraid Tam-riko may be affected too. I'm worried about her blood pressure. She came home yesterday and when she sat down she said, 'I have a gun. Do you want to see it?' And then she pulled a little gun out of her purse. Imagine! Slims, do you know where she got a gun?"

"No," I said. "Maybe from Gocha. You should get her away from that guy."

"Have you heard the saying, 'Don't take away someone's hope because it may be all they have left'? In his case, our only hope is this new Saakashvili. Have you heard of him? I believe he knows how to harness the energy of our young men. He'll teach them to get rid of their guns and fight with swords again. Here, drink this," she said and handed me a cup of instant coffee. "Oh, Slims, what is happening to our people? My students used to cry at the orphanages and the boys brought flowers for them. Our women used to be so beautiful. Do you remember when Gamsakhurdia said, 'If you shoot bullets we will throw roses at you'? In those days people loved each other very much."

* * *

That evening while I was looking out the window watching out for Tamriko, I saw Malkhazi drive up. He parked, locked his car, and then he yelled Juliet's name. "Juliet!" he called.

"*Sheni deyda!*" Juliet said from the table. "Does he think he is in a Shakespeare play? I just spilled my hawthorn tea all over the papers I was proofing."

"Juliet!" Malkhazi called again. "Are you still waiting for your white English prince?"

Malkhazi thumped up the stairs and came inside, holding a large lump of dough in his hands.

"Where have *you* been?" I asked.

"Here. Take it," he said, pushing it into my hands. "I brought it from the bakers. I know how you don't like to cook, but have you heard? Most of the bread supplies have been infected by a strange Korean curse, but I know the baker who makes this bread and I know it's clean. Though when I went to his shop and asked him for it, he thought I was on drugs."

I put the dough into a bowl, and Juliet came into the kitchen waving her papers, trying to dry them. "Where have you been?" she asked.

"Juliet!" he said brightly. "What are you up to?"

"Just now?" she asked. "I was imagining a beautiful image. I was imagining shooting you with a gun. Ah, so beautiful."

He raised his eyebrows, pulled a gun from his pocket, and gave it to her. "You're right. I would probably be better off dead."

"Actually Juliet," I told her, "he brought you some pretty nice dough. But where *have* you been, Malkhazi?"

He smiled at me and then turned to her, "You came to my work today looking for me, didn't you? I know you were there because you left your empty glass of apricot compote on my desk. Can I sit down? No. Excuse me," he said, switching to English. "*May* I sit down?"

She pointed to a kitchen chair.

"Okay, I'll tell you if you sit down too. Both of you. It's really a stupid business. Last winter the Turkish ships were in an auction. Well, Slims knows this. Anyway, I convinced a British master to buy one. Okay, Slims you don't know this part. No, not Anthony. It's a long story. Anyway, a British master bought the ship with some investors, but now after only one voyage he thinks I stole oil from his Turkish ship, that I didn't discharge the correct amount. Over five hundred tonnes. So little for such a big headache."

"Well, did you?" Juliet said.

"Juliet, haven't you seen those Turkish ships?" he pleaded. "They are so old. The oil gets lost in the cracks." He stood up, went to the sink, and grabbed a bottle of dishwashing soap. "It's like this bottle of dish soap. If you squeeze it widthwise like this, there appears to be more, but this way, it appears to be less. But don't worry. I know that the missing oil is there somewhere. But I couldn't get anyone to sign off on anything. For ten days we had to stand like this, with our arms crossed. I wanted to sneak back in the middle of the night to come talk to you. But the British master was so angry. I didn't want to tell you because I didn't want you to worry. I had to spend two weeks trying to convince them that I had discharged the correct amount into their ship. Do not be angry with me. Please? You should pity me instead. I had to spend this whole time with a bunch of English people."

"You sound like such a bigot when you talk like that," she said.

"Thank you," he said and bowed. "You use that word with me very often. So I looked it up in the dictionary and found the meaning. The word *bigot* refers to a man's mustache, that it looks like a herd of horses stampeding in one direction. Do you think that I stampede in one direction, Juliet? Ach! I need to find a solution," he said and stood by her side. He put his palm on her shoulder. "What am I going to do? *Vaimay!* I don't understand these laws. This *sue*. How do you say this word in English? Sewage? English people are not better than us. I understand Filipino people. I understand Greeks. I understand the Spanish. Well, they are easy to understand because they invented Don Quixote. With anybody else, we could just give them wine and a sword and they would remember what a true human is, but in this case, I'm afraid that won't work. I don't know anything about this court of law. And now Gocha is going to send me to England to go on trial."

Juliet began laughing.

"Why are you laughing?" he asked her.

I was definitely not laughing. I was sent home from abroad because I broke the law and Malkhazi was being sent abroad *because* he broke the law?

"I was just trying to imagine you in a British court of law," Juliet said.

"Yes, I will bribe them," he said. "Is that what you are thinking? No, I will tell them the truth. I will go there and I will find some Georgians and we will get drunk in one of their parks so that we can remember that British people are not better than us. When they ask me a question that I don't want to answer I will just say, 'I don't understand the question.' Soon they will get bored, and finally they will point at me and say, 'Let him be right.'"

"Malkhazi, I'm a lawyer," I said. "I can represent you."

"I'm sorry, Slims. I don't want you to feel strange about this, but I do not know if your American methods will help me in this case. I need a true Georgian like Gocha to help me out. Besides, I don't think they'll let you out of this country. Please, Juliet," he said. "Give me my gun back."

"Where are you going now?" she asked.

"I must go," he said and left.

"They say that the Georgian man always speaks the truth," Juliet said while looking out the window. "The problem is that if he cannot speak the truth, then he does not speak."

But I could not listen to her words. Instead, these were the thoughts searing through my mind: Malkhazi thinks I am not a true Georgian? He thinks I don't understand how to do things the Georgian way? Oh, Mr. Inspector, big Georgian man of the town, big-*nosed* Georgian man of the town, no matter how proud you are of your bigness, in a fat contest you would always lose because your nose, no matter how big your stomach is, would always touch the wall first! I tried to figure out what to do. I was ready to go to Tamriko, ask for her gun, and go shoot Gocha. With his own gun. Is that what it would take to prove to Malkhazi that I knew how to do things the Georgian way?

But I wasn't interested in starting a new nine-generation vendetta. I squeezed the little @ ball I still had in my pocket until I could feel myself calm down a little. The Georgian heart is always divided between punishing his enemy and being a good host to his friend. When we put hospitality before all else, then all our fears fly away.

But I needed a guest in order to feel Georgian again. I began to really understand why Malkhazi valued his job so much: he could always be a host to these foreign sailors. The only guest I knew was Anthony. I felt a soft feeling for Anthony, especially now that I knew he was trying to protect my village from the pipeline. I wondered if the feeling was the same as the feeling Oprah Winfrey described in that show I watched of hers on how to have good relations with yourself. Maybe Anthony was my only true friend—the only one I could really understand anymore because as different as we were, we were both caught in between two cultures.

25.

I WAITED A FEW DAYS UNTIL THE NEXT TIME A FOREIGN SHIP ARRIVED at the port filled with beer. I knew that in order to measure the quality, Malkhazi usually took one bottle from each case. By the end of the day there were eighty-five bottles of beer in his backseat. Then I asked Malkhazi if I could borrow his car. I knew that Anthony liked beer very much so I waited for him outside the Center for Democracy, where I had heard from Juliet that he was trying to appeal to our local dictator about the sealants used in the pipeline. When I saw him leave the building, he was shuffling down the street with his head down, looking like some sort of coward. I drove alongside him and said, "You are looking depressed today, and probably for good reason, but it's always possible to turn the day into a holiday. Look in the back." His face lit up when he saw so much beer. "Come," I told him. "Let's go for a drive." He agreed, but only if I let him drive because he didn't like the way I drove. "Wait until we're a little bit away from the traffic," I told him.

"What traffic?" he said.

"Ho ho! Okay!" I said. I told him the clutch was stiff, that maybe he didn't know how to drive a Russian car, but he drove decently, except he kept stopping at the intersections. I had to tell him, "What are you doing? You have the right of way. All the streets that lead to the sea have the right of way." While he was waiting for a red light to change, I said, "What are you doing?"

"You want me to just drive though the red light?" he asked.

"Well everyone else does because they are so used to the light never working, so you must too if you want to continue to live." There is something about Georgia. When people get behind a steering wheel, they start to feel a little crazy, and I knew this would probably happen to him too. He drove through the red light and then he said, "Can I do that again?"

"Sure," I said. "As many times as you like."

He didn't drive very well and kept hitting all the potholes. "I feel like a baby in a cradle because of all the bouncing," I told him. We drove out of town, over the train tracks, and then he told me why he was depressed. He said, "Yesterday I was fired from my job. BP doesn't want a whistle-blower complaining about pipeline connectors."

"Let's just drive," I said.

I told him where to drive on all the back roads to avoid the police checkpoints. When we got to the river, at the base of the mountains, I told him to pull over. I reached in the back, opened a beer, and handed it to him. I told him how the first night we had met him we had been planning to kidnap him, but how it would have been really impossible to carry out because higher than the law is the guest. I pointed to Crying Mountain, the hill that Malkhazi's uncle used to own, and told him the story about it—how when the invaders came they killed everyone on it. He became sad about that and then asked for another beer. We started driving again and then, up ahead, I saw Shalva the policeman, dressed all in black, near the rail station. He was flagging us down.

"Oh my God!" Anthony started yelling, "It's a bandit!"

"Actually, it's a policeman," I said.

"Even worse!" he said. "They are all criminals."

I told him it was no problem, that I am a Makashvili.

"Easy for you to say," he told me. "I'm the one driving the car. And we have I don't know how much beer in the backseat. And yesterday, BP canceled my visa. They want me out of this country."

"I thought you understood!" I told him. "Higher than the law is the guest. Even if a *bandit* sees an Englishman he won't bother us. I am so safe with you," I said.

"Should I just keep driving through?" he asked.

"It's better to stop," I said and leaned back in my seat pretending to take a nap. And of course, as I knew he would, Shalva went to my side of the car and asked for *my* papers and I had a little private talk with him. He went back to Anthony's side, leaned his head in the window, took a beer, and then bid us goodbye. "Adieu," he said, blowing Anthony a kiss.

"What kind of a country is this?" Anthony asked. He was laughing so hard he almost drove into the river. "Oh sorry, sorry," he said.

"What is this *sorry* all the time?" I asked him. "I am not afraid to die. Death is afraid of me."

The next evening I walked to Tamriko's house with some tools. "I've come to fix your sink," I said. "The last time I was here, I saw that it was leaking."

"There, I have fixed your sink," I said when I had finished.

"Thank you," she said.

"Now I must go," I said. But I didn't make a move toward the door.

"Our block still has no electricity," I said. "So I will leave my phone here to recharge it." I still waited for her to say something.

"What?" she asked. "Why are you looking at me like that?"

Aah! Feelings. Words. They came together somewhere inside me.

I wanted to ask her if she had ever met a fairly fearless man. I wanted to tell her that I could help her if she had a problem with her car or with her cat. I wanted to tell her the story about one of my sister's students who got drunk and confessed his love to her but how she had told him, "You are like a son to me." He went away for many days and took the narcotics that grow up by the railroad tracks. Everyone was worried about him. When he came back he begged Juliet to marry him, but instead of telling him, "It's impossible," she said, "Well, maybe if you get over your drug habit." Maybe this. Maybe that. I became so angry at her. It wasn't direct and kind. I wanted to be direct and kind to Tamriko. I wanted her to be direct and kind to me, to tell me if it would ever be possible or not possible to be with her. But she spoke instead.

"What are your ambitions, Slims?" she asked. "What are your dreams?"

"Don't you know that the Makashvilis are famous for our dreams?" I cried.

"So what are they?"

"My dream is to live in nature. With you. I could build for you a little house."

"No, I mean as in a career."

"I can do anything."

"I know. But what do you *want* to do?"

"Maybe something with the sea. I love the sea."

"Maybe you could be a marine biologist."

"I don't want to do any more *research*!"

"I'm just saying, if you could do anything in the world, what would it be?"

"I wanted to be a lawyer but no one follows the law here," I said. "One time, I wanted to be a nature scientist and draw animals in the dark like that dark therapy tradition in the Czech Republic, but no one has any money to buy art in Georgia. Anyway, I will leave my phone here to recharge it," I said. "I will be back tomorrow to get it."

"Slims," she said when I had turned to leave. "If no one follows the law here, then how come you never became *kurdi*?"

"You too?" I said and grabbed my phone. "You want to marry a criminal? How very romantic. Maybe you *are* better off with Gocha."

But when I walked outside, the fading light painted slants on all the buildings, marrying shadows to earth. It was that ecstatic time of the day in between day and night when the light is trying to prove that the purpose of life is love. I headed toward Malkhazi's office. If Tamriko wanted *kurdi* then I would become *kurdi*.

The doorbell of Malkhazi's office didn't work so I pushed open the door and saw the guard asleep on a chair. The hall smelled of boiled cabbage. Malkhazi's head was slumped over on his desk, fast asleep. I noticed that the stress of his job had started to gray some of his hair.

When he woke up I told him, "I want to come with you onto that Turkish ship." I actually didn't want to go for a number of reasons. Here I was, Mr. Slims Achmed Makashvili, tireless worker for anticorruption, trying to bring the modern law to Georgia, but higher than the law is the woman.

"The Turkish ship with the British master is on its second voyage. We'll have to wait until it gets back if you want to help me out," he said.

"No," I said. "I just want to steal some plastic flowers off a Turkish ship for Tamriko. That girl is crazy for *kurdi*."

Malkhazi laughed heartily. "Maybe *she* will appreciate it."

When we got to the port Malkhazi pointed to a ship lit up like a glow-in-the-dark dragon. "See that monster?" he said. "It's another Turkish vessel. Look at it. Would you believe this one is new though? Now crouch low. We are driving through a restricted area. You would think that this Turkish master on his voyage to Batumi would have gotten used to the controls. If you were the master of such a vessel, you would get to know the controls if you had to navigate your way though the straits of Bosporus across the Black Sea, right?"

"Of course," I said.

"And you would know how to balance the weight. But look how all the weight is on the starboard side!"

Malkhazi parked his car in the space reserved for oil inspectors. "Here, you can wear my jacket," Malkhazi said, throwing it to me. "It has my badge on it."

Inside, he pointed to a room humming with the sound of a generator and equipped with a green vinyl couch. "Wait here. I have to go sign some papers before we can go on the Turkish ship. Here, you can read this." He handed me a magazine about the American sport of snowboarding. "An American sailor left it here. It will be quiet because everyone has left, but don't fall asleep. I may need your help.

Here are some binoculars. You can see the port through that window. Make sure the Turkish ship doesn't start to sink."

Looking around, I realized that perhaps the reason Malkhazi liked his job so much was because it allowed him to work in such a modern environment. The colors were neutral and the paint wasn't chipping. There was a NO SMOKING sign on the wall in English. I grabbed a handful of pens from the office supply drawer. I could give Tamriko some stolen pens.

Malkhazi's boss from Azerbaijan came into the room wearing a green business sweater with orange diamonds on the sleeves, looking like he was trying to uphold the standards of professional dress that were becoming lax in our city. Everyone feels better when he has a purpose. Malkhazi's Azeri boss stared at me enjoying the warmth of his heater.

"Do you mind if I sit here?" I asked.

"Do what you like," he said and turned to his desk.

The waiting room was warm with the blaze of the blue gas heat. The lulling hum of the generator and the white noise of the Western refrigerator soon blurred the lights of the Turkish ship in the harbor and put me to sleep.

I woke up in the middle of the night to the sound of documents printing and Malkhazi swearing at the print button. "Oh, I am having some difficult times," he said when he saw I was awake. "None of these Turkish sailors speak one word of Georgian. Turkey is our neighbor! Don't you think they should at least know how to say *hello* in Georgian to their neighbor? They go to school only to learn how to do strange tricks with their cigarette lighters. You can come with me now, Slims."

So I finally went aboard the Turkish ship.

At first I was afraid, but to my surprise, the Turkish sailors were very friendly. Some stood by the rails looking wistfully south, in the direction of their home. I asked one for a cigarette and he gave me his whole pack.

I watched Malkhazi measure the oil. He stuck a tape measure into the hatch of the oil container and wrote the number down. But no one here could understand his measurements. Finally, a Turkish sailor who could speak a little English said that they measured, like the Americans, in feet and *inchus*. At first I thought he was joking because *inchus* means *what* in Armenian. I thought he was saying, "What? What?"

While Malkhazi finished with the measuring I walked around the ship but couldn't find a single plastic flower. "There is nothing to steal on this ship," I told Malkhazi.

"Of course not," he said. "I thought you were joking."

"But *you* stole plastic flowers off a ship!"

"No, I didn't. I bought them in a shop! Come with me to the American ship. You'll like it there."

But on the American ship they weren't quite as friendly. When I pointed to the Turkish pack of cigarettes and said, "No good, no good. Do you have good cigarettes?" an American sailor pulled out a pack of Marlboro Lights, said, "Good cigarettes," and then put them back in his pocket. Foo.

A few days later Malkhazi bounded into our flat and said, "Juliet! Cook me a cutlet!"

"Pardon?" she asked.

"Or, I will buy you a cutlet. Come Juliet, Slims too! Let's go for a drive."

"Why are you in such a good mood?" I asked him. "What happened? Did you give the English captain wine and a sword? Because that might actually work. Anthony . . ."

"No, Slims," he said. "You joke. You joke. To tell you the truth, the Turkish ship came back yesterday from its second voyage. This time I said to the British master, 'You measure.' I stood there staring at him with my arms crossed, just watching him do his own measurements. Every time he looked at me I just said, 'Go ahead.' And then he found a discrepancy, himself, of five hundred and thirty tons. So his company decided not to sue after all. I told him, 'After you take that ship on about twelve more voyages, you'll be able to find the average and can then adjust the calculations correctly.' I am friends with all the Turkish sailors now. One of them even suggested I marry his daughter. I told him, 'Even though I am learning to love Turkish people, I could never marry into your family because you like sugar on your meat dishes. Meat is not a cookie.'"

It was the beginning of summer now and the tourists were returning to Batumi. So many Armenians were driving their Mercedes to our beaches again. I thought about how already a year had passed since Malkhazi and I had sat on the beach without a job, only listening to the radio. Now, already, a new ice cream shop had opened in Batumi that claimed to have American flavors. When we drove past it I told Malkhazi, "You must try American ice cream." We ordered pistachio and Juliet ordered cinnamon. We took our ice creams outside.

"This is so delicious," Malkhazi said and threw his ice cream into the street. He was developing a modern man's flair for sarcasm.

"Try this one," Juliet said, handing him her ice cream cone. "It's spicy."

Malkhazi took a bite and made a face. "Next they will be making goulash ice cream."

When we got back to the car Malkhazi took eight thousand lari from his pocket, put it into both of our faces, and laughed. "I was paid today by the British captain. It's enough to buy my own visa to England. Juliet, if you go there I will join you. You better not let me have any wine today or I really might do it."

"Do you have any wine?" Juliet whispered to me.

"No," I said.

"Neither do I," she said.

Malkhazi drove to Gocha's new cafe near the bus depot. We stayed in the car while Malkhazi gave Gocha four thousand lari. Gocha counted it and nodded his head.

I still had the pens I had stolen off the ship. As we drove away I threw them to Gocha and said, "Give these to Tamriko. I stole them." Gocha gave me a puzzled expression.

"Ha!" Malkhazi said, pounding his fist on the steering wheel and driving away. "Did you just see that? I had eight thousand lari, enough to buy a visa to leave this country! And I didn't do it! I will remember this day forever. Now we really must celebrate!"

We flew up the road, through the familiar mountains, listening to the lyrics, "I belong to you, you belong to me." As we drove, the world of green trees was waving at us outside the windows of the car. We stopped at a bean bread place and bought six breads. There was no place to buy wine so we had to buy it at a Russian store, the one that only sells port. "The Russians always love to go to the forest and sing songs about their port," Malkhazi said. "'Ooh, ooh, me and my port,'" Malkhazi sang and then wiped his sweating forehead with a handkerchief. We parked the car and from there walked into the mountains, lighting people's cigarettes along the way.

We walked farther on, to Maxunseti, the waterfall near Queen Tamar's arched stone bridge, and drank from the water there. Malkhazi proffered wild honey, cheese, and the bean breads. We made a huge bonfire.

The trees were heavy with plums. We meandered down to the river. "Here!" Malkhazi demanded to Juliet. "Sit on this rock!"

She told him that the more polite way to say this was, "Would you *please* sit on this rock?"

"Really?" he asked, starting to laugh. "That is the English way? I must say *please* if I want to help you from getting wet? This water is cold! I just don't want you to catch a cold."

We opened the bottle of port and Malkhazi drank without making a toast. "I can be an English person too," he said, sipping experimentally. "I can adjust to anything. I am ready to give up toasting."

"Please, don't," Juliet said.

I sat silently, staring at waterfall gush.

"Juliet," Malkhazi said. "Do you understand me? I am ready to give up my culture. For you."

"Please," I said. "Don't."

We all sat in silence. The rocks reflected the shimmers of the river water.

It was late now; the light was gone. We walked back to the car, all of us silent. The drive home was long.

I had fallen asleep but I woke up when Malkhazi pulled up to the entrance of our flat.

"So here we are," Malkhazi said softly to Juliet. "Sitting in this car in the middle of the night."

"Here we are," she said.

"It's the middle of the night. Juliet, aren't you ever afraid of me?"

"Well, my brother is asleep in the backseat," she said.

"If *I* were a woman I would be scared of me. I can't understand why no woman is ever afraid of me. I am like *kurdi*. I thought Georgian girls were crazy for *kurdi*."

I opened my eyes and saw him yawn and look at his watch. "It's three in the morning." He indicated the first-floor flat where the light was still on. "What are they doing awake? Maybe I will go to sleep right here," he said, leaning back in his seat and closing his eyes. "But unfortunately, I can't sleep. I must go back to the damn Turkish ship. First, though, I will carry you to your door."

"No," she said.

"Why? Give me one good reason why not."

"Because I have my own legs."

"That is a weak excuse."

"Because I am too heavy."

"I am waiting. You are only giving weak excuses."

"Because we . . ."

"I think you were about to say it."

"Because the whole town would be talking about it the next day."

"That's the correct answer," he said and shook her hand. "But at least I will walk you to the door."

Neither of them got out of the car. They just sat in the silence. I imagined Armenians being born.

"Those damned Russians who created this car," he said. "This is supposed to be car for a couple, yes? And look at this space in between the seats."

I laughed out loud at the two feet between them.

26.

ON AUGUST 19, 2003, THE DAY OF TURNING THIS YEAR, THE weather just got hotter. All the grapes withered and turned to raisins before the harvest. The icons in the churches started weeping again, but this time everyone was so riveted by the politicians arguing on TV that no one noticed. My cousin Ben Hur, in the village, told me later that only when a neighbor's cow fell off a cliff did the whole village turn off their TV sets and mourn.

For two months we listened to battery-powered radios while the politicians argued. Even Mr. Fax kept the radio on at work. A week before the elections, Fax and I were sitting in the conference room with some Ukrainian soldiers when the news announcer told us that our own local dictator had just arrived back home from Switzerland. The dictator announced over Adjarian radio, "Oh, my people! You lacked electricity while I was away in Switzerland?" In a sweet voice he said to whoever must have been sitting beside him, "Why didn't you tell me?" Pretending to be a superhero, he must have pulled some sort of lever because he lit up the whole city at once. He spewed electricity into every house, every hut, every barn.

I had thought that Anthony had left the country by now, but in fact he had continued to live (or perhaps hide out) at the Paradise Hotel, and he told me later that even that place got its electricity back. And such a high quality of electricity it was! The refrigerators didn't shake. The water, scalding, came all the way up to the eighth floors. The communal vacuum hummed continuously through the flats. Everyone was so saturated with light that after a week we forgot there had ever been darkness. We took hot baths at home, invited people over, ironed our clothes, slept with the lights on. Now that there was light in the hallways, I thought that I might catch a glimpse of Tamriko. But I saw her only once, when she passed me the vacuum.

I even heard someone on the street reciting a snatch of the old socialist poem that Joseph Grishashvili wrote fifty years ago in honor of the opening of the hydroelectric station in Khrami:

I drink in pride a toast to my dear native land!
As I behold electric lamps gleam everywhere,
To demagogues of foreign countries I declare—
These piecing rays have struck you blind, you fear the light;
You are the slaves of night, corrupting truth and right.
No man can cleave these waters with a mighty sword,
No force can dissever us, no enemy horde!

And with electricity came TV! The entire day we could watch the local station broadcasting the surging violence far away in the capital—young men hoarding stones to throw at the parliament, old women in the market surrounding the electric company's representative, and other images of the suspicion generated in Tbilisi that usually comes before an election: people marching in front of the parliament, too poor to afford artillery equipment, but with a rage far beyond indignation, a desperate appeal for a regime change that would bring back the electricity once and for all.

Once, many years ago, as a result of remonstrations like these, President Shevardnadze canceled sessions for the day. That afternoon he even resigned. Ten minutes later he changed his mind, promising, however, that he would not run again. But he reneged on his promise and ran again. And still again, for ten years. "And here we go again," I told Malkhazi.

* * *

November, the month of the parliamentary elections, is also called the month of truth because it is the month of Saint Giorgi's Day, our patron saint of Georgia. In Georgia we like holidays very much—so much that we have two or more of every kind. We have many days for women and we have two days for love: the first one is for romantic love, and only romantic songs are allowed to be played over the radio; the second is the Day of Spiritual Love and you don't have to be in a couple to celebrate that one. We have two Christmases, and two New Years, but that is because we have two calendars. But even before we had two calendars we had two Saint Giorgi Days—the first is to remember the time he died, the second is just to remember him. But this is nothing because we used to celebrate his day *every day*.

To celebrate the first Saint Giorgi's Day in November, my mother agreed to make honey walnut brittle for Zuka's class if he cracked the walnuts. As we say in Georgian, "A small walnut can be divided among nine brothers." It means love is limitlessness. But Zuka had already cracked about seven kilos of walnuts, enough to fortify all of the beer factory district with candy. He had reached the bottom of the walnut barrel. Juliet was singing an old Svani mountain lullaby on her guitar, something about crossing a wide sea with only a little candle, I can't remember the exact words because right in the middle of it, Zuka cracked open one of the remaining walnuts and there, on the face of the crinkly meat, was a green and blue icon of Saint Giorgi. The image was tiny but I could clearly see him riding his rearing white horse and slaying a dragon with the tip of his spear. My mother stopped stirring the syrup and put the walnut on the table under the icon lamp. She lit another candle, said a little prayer, made us all say a little prayer, and sent Zuka off to the bishop. When Zuka showed him Saint Giorgi, Zuka said that the bishop said solemnly, "Saint Giorgi always leads our troops in battle." But Zuka said he was tired of wars so he put it back in his pocket. But then the bishop stretched out his palm and demanded, "Give it to me!" But when Zuka fetched the walnut, the icon had disappeared. When he turned his pocket inside out, he saw that the blue and green color had rubbed off on his pocket lining.

Herbalife tells us that since walnuts resemble the shape of the brain, it's good for your health to fill a sack up with walnuts and balance it on your head for twenty minutes. I tried this once and it made me feel giddy. But the walnut that Zuka found that day was not the *brain* of Saint Giorgi. It was his image.

Neither Zuka nor I was afraid of war but we were afraid of invaders always trying to light fire to our forests. And I was afraid of our military parachutes because they didn't often open. We had been invaded in our history so many times you would think we would have gotten used to it, though whenever it happened we still ran off to hide in a fortress or a village somewhere. But on the day that Zuka saw the icon of Saint Giorgi on the walnut, and still now, I do not know if Saint Giorgi was warning us of the invasion by our neighbors across the border or a different type of invasion.

Herbalife says that if you take a bath in boiled walnut shells and think about something you are willing to give up the contours of the walnut shells collect your old habits and you are no longer burdened by them. But when I put the shells on to boil, I forgot about them, left them on the stove, and all the walnuts scorched the bottom of the pot. All the contours disintegrated so they would not hold any more histories. I couldn't help wondering if my history with Tamriko was scorched at the bottom of a pot.

November 23 was the second Saint Giorgi's Day, and the bells were ringing in the churches. My mother laid the table with a white cloth, and everyone took the day off. On Saint Giorgi's Day you must give a present to everyone whose name is Giorgi. Most everyone's name is Giorgi, so everyone was shopping.

For the elections this year, the officials, with the advice of an American think tank, decided to mark everyone who voted with ink.

"But it must be invisible ink," insisted the bishop.

"Ah yes," agreed the American think tank. "So that no one can find it in order to wash it off."

"No," retorted the bishop. "So they will vote. Only the devil marks people. People already believe that the politicians are the devil. You think they will vote if they are going to be marked by the devil?"

On Election Day the morning was crisp. November's leaves lay like ripped orange wrapping paper after a birthday party. I alighted from the bus and walked to the Center for Democracy feeling like an American prepared to participate in my civic duty. Juliet had helped me iron my pants so that, like in Soviet times, they had only one crease. And on the bus I had flipped through my stack of cards on which I had written my favorite English verbs. *To hope. To aspire. To strive. To achieve.* A man behind me, some sort of jokester, reading over my shoulder, had announced the name of a girl to everyone on the bus every time I flipped a card: "Nino . . . Mzia . . . Salome . . . Marika," as if, instead of preparing to vote, I was trying to decide which girl to call. I glared at him and asked, "Are you going to vote?"

Of course he was, he said. He had come all the way from the village. In the village, huddled around the heater, they talk politics so much they even know what George Bush will do next—before Bush himself knows.

At the Center for Democracy I nodded to Geloti, the security guard. In Georgian the name Geloti is given to the first son of a family who has only had daughters. It means, "We have been waiting for you." But apparently he had not been waiting for me. "So sorry, Slims," he said. "But we have run out of ballots."

At first I believed him. I was extremely disappointed and blamed myself for not arriving earlier. After all, paper is very expensive and it is for this reason that Batumi's publishing house could only afford to publish *Volume I*, up to the letter *N*, of our Georgian/English Dictionary.

But then I saw Geloti open the door for a woman who was traipsing out on extremely high heels, a distant cousin of our local dictator. He helped her to walk down the steps, leaving me to peer through the open door. And that's when I saw Gocha, mini-mafioso of the peewee golf course, cramming a baker's dozen of ballots into the box.

I became extremely irritated. So did a man inside who began

yelling that his name and his wife's name were not on the voter registration list. I looked around for some kind of justice, but it wasn't easily located. I sat down on the steps and proceeded to watch who was allowed to vote and who was turned away. Niko, the finger puppet theater director, was turned away, probably for the candid remark he had made last week in the newspaper, "I like the dictator. But I like his wife even more."

After Gocha left the building he was allowed to vote once again, half an hour later, even though he had already voted quite a number of times.

I tried to cheer myself up about not voting by telling myself that I must be a very important person that they would deny me this right. Perhaps our imperious dictator, through one of his assistants, or through a hypersensitive recording device in a ceiling vent, had concluded that since I had gone to America I might have cultivated certain sensibilities toward Tbilisi, the capital, and away from the provincial interests of Batumi.

I bought a Kazbegi beer. Under the beer's influence—and noticing the sun sparkling on the warm, emerald bottle—I became sensitive to the beauty of the winter light. "Light. It is light that is important. Whoever wins this election, may the sun always shine on his head," I said, and raised my glass to Shalva, the policeman, who was standing by the side of the road, bowing and waving at the women who drove past. One stopped her car and gave him a bag of apples. Shalva divvied them up on the curb and gave me half. I spit out the seeds for the blackbirds.

At the end of the voting day, the electricity quivered, and like the candle in Vaja Pshavela's poem, "its light embraced the hearths, and at times gleamed brighter still, but then flickered low and died."

A pair of European election observers—some sort of official scrutineers—emerged from the Center for Democracy rolling their necks, which were so stiff from their intense observation work. They wore bright yellow badges advertising the importance of their work. Fortunately, they hadn't already made an appointment, as I could tell by their halfhearted steps shuffling in one direction and then in the other. I knew I must address this issue very diplomatically so I shuffled, a little experimentally, until my strides matched theirs, and asked them, "*Romeli satia*"—what is the time, in Georgian. They didn't understand Georgian and made this clear to me by using the un-Georgian body language of raising their eyebrows and bobbing their heads.

"Ah, you are foreigners!" I said. "Do you know Anthony?"

"Who's Anthony?" they asked.

"It's a joke," I said. "But you should meet him. You would all really like each other, I think." I gave them my business card—it had an emblem of a sheriff's star in the left-hand corner—to let them know I was not merely a Georgian peasant. I led them to the Cafe Soviet Nostalgia because I knew today was the day that the violin player played in the basement.

"The electricity is out here," one of the election observers said while adjusting his ski cap. "Let's go to a different place."

"Ah, but the elections are over so the electricity is out everywhere," I said. "We can sit by the window for some light. Also the women are the most beautiful here." From Tamriko, I ordered some *khachapuri* and Kazbegi beer.

I couldn't understand everything they spoke about because as we waited for our food the two only cavorted in Swedish to each other. When I began to feel a little bored I ordered another beer and demonstrated to Tamriko how I could open it with my belly button.

When our food arrived, with the golden yolk of the hen floating on top of a steaming boat of farmer cheese, I said, "Sunny-side up!" in order to assure them that I was no mere dilettante of the English language and it wasn't my intention to use them only to practice my English, but that I had more serious matters to discuss. I wanted to wink at them but felt so sorry for them as I watched their struggle with the *khachapuri*, cutting into it with their knives and forks, all the butter leaking off the bread into a puddle on the platter.

"It's okay to use your fingers," I said and tore off the outer railing of the bread boat to demonstrate how to scoop up some cheese and dip it in the yolk.

After they had taken a few sips of beer and had spoken to me about the exaggerated alcoholic content of it, I stooped my head toward theirs and whispered, "What would you do if you saw someone, one person, stuffing fifteen ballots into the ballot box?"

They looked at each other. One man cleared his throat; looked down at his beer; and turned it, slowly, counterclockwise on the table. He said that they were sent to observe, not to interfere, and that he had seen these *irregularities* and had noted them in his book with the date and the time. His voice lacked contrition, didn't even try to feign it.

"But what is the use of that?" I asked. "Don't you know, we Georgians will try to get away with anything?"

"We are here only to observe," he said. "Not to act as police."

"But what is the use?"

"Diplomatic purposes," the other man said.

"Georgian elections are like women," the first said. "So changeable." He was trying to change the subject.

Right then the electricity came on. "Ah," I said, pointing to the light. "A sign. Perhaps you are right. Tamriko!" I yelled. "He says the elections are like women. Would you agree?"

But she hadn't heard me because a newly electrified radio in the kitchen crackled forth, "I wear my sunglasses at night."

Even though I usually had the *chonguri* in my heart, filling my blood with the resonance of a traditional Georgian instrument, reminding me what and who is a Georgian, this modern disco music, this doom-boom-doom music, started to speed everything up. Now I had to align my heart to *that* beat, and where there is speed there is no feeling. It reminded us all, sitting in the restaurant, what people in Western modern countries were feeling. Subversively, the music whispered to us *catch up!* with the heroic rhythm of a UN rescue helicopter on the slopes of Mount Kazbegi, evacuating skiers out of the snow—those who got stuck in the chairlift when the electricity went out.

The sun was setting like a huge pimento, gilding the restaurant tables in goodbye light. But nobody was noticing because we were all nodding our heads up and down to the rhythm of this American song.

I said, "Listening to this music is the way that we feel close to you in the West because it is your main emotional reality."

They became indignant; they claimed that this had nothing to do with their emotional reality. "It's music from the eighties," one of them said. "And we're Swedish." Yet even *they* couldn't help nodding their heads up and down to its dictatorial rhythm. I watched them: one spoke into the ear of the other. The man nodded and waited his turn to respond. Both of their hands were splayed on the checkered red-and-white tablecloth, hunching over their foamy tankards of high alcohol content beer.

It was only then, while listening to this Western music, watching everyone nod in tune to an unelected melody, something native to neither our soil nor our soul, did I remember my promise to the eternal Toastmaster in the sky, how I had once wanted to put forth an individual effort. But to bring real democracy to Georgia could only be accomplished through collective effort.

"Are you writing a political document?" Malkhazi asked leaning over my shoulder to try to see what I was writing. "Because if it is, it's going to be the most boring thing in the world to read."

"Do you think the politicians will be offended at what I write?" I asked.

"Well now," he considered. "That depends entirely upon whom you dedicate it to."

That evening, after the results from the elections had been tallied, we learned that old Shevardnadze had won again! One hundred and twenty percent of the population had purportedly voted for him. And so, it seemed that once again democratic values were thrown into the rubbish bin.

"Looks like you're going to have to dedicate your book to *him*," Malkhazi said as we watched the election programming on TV. A big brass band was playing our anthem and ol' Shevardnadze was smiling.

He still wore a suit that looked like it was from communist times, but the later period, around the time the first lightbulb commercials appeared. The program was interrupted, however, to show the beginning of a ferment in front of the Parliament Building. Usually, the only protesters were the retired grandfathers. But now, after fourteen years without light, water, and movement, the people's resentment had increased to such a degree that the usual posse of old men, women, and communists were joined by young people. I even saw some old school friends from the university on TV. They, and so many others, were gathering on the steps, under the columns, in the middle of the intersection where the statue of King David on his horse seemed to be girding people up. It was becoming clear that something was going to happen. I wanted to join them.

This new Saakashvili was using the high quality, advanced, technical diplomatic skills of the West. There were so many people gathered in the main square, even the ice cream seller was getting some good business. Saakashvili wrestled the ice cream seller's megaphone away from him and shouted to the people to come together side-by-side. "Sing!" he shouted. At first only one or two obeyed. But soon others began to harmonize in a polyphonic tune.

Eduard Shevardnadze fortified the parliament with more of his guards. In the air was the old familiar aroma of civil war. But both parties knew what civil war meant; Mikheil Saakashvili knew he had to be careful. Everyone knew that if even one person was shot, too much blood would be spilt. Saakashvili decided that none of the protestors should be armed. He took away their guns and their swords and announced that true victory could only be achieved with flowers —in particular, a rose.

"If there was ever a time to steal a flower for your girl, this is the time," Malkhazi told me.

People from every corner of Georgia came to Tbilisi in transports filled with roses. The military watched wearily, but to speak truthfully, they were bored with old Eddy Shevy's policies too. In fact, the soldiers could not suppress their astonishment and admiration. They had not expected such an immense crowd. "There isn't even room to swing a cat," one of them was quoted as saying the next day in the newspaper.

At home, Juliet was even preparing to join them. She was wearing all kinds of bags over her shoulder. One of the straps had broken so she had replaced it with a telephone cord. "Brotherhood has come back to Georgia," she said. "They are all holding hands in front of the parliament building. Saakashvili has called for people to join him, even from Western Georgia."

In the villages, the atrophied rosebushes, the ones garlanding the Stalin statues, perked up. We gathered them by the bushel, all the unruly ones growing out of control up the balconies. We gathered the *Rhododendron caucasicum*, also known as the snow rose of the alpine meadows—the secret to long life when you drink it. We gathered the five-petaled roses, associated with the five wounds of Christ, and the blood red ones symbolizing the blood of the martyrs. Like Georgian Don Quixotes we held out our roses like swords.

Malkhazi said he would drive. But as soon as our local dictator realized that Saakashvili meant to reunify Georgia, to take over Adjaria, he declared a state of emergency and closed down the borders to our province. His own residence was no longer safe. His Russian soldiers roamed the streets trying to protect him. Putin called Bush and left a voice mail. A bridge exploded. The dictator had blown up the bridge over the Choloki River, which united our province with the rest of Georgia. Bush called Putin back.

Our local dictator blew up all the bridges, but the Georgian army came into our town by way of the sea. Ten-year-old boys climbed onto tanks and waved Georgian flags.

The dictator had thought that he had the whole of Adjaria in his pocket. He had thrown little salaries and pensions to us like bones to a dog. But now all of Western Georgia was in chaos. In the local villages people harvested the rest of their roses.

Those of us who couldn't come to Tbilisi because of the blocked roads watched the Rustavi 2 news station and saw the streams of vehicles, fifty thousand people filling Freedom Square and Rustaveli Avenue in front of the parliament building. Saakashvili entered the crowd bellowing songs. Every evening and into the morning for almost a whole week they sang, while President Shevardnadze still insisted that he wanted a face-to-face discussion, he wanted a peaceful solution and, if given another chance, he would fight corruption.

At dawn on the day when Shevardnadze would be sworn into office, yet again the hymn sounded in the parliament. It was time for old Eddy Shevardnadze to make his acceptance speech. But the noise of the crowd outside, being urged to sing, was so huge it was like something by Shostakovich—those first seconds, which sound like frying or the static sound we used to have to listen to when we couldn't reach the top button of the old Soviet push button televisions. And then the crowd got its melody back. Mikheil Saakashvili yelled to Edward Shevardnadze through an official bullhorn, "Look here at this crowd. Restore justice to them or resign. If you want a revolution, you will get it!"

Edward Shevardnadze responded, "I tell you there must be no protest meetings. Or disorder! People must calm down, become quiet, and mind their own business. If they do not refrain from using force, the police and the internal army can take care of them!"

"Now or never!" yelled Mikheil Saakashvili.

At exactly that moment the police guarding Shevardnadze realized that their deeds could awe the world. The world would never see again such a peaceful protest or such happiness. Shevy's soldiers, his own military men, refused to defend him against their fellow Georgians. They broke their own cordon and let the people wielding their rose petal weapons into the parliament building. Mikheil Saakashvili and a hundred other young people stormed the parliament carrying so many roses into the hall at the moment Edward Shevardnadze was making his welcoming speech that many wondered if it was actually another holiday for women.

"Resign, resign!" shouted our Saakashvili to Shevardnadze.

"I will not resign!" replied Eduard Shevardnadze. But Shevardnadze's chief guard soon deciphered the situation, surrounded his object of protection, gathered him from his chair, and escaped out of the building.

"I feel hungry," Saakashvili said, and in one sip, finished the cup of tea prepared for Shevardnadze.

That evening Edward Shevardnadze officially resigned and promised journalists that he would write his memoirs.

Euphoria had begun in Georgia. Some began to speak aloud about past violations. Some were so happy they spoke to themselves. "They have gone through a lot of suffering to get here!" reported Western newspapers.

The women leaders thanked the youth who had been particularly active and asked them to be peaceful. The male leaders asked the new troops to be clever and careful. Even the old communists supported Saakashvili.

"We have got a very important mandate from the people to clean up Georgia, to make it peaceful and prosperous, to make Georgia efficient, investor-friendly, to consolidate power," Mikheil Saakashvili said that evening on TV. Comedians were having a field day. "Please don't drink *my* tea," they told him. He ignored their bantering and became stern. "I realize how big a burden I have taken on my shoulders, how big a burden all of us have taken on our shoulders. We are dealing with a failed country, where democracy and success don't even come as natural words for us."

"Will we become part of NATO?" one TV commentator asked.

"Europe has their own problems. They feel nervous all the time. We don't want to increase their headache." He girded himself up like the statue of King David on the square. "We cannot do everything in one day," he reminded us. "We will go step-by-step."

"I hope it's not another step off a cliff," Malkhazi said.

27.

THE FIRST THING SAAKASHVILI DID WHEN HE BECAME PRESIDENT WAS restore the electricity. Like the Great Toastmaster on the first day of creation, he said, "Let there be electric power!" And we examined the light and saw that it was good. Like wine (also like vodka), the light made everyone's thoughts more tender. The old people from the village who had suffered the most especially praised him. Even now my grandfather raises his glass of *chacha* to him when he shows up on TV and says, "At least he brought light. He is a good boy."

But Saakashvili also brought other kinds of light: Marlboro Light, Coca-Cola Light, Christianity Light, Eggplant Light.

"What is eggplant light?" Malkhazi asked at first.

"A banana," I told him.

"I brought bananas to Georgia before Saakashvili," Malkhazi insisted.

Saakashvili, our Misha, he was called, was also called the fountain king because he loves fountains. He also loves little parks with statues of women—especially he loves Ukrainian women, especially in his bed.

On Seaside Boulevard, Saakashvili built a new dancing French fountain operated by a salaried DJ for all the pedestrians to promenade in front of in the evenings. On TV, instead of an old army boot, they show us a close-up of our fountain.

"But our fountain doesn't compare to Barcelona's," Juliet said the first time she visited it.

But it does play Viennese waltzes. Sometimes the DJ gets drunk and pushes all the buttons at once. But then the younger children stopped visiting the fountains. They went to the SuperHyper Market instead, to play with the new American doors, the kind that open and close automatically.

It even became quite stupid to talk about electricity. We didn't have it for thirteen years and now no one wanted to think about that time. "That was a dark time," people said. "Why think about that time?"

The whole town of Batumi was suddenly illuminated, a mockery of darkness. New streetlights splattered light onto every road, and even onto vacant land where there were no roads. Every major municipal building, church, and historical building of any significance—every modern, historic, and even prehistoric cafe glowed with fuchsia, lime, and peacock blue lights. Glimmering plastic palm trees shimmied up and down Seaside Boulevard like showgirls. And in the boulevard the government gave us a Ferris wheel for free—at first it was a gift to make up for all of our suffering, but ten days later they started charging money.

"They want to light up the boulevard when people are still hungry?" Malkhazi complained.

Pop music began to pump through the loudspeakers, ricocheting across the sea. We suddenly had one of the best sound systems in the region. Then I saw a billboard advertising Wi-Fi for the tourists. But the bungalows on the beach, the little thatched holiday shacks run by tough guys—Gocha's former bodyguards—were still empty. "Where-oh-where are the tourists that Saakashvili promised?" I heard an old woman say on the bus, looking out at all the changes. She was whimpering, "Oh, I don't want Saakashvili." She wiped her eyes with her headscarf and the woman sitting next to her patted her back.

Saakashvili's government acquired some paint and slathered grape, strawberry, and lemon candy colors over all of the buildings in our beer factory district. He didn't ask anyone's opinion of what color they preferred because it would have taken too long for us all to agree. Now we were no longer called the beer factory district but "cartoon village showcase." It became a very prestigious part of town.

"We are now part of the beau monde," Juliet said, excited at first. But then she had to start telling our guests, "Don't look in that direction," pointing to the Turkish cranes demolishing the old buildings. "It's not beautiful. Only look in that direction, at the sea."

"*Vai may!* An earthquake," Tamriko started frequently yelling from her balcony.

"It's not an earthquake," Juliet would reassure her. "It's just the Turkish businessmen jackhammering the sidewalk."

Saakashvili and his cohort also repainted the streets in Tbilisi, but only the ones that President George Bush would see when he rode by in his entourage. And they garlanded all the balconies along the route from the airport with plastic flowers. Saakashvili liked George Bush very much. He liked his style. He liked the prefab, golf pro look. I think they both belonged to the same country club.

After Saakashvili gave us our light back, the next thing he did was build a new airport.

The news broadcasters announced on TV: "He is doing so much work, working so fast that some people think America is giving him drugs. How else could he be working so fast?"

When people asked our Misha what kind of drugs he was taking he said, "Some people are accusing me of walking too fast, of being too frantic, but that's because I'm in a hurry to help Georgia. We've lost a lot of time. I hope we can make up for it."

On the day he completed his airport project he was very proud. Naturally, he showed it off on TV. But that evening the roof blew off. He was very confounded. Isn't that a good word? Or is dumbfounded a better word? It describes his expression exactly, as well as everyone else's.

Then a Georgian billionaire from Moscow built a theme park—complete with roller coasters and an inflatable castle—on the main highway not far from my village. Entrance was free all summer. A sign out front said, "With love, a cottage becomes a castle." But I think this wasn't the proper meaning of the proverb. This billionaire wanted to show Georgians, "You see? Investment can benefit you directly." People were still suspicious though. They said, "We thought the *Ferris wheel* was free, but now they have started charging for *that*." This billionaire also bought up four kilometers of beach, the cleanest part where the sand is fine, and we lost all our public access.

People started complaining to Saakashvili when the Kazakh businessmen began construction on a Sheraton Hotel in Batumi. They said, "You want us to look like a tourist resort in Florida?" That night Saakashvili made an announcement on television. He said, "Some people are accusing me of trying to make Batumi look like Florida. They say that I watched too much *Baywatch* when I lived in America. But soon Batumi will look like Cádiz, or some other such European coastal town, because we are an ancient culture."

"What's wrong with looking like Florida?" Zuka asked.

Saakashvili even moved our national statue of King David the Builder in Tbilisi to the suburbs. He replaced it with a statue of Ronald Reagan. Then he added another monument to a Kazakh hero to honor all the Kazakh businessmen who were now investing in Georgia. The investment project was called the new Silk Road Project. And in Batumi the minister of finance built a statue of Medea, the Georgian wife of Jason of the ship of Argo, who searched throughout Georgia for the Golden Fleece. On the streets you could hear the taxi drivers discussing it. "Have you seen the new statue of Medea?" they would ask.

"Her nose is disproportioned. She's so unattractive I don't want to go to the square anymore."

"But why build a monument to that woman? She betrayed her father and killed her brother and her two sons."

At first these new developments were surprising, in the same way that miracles surprise us. But then I went to the post office and saw that it was for sale. Saakashvili doesn't like post offices?

"It's worse than five years ago," Malkhazi complained. "*Everything* is for sale. It's a catastrophe."

"Cata*strophe*," Juliet added. It seemed she had now decided to forget about English and learn French!

And for Malkhazi, especially, it was a catastrophe. He lost his job in the port. Saakashvili's men had put everyone who had made any money in oil into jail. Malkhazi began to grow anxious waiting for when he might be put in jail too. The biggest construction project Saakashvili had started was his new psychological project: constructing a Georgian mentality layered with fear.

"The university *and* the hospital are for sale," Malkhazi said. "Turkey and China are buying up everything. At least the beer factory district is now considered a *good* area, but I have no money for anything extra. I finally have time to go to the forest to relax, but I can't afford the gas to get there. No one can afford to put more than twenty-two tetri on their cell phones these days. You never get to finish a conversation."

"Don't be very stupid," Zuka said. "Now we have everything. Datsun. Daewoo. Hyundai."

"No, Zuka," Malkhazi said. "Just go outside and listen for yourself. Listen to what the taxi drivers are saying." We could hear them complaining through the open windows of our flat. "Who can buy their own flat now for seven and three zeros?" they were saying. "Now a flat costs twenty-five and three zeros."

But good things were happening too. Since so many hotels were being built, Tamriko quit her job at the Cafe Soviet Nostalgia and got a good job as a secretary for a building supply company. She said Saakashvili planned to build a Dutch restaurant in the shape of a windmill, and even a restaurant for tourists that was upside down. Our crazy president was even going to build a business institute with a swirling restaurant on top. It would be decorated with the letters of the Georgian alphabet because many say the Georgian alphabet resembles strands of DNA.

I wondered where Saakashvili was getting all his money.

Some change had come over Fax. At work he started drinking only one cup of coffee a day instead of his usual eight. He stopped smoking and started speaking in a placating manner, and he even asked about me, as if he was concerned about me. But then, he was put in jail too.

* * *

And we were really becoming a cosmopolitan country! When some Turkish businessmen opened a restaurant-uniform factory in Sarpi, the town bordering Georgia and Turkey, Zuka quit making furniture and started working there instead. We all went to the opening ceremony because they promised to have a good buffet afterwards. Saakashvili was there too, surrounded by bodyguards, their arms crossed in front of them.

Saakashvili stood at the podium in front of the factory, robust and rather pink, next to tables neatly lined with champagne flutes on little doilies and attended to by attractive Ukrainian women. They were modern women; they wore short skirts and heels. Saakashvili tightened his purple tie and announced, "Today is a great day. It represents great progress for our country. Our guests from Turkey used to be afraid of us, afraid to open up factories in Georgia." The fountain king stopped talking in order to smile at his Turkish customers. "But now everything is peaceful and they can begin bringing in employment opportunities. We now invite our guests to come up."

The Turkish factory owner stood before us, also robust, corporeal, giving us advice. "You may look at me now and think that I have had certain advantages I was born into," he said. "But I started working when I was seven years old. I had five brothers and we all shared the same room growing up. I am here to tell you, if you have a head on your shoulders and two good hands, if you're willing to work hard, you can succeed in anything you do. To do something great, it's not necessary to be Superman, just to be willing to work hard, to pull yourself up."

We were appalled! We had *heard* the Turks made their little children work when they were only seven years old. We didn't realize it was *true*. "How uncivilized!" I heard someone remark to another.

28.

THEN THE JEHOVAH'S WITNESSES TOOK OVER THE SIDEWALK. THEY WERE
setting up a display table near the entrance of the church. When I
walked by I whispered, "Please God, if I'm ever hungry, don't let me
be tempted by the Jehovah's Witnesses." The Jehovah's Witnesses are
very rich people. They brought a lot of money to Georgia. The quality
of the paper in their teaching books is the highest level. Even if you
try to burn the pages, you can't.

The main problem was that Batumi's bishop had a scenic face,
like a movie star, and people were suspicious of this. He should have
had a common face. He also took vacations in five different countries.
When people were hungry and they saw his face they said, "Look at
him! He preaches one thing but does another, and he resembles that
actor from that new Brazilian serial, *Blanca's Widow*."

So our own village priest came to town and began to speak of the
time that Jerusalem was destroyed, described the time when people had
grown weary of waiting for God. They had been invaded and their holy
city had fallen apart. "How long did they have to wait?" the village priest
asked. "How long do we have to wait until our lives are restored? When
will God bring the promised blessing? When will we be renewed? We do
not always feel that we are moving forward toward love. Sometimes it
feels like a lunatic world. But we are living in the same world as Isaiah.

The loss I speak of today is not only the loss of our ancient culture, the loss I speak of is the loss of the act of waiting. When I say we have lost the act of waiting, I don't mean only the loss of waiting for light. We've lost the hope and life that happens within the waiting, the love that happens within the waiting. We've all had losses and you've all had to wait out the grieving. But now these Jehovah's Witnesses, brothers, will give you a car. You want a car? Oh it looks so shiny. Washed clean after its drive here through Bulgaria. But now you no longer know how to wait out your impulses of wanting that car. I say it's better to wait it out." He suddenly became so angry that he grabbed a Jehovah's Witness by the neck, bent his head down, and shaved a cross on his head.

Saakashvili came after the old priest with his entourage of snipers, though, and put that father, our very own, in jail.

On TV the new priests were blessing the gas stations. It was a little embarrassing. They were blessing the brandy, the meat, forcing the public to drink, even the pregnant women. On the street children were singing the song from the commercial now playing on TV: "Coca-Cola goes with *pelamooshi, kingkali, padrajani.*"

I overhead Tamriko at a cafe complaining to Juliet. "I have lost my spiritual father," she said. "I haven't been able to make any confessions. In church the new patriarch only speaks about how you must be kind, you must help each other, give to beggars. Foo! I know that. Who doesn't? Who doesn't already do that? It's nothing new. He says, 'All nations are brothers.' He should speak about something more relevant. He should speak about our land! About life! Flesh! Saints! Give us some *true* feeling. *Vaimay!* Forgive me. Oy!" she said and crossed herself. When I heard that I felt like punching my thigh.

In the villages people had started to drink. I mean, even more than they used to. According to some reports in the newspaper, ninety-five percent of the people were drunk when they were on their deathbeds. This meant they met their creator in a tipsy state. But really they drank so they could understand modern economics better and judge it more correctly. They would drink and then say, "If I give *you* wine, then actually you should give *me* five kilos of *beans*!" They used to give more freely. For the village women it was worse. Prostitution was at the highest level. If one man had a lot of money, like a sheriff in a small state, he had many women.

When Saakashvili started shutting down the universities, Juliet began to worry she would lose her job. Saakashvili said that too many people in Georgia were overly educated and with such high degrees no one would want to do the service work in hotels. "I'm afraid that soon I will lose my job at the university and will have to get a job working as a housekeeper in the Sheraton," Juliet said.

"They are trying to make Georgia without Georgians," Malkhazi complained. "During Soviet times we had to speak Russian. Now we must all speak English?" Actually, *all* the men started complaining about it. They said, "Now we must learn this *girly* language?"

Dear Hillary,

I take it back. I didn't mean it. I wanted the law but not like this. I didn't mean the American *law.*

We had two bank robberies last week in Tbilisi. The police surrounded the bank robbers and began shooting at them. A policeman was shot in the forehead. Wait! I will explain it to you. They ordered the robbers to put their hands up. You know, "Don't move!" like they do in America, but the robbers weren't accustomed to this type of American tradition so they moved and the police started shooting. Ax!! Everything takes after America now. Before, the police and the criminals were on the same side. One of the bank robbers was the director of an elementary school. He just wanted to give his teachers better salaries. On the news they are showing how they are arresting everyone who the bank robbers had contact with.

"*Sheni deyda!*" Malkhazi yelled at the news on TV. "It's so stupid. If your best friend calls and has just committed a crime in order to feed his family and he pleads to you, 'I need help,' how can you possibly refuse?"

"Some counterfeiters are also on the loose," Juliet said. "If we see them we are supposed to call this new police force. But I don't know that telephone number. Even if I did I wouldn't call. If the people were making fake money, obviously they needed it."

"Before," Malkhazi complained, "if you didn't have anything, at least you could steal something. Now we have all these new police putting people in prison."

On television the politicians were yelling louder, explaining why they were putting each other in jail. "Do not think that I put you in jail because I'm trying to get revenge. I put you in jail because you *should* be put in jail."

America also gave Georgia technologically advanced spying equipment. If an official from Kutaisi took a bribe they made a big show of it on TV. Forty official police cars would flash their lights. They would escort the bribery-maker out of the building. The police were not good actors though because when they saw all those cameras up close they couldn't stop smiling. But if you looked at any young security guard in front of a bank, he was biting his fingernails, afraid to be bribed, afraid to be caught. Even the police station walls were knocked down and replaced with glass as a symbol of transparency. Saakashvili forced the police to pay back the money that they had taken as bribes. They were forced to pay back a hundred million dollars.

"One hundred and twenty million dollars," Malkhazi corrected me. "Or else they go to jail. One third of Georgia is in jail now. But who knows what happens there? Why don't they make the jails transparent? If you fight in the middle of the street and block the traffic it's ten years in prison or ten thousand dollars. If you have some black market operation where you take a bribe for three thousand dollars and divide it between five people, and if you are caught, each person must pay Saakashvili ten thousand dollars each. You must sell your car, mortgage your house. I don't know what's going to happen. I want to go back to the village before they get me for something. Oh, I don't know anything anymore. Maybe it's better to follow the law like in America. Then you have a stable society. But we like freedom too much." Malkhazi was so tired, his balding head so shiny. He sighed and sighed. "Ah, I will clean my gun now."

I thought it was only happening to young boys on the street—other boys—but then our own Zuka was thrown into jail. He had stolen a mobile phone from a girl, hoping that she would chase after him. "Oh, it's so stupid!" Malkhazi groaned when he heard. "Ai yai yai! Why didn't I teach him better? Zuka thinks that is romance?" Malkhazi went to the police station and, due to his ability to talk to policemen, was able to extricate Zuka from jail, but all the way home he lectured him. "Zuka, listen, these days, if you take someone's mobile phone it's five years in jail! That's the new law now."

"But you always said that girls like *kurdi*."

"Foo! You don't know what *kurdi* are. *Kurdi* are noble men. They never take someone else's *property*. Do you know what prison is like? Ten men in a cell. There is not even enough room to sit. They have to take turns."

Dear Hillary,

Everyone is confused. It's too complicated, not simple anymore. Saakashvili is tearing down people's homes. They must live in the yard. The new government is checking everyone's papers now to ensure that they are the official owners of their houses, scouring the countryside for people without papers, trying to implement these new American laws. But in some mountains, like Svanetia, the people have lived in their towers for 1,200 years and now they must show their papers, these proofs of purchase? I can understand if it's in a town. But the president is requiring this even from the hard workers next to my village, the ones who are living in the abandoned tea factory because their villages fell off the mountain. You understand, Hillary, right? Before, there were no laws. There was no one here thinking about private property. People built houses at the bottom of the hill or inhabited old factories. Now this president is asking for the paperwork. If they don't produce it he will move them to the border with Armenia. Their land is valuable seaside property, you know.

Everything comes from America now, even this Saturday night live show on TV. They show Playboy pictures and sing about the sexy daughter-in-law in the background. It is important to have something sacred inside. Yes? What is going to happen with this capitalism? I worry. Money makes people crazy and they lose the sacred thing inside. We are not like Turkish people who work all the time. We Georgians believe we were put on this earth to relax, to enjoy the Paradise that God gave us, to have good thoughts and good deeds. It is not noble to think one thing, speak another, write another, and do another. So I will stop writing to you now. Remember me. My name is Slims Achmed Makashvili and I am from the twelfth century.

p.s. If your country ever experiences the economic problems that we did, and heads toward a collapse, remember that it happens so quickly. Soon the roads become like the garden. But remember this: when you only think about how to put bread on the table there is no more time for metaphysics, no more time for depression. And if that ever happens, don't worry, be happy! Soon you will have rich Georgian tourists crazy for American nostalgia.

Now that Fax was in jail our little Maritime Ministry of Law became a completely volunteer organization. Since most men won't work for free, only the women kept working. The good thing about this was that for once I could work full time with Anthony—without Fax's resistance—to convince BP and the Georgian government to spend more money in order to use a different sealant on the pipelines to prevent them from leaking. And for the first time in my life, with Anthony's help, my little law firm won a case against the government. None of my friends believed me when I told them. They said, "How is it possible to beat the government? No it isn't possible, I don't believe you, you are lying." But I told them, "Of course the government will repeal, but a great thing has happened. I stumped the judge. Anthony and I presented before her fifty-two pages of American- and British-style facts, of why they must use a better sealant."

The judge crumpled under the weight of so many facts, banged her hammer on the Turkish desk, called a recess, and said that for now, we, the little people had won. But the little people didn't believe me. They said, "We are the little people. We do not win such things. It is our destiny to suffer, we are Georgians," and so on and so on. They are more difficult to convince than the opposition.

"Actually," I told Juliet the evening I heard, "instead of Medea in the square, they should erect a monument to Anthony."

Now with electricity, we spent all our time at home watching TV. Malkhazi had started questioning everything. He even started defending Saakashvili. On the news a crowd of people were yelling, "Misha, go to Holland and sell your roses there and let us sell our own wine!" Saakashvili had just bought up all the wine in Kakheti.

"Saakashvili wants to change the character of our wine to make it more palatable to Western financiers," I complained to Malkhazi. "He's watering it down. So of course the Russians say, 'We don't want your wine.'"

"Oh, *sheni deyda*, Slims! *You* don't know," Malkhazi suddenly shouted at me. "What are you saying? Saakashvili still loves Georgia. If he found out that someone was watering down Georgian wine he would *kill* that person. At least he *bought* the wine. The Kakhetian men in their vineyards were just sitting there, moaning, with their heads in their hands. 'Oh, the Russians won't buy our wine. Boo hoo. The Russians just want to bomb us.' Just whining. Doing nothing. 'For two hundred years,' they moan, 'we sold to the Russians and now what do we do? Who will we sell to?' So Saakashvili bought it and implemented his public relations marketing technology. He personally took the wine around Europe to fancy restaurants and said, 'Try our wine.' Don't you understand, Slims? At least he is trying to do *something*. He is trying to make Georgian wine famous."

"But you can't drink Georgian wine at a fancy French restaurant," I told Malkhazi. "You cannot take little sips like they do in America. You must drink it outside near a stream, singing a song, or at a table eating Georgian food and remembering the true life. Is he teaching these restaurant people our songs?"

"Oh, I don't know *anything* anymore," Malkhazi said putting his head in his hands. "What is the point of all these toasts? We say profound things, vow eternal friendship, go into a state of *mona-treba*—so stunned and touched by hospitality that we can't speak—and then it's all forgotten in the morning."

One day when we were driving and we passed a beach resort I pointed to a tree some highway workers were cutting down. "Look!" I told him. "They are cutting down another tree. You see? Saakashvili doesn't even like trees! He is trying to make Georgia just like America."

But Malkhazi said, "That tree was about to fall down. It's not *all* his fault."

We were listening to the radio, to Enrique Iglesias's "Escape," and when I said, "This song makes me want to stand up and fight," Malkhazi just shook his head a little.

A line of black Mercedes edged the parking lot of the beach resort. Malkhazi whistled. "I have never seen so many Armenians. This is the thing, Slims. Armenians are doing fine, even though Azerbaijan shut them off from everything, and now they have no access to Russia either. But somehow they are able to obtain these luxury cars to drive to our beaches. They get up early. Five, six in the morning and start working. Actually, Slims, I am beginning to think that maybe *Georgians* are the strange ones. Do you remember how in school we had to read Alexandre Dumas? He said that Georgians were like lions and deserved to rule the world. But the world is different now. I don't know how to live in this world. Oh, I don't know what will happen. Maybe I should move to Uzbekistan."

"I can't believe your attitude," I told him. Actually, I was still mad about how Saakashvili bought up all the grapes. After we heard that Saakashvili had bought all the wine, Zuka and I went from door to door. "Do you have wine? Do you have wine?" But it was all gone. Now we had to make our toasts with beer. "How can a president buy up all the grapes of a country? He made all the parliamentary leaders stomp on them, even if they didn't want to, so they could be in *The Guinness Book of World Records*. But they didn't know how to step on them. They used their boots! It was too hard on the wine so it made the wine hot. Now, like the rest of the world, we will be drinking hot-tempered wine, getting hangovers, and feeling ill the next day. When you drink market wine," I told Malkhazi, "you are drinking Saakashvili's feet."

"Foo, you don't know," Malkhazi said. "Maybe that was part of his marketing campaign, to draw attention. You think he *likes* stomping on grapes? Maybe it's better to make peace with the Russians. They're Orthodox and they are the only ones who understand our wine."

Everything was changing. Tamriko was becoming a political activist. When I saw her on King Parnavaz Street, she began complaining to me.

"The government says they want to be like America but I haven't been paid my salary in eighteen days."

"Maybe that *is* like America," I said.

She turned a corner and yelled down an alley to some men leaning against a wall, "Where is the Armenian restaurant where the electricians eat lunch?" She turned back to me. "Saakashvili promised that on the first of the month my salary would come. He *promised* this. And now the coordinator from the building supply company said the financial backing for the casino project was financed by the World Bank. And now this *coordinator* says she can't pay me, that we must pay back the World Bank for their loan. Imagine!"

She was on her way to pay her electricity bill because the new privately owned electricity company had cut hers off without any warning. "But at least now we know who to talk to. Slims, do you know where the Armenian restaurant is? Oy! The people at the bank said that I'd find the electrical engineers in front of the Armenian restaurant. It's called Marouch."

To some passersby Tamriko yelled, "Where's Marouch?"

"It's behind the hotel," one of them replied.

"Is this the restaurant? Where are the engineers? Is this their house?" she asked a man sweeping the street.

Bang bang bang on the door. Some disheveled cosmopolitans answered.

"Are you the people who can turn on my electricity?" Tamriko asked.

"No, we're tourists from Tbilisi."

"*Vaimay!* Where's the restaurant?" she asked a man selling watermelons. "Kindly tell me, do you know where the restaurant Marouch is, where the electricians eat their lunch?"

"It's behind the auto repair shop," he said.

"Did you see how expensive his watermelons were?" she said as we walked to the auto repair shop.

When we finally found the men, Tamriko asked them, "When can you turn my electricity back on?"

"In two days. I have a sick mother at home."

"Two days!"

"We're just joking."

"Oh, you almost gave me a heart attack."

Walking home together we passed Gocha's house. His mother was in the garden, behind a very high gate. "Come in. Come in and visit," Gocha's mother called to us. I didn't want to go in there but I also didn't want Tamriko to go in alone.

"Here is my American television set," she showed us. "Here is my waterfall. Here is my shish kebab grill," she boasted. "Everyone slows down when they pass my house because they think it's so enormous. One morning when I went outside only in my housedress I saw the police glaring through the gate. Oh, but it's such a small house. I have a bigger house in Tbilisi. But, I'm so bored here now that they've put poor Gocha in jail."

"Gocha is in jail?" I asked, trying to hide the jubilation in my voice.

But Tamriko could hear my happiness and she glared at me.

"That's why I want to go back to Geneva," Gocha's mother said. "Did I show you my roof terrace where we're growing grapes? There's room for a big table and a big feast. Oh, look at this. My husband bought a watermelon."

When we left I was ecstatic but Tamriko was furious. "The aristocratic society we have now are not the originals," she said. "I can count the originals on one hand. The new ones call themselves *the cream*. Imagine!"

"Why do you think she introduced us to the watermelon," I asked, "if she wasn't going to give us any?"

"Because no one can afford watermelon anymore. To destroy the country you don't need to throw a bomb from someplace, just triple the price of watermelon." It was true. In addition to everything else, the price of food was going up.

As I was walking home from work a few evenings later I saw Anthony slowly cruising down the street in a new black Volga he had just bought. It looked like the kind of car Batman would drive. He wore a gray felted Svani mountain hat pulled down over his eyebrows like some sort of Georgian gangster. When he turned to me his eyes were sort of stupid looking, as if he couldn't count to ten, like some sort of blockhead, or someone who had consumed too much fizzy tarragon water.

"What has happened to you?" I asked him through the window, which he had rolled down. "I didn't even recognize you from over there."

"I don't know how this happened," he said, motioning me to lean closer, as if he had a great secret to reveal. "I have fallen in love with Georgia."

"You even speak English with a Georgian village accent now!" I told him.

"Maybe that's because I've been spending so much time in Svanetia. I bought one of those stone towers up there. I'll have to do a little repair work . . ."

"It's dangerous there! Don't you know the story of the Svani man who brings his guest up to the top of his tower for a view? The guest says, 'Your neighbor is pointing a gun at me.' 'Don't worry,' the host says. 'He'll have a guest next weekend.'"

"All my life I've lived in fear," he said. "I come from a fear-driven culture. I didn't know that until coming here, and living in a land that is not based on fear. After I lost my job, and after you taught me not to be afraid of the police, I felt free all at once. I can be myself here. I stayed past my visa expiration and no one has even noticed."

"But you see what Georgia is now? Before, everyone would try to catch you to bring you home to eat something. Do you remember when you ate dinner at our house? Everyone wanted to sit you down at the table. Now they try to avoid it."

"That's not true," he said.

"Didn't you hear the story recently about the man who was sleeping and he heard some knocking? 'Open the door! Open the door!' the people outside yelled. The man got out of his bed and said, 'Who is it?' 'It's robbers,' they said. 'Oh, thank God!' the man said, throwing open the door. 'Come in. I thought it was guests.' You see Anthony, he had nothing to take. If it had been guests he would have had to give them food. No one will tell you this—not the politicians nor the news broadcasters—but due to globalization, our culture is finished. C'est la vie Georgia. What can we do with this artificial myth of happiness in this new dream of capitalism when it only works sometimes? How can it become more optional? Perhaps the October Revolution was the right way, the right story for us, but there were a lot of mistakes. A distortion. Now is the synthesis of the natural dialectic, but I think it is not the real synthesis. It is only the grotesque repetition of the previous stages."

"But I bought a tower in Svanetia," Anthony said. "We can escape all this. Do you think Juliet will move there with me? You can come too. I need to marry a Georgian in order to be able to stay here. I mean, of course that's not the only reason. I love her too."

"I don't have any control over that. You'll have to ask her yourself," I told him. I got into his Batman car and together we drove to the beer factory district. We parked outside our flat and I sighed. I didn't know how this was going to go.

"Juliet," he called up to her. She came down to the car. "Get in," he said. "I have something to ask you."

When she got in he told her his news. "I bought a tower in Svanetia."

"You too?" she cried. "All these foreign people are buying up our land!"

"No, no," he said. "I meant you can move there too. With me."

"You want me to move to a tower and just brew alcoholic beverages out of milk products all winter?" she asked.

"No! Of course not. Okay, what if we moved back to England? We could live with my mother in her little village in the Cotswolds," he said.

As the words to our first Georgian folktale say, "Once there was." Once there was a time when Juliet imagined it was possible to live in England. She could imagine it again and again. It fit into another story called *The Great Georgian Exodus*. So many people already knew this story and followed it. Once there was an Englishman who worked for an oil company, who came to Georgia. He met a lovely woman from the Caucasus and promised her a more organized life with a great many kitchen appliances to keep her company. It resembled the story of Jason and the Argonauts that every dramatist keeps revising according to which political party is in power. Jason comes to Georgia and steals the gold—the oil—and he brings Medea back to Greece with him. But in order for them to not live under tyranny, she ends up killing her sons. It's a bad ending. Juliet began to sing:

> *Christopher Columbus traveled the shore*
> *He should have stayed at home*
> *at his own shores*
> *It's better not to run here or there*
> *even if your name is Christopher*
> *Better to obey your own fate*
> *on your own shores*

This next part becomes difficult to describe. Our Georgian hospitality has been known to ruin people. Maybe it had washed over Anthony so strongly that he became like that new seaside fish restaurant that was broken apart by unruly waves after a storm. Maybe the Georgian kamikaze pride, the careening-around-the-corner-trying-to-get-to-the-next-bowl-of-*chacha*-on-the-porch sensibility was contagious. But Anthony finally took one of our stories and appropriated it for his own. "You think I don't understand your traditions?" he asked, swollen with indignation and red-faced—his nose had even grown a little. He started to drive. Juliet and I put on our seatbelts, not because he was drunk but because Saakashvili's wife had ordered us all to wear seatbelts.

"You understand some of them," I said.

"Where are you taking us?" Juliet asked.

"I just want to show you the tower I bought. I could never just buy my own tower in England. I'm going to take you there."

"We could go another day," I said.

"According to your Georgian traditions the most romantic and beautiful wedding ritual is the abduction of the bride."

"Yes," Juliet said. "But you did not ask for my consent. The abduction only ever happens with the consent of the bride and her parents."

"And usually her brother isn't in the car," I added.

Anthony didn't seem to hear us though. He sped north, in the direction of Mount Kazbegi. A picture of a coconut dangled from the rearview mirror, some kind of air freshener that made me feel, oddly, as if I were on a coconut holiday. We clambered up the pot-holed highway, now urgently being repaired by the new government.

"Oh, Georgian woman," I sang. "Don't let your children fall into enemy hands." I consoled myself slightly that if the police pulled us over nothing would happen because they might think Anthony was working for the government, because on the floor was a stack of his old anticorruption pamphlets. If the police pulled us over we could say we were part of their own anticorruption campaign.

"Who is kidnapping who?" Juliet asked and pulled out a little handgun. "I told you I am a bandit English teacher." The excitement didn't last long though, unfortunately for us all. He was driving too fast, and a policeman was flagging him down.

"Why are we pulling over?" I asked. "It's better to just keep driving through!"

"I know how to handle this now," he said, and pulled over to the side of the road.

"It's Shalva!" I said. But Shalva didn't look as happy as he used to—he looked as if he was under a lot of stress. He slowly walked to the car.

"Here, do you want this?" Anthony asked him, waving a hundred-pound note. Shalva looked at him with pity, looked over at me apologetically. With his head he motioned to the loitering group of policemen behind him.

"They keep surveillance on us," he said. "We'll have to take him in." He pulled Anthony out of the car, and strapped handcuffs on him. Poor Anthony, he was in the right country but at the wrong time.

"*Vaimay*," my mother said. "The poor Englishman's in jail?"

"Don't worry, don't worry," I told her. "Malkhazi will get him out. When you worry so much it puts God out of work."

We had electricity all the time, but now Georgia was waiting for the light of Mary. We were always waiting for something. "But maybe when She comes there will only be Turkish people left here," Juliet said. "The Turkish man will say, 'We can buy this too?'"

"Oh, there are some more Turkish people!" Juliet cried every time she walked on the boulevard. "Axh! They are looking at what they want to buy. They don't think about King Irakli, only, 'Oh what I beautiful view I will have when I wake up in the morning.' They don't even know any songs about Prince Irakli."

Juliet had begun to sing the old songs about King Irakli. She sang them while knitting chain mail suits on the balcony.

"Stop it with these folk songs!" Tamriko yelled from her balcony. "Are you trying to be Saakashvili? Be careful! He also is trying to celebrate our traditions through the old songs and dances. But that is only for the tourists. It doesn't have anything to do with the regular people. And I don't believe those folk dances anyway. A whole army fights over one woman? If *only*."

Oh Tamriko, I wondered. Do you need a whole nation to fight for you?

The next day I brought Tamriko some roses. "Do you know what day it is today?" I asked her.

"Wednesday."

"No. Well yes," I said. "But it's also Women's Day."

"I thought Women's Day was in May," she said.

"No, that's Mother's Day. Next week is Sister's Day. The week after that there's the Day of Love, devoted to women, of course. And then the Day of Beauty. Devoted to the woman again. And then late summer is devoted to the older woman. And then Saint Nino's Day. But isn't it strange that there is only one day for the soldiers?"

She took the flowers and arranged them in a vase while I watched her. They didn't all fit. She was trying to squeeze them inside.

"You don't have to fit them all in," I suggested.

She shrugged and put one in her hair. I had told Hillary that it was a sin to think one thing, speak another, and do another, and I had vowed that I would try not to do this, but I didn't think I should speak my current thought aloud.

But then Tamriko forced me to. She turned to me and asked, "What are you thinking?"

I quickly tried to think of something else, but I couldn't. "Is it true that Georgian girls still don't believe in sex before marriage?" I asked her.

"Yes, but some Georgian girls don't believe in marriage anymore," she said sadly. Oh no! The tears. The woman always overpowers the man with the hydraulic force of her tears!

"Are you crying because Gocha is in jail?" I asked.

"Oh no, it's not that. He became a different person. I couldn't be with the person he became. Maybe I'm sad because people change so much these days. The last time I was with him he brought me flowers too. We were at the cafe in the port. But his eyes were

just scanning over the white plastic tables to see what other friends
he could kiss, besides me. He bought me flowers from the flower
lady but he gave them to all the women sitting at the table, throwing me mine on my plate. When I looked into his eyes they had that
cold look, the same look as the customs inspector at the border with
Turkey, so accustomed to taking bribes that I don't think he feels
the pang in his conscience anymore."

I didn't tell her that maybe some people don't change, they just
become more of themselves. Instead I said, "Do you want to get out
of here?" So we went to the market and bought a kilo of one long
strip of apricot fruit roll-up. We walked along the boulevard and our
political discussions became heady like *prianiki*, Russian gingerbread.
And then, afterwards: *shashliki*, fireworks, and singing with Gocha's
mafioso karaoke machine on his peewee golf course. Everyone was
using it now that he wasn't there.

In Tamriko's bedroom there was the glow-in-the-dark Jimi Hen-
drix poster I had given her a long time ago on the wall—it had lost
all its glow. But the pop-up *Kama Sutra* book on the bedside table
still popped up!

I thought about how some stories save us and other stories can
kill us. I remembered a film I had once seen about what happens in
the mountains of Svanetia. I think it wasn't even a Georgian story. I
think they borrowed it from a Norwegian myth, but maybe Georgians
had read the myth and liked it and adopted it as their own. I went into
the kitchen and rummaged through the drawers for a knife. I looked
for the biggest one but I could only find her cucumber-peeling knife. I
wished I had a sword, the male one, shaped like a cross, not the Turkish kind curved like the moon. I sharpened the knife on the bottom of
a teacup. I brought it back to the bedroom, where Tamriko hunched
hesitantly on a chair. I threw the knife in the middle of the bed and
said, "If I cross that knife you can kill me with it in the morning."

She looked at me and smiled. "But what if I cross that knife."

"Then you'll have to marry me."

In the middle of the night I threw it off the bed. "Let's just get
rid of the damn knife!"

29.

ON THE INTERNET, I READ ABOUT A NEW MOVEMENT. IN MOST OF THE world's poor countries, people are moving from the villages to the cities. But in Eastern Europe (at least according to the Internet) there is a movement called village syndrome, where people from the industrial cities are moving back to the villages. They go back to the village and buy a nice house. Maybe only six people live in the village. There is no market. Nothing. They go back to the land and grow vegetables and watch the chickens lay eggs. Do woodwork. They sit in front of a fireplace eating Albanian gypsy sausages and say, "Here is some fresh pasta for you right now!"

That's why I decided to invent in Georgia the American weekend, so that at the end of every week I could go back to the fields to work, not only to hoe the corn, but to help repair the electrical meters that had been sitting broken for fourteen years. The whole village had finally agreed to be united by a communal meter. The meter even helped the priest and the imam get along better. Instead of competing about who could sing the loudest, they helped each other translate the instructions off the Internet on how to repair each meter and connect them communally. It is amazing that their religious dispute, which could not be settled by relatives, was resolved with the help of a metal box. Now the old men were raising toasts to the communal meters.

In the village everyday is the same. This chattering life. This heavy seaward slowness. The men start playing backgammon at nine a.m., hunching around the picnic tables in the yard. By eleven they've removed their shirts. At noon their wives bring them homemade muskmelon vodka, black bread, and salted cucumbers. When they begin to sing, women clap from their open windows.

But by one o'clock all is quiet. Women have gathered in the living rooms in their black mourning robes. My aunt grinds Turkish coffee on her lap. Men come in from the cornfields wiping their brows. Even their lazy brothers-in-law wake up from their naps. It is time to watch *Blanca's Widow*, the Brazilian serial.

When my aunt started daubing her eyes over the bronze men and the scantily clad women loving each other, I asked her, "What do you think about all the kissing those Brazilians do outside of marriage?"

"That's okay. That's their tradition," she said.

My aunt was wearing new purple plastic slippers, a black woolen skirt, and blue stockings bunched at the ankles, and caressing a baby chicken in her palm. She put the chick down and pointed at her hands, laughing at the purple stains from the plum sauce she had been squeezing.

"Your Tamriko brought me a new chicken," she said. The neighbor Soso, on the piano, now accompanied my aunt for a duet of Kazbegi mountain songs. I told Tamriko, "Here in the village is nothing. No technology. No money. No work. But do you like the way our frogs sing?"

We sang with the frogs, "I thank my heart because it can love so well," and we sang to each other, "No one can so charmingly as I express how I love you."

"Let's make a toast to the twenty-two Gurulians who brought a hundred horses to America a long time ago," I said. We toasted to that, and to the very moment we made the decision that led us to where we are today. We toasted to the new sealant on the pipeline. We toasted to the old woman who had recently died in the village. We toasted to the unemployed men who had time to make her a coffin from the scrap metal at a rich man's construction site. We toasted to freedom, to children that they should have a better future, to the roots of the hazelnut trees. We toasted to journeys; to friendship, whatever that meant; and to native people everywhere. I toasted to Parajanov, my favorite film director, even though some say he is Armenian. And then we toasted to, "Oh, hollyhocks," Tamriko said. "I'm tired of toasting. Let the reader fill in the blank_____."

We toasted until early dawn and my strength started to ebb. It was that time in the morning when everything becomes giddy and unrevealed truths can no longer hide, so we began to sing those songs that are jokes but that have a little bit of truth left in them. Tamriko sang to me, "I waited for you, but maybe you were lost because, you know, your strength is kind of weak." Of course it couldn't have been a real love song. Who sings real love songs so early in the morning?

And then it was time for us to leave and go to the next house. But first, at the door, Tamriko's relatives were calling, "Goodbye. Safe journey. May everything be good for you." And then again on the balcony, "Come again soon. You're a good girl. You're a good boy. Be well!" Waving and kissing and shouting our names.

Back in Batumi I was very surprised to see a garbageman sweeping the streets early one morning. He was young, only twenty-two or twenty-three. He even wore a uniform. Usually, only the old men would do that kind of work. The young men were too proud. He had started winking at Juliet on the balcony.

"I'm going to marry a garbageman," Juliet said to Malkhazi, trying to provoke him.

"Oh, how very romantic," Malkhazi said. "You can be a garbage woman. Sit beside him ringing the little bell."

"If he has a good salary, what's the problem?" my mother said.

"What do you think will save Georgia?" I asked Malkhazi.

"The only thing that will save Georgia is if everyone asks that question," Malkhazi said. "In ten years Georgia will either be very good or it will be very bad. Who can tell? You heard the antidrug concert they had in the boulevard last night, sponsored by the cell phone company? All night they were singing, 'Choose life.' Okay, so I choose life. Then what? What is this life?"

At Batumi's market the women were yelling, "Welcome. Come buy my meat. Come look at my meat. I know you want the meat. I killed it this morning. You won't find fresher. All is well with my meat." So many sellers but no one was buying.

"How much is it?" Tamriko asked.

"Eh?" asked the vendor but Tamriko had already turned away. "Go to hell! Why did you ask how much it is if you're not going to buy it?"

Everything anyone would ever need was there. Two kinds of cheese—imeruli and sulguni—walnuts, *churchella*, all fruits, figs, peaches, cans of peas, ketchup, sunflower oil, olives, hard candies, cutting boards, and backgammon sets. But we were in the meat section because Malkhazi knows how to buy meat. He is Meat Master Technologue. He buys the meat that looks like Snickers bars, layers of caramel-colored fat and layers of meat. He can tell by the color of the fat when it was killed. He can tell by the smell and the way the fat rolls which mountain or valley it came from. He picks it up, handles it, asks the woman to trim off just an inch of fat. She does so, smiling insipidly, holding the knife high in the air. A half-inch of fat remains. Juliet wanted the meat that had been marinating in the hot spices of *adjika*. "*Adjika. Adjika*," Malkhazi said scornfully. "They only add these spices to hide the color of it, to hide the age." He bought her a little bag of *adjika*-marinated meat anyway.

We went to the botanical garden. Malkhazi and I sat in the front and Juliet and Tamriko sat in the back. First we drove through the Himalayan region, past the demonstration Himalayan grasses. Then we drove through Australia, Northeast Asia, and North America, past crumbling sanatoriums, ponds full of oriental fish, pine forests, palms, greenhouses growing never-ripening banana trees, and then the dry foliage of Eastern Turkey.

"Eastern Turkey has no civilization," I said. "But if you look around, every kind of flower grows here in this garden. We have New York flowers. Flowers from China. I think that's why when foreigners come, they feel so at home here."

In the subtropical jungle of Cuba, thick hawsers of vine thunked our car. Malkhazi turned up the volume of his Cuban music coming from the tape player: Buena Vista Social Club, appropriated from a Scottish sailor he had met at the port. We parked at the end of the road and walked to the cove, near the railway tunnel, the one that used to be Stalin's secret vacation spot. Malkhazi built a fire, a little stick tipi. He blew on it, standing over it tenderly. "It's too hot," he said. He threw salt on it to quench it and then whittled some sticks and plunged them through the thick hunks of meat, slowly turning them over the heat. What were the flavors? Salt and smoke. But sweet as a freshly killed chicken. "It doesn't even need plum sauce," Malkhazi said, holding the meat up, juices dripping.

"It's like candy," Juliet said. "It melts. I don't need wine with this meat. I'm drunk already."

"Me too," Tamriko said. For me, pulling off this meat from the stick with my teeth made me feel as if I were a twelfth-century nobleman after an invader had sacked my castle, and I had just come across a church builder squaring boulders in a little wood.

"Now for Juliet's meat," Malkhazi said. He blew at the fire to wake it up and threw the orange-stained *adjika* meat on it. "Juliet, we used all the salt. Oh, but we don't need salt. You like this premarinated. *Adjika*," Malkhazi said scornfully. "*Adjika, adjika*," he repeated and shook his head.

"You're cooking it for a long time on purpose so it will be tough," Juliet said.

When he had finished cooking Juliet's meat, he brought us the little precut pieces on some newspaper. But we were already full.

"What do you think of this meat?" I asked Malkhazi.

"It's like candy," he said. "Like gum."

"But the flavor is still good if you lick it—lick off the *adjika*," Juliet said.

"Ah? You see?" Malkhazi wailed. "Why didn't you *listen* to me? You should listen to me." Now, he was slaughtering the watermelon as if it were a calf. He lifted half the watermelon to his mouth and let the juice fall into it. Shook the juice off his fingers. He lay down in the grass. He pulled the weeds up by the roots, the ones near his head, throwing green-speckled foliage at Juliet. "Actually, I should have listened to you," he said.

She grabbed some watermelon entrails and threw them at him. Watermelon guts landed on his neck. He swatted them off and threw a tomato at her, a few tomatoes. She threw more watermelon at him, teardrop sized. His hair was now wet with watermelon. Her back was grubby with grass roots.

I pulled up some grass to throw at Tamriko but she was holding her guitar. "Don't you dare," she said.

Malkhazi went to the spring and washed his face, his neck, his head. He threw some of the water at Juliet. She was laughing and shrieking. She washed her hands and wiped them off on the grass. Juliet took Tamriko's guitar and started playing while Tamriko sang along:

> *Like the teapot boiling*
> *it must let off steam*
> *or it will blow off its hat*
> *like a person.*
> *All the world is crazy*
> *clever or stupid.*
>
> *The roof is flying off the house.*
> *Now is the time to speak*
> *about what is inside*
>
> *Whoever's heart is hungry for the living come to me*
> *I am crazy for this world.*
>
> *My body is a ship with a pipe*

and it's polluted with too much steam.
It's time for it to return to sunny and clean lands.

Don't believe the crocodile tears.
It's real rain.

It's the fashion to build cities out of ice
but the sun will melt it.

Forgive me my fortune
for I cannot accompany you.
In heaven there are also countries.
There is a Georgia there too
but it is not for sale.

"Come, Tamriko," Juliet said. "Let's move back to the village."
"I'll follow you," Malkhazi said.
"I'll follow you, too," I said.

Acknowledgments

This book would not have been possible without those who taught me to see with a Georgian lens. My deepest thanks go to Giorgi Murvanidze, Zviadi Mikeladze, Anzor Katamadze, Nona Mikeladze, Manana Mitaishvili, Tamuna Kiknadze, Tornike Tsotsoria, Tamuna Kobelashvili, Manana Antidze, Tamriko Siradze, Marina Giorgadze, Nino Inaishvili, Vano Kobelashvili, his wife Qeti Goguadze, and everyone in their village. I would also like to thank Inga Goguadze for her songs. Also thanks to Kuba Sheshenkojoyev for teaching me what a village can be, and to Mathjis Pelkmans for his far-reaching perspectives. I am also deeply grateful for those who supported me in a variety of ways: Dana Dizon, Susan Lindauer, Amber Mahler, Mehera Kleiner, Susan Marshall, Izida Zolde, Naveen Chauduri, Nan Wicker, Cate Calson, Julia Weidmann, Smita Patel, Laurissa Kowalchuck, and Marjorie Thomas for their steadfast friendship throughout this process. I am grateful to Rebecca Kunin for offering to be my New Zealand wife if I ever needed to immigrate; Allison Siebecker for plying me with chocolate chip cookies and prune alcohol; David White and his barbecue and Shop-Vac; Chandra Shukla, who remembered what I wrote; Micol Hammack to compare notes with; Markus Bennett—the metaphor man—and his lovely Cecilia for their garden-talk rejuvenations; Larry Thrasher, who set out an extra plate at the dinner table for Slims, and Larry's mother who prayed that Slims's life would improve; Ken Paul Rosenthal for his courageous experiments; David Kay for offering to host a radio show for Slims to give advice to four blocks in Brooklyn; Daniel Smith, who actually read the Juliet parts and liked them better; Lulu Torbet, who was the very first to read it and said I might have something; Martha Gies, who told me the oil industry was more important to write about than Kyrgyz kidnapping; Laura Didyk for hawk jokes and her intuition; Jeff Gillon, who could also write something really funny; Tom Parker, who still believed in this book after a long time; Joan Gelfand, who still believed in the pursuit of truth after a long time; Garth Dyke for his creative support and the huge table he gave me to write on; David Leavitt for his valuable suggestions; Padgett Powell for his stories that are so funny it's hard to really believe it; Mary Robison for the way she articulates her sentences; Jill Ciment for consistently pushing me in the right direction; John Cech for his childhood looking-glass; Vince Amlin for his touchstone of wisdom and humor; Larry Reimer for the same, and for his sermon on waiting; Roger Beebe for daring to read the thing; Stu Crosby for actually laminating the manuscript so he could read it in the bathtub; the MacDowell Colony for the time and quietude and company; Peter Demek for being himself; Melinda Stone for her homemade fellowship; the MFA@FLA gang, most especially Sarah Sheldon, Harry Leeds, Rachel Khong, and Elizabeth Bevilaqua (oh heck, everyone there!); the magnificent support of the Rona Jaffe Foundation; Merwan Irani, for consistently keeping my funny bone tickled; Joyce Barison for her avocado, wasabi, and sardine sandwiches; Shanti Elliott, for her far-reaching magic and rituals; Mark Thomas for appreciating my humor; my cousin's children; my other cousins, Matt, Maria, and Miguel; Chris Fortin, who taught me to trust my feet again; my Aunt Francis, whose very existence helps me connect my feet with my heart; my Uncle Bruce for reminding me of the economic reality of sheep; Bill Offermann and my mother, Kate Frazier, for the deep solace of their coffee talks; my father Allan, who told me he wouldn't speak to me unless I quit my job and started writing; my sisters Jessica and Annie, also true storytellers and interpreters in their own right; my brother, David, for his grand generosity and his big deck to write on; my sister-in-law Lelah for the same; my nephew Julian who thought I was writing *Waiting for the Electron*; my tireless advocate of an agent Irene Skolnick; and my ineffably brilliant editor Mark Krotov.

CHRISTINA NICHOL is a 2012 recipient of a Rona Jaffe Foundation Writers' Award. Nichol grew up in the Bay Area, studied at the University of Oregon, and received her MFA from the University of Florida. She has traveled widely, worked for nonprofit film companies, and taught English in India, South Korea, Kyrgyzstan, Kazakhstan, Kosovo, and, of course, Georgia. Her work has been published in *Guernica* and *Lucky Peach*. *Waiting for the Electricity* is her first book.